Praise for *Cruel Beautiful World*

"Marvelous . . . Leavitt brings to life the chaotic days of Vietnam War protests, the assassination of Martin Luther King Jr. and the Manson murders as the setting for a complex story of the relationship between two sisters and a predatory teacher. The result is a captivating, timely feeling thriller."

—*Los Angeles Times*

"The war in Vietnam, the Charles Manson murder trial and other touchstones of that era provide the backdrop for *Cruel Beautiful World*, Caroline Leavitt's moving novel about three women connected by fate and a spate of tragic deaths . . . As in her other novels, including *Pictures of You* and *Is This Tomorrow*, Leavitt expertly draws us into the stormy lives of her female characters and deftly narrates their coming-of-age in a world in which women's roles are changing."

—*The Washington Post*

"Backdropped by the Vietnam War and the Manson murders, *Cruel Beautiful World* is a fast-moving page-turner about the naïveté of youth and the malignity of power. Leavitt explores with a keen eye the intersection of love, family, and the anxiety of an era."

—Lily King, author of *Euphoria*

"From its first sentence, Caroline Leavitt's new novel, *Cruel Beautiful World*, draws the reader into a seductive page-turner that ripples with an undercurrent of suspense and is fueled by the foibles of the human heart . . . Though the novel unspools with the edge of a psychological thriller, read too quickly for plot and one might miss these nuanced moments of insight, which seed Leavitt's prose like tips of crocuses pushing up through snow. Best to slow down and savor."

—*The Boston Globe*

"The author of *Is This Tomorrow* and *Pictures of You* once again skillfully animates themes of disappearance, abandonment and loss . . . With *Cruel Beautiful World*, Leavitt successfully reminds the reader of the ephemeral and lifelong nature of sisterly love, and how it always leaves behind a certain kind of sadness and beauty." —*San Francisco Chronicle*

"A riveting novel about love and loss, secrets and lies, and what it means to be a family. Its twists and turns will keep you reading late into the night."
—Christina Baker Kline, author of *Orphan Train*

"Marvelous . . . Leavitt brings to life the chaotic days of Vietnam War protests, the assassination of Martin Luther King, and the Manson murders as the setting for a complex story of the relationship between two sisters and a predatory teacher. The result is a captivating, timely-feeling thriller."
—*The National Book Review*

"A plot-driven exploration of how love can impel one to terrible depths and lofty heights . . . The story moves along at a breathless clip . . . A compulsive yet touching page-turner . . . A devastating portrayal of how at any age, we alone are responsible for how we let our love for the people in our lives affect us. Too few books truly challenge our own hearts, no matter how hard they may aim for them; *Cruel Beautiful World* hits its target." —*Pittsburgh Post-Gazette*

"Tender and tragic, with a shooting star of hope, Leavitt's profound latest is about the connections of siblings, the mystery of love—first, last, and dangerous—and the struggle to accept what can never be changed."
—Sara Gruen, author of *At the Water's Edge*

"Leavitt engages the reader by avoiding simple answers. Life isn't straightforward, and the lives of William, Lucy, Charlotte and Iris carry their own secrets and surprises. Gripping and suspenseful, *Cruel Beautiful World* will leave the reader pondering who, exactly, these people are—and perhaps, how thoroughly we can understand any individual."   —*BookPage*

"Leavitt paints her characters with deep flaws and yet hugely redeeming qualities. The writing is rich and real and provocative, with scenes that bring tears of sadness and of joy as we watch America struggle with its growing pains and wonder if our young protagonist will make it through her own."
                                        —*Minneapolis Star Tribune*

"At once a page-turner that leaves you holding your breath and a gorgeous meditation on love and family, *Cruel Beautiful World* had me in its thrall from start to finish."
        —J. Courtney Sullivan, author of *The Engagements*

"Leavitt builds her story around characters who are warm and engaging but very much flawed. The 1960s setting provides a few unsettling details that murmur in the background—the Manson murders, the Kent State shootings—but this is essentially the timeless story of a family, one that's unorthodox and fractured but rings emotionally true."   —*Tampa Bay Times*

"*Cruel Beautiful World* is a masterwork, a book that is so well-crafted and emotionally resonant that the reader will be loath to hand it off to the next willing reader until he or she has read it over again. Congratulations to Caroline Leavitt for an upstanding and inspiring literary masterpiece."
                                        —Bookreporter.com

"I was mesmerized . . . It is hard to read this novel and not think of *Lolita* and also of Dan Chaon's psychological thriller *Await Your Reply* . . . This poignant and complex novel is a story about how we tell stories and the narratives that become our lives." —Mary Morris, author of *The Jazz Palace*

"For fans of Emma Cline's bestselling debut, *The Girls*, Caroline Leavitt's *Cruel Beautiful World* offers another opportunity to spend time in the wild, off-kilter America of the late 1960s, the period when peace-and-love idealism began to curdle into something far less wholesome, a period reigned over in the collective imagination by Charles Manson. Leavitt's title—and lovely period book cover—get it just right . . . *Cruel Beautiful World* is a page-turner—recommended reading for those reveling in the current literary '60s revival." —*Newsday*

"Caroline Leavitt knows how to pull a reader into the page . . . An intense page-turner . . . Leavitt is on to something here— the vulnerability of young girls, sexually advanced, perhaps, but naïve when it comes to human nature. The novel reminds us, too, of our own peril. Oh, how thin the line between good fortune and tragedy; how tenuous our hold on a safe haven from life's calamities." —*Milwaukee Journal Sentinel*

"Leavitt is a magician at creating unforgettable characters, and the two sisters at the heart of this tale will stay with me in all their complicated humanity. A brave book, and a powerfully moving one." —Robin Black, author of *Life Drawing*

"*Cruel Beautiful World* hits the sweet-spot between popular and literary fiction with finely honed writing, complexity of character motives, and enough guilt and secrecy to sustain the page-turning suspense." —*New York Journal of Books*

"This hauntingly brilliant novel is one no reader should miss this fall. It speaks to one of the deepest human fears: What if you can't repair the damage you caused? When 16-year-old Lucy wants to run away from her rural Pennsylvanian life, she risks ruining not only her future, but her sister's as well. A vibrant portrait on the intricacies of family and the consequences of abandoning responsibility, *Cruel Beautiful World* will remind you of the value found in familial bonds."

—*Coastal Living*

"Peopled with gorgeously flawed characters, *Cruel Beautiful World* is a wonder of triumph and tragedy."

—Miranda Beverly-Whittemore, author of *Bittersweet*

"Set in the same tumultuous period as Woodstock and the Manson family murders, Caroline Leavitt's astute family drama in *Cruel Beautiful World* is as vintage as a pair of bell-bottoms and as timeless as the bond between sisters. Leavitt (*Is This Tomorrow*) perfectly captures the essence of the teen years adults tend to look back on fondly through the lens of nostalgia, reminding the reader of the uncertainty, insecurity, naïve expectations and broken dreams that came with growing up. Deeply resonant and quietly powerful, *Cruel Beautiful World* has the heart-pounding moments of a thriller and the heart-warming moments of a perfect coming-of-age story. In her 11th novel, Caroline Leavitt weaves an absorbing story of family, love and tragedy set at the dawn of the 1970s."

—*Shelf Awareness*

"This haunting examination of the duty we have to family— and the irreparable consequences we abandon it—will leave every mother moved." —Workingmother.com

Cruel Beautiful World

Also by Caroline Leavitt

Is This Tomorrow

Pictures of You

Girls in Trouble

Coming Back to Me

Living Other Lives

Into Thin Air

Family

Jealousies

Lifelines

Meeting Rozzy Halfway

Cruel
Beautiful
World

a novel

Caroline Leavitt

ALGONQUIN BOOKS OF CHAPEL HILL   2017

Published by
Algonquin Books of Chapel Hill
Post Office Box 2225
Chapel Hill, North Carolina 27515-2225

a division of
Workman Publishing
225 Varick Street
New York, New York 10014

First paperback edition, Algonquin Books of Chapel Hill,
August 2017. Originally published in hardcover by
Algonquin Books of Chapel Hill in October 2016.
Printed in the United States of America.
Published simultaneously in Canada by Thomas Allen & Son Limited.
Design by Steve Godwin.

This is a work of fiction. While, as in all fiction, the literary
perceptions and insights are based on experience, all names,
characters, places, and incidents either are products of the author's
imagination or are used fictitiously.

Library of Congress Cataloging-in-Publication Data
Names: Leavitt, Caroline, author.
Title: Cruel beautiful world / a novel by Caroline Leavitt.
Description: First edition. | Chapel Hill, North Carolina :
Algonquin Books of Chapel Hill, 2016. | "Published simultaneously
in Canada by Thomas Allen & Son Limited."
Identifiers: LCCN 2016018796 | ISBN 9781616203634 (HC)
Subjects: LCSH: Sisters—Fiction. | Runaway teenagers—
Fiction. | Life change events—Fiction.
Classification: LCC PS3562.E2617 C78 2016 | DDC 813/.54—dc23
LC record available at https://lccn.loc.gov/2016018796

ISBN 978-1-61620-737-3 (PB)

10 9 8 7 6 5 4 3 2 1
First Paperback Edition

For Jeff and Max.
You make my heart grow nine sizes.

Cruel Beautiful World

Chapter 1

1969

Lucy runs away with her high school teacher, William, on a Friday, the last day of school, a June morning shiny with heat. She's downstairs in the kitchen, and Iris has the TV on. The weather guy, his skin golden as a cashew, is smiling about power outages, urging the elderly and the sick to stay inside, his voice sliding like a trombone, and as soon as she hears the word "elderly," Lucy glances uneasily at Iris.

"He doesn't mean me, honey," Iris says mildly, putting more bacon to snap in the pan. "I'm perfectly fine."

Good, Lucy thinks, good, because it makes it that much easier for her to do what she's going to do. Lucy is terrified, but she acts as if everything is ordinary. She eats the bacon, the triangles of rye toast, and the scrambled eggs that Iris leaves her, freckling them with pepper and pushing the lumpy curds around her plate. Lucy drinks the orange juice Iris pours for her and picks up the square multivitamin next to her plate, pretending to swallow it but then spitting it out in her napkin moments later because it has this silty undertaste. She wants to tell Iris to take more vitamins, since she won't be around to remind her. It's nearly impossible for her to believe that Iris turned seventy-nine in May. Everyone always says Iris barely looks in her late sixties, and just last week Lucy spotted an old man giving Iris the once-over at a restaurant, his eyes drifting over her body, lingering on her legs. Lucy knows three kids at school whose parents—far younger than Iris—have died suddenly: two fathers felled by heart attacks, a mother who suffered a stroke while walking the dog. Lucy knows that anything can happen and age is the hand at your back, giving you an extra push toward the abyss.

She tells herself Iris will be fine. Iris hasn't had to work for years, since receiving sizable insurance money from her husband, who died in his sixties. Plus, she has money from Lucy's parents. Lucy had never heard her parents talk about Iris, but Iris told Lucy and Charlotte it was because she was only very distantly related.

Lucy was only five when her parents died, Charlotte a year and a half older, and she doesn't remember much about that life, though she's seen the photos, two big red albums Iris keeps on a high shelf. She's in more of the photos with her parents than Charlotte is, and she wonders whether that's because Charlotte didn't like being photographed then any more than she does now. There are lots of photos of Charlotte and Lucy together, jumping rope, sitting in a circle of dolls, laughing. But the photos of her parents alone! Her mother, winking into the camera, is all banana blond in a printed dress, her legs long and lean as a colt's. Her father, burly and white-haired, with a mustache so thick it looks like a scrub brush, is kissing her mother's cheek. They hold hands in the pictures. They smooch over a Thanksgiving turkey. Her dad was much older than her mom, but he didn't act like it. They were at a supper club, dancing and having dinner, the girls at home with a sitter, when the fire broke out. Later, the news reports said it was someone's cigarette igniting a curtain into flames so heavy most of the people there never made it out.

When she thinks about her parents, Lucy feels as if there is a mosquito trapped and buzzing in her body. She tells herself the stories Charlotte has told her, the few Charlotte can remember.

There was the time their parents took them to Florida and they rode ponies on the beach. The time they all went to New York City to look at the Christmas lights and Lucy cried because the multitude of Santa Clauses confused her. She has told herself all these stories so many times she can almost convince herself that she really remembers them. Iris has no stories about the girls' parents. "Our lives were all so busy," Iris says. "We just never got together."

Lucy glances at Iris bustling around the kitchen, pouring coffee, reaching for the sugar. She looks old, her skin lined, her hands embroidered with blue veins. Iris has never seemed old before, Lucy thinks. Iris took the girls to the park, she threw and sometimes caught Frisbees. The only thing she couldn't do was take the girls to a movie in the evening, because she didn't like driving at night. Plus, she preferred to go to bed early. Charlotte was always Iris's "big-girl helper," watching Lucy on the swings, running after her, and, a lot of the time, just sitting on one of the benches with Iris, the two of them with their heads dipped together, laughing, so that Lucy would have to stand on the swings and go higher just to blot out the surprise of being the odd person out.

Iris turns the TV to another channel. She shakes her head when she sees the hippies on the news, a sudden influx of them congregated and camping out in Boston Common, spread out on the green lawn like wildflowers, all of them in tie-dyes and striped or polka-dot pants and bare feet, some of the girls in flowing dresses or minis so tiny they barely cover their thighs, but Lucy finds herself glued to the set. "Like sheep!" Iris says, pointing to the way the cops are herding the kids back onto the streets. "Look at how they dress!" Iris marvels.

Lucy sighs. Iris wears jewel-tone silk dresses every day, or blouses and skirts. She's always in low-heeled, strappy shoes. Her white hair is braided into a fussy ring around her head, like Heidi, and her earrings are always button ones, instead of the long, jangly ones Lucy wears. "Look at that one," Iris says when the camera focuses on a boy with ringlets skimming his shoulders. "What a world," Iris marvels, and she shuts the set off. But Lucy loves the way the hippies look, the multitude of rings on their toes and fingers, the clashing clothes. These kids are part of a life glittering just inches away from her, and all she has to do is grab hold, the way she does with William's hair, thick and shiny as satin. She can almost feel her hands in it, tugging him closer to kiss her.

She wants to tell Iris and Charlotte. She wants to tell someone, but she can't.

Iris hands Lucy a brown paper bag filled with a peanut butter sandwich and an apple, the same lunch Lucy's had since elementary school. Iris sits down and pulls out the crossword puzzle from the daily newspaper. This is her favorite part of the day. She picks up a pencil and chews on the end and then glances at Lucy again. "Honey, go find a hairbrush before you go," Iris says.

Lucy pats down her cap of curls and then sits and finishes her juice. She looks around the kitchen as if she's memorizing every detail—the oak table and chairs, the braided rug—because until she's eighteen, just two years from now, when no one can legally stop her from being with William, she won't see this room again.

She has to leave the house before Charlotte can catch up and ask why her knapsack is so heavy, why Lucy seems so nervous, why she's in such a hurry. Charlotte worries over Lucy the same way she worries about everything, and though Lucy used to like that, now it's a burden. She's taken only what she thinks she'll need, because William says that the whole idea is to simplify their lives, that people today are too hung up on having stuff. She packed two pairs of bell-bottom jeans, one of them elephant bells, a paisley minidress, her favorite pink felt shift

dress—the same one Twiggy wore on the cover of *Seventeen*—
and her Love's Baby Soft shampoo. She has a brand-new Lanz
nightgown with black lace trim and a pair of yellow marabou
slippers she found on sale for two dollars, crumpled in a bin at
Zayre, the feathers fluffed around the toes. And of course, she
has her blue journal, a new one that she's already started to use.

She wonders whether Charlotte will miss her. Though they
go to the same school, Lucy is a sophomore, while Charlotte
is a senior, and that makes a big difference. Charlotte loves
every stupid brick of Waltham High, but Lucy is in misery. The
school is so small minded. Last year, while all the world and
other high schools were protesting the Vietnam War, Waltham
High had a tiny walkout of just twenty kids, mostly the art
and drama students, and by the time everyone spilled onto the
blacktop outside, the protest had changed from being against
the war to wanting a Coke machine in the cafeteria. "What do
we want?" someone screamed. "When do we want it? Coke!
Now!"As soon as all the kids came back inside, sweaty from
the heat, jazzed up, they all got detention, including Lucy. "The
president knows better than you what should be done with the
war," Iris said to her. "What if people did this during World
War Two? What if all the soldiers decided they didn't want to
go? We'd all be under Nazi rule."

The day of the walkout, Charlotte didn't get detention, because she was taking her SATs for the third time, as if her stellar scores the first two times weren't high enough. But even if
Charlotte had been there, she probably wouldn't have joined
the protest, because she'd have been worrying what would
happen, whether getting detention would spoil her chances of
landing her choice college. She'd have made a list of every positive and negative, and by the time she was done, the war would
have been over and she wouldn't have had to make a decision
at all.

Charlotte has no idea how good she has it. She's always

been in the accelerated honors program. She's completely gorgeous, with startling eyes, green as limes, and the kind of thick, straight cocoa hair that Lucy yearns for. But instead of growing it to her waist, parting it in the middle, the way Lucy would have, Charlotte chops it to her chin, cutting it herself with scissors in the bathroom because she's afraid that the hair salons won't listen to her, that they might give her an artichoke or a pixie style instead. Plus, Charlotte has already decided her whole life. She loves animals and she wants to be a veterinarian, and she got a full scholarship at Brandeis. "It's only ten minutes away," Charlotte tells them, but Lucy gets this ache behind her eyes when she thinks about it. Her sister has always been in the house with her. How can she so easily leave Lucy behind?

Ever since Charlotte started worrying about college, the only person she hangs out with is her friend Birdie, another study-all-the-time girl who's going to be a theater major at Emerson, and when Lucy listens in on their conversations, all they talk about is leaving home.

Charlotte bought saffron-colored Indian bedspreads for her dorm room from the Harvard Coop, and a funny lamp shaped like a pineapple. She's already written to her roommate, a girl from California named Cherry Mossman, who sent Charlotte a photo of herself and her beagle, both wearing angel wings for Halloween.

Lucy knows from friends of hers how it is, how their brothers or sisters went off to college and made lives there and didn't come back, and even if they did, the person who returned was different. Just like William told her. "People move on. They change. They go on and make new families."

"What's a three-letter word for pies starting with the letter z?" Iris asks, readjusting a white bobby pin in her hair.

"*Zas,*" Lucy says, and Iris frowns. "Are you sure?" she says. "Is that really a word?"

Lucy has a feeling that if Charlotte answered the question, Iris wouldn't doubt her. "It means pizza," she says. She hesitates and then gets up from the table and kisses Iris on the cheek. Iris flushes. "Well, what have I done to deserve something that nice today?" Iris says. "Did you eat enough? Are you taking a jacket? It might get cool later."

Lucy nods. Sometimes Lucy feels that Iris worries over her more than she does Charlotte, and it makes Lucy feel deficient, as if she can't take care of herself. She keeps thinking that soon she will be one less thing for Iris to worry about.

Lucy hears Charlotte coming into the kitchen, the rat-a-tat-tat of the green cowboy boots she insists on wearing every day, the heavy way she walks as if she needs to weight herself to the earth or she'll fly away. There she is, Lucy's sister, as startling as an exclamation point, in a purple mini and orange tights.

"Morning," Charlotte says, reaching for a bagel on the counter, brushing close.

Lucy breathes in deeply. "Hey," she says.

Her sister, who never eats much, takes neat bites out of her bagel. "If you wait a few minutes, I'll walk to school with you," Charlotte offers.

The thought scares Lucy. She knows if she has to speak, her plans will be doomed, they will helplessly leak from her. She's never been able to keep much from her sister.

"I can't. I have to see the science teacher before class," Lucy says, and she bolts toward the front door.

"See you later, then," Charlotte says, waving a hand.

On the way out, Lucy spots the long red silk scarf Charlotte's taken to wearing, which is hanging on the doorknob. She grabs it. She's taking this part of Charlotte with her. She has to have something. She wraps it around her neck, lets it flutter to her waist, and races outside.

BEING IN SCHOOL is tricky because Lucy keeps dodging people she knows so she won't have to talk to them. The less anyone knows, the better. She winds in and out of couples and groups of girls, her heart hammering against her ribs. She ignores the catcalls of the boys, the sly way they take her in, their eyes fastened on her. "Hey, frizzy, you busy?" someone yells, but she pretends not to hear. She's so not interested in any of them. She hums so that her whole body seems to vibrate, something Mr. Hobert, her science teacher, had told them was actually good for people, because vibrations can heal by the power of sound. She leans against the hallway walls, trying to compose herself. She presses her toes together in her shoes and feels the forty dollars she tucked into her sneakers. Ever since Iris started giving her an allowance, she's been saving every bit she can, and now she has all of it stuffed in her shoes. She's walking on money. This waiting is drumming inside her. Every sound makes her flinch. Please, she wants to say out loud. Please let this happen to me.

At second period, she's in Algebra with Miss Grimes, who wears pop beads and pink lipstick. There's a smell of stale bubblegum (most of it stuck to the underside of her desk) and sour milk, and Lucy isn't sure she can stand it another second.

"Homework," says Miss Grimes, and Lucy can see there is a freckle of lipstick on her front tooth. Everyone passes the papers forward except for Lucy, who tried to do the quadratic equations the night before and got so confused she finally gave up. She tried and tried, but she just didn't get it. Miss Grimes looks at her. "Really, Lucy, even on the last day of class?" Lucy lowers her head, but she knows she will never have to do this humbling before a teacher again.

At lunch in the cafeteria, Lucy sits at the same table she always does, with Sable and Heather, her friends but not really her friends, girls she's known since grade school who live conveniently near her. They talk about a party that night, held at some girl's house. While Lucy picks at the cafeteria pizza, pulling off the gluey cheese, finding the crust, Heather and Sable scope out the boys they have crushes on. The girls twirl their hair and examine their split ends. Lucy knows the boys look at her, and sometimes she thinks that's the only reason Sable and Heather hang around her, so that they can get the ones Lucy doesn't want. Lucy's had dates, but her initial attraction always fades after a week or two, something that worries her a little. "You just haven't found the right guy," Sable told her, and now Lucy knows that was true.

"Older kids are supposed to be at this party," Heather says.

"We'll pick you up," Sable confirms.

"No, no. I'll meet you guys there," Lucy tells them.

It's so easy to lie. It's getting easier all the time.

Then, there it is, after a whole day of staring at the clock, three in the afternoon, and Lucy swears that for a moment all the color has bled out of the school. Every person seems smudged. She leans against her locker, gulping air, averting her whole body so she can't tell if anyone is looking at her. Luckily she hasn't run into Charlotte all day, but then she's been racing out of one class to the next, taking weird routes to get there, hallways where she knows her sister won't be.

Lucy walks through the school's main entrance for the last time, keeping her head down. She'll always remember this day. She'll never forget it. Worry thumps in her head.

She had debated with herself how to leave, over and over, pulled like elastic. She didn't want to be cruel, didn't want anyone to worry. "We need to just go," William had told her quietly, but she couldn't do that. Instead she left a note, tucked under her pillow. They won't think to worry about her until she isn't there for dinner, and even then they'll chalk up her absence to her forgetting the time while she's out carousing after the last day of school. No one will even think to scour her bedroom until Sable or Heather calls, wanting to know where Lucy is, why she isn't at the party. Then Iris and Charlotte will search her room and they'll find the note. Then they'll realize that Lucy's fine. She's doing this of her own volition. *I love you but I have to do this. I am happy and safe and I will call you soon and explain everything. Please don't worry.*

LUCY LEANS AGAINST the side of the school until she sees Mr. Lallo—William—striding out the door, pulling off his jacket so he's wearing just a black T-shirt, acting as if it's ordinary for a teacher to leave at the same time as the kids. All the teachers are expected to stay until four, to make themselves available to the kids, though most of them just end up hanging around in empty classrooms, drumming their fingers on their desks or reading the newspaper. But of course, today is different.

Lucy watches William, admires his graceful lope. He's thirty years old and he came to the school a year ago from a free school in California called the Paradise School, and he's different from all the other teachers, full of new ideas. The first thing he did was to take apart the rows and put all the desks in a circle. The kids watched him, astonished, unsure what to do or where to go. "Sit wherever you like," he told them, and the kids looked so confused he had to repeat it again. "Wherever you want. Claim your space," he said. "It can be different every day."

At first, Lucy was anxious in his class. She wanted to do well, but she had always struggled in school. She wondered whether she was all that smart, something so dark and shameful she tried not to think about it too much. Could she really be stupid? Charlotte was worlds smarter. Charlotte could read before she even hit kindergarten, while Lucy was always in the third reading group, the one where all the dummies were. Whenever Lucy got a teacher that Charlotte had had, the teacher was always delighted. "You're Charlotte's sister!" they said, as if they'd just discovered a new planet. But then Lucy would start failing, and she would feel their disappointment like a fog settling over her.

Charlotte helped her with her homework, but even so, Lucy brought home Cs and even a few Ds. It wasn't long before Lucy was stuck in general ed with all the kids whose only possibilities after high school were the armed forces or marriage or being a cashier at Woolworth's. Lucy felt her heart knot. How many evenings had Charlotte sat with her, patiently explaining quadratic equations and the Magna Carta, not caring if it took all evening, making Lucy laugh, being as excited as Lucy when Lucy brought home Bs? But then Charlotte started worrying about PSATs and then SATS, about colleges and essays. She began studying through the evenings, sometimes even taking her dinner into her room so she wouldn't waste time. Charlotte looked helplessly at Lucy when Lucy was frowning over her books. "I'm fine. I can do it on my own," Lucy said, and she saw the relief bloom on her sister's face. After that, Lucy just stopped asking.

Lucy studied for hours—the history dates, the math theorems, the French verbs—but it all flew out of her head. She tried everything. Flash cards. Repeating facts before she went to sleep like a mantra, because she had heard that information would imprint on your brain almost the way it did under hypnosis. She had gone to her teachers for help after class, but all the teachers did was to give her more take-home worksheets that she still didn't understand. She knew her PSAT scores were so low she wouldn't get in anywhere she applied, let alone get a scholarship.

Even the guidance counselor had given up on her, telling her, "Not everyone is meant to go to college," as if that was supposed to make her feel better. Iris told her brightly, "There's always Katie Gibbs," and Lucy knew she meant Katherine Gibbs, the secretarial school in the city where you had to wear white gloves and skirts and stockings and the best you could hope for was a boring job typing for some man who looked down on you. "I'm not going to Katie Gibbs," Lucy insisted.

"It leads to jobs," Iris said. "I just want you to have a great life. To be able to take care of yourself." But Lucy wasn't so sure how great a life that would be. Not then, anyway.

THE FIRST CLASS Lucy ever did well in was William's English class.

He took the gray Manter Hall vocabulary books and put them in his closet. "You can learn vocabulary by reading." He had the students underline words they didn't know in books and look them up. He said that you should write about how a story made you feel rather than parrot what you thought the symbolism was and what the author really meant, because no one really knew that other than the author, and sometimes the author was clueless. "A table can be green just because that's the first color the writer thought of," William said. He made them all buy notebooks, which they were to call their journals, and when Lucy stared at the page, paralyzed, he crouched down by her desk. "Write about the thing that scares you the most," he encouraged. That night, she wrote four pages about how afraid she was of getting stuck in Waltham, having to be a secretary or a cashier, living at home because she couldn't afford her own place. She wrote about missing her sister, who was always studying now, how it felt as if she had lost her partner in crime. When she read her story over, it surprised her that her writing didn't seem that bad. That it actually felt honest and even fun, like when she and Charlotte made up stories when they were kids. Later, when William handed it back to her, he was grinning. "I liked this lots, Lucy," he said, and then she looked from him to her journal and saw the big inky A. She had never received an A, not even in Home Ec, where all you had to do was show up and make sure your apron was ironed and clean. She couldn't wait to write more in the journal, just to get an A again, maybe on something a little less personal so she could show it to Iris and Charlotte. *This is something I can do.*

William played movies in class, clips from Fellini and Antonioni. The films were surprising and strange, and while a lot of the kids put their heads on their arms and dozed, Lucy loved them. She even sort of understood them, which made her begin to wonder whether maybe she wasn't as dim as everyone seemed to think. When William asked what they thought about the imaginary game of tennis at the end of *Blow-Up*, kids hunkered down in their seats, trying to be invisible, but Lucy hesitantly raised her hand. "Isn't it about what's real and what isn't? How we can't tell the difference sometimes?" she said. William beamed. "What a good point, Lucy," he said, and she felt the flush rise up to her cheekbones. He actually thought she was smart, and it made her feel like a light that had just been switched on.

"Ask me anything," William would say, and slowly, hesitantly, their hands popped up. He had never been married. He had had lots of girlfriends. He had been born in Belmont and gone to college at Tufts. His father was dead, but his mother still lived in the house where he grew up. He'd tried grass, opium, acid, but was completely straight now. Yes, it had felt great, that's why people got addicted. That was the whole point and why drugs were so dangerous. "And no, none of you should even think of trying any," he said.

Not only did he support the antiwar movement, but he'd marched in Boston a few months ago and even got to talk to Abbie Hoffman, who was there giving a speech. William wore a Not-So-Silent Spring button on his jacket lapel, a dot of yellow imprinted with an upraised red fist that held a sprig of greenery. "Hey, hey, LBJ. How many kids did you kill today?" he chanted, and then he told them the answer, writing on the board the Vietnam death toll for 1968—16,899—a number so staggeringly high that the kids shifted uneasily in their seats, because they knew there was a draft. The boys could be called up one day. Their lives could end, just like that. "Not if you resist the draft," William assured them. He drew a map of Canada on the blackboard and tapped the chalk on it. "Or go here," he said. "What a beautiful country." His voice was silky as a promise. "It's possible to live in a perfect world," he said. "Peace. Love. They aren't just dreams, but you have to fight for them."

William believed in civil rights, women's lib, and progressive education, in teaching to the kids' own personal level. School curricula were too regimented for him. They killed any desire for what he called never-ending learning. He talked about this school Summerhill in England, where there were no classes at all and you could learn whatever you wanted on whatever day you wanted. Success there was defined not by grades but by what the child himself thought was successful. "What's a grade?" he said dismissively. "Einstein flunked math. I give grades because the school requires it, but don't think for a moment that grade is all you are. You're all so much more." Lucy thought of the F on her latest French test, all those past-perfect verbs swimming by her like a school of wild fish. She thought of the As and Bs he was giving her, his constant praise.

The kids all loved him (except for Charlotte, who actually dropped out of his class the year before because she said she wasn't learning enough). The kids all thought he was hip and cool and wonderful. He wore a tie and jacket like the other teachers, but his tie had dancing dogs on it, or words in French that he would teach them. *C'est si bon.* It's so good. His suit jacket was sometimes bright purple or paisley, and even though boys were being sent home for having their hair too long, forced to cut it or slick it back with grease, William's hair dusted his collar.

Lucy saw the way some of the other teachers eyed him suspiciously. She heard that parents had begun to complain about the antiwar articles William handed out in class, taken from love-me-I'm-a-liberal magazines like the *New Yorker* or the *Atlantic Monthly*. Where were the things these kids really needed to know, like grammar and vocabulary, and the tests to prove they had mastered them? Shouldn't they be writing research papers? Parents complained that instead of having students in Lucy's class read *Romeo and Juliet*, which the other English class was reading, he had handed out paperbacks of *One Flew Over the Cuckoo's Nest*, and even though he had paid for the books himself, the principal had made all the kids give them back, standing over William to make sure it was done. "The book is subversive," Mr. Socker said. "It's inappropriate. Plus, the author is one of those nut jobs who rides around in a painted bus and takes LSD, and why give these kids ideas?"

"Why not?" William asked. "Isn't that what school is about, ideas?" Mr. Socker just gave him a pained look and walked away.

The next story William had the class read was taken from the *Atlantic Monthly*, put on ditto sheets. The kids all put the pages to their faces to inhale the fumes, eyes closed, and then Lucy saw the pages were censored, whole paragraphs blacked out. William refused to meet anyone's eyes. His mouth was a line. All Lucy could get from the story was that it was about a soldier in Vietnam and he had killed someone and now he was wandering lost in the jungle and everything was rotting: his clothes, his skin, his mind. Too much of the story was gone for her to follow it. She was lost and she began to feel thick and stupid again. One kid complained, "This doesn't make sense with all these words crossed out," and William said, "You're right, it sure doesn't," but his voice was weary, his head lowered, when he said it. "Put the story away," he said finally. "Open up your vocabulary books."

"But we never use them—" someone said, and then William narrowed his eyes. "Just do it," he said, and everyone dug out their Manter Halls.

It wasn't long before it became official, before everyone somehow knew. William had been warned, not just by the principal, but by the school board. There had been too many complaints from parents, and a few from other teachers. There had been meetings with everyone trying to decide what to do. Lucy said nothing about any of this at home, afraid that Iris would think the warning was appropriate, that Charlotte would chime in and agree. William was put on probation for not following the curriculum, for talking about the war, for discussing his personal life, for encouraging the students to call him William, which was not school policy, and which certainly broke the barriers that needed to be there.

One day, William was absent from class. They had a substitute, an older woman in a green suit and tight, dry curls, who scratched her name across the green board in chalk: Mrs. Marmoset. "Like the animal," she told them, and one of the boys in the back made his hands into claws. "I saw that," Mrs. Marmoset said. "And my talons leave scars. Just so you know."

"Let's get this room in order, shall we?" she said. She made them put the desks back in rows, took attendance so she could seat them alphabetically, and then drilled them on vocabulary words, raising her arms as if she were conducting an orchestra, shocked at how they couldn't conjugate irregular verbs or diagram a sentence or use the word *mendacious* in a sentence. She shook her head, clucking her teeth. "This is not good, people," she said. "What have you been doing all year?"

Halfway through a drill of past-perfect verbs, William showed up in the doorway, his shirt rumpled, his hair askew, his tie like a noose around his neck. As soon as he strode into the room, the air felt charged. "I'll take over now," he said to Mrs. Marmoset. He said something to her quietly. Mrs. Marmoset looked at him doubtfully. "Well, I don't think—" she said in her normal voice, but he murmured something else to her, something more insistent, and then she nodded reluctantly.

"Work hard, people," she said to the class. Then she left the room.

Everyone waited, rustling in their seats, but William didn't teach. Instead he surveyed the class, as if he were taking their measure, as if he expected them to do something for him. He looked at all the conjugated verbs on the blackboard, the books open on their desks, all set in fierce rows, and then he sat at his desk and put his head in his hands. "Mr. Lallo?" someone in the back said, but William stayed motionless. "William?" a girl called, and he lifted his head for a moment and then lowered it again. They could see he was crying. Lucy sat frozen at her desk. No one spoke, and then the bell rang and everyone quietly filed out.

After that, William's classes weren't as much fun. He stopped showing movies except for one he said he was required to show, which was about the dangers of drugs. A boy in the film went crazy after taking one drag of a joint and was put in a straitjacket and led away by two doctors, while his parents helplessly cried. A girl took a tab of acid and then shouted, "I can fly!" and jumped off a roof, flapping her arms, while her friends cheered. Lucy glanced at William to see whether he thought this film was as moronic as she did, but he was staring at his hands, his face unreadable.

He began using textbooks, and everyone knew it was because the principal kept showing up without notice, sitting at the back of the class, almost as if he were daring William to go ahead, make trouble, and see what would happen.

It made the kids love William more, making him an even greater hero. Everyone swapped William stories as if they were trading cards. This kid, Ronnie Bortman, had called him at two in the morning, wanting to kill himself, and William had stayed on the phone with him until dawn, talking him down. Now, thanks to William's recommendation letter, Ronnie was headed to Berkeley. There were rumors that he had helped a girl get an abortion, a safe one, even though it was illegal, because William had a doctor friend who owed him a favor. No one even knew who the girl was. That was how good William was at keeping your secrets.

Now, walking out of the school, William doesn't even glance at Lucy. His gaze is a laser, straight ahead. Debbie Polley and Andrea Dickens, two other girls who have crushes on him, are running to talk to him now, and Lucy feels a whip of jealousy, before she reminds herself that the only one he loves is her.

It's been going on for six months now and they are both very careful. Today they are leaving Waltham and moving to rural Pennsylvania, where he has a new job lined up, where they can be together all the time, where Lucy won't have to feel that she is about to spontaneously combust if she can't touch his face, his hand, the slope of his back. Lucy will never feel alone again. No one will ever call her stupid. She can write all she wants—which is all she's been doing now—and he will help her. But she knows what else could happen. She's a minor. William could be arrested, especially for taking her over state lines. She shakes the doom-and-gloom feeling off. No one will find them, she tells herself.

As soon as Lucy sees William, she wants to run and kiss him, but instead she sticks to their plan, checking her watch and pretending to be waiting for someone. Out of the corner of her eye, she sees him get into his little yellow Bug and peel out. She knows exactly where he's going.

When the crowd of students has thinned out, when she's just about the last one left, she walks over to the Star Market, two blocks away. She strides casually across the parking lot, past the silver skeletons of the shopping carts, the occasional shopper wearily getting into a car, probably pondering the price of groceries and not taking any note of Lucy. She remembers the way William looks at her when they are making love (she would never call it balling, the way the other kids do, a coarse, ugly word—that's not what they do), the way he always says, "I love you so fucking much," when he comes, as if he is crying it, while she lies quietly underneath him, just watching his face. He tells her not to worry that she hasn't had an orgasm yet, he will teach her. But she doesn't really care. What she loves is the feel of his skin against hers, the way he keeps saying, "How did I get so lucky?"

She remembers the day he found her eating lunch in his empty classroom way back in December, because it was the only room that was open all the time, the one place where she might have some privacy. She was crying into her peanut butter sandwich because she had come out of gym class to find that one of the tough girls who didn't like her—and for no reason at all, as far as Lucy could see—had tied her tights in a knot again, that the silver bracelet she had hidden in her shoe was missing. She walked out of the dressing room to look around, and the girls were watching her, smiling. "You ever hear of one of these?" one girl said, holding up a comb, and the others laughed while Lucy's face flamed and her hands flew to her hair. Lucy had strode past them to the gym teacher's office, but the teacher had sighed. "Who wears an expensive silver bracelet to gym class?" she asked Lucy.

"I shouldn't cry in school," she sobbed to William, and he shook his head.

"Chemicals in tears release stress. It's good to cry," he said. "Plus, you're in touch with your feelings. I wish I were that open."

She looked up at him, astonished. "You are. Of course you are," she said. "You're the most open person I know."

He shook his head again. "I try and fail."

He handed her tissues from a box on his desk. "Keep crying. Let it all out," he told her. He smelled good, like pine or new wood floors, and it made her stop crying a little. When she was finally finished, snuffling into a bloom of Kleenex, he picked up her journal and browsed through it and she sat frozen, because she had begun to write stories on her own, not just for class. It was fun to write, to be someone else, but she wasn't sure whether her stories were any good. She wanted to tear the journal out of his hands, but instead she watched his face, his eyes unwavering. He read the first story, about a pregnant waitress whose boyfriend has left her, and the whole time she was terrified he was going to tell her to write about what she knew or to watch her spelling and grammar. Instead he shut the journal. "Well, well. This is really excellent," he said.

She blushed, looking down at her hands, at her bitten nails, painted red.

"Why didn't you show this to me before?"

She shrugged, embarrassed.

"You have real talent. You shouldn't hide that."

"You think so?" She looked up at him.

"This is really good, but you need to tighten it up." Casually, as if he were telling her how to put in a kitchen faucet, he pointed out how she didn't need all the backstory about her main character, how the waitress didn't have to yell at a nasty customer but should simply slam down the coffee cup instead to show her anger. "I could work with you on your writing," he told her. "If you want. You could come in during lunchtime. Or after school." He leaned forward and she felt the heat from his body. "Are you willing to work hard?" he asked. "Are you willing to struggle for greatness?"

Every day after that they ate lunch together and talked about her work. He covered her pages with red marks, like slashes with a razor, but she didn't mind because she knew he was on her side. "Go deeper. Think harder," he said. He made her rewrite and rewrite, crossing out her adjectives and adverbs, which he said made you see the writer trying to craft a beautiful flow of words instead of letting the reader get lost in the story. "I want you to disappear," he told her. "There should be no Lucy on this page."

When they were done working, they talked. He admitted that the reason this mattered so much to him was that he was actually a writer, too. "You're kidding!" she said. They had something in common. "You never told us that in class."

"I don't share it with everyone," he said, and she felt herself gleam. He said that he had a novel that was almost finished, that there was real interest from a New York publisher about it, too. "I just need the time to finish it," he said.

"Can I read it?" she asked. "What's it about?"

"Let's focus on you, first," he told her, which both thrilled and disappointed her.

"Did you have someone who helped you, like you're helping me?" she asked.

He shook his head. "My father was a CEO of a big business

company that made sprockets. He wanted me to come work for him, but I refused. He pulled all these strings to get me into business school, and I wouldn't go. Every interview he set up for me I deliberately flubbed. As soon as he figured it out, he lost all interest in me. And in my mom."

"What does he know?" Lucy said. "What a doofus."

"I don't know. Sometimes I think he was right. The truth is that here I am, at a fifth-rate high school with an unfinished novel sitting in my sad, tiny apartment."

"All the kids love you. I hear them. I know. And you'll finish your book. I know it's genius, I just know it. And I bet your apartment's cool, too."

"Sometimes I think that the kids love me because I'm their friend. Not because I'm a good teacher."

"But that's just not true. You've taught me so much. You really helped me. No teacher's ever taken me seriously before."

He studied her. "Maybe we should start sending your stories out and get you published. There's lots of great magazines for young writers."

She met his eyes. He had a fleck of gold in his left iris and she couldn't stop staring at it. "Really?" She looked at him in wonder.

IN THE WEEKS that followed, Lucy began to be more careful about how she dressed for school, trying to look older, more sophisticated. She borrowed Iris's soft silk blouses and rolled the waistbands of her skirts to shorten them as soon as she left the house. ("Don't you look pretty," Iris said.) Lucy couldn't do anything about her hair, so she festooned jeweled clip earrings into her curls like barrettes. She made lists of things she could talk to William about, topics of conversation that might make her seem more interesting, more valuable to be around, more grown up. He had brought a camera to class to snap all their photos. She lied and told him she was learning photography, maybe he could give her pointers. She knew he loved the country, so she spent one evening in the library reading about birds and plants and chickens, and the next time she saw him, she casually mentioned how wild dandelions greens could make a spectacular soup, how brown speckled eggs might not be the prettiest but they were the most nutritious. "You are full of surprises," he said.

One morning at lunchtime, she walked into William's room and he was grinning. He waved a letter at her. "Well, would you look at this," he said, and when she took the paper, her hands were shaking. Honorable mention in *Boston Kids* magazine, a little journal held together with staples. No money, but still, it was a prize, and she would be published in their next issue. He was smiling at her.

"You did this," she said.

"I think we can say that we both did."

She impulsively hugged him, her arms around his ribs, her cheek against his neck. His stubble scratched. He smelled like cigarettes and toothpaste and she couldn't help it, she kissed his mouth, feeling a shock of heat, her eyes fluttering. "I love you," she blurted out, and he pushed her away from him, so that she stumbled, bumping into a chair. She felt like an idiot, as if she had ruined everything. He brushed himself off and moved behind his desk.

"No. You don't," he said. "You're a student. I'm a teacher. It's totally inappropriate."

She wavered on her heels, blinking back tears. "You like me. I know you like me." She felt as if she were pleading.

"I like all my students," he said. His voice was metallic. "But not like that. Never like that." He shook his head. "I think you had better go, Lucy."

After that, he kept his distance. He didn't call on her in

class, even when her hand was the only one raised, and when she spoke out anyway, he looked as if he hadn't heard her. She sat hunched over. When she came to see him at lunchtime, stories gathered under her arm, he said curtly, "I'm busy." One day she came by and he was talking to Miss Silva, the French teacher, smiling sleepily, and when he touched Miss Silva's hand, Lucy felt as if she had been sucker punched. "Tonight would be great," Miss Silva said. "But this time, I'm beating you at pool, buddy."

"Mr. Lallo," Lucy said, and then he turned and looked at her as if he didn't recognize her. Miss Silva took a step back from William. "I have a story. Would you read it?" she asked.

"You can leave it for me on my desk," he said. He turned back to Miss Silva.

The next day in class, William returned her pages. Her story was covered in red marks, his usual slashes. He crossed out all her adjectives and adverbs. *Be more precise*, he wrote. She touched the red ink with her fingertips.

She walked home crying. Everything was ruined. How could she have been so stupid? What was wrong with her? She was crying so hard she couldn't see in front of her. It was cold out, starting to snow, and she was shivering. She swiped at her eyes, at her running nose. A woman walking past gave her a strange look but kept going. Two girls in identical red maxicoats stared at Lucy and then whispered behind their hands.

She didn't go to school the next day, lying to Iris about a fever. She skipped the day after that as well, sitting in her room, painting watercolors on a card, blue stars and moons floating out of a silver cup. It looked impossibly beautiful to her. She thought about signing it but instead tucked it into an envelope and then looked up William's address in the white pages. Iris was watching a movie on TV, so engrossed that she didn't hear

Lucy slipping out the front door. Lucy hitchhiked to William's, and as soon as she got into the foyer of his apartment building, she hit all the buzzers except for his until someone let her in. Then she ran up the stairs and slid the card under his door. Her boots made snowy prints on the hallway rug. By the time she got home, she was feverish with need. She lay on her bed, feeling sick that she had left the card. It was something someone crazy would do. Someone obsessed. At least she hadn't signed her name. She hadn't written anything that would give her away.

On the third day, she returned to school and walked into William's class. "Nice to see you back," he said shortly, and then she felt his hand on the small of her back, just for a moment, like an electrical current. "Go take a seat," he said, and, flustered, she did. She sleepwalked through her classes, but the teachers thought she had been sick, so they gave her leeway.

At the end of school, as she was about to walk home, she saw William standing by his car, in the lot, looking at her as if he were waiting for her. He was perfectly still until she was close to him, and then he bent, as if he were going to tell her a secret. "Do you think you could get to Belmont today?" he said finally. His voice splintered.

"What?" The sun was in her eyes and she squinted at him. It looked as if he had a halo shimmering around his head.

"We can't go there together," he said. He wrote something on a piece of paper and then folded it like origami and handed it to her. She saw his hands were shaking. She opened the paper. *1214 Winston Drive. Apartment 4B*. It was the same address where she had delivered the watercolor. She saw the same elevator she had snuck up to give him the card, his hallway carpeted in blue. She nodded and tucked the paper into her hand.

"I'm suffering, too, Lucy," he told her.

SHE FOUND A pay phone to call Iris. "I'm hanging with friends," she said. "Be home later." Then she hitched a ride from a woman in a purple snow jacket, who was silent the whole time. When they arrived, Lucy practically ran into the apartment building. She rang William's buzzer and walked up the two flights. She could hear music, an itchy slide of jazz, and when she got to William's floor, she smelled coffee, and there he was standing in the hall, in jeans and a white shirt, his door open. His hair was loose around his shoulders and she thought she had never seen him more beautiful. He looked away from her, pained.

"Did you change your mind?" she said.

"Yes. No. Come inside."

His place was small and bright with sun. There was a big painting of a red dog on the wall. She didn't know what to do, so she waited. "Sit," he ordered. "We have to talk about this." She moved gingerly to the edge of his nubby white couch, but he kept moving around the room, pacing.

"You think it's just you, and it's not," he said finally.

"What's not?"

"I get to school and you're the only person I want to talk to," he said. "How insane is that?"

"Me, too—" she said, but he lifted his hand. "Let me finish," he said. "All day, things happen and I keep thinking, I want to tell Lucy this. I want to show Lucy this article. I wonder what Lucy would think of this piece I heard on the radio, if she likes this song, this dish, this color—"

"I feel like that about you."

"Don't say that. Please don't say that. This whole situation is ridiculous. All I wanted was to help you get better as a writer, help you shine a little. That was my job as a teacher and I did that."

He dug his hands into his pockets, his face tense and miserable. "I can't stop thinking about you," he said abruptly.

"What's wrong with me that I can't?" He shook his head. "You don't look sixteen. You don't act sixteen." He hesitated. "You sent me that card. I know it was you. It was the most shockingly beautiful thing I've ever seen. Who knew you could paint?"

"I can't. Not really. I sort of mess around—"

"No. No. This wasn't messing around. This was truly amazing. It spoke to me."

She flushed.

"I have a friend who met his wife when she was fifteen and he was twenty-five. Everyone told them it would never work, that he was too old for her, that it was wrong. But they didn't listen. She's seventy now and he's eighty. The age difference means nothing. It's a blink. Can you imagine? Way back then, they just knew. They just recognized something in the other. What's age, really? Haven't you known some impossibly immature adults? Some really wise young people?" He finally stopped pacing. "You're an old soul, Lucy. You don't think like sixteen."

"You don't think like thirty," she said abruptly, and he laughed, dry as a cough. "How would you know what thirty thinks like?" he said.

"My dad was a lot older than my mom," Lucy said.

"Well, there you go," William said.

Lucy stood up and moved toward him and kissed his mouth. His lips were soft and warm and she sighed against them. He pushed her back but she kissed him again and then she felt him kissing her back, gently at first, and then harder, lowering her to the floor as if she were a captive. She had had sex with only one boy before, at a party, in a dark bedroom, when she was drunk, and he had jammed himself into her, finishing in what seemed like seconds, and then, as soon as it was over, he had freaked out at her for getting blood on the sheets.

But William took his time. He traced the curve of her hip

with his hand. He touched her hair and she flinched, smoothing her hands over it, but he grabbed at her wrists so that when she tried to move, she couldn't. "Don't do that," he said. "Your hair is beautiful, exotic. It's all you." His voice sounded strange and foreign to her, as if he had a fishhook caught in it. He set her hands free and she felt a roaring through her body. She took a breath when he unbuttoned her blouse. He slid her skirt off her hips, down her legs, taking everything off as gently as if it were made of glass. She was naked on the floor and then he moved his hand along her knees, up along her thigh, and then he touched her ass, staying his hand there for a moment, and she tensed, a pulse of fear running along her spine, not sure what he was going to do, whether she'd like it or not, and only knowing that she didn't want him to stop, that she had to move closer to him. "You're a beautiful woman, Lucy," he said, and when she heard that word—"woman"—she shut her eyes. She heard a pulling of plastic—a condom—and then he was inside her and her eyes flew open.

Her head bumped on the floor. Something was digging into her naked hip, but his breath against her face was warm. His hands cupped her ass and then he slid a finger into her, and she gasped and felt a flare of desire. "Look at me," he said, "please. Look at me," and when she did, he shuddered inside her. Afterward he held her, sweaty and close against him, rocking her, the two of them sticky and damp. He fell away from her, panting. "It will get better," he promised. "I'll show you." He kissed her nose, her mouth, the curve of her shoulder.

He helped her up. He ran the shower for her, hot the way she liked it, and set out a soft green towel for her, and when she came out, he had cheese and bread and apples for them on the table, though neither one of them could eat. Finally he got up and went into the other room, coming back with money that he pressed into her hands. "For a cab," he said. He told her why he couldn't come outside with her to wait for the taxi, that they couldn't risk anyone's seeing him with her, because now everything was different. If anyone saw her alone, they'd think she had come to visit a friend. "Get home safe," he said, cupping her face with his hands, and she thought she had never felt so happy or seen him so sad.

OF COURSE THEY couldn't tell anyone. "Some people wouldn't understand this," William told her. "I'm not sure I understand it myself." Every time she came to his place, which was at least three times a week, he acted strange at first, as if he wanted her to go, as if he was furious with himself for wanting her there. "It's my fault, not yours," he kept saying. He wouldn't touch her, and he flinched when she touched him. He was curt with her. "You're a child," he told her, but then gradually he'd soften. He'd move closer and talk about her being an old soul again.

He gave her cab fare to and from his apartment because he didn't like her hitching. He didn't care that everyone did it, he didn't want her to. In class, he treated her the way he treated everyone else, polite, teasing, respectful, not calling on her more than on anyone else.

Lucy began to feel as if she had a sparkler inside her, glowing and growing. She couldn't sleep at night but got up and alphabetized her books or rearranged her closet and once did a hundred sit-ups. She leaped out of bed in the morning, her heart jittering as if she had just drunk coffee. Though sneaking around really seemed to disturb William, Lucy had to admit she found it thrilling. Everything seemed heightened. Every color seemed to vibrate, from the grass on the abandoned ski slope near Piety Corner to the way the air drifted against her skin like a swatch of silk. She used to think that Waltham was a stomach cramp of a town, a way station to the more exciting

Cambridge and Boston, but now she loved everything about it, the brick library smack in the middle of town, the winding suburban streets, the little fire station down the block—even the terrifying psychiatric hospital, which boomed an air horn when someone escaped. When she was at home, she looked at Charlotte and thought: If you could only be this happy, too. If I could only tell you and share this.

AFTER CLASS, AT his place, they worked on her writing, but he also taught her how to cook a few simple things, spaghetti and sauce, fish sautéed in a pan. He showed her how to put a clean nail inside a baking potato, because it would conduct heat and cook the potato faster, and how to rewire a lamp and fix a leaky faucet. He explained why she should always wear dark colors instead of the pastels she liked because it emphasized her pale skin and hair and made her beauty more extraordinary. He told her how she was going to be a very famous writer if she just listened to him. Then they sprawled out on his bed, and every time, he showed her something new she could do with her body. Something new she could do with his. They made love until it was time for her to go home.

ONE DAY IN April, William was called out of his class again, and when he came back, Mr. Socker was with him. Mr. Socker sat in the back, his arms folded, and William handed out copies of *Romeo and Juliet* while the kids groaned. "No carrying on," he said, but he wouldn't meet anyone's eyes.

For the next three weeks, all he did in class was *Romeo and Juliet*, with Mr. Socker sitting in the back. Most of the kids thought it was a big bore, but every time Romeo was barred from seeing Juliet, Lucy sighed. It was like William and her, except their story would have a happy ending.

Even following the curriculum, though, William still couldn't

seem to avoid trouble. Rumors flew again that he was too familiar with his students, that he had skipped a vocabulary lesson. When Lucy went to his apartment, when she tried to talk
to him about it, he shook his head. "We can get a petition together," she said. "Get all the kids to sign it, to fight for you—"

"No," he said. "Let me handle it."

She worried. Of course she worried. If William left, what
would she do? How could she possibly live? She rubbed
William's back. She told him, "Everything's going to be fine,"
even though she was sick with panic. "Maybe you could get a
lawyer," she said, and he shrugged. "Lawyers cost money," he
said.

But then, two weeks later, when she came over, his apartment was filled with candles and he was beaming at her.

"You're all right?" she whispered.

"I resigned, Lucy."

"What?" The room blurred in front of her, flickering with
lights. "When? Why didn't you tell me?"

"I'm telling you now, honey. This has been a long time coming, and I wanted to do it right."

"To do what right?"

"You're looking at the new teacher at Spirit Free School.
It's totally progressive, modeled after Summerhill, and in the
sweetest little town in Pennsylvania, where the air's clean, the
food's fresh, and they're dying to have me. They even pay their
teachers in cash, because they want as little tax money as possible going to the war."

He was leaving here, leaving her. He was so happy he was
vibrating around the room.

"When?" she said.

"I'm teaching out the end of the year. But I don't want
anyone knowing this, Luce. No good-bye party. No gossip. I
wouldn't even tell Socker where I was going. I don't want him

calling the school and souring them on me. I even gave the school a new name, like a fresh start. Billy Lalo. One *l*. Different enough, yet still me."

"But don't you have to tell him?"

"Lucy, it's a new start. I don't want anything to ruin this."

"Pennsylvania." Tears pricked behind her eyes. There might be trains to the city, but not to a rural town, and how would she be able to see him so far away? He'd be lost to her. He'd meet some beautiful hippie teacher who had long hair and wore those lovely Indian gauze dresses, and Lucy would be back in high school, dragging through the corridors.

He tilted her chin up. "What's with this sad puss?"

The room was whirling. "I thought you loved me."

"Of course I love you. What do you think this is about?"

"You're going away."

"Would you want to come with me?"

His smile grew. She leaned against the wall, weak with relief. "You're taking me with you?"

"If you want to."

"Of course I want to. You're my life."

He moved so he was balanced against the wall, too. He told her that as soon as he'd known he had the job, he'd begun looking around for somewhere to live, driving out to Pennsylvania on weekends, not saying a word to anyone, not even Lucy. His excitement about the job kept bumping up against his grief at having to leave Lucy behind. But he was so trapped, and she was a minor. What else could he do? He even told himself that it was for the best to make a clean break, that a girl like Lucy would easily find someone worthy of her.

"Wait—you weren't going to take me?" Lucy frowned, stung.

"I tried not to, Luce. I really tried." At first he just looked at studios. He didn't need very much—and think of the money he would save! But then, in the back of his mind, like a dream, he kept seeing Lucy in the kitchens he looked at, standing by the stove, smiling. He saw her in the bathrooms, wet and silky from her shower, or standing in the woods behind the houses. Stop, he told himself. Stop. He needed to give her up, to move on. She was too young. It was too dangerous. But he couldn't leave her. "We'll figure it out. We'll make it work," he said.

She rested her head along his shoulder. "You make me feel like I can do anything."

"It's our life. But it belongs to us, not to Iris or your sister or anyone else. We have to keep it secret—just for a little while—just until you turn eighteen. That's not so long, is it?"

There it was. Her future. She thought of Iris's wanting her to go to secretarial school, and of Charlotte's already throwing herself into college life before she was even in college. "I could be anywhere with you," she said. She lifted her head up and kissed his mouth.

Now, she sees William's car. He's sitting in the front seat but he doesn't look at her. His face is in shadow. She strides over and gets into his car.

Once she's inside, he finally turns toward her, his smile deepening. Lucy feels as if she were dipped in gold.

She wants to say, I love you. She wants to thank him for rescuing her, but when she does, he shakes his head. "You are the one who rescued me," he says.

"I'm so ready for this," she tells him. She buckles herself into the seat belt. Her whole life is ahead of her, thrumming like angel wings.

For a moment, before the car peels out, she wonders whether she's left anything behind. Whether she's making the right decision. She feels a pang for Iris, how Iris will be hurt when she discovers that Lucy is gone. How maybe she'll be frightened.

She wonders whether Iris will call the police, and what they'll do and how they'll do it. She fingers Charlotte's red scarf and knows her sister will be angry with her. But she'll forgive Lucy when she eventually learns the truth. She just has to. Lucy will miss them a lot, but there's no other way for her. She doesn't know, can't yet imagine, what this will do to them. What will happen to her. How it will all end up splashed across the newspapers, but she won't be around to read it.

Chapter 2

The night Lucy ran away, Charlotte and Iris were camped out in the living room, watching the old Bette Davis movie *Jezebel*. Charlotte had made popcorn, and she was trying not to cry as Bette Davis sacrificed herself to take care of her married lover, who had yellow fever, and when the credits began to roll, Iris sighed and said, "They don't make movies like this anymore." Was it worth it, to die with the one you loved, the way Bette had, Charlotte wondered, especially when he wouldn't even know it? Did people really fall in love like that? She never had, and it made her a little sad. She was so awkward around boys. She could never think of what to say or do, and when she blurted out something about a movie she'd just seen or a book she loved, the boy usually just gaped at her and moved away. Who was she kidding? She was awkward around girls, too, and she was lucky she had her friend Birdie to hang out with. Charlotte turned off the set.

"Your sister's late again," Iris said.

Lucy was home less and less these days, and even though she had an eleven o'clock curfew, she never kept it. No, Lucy made a show of going to bed early, and then two hours later, Charlotte would hear a noise and look out her window, and there would be Lucy, in a glittery short skirt and tube top, running out to a car idling in front of their house. Lucy would come home at four, quietly fitting her key into the lock. Charlotte was always worried. "Where were you?" Charlotte asked, following Lucy into her room. "Were you with a boy? Where do you really go?" Lucy was always full of excuses. "I fell asleep at a friend's," Lucy said. "If you don't believe me, you can call her," Lucy said, but Charlotte never did.

The few times Iris woke up, wanting to know what was going on, Lucy made it seem innocent. She didn't stink of booze or grass. Her clothes were never torn or stained. "Don't you know the things that can happen to a young girl out at night?" Iris asked her.

Lucy sighed. "Why do you always have to think about the worst things?"

"Because the worst things happen all the time."

"Not to me," Lucy insisted. "Look, I'm fine. I'm perfectly fine. And I promise it won't happen again." She yawned, stretching her arms over her head, and left the room. "I'm going to bed."

Five minutes later, Charlotte could hear the soft rumble of her snore.

Who knew where Lucy was now? And with whom? Charlotte tried to think where she might be if she were Lucy, but her mind went blank. She could never be Lucy, no matter what she did.

Even when they were little, and their parents were alive, Charlotte had been the plain Jane, the coltish girl who was thoughtful and liked to look at the pictures in her books, play the piano, or sing along to her *Peter Pan* record, unlike her parents, who were always having parties at the house or going out to them. Before Lucy was born, when Charlotte's parents wanted her to dress up and show off to their friends by singing or playing the piano, she got so anxious she couldn't do it. She saw the disappointment on their faces. "Why do you have to be such a mouse?" her mother asked her later. Her father slung his arm around her mother. "How did we two life-of-the-parties end up with a wallflower?" he said, shaking his head.

But then there was Lucy. Rosy as a peach, with blond curly hair and lashes so long they left shadows on her cheeks. Of course, when she was born, Charlotte was jealous. Of course. She saw how her parents doted on Lucy, how they stopped begging Charlotte to come out at parties and instead paraded Lucy, letting everyone hold and admire her. And Lucy loved the attention, laughing and stretching out her hands to whoever was nearby. "What a flirt!" their mother said, admiration in her voice. But Charlotte couldn't help herself from falling in love with her baby sister, too. Lucy smiled as soon as Charlotte entered the room. Lucy grabbed her hand and wouldn't let go. Her eyes were always searching Charlotte out.

Lucy turned two, and then three and four, and she tore around the house, singing songs so loudly they were almost a shout. She got into the canister of flour and dumped it on her head, laughing, saying, "Now I have white hair like Daddy!" and making their parents laugh, too. "You little live wire!" their mother said.

Charlotte realized there was something she could give Lucy that her parents couldn't. She could protect her from them. She could make sure that every night, she was lying in Lucy's bed with her, their legs and arms entangled, so her parents couldn't easily lift Lucy up and make her dance the twist to entertain their friends. She stayed in the backyard when Lucy was playing— and their mother was napping, in the chaise longue—to make sure the big dog next door didn't come over and frighten her. Charlotte began reading stories to Lucy, too, until Lucy began to follow Charlotte around, yearning to hear another.

And then their parents died, and Charlotte was terrified. What if she and her sister were split apart? If they were to get another family, wouldn't the family want the pretty towhead rather than the one who was so shy she barely spoke? Even when Iris took them home, Charlotte steeled herself, thinking that at any moment Iris could give her back.

But to Charlotte's astonishment, Iris didn't. Instead she loved both girls. She took them to the park every day, even though Charlotte didn't like to run around wild the way Lucy did, preferring to sit on a bench reading or just watching. One day, Charlotte cautiously leaned against Iris. Iris stayed perfectly still until Charlotte curled closer, and then she lifted up her arm and hugged the girl near.

THE NIGHT LUCY disappeared, Charlotte prowled the house after Iris went to sleep. She passed Lucy's room, the empty bed, the cover carelessly thrown over it. Just the year before, Lucy had painted her walls red, which Charlotte had thought would look awful, but instead it made the room glow. Nothing looked any different. There was the poster of the Beatles tacked up beside one of the Rolling Stones. There was Lucy's dresser, with all the cheap drugstore makeup she liked. Maybe Charlotte could take more time to spend with her sister. Maybe on the weekend they could bike into Harvard Square the way they used to and get raspberry lime rickeys and burgers at Brigham's. She sat on Lucy's bed and heard something rustle under the pillow. She pulled the sheet back and there it was. A white envelope. Writing on it. *To Iris and Charlotte.* Charlotte tore it open.

Charlotte didn't realize she was shaking until the paper flew out of her hands. "Iris!" she yelled. "Iris!"

Iris called the police, her voice breaking on the phone. "Please!" she cried. "Hurry!"

Two young cops came over and both read Lucy's letter with uninterest. "Girls that age come back," one cop said. He told her that all the kids today were like lemmings, making their way to San Francisco, poking flowers in their hair like idiots. Kids today smoked so much dope it's a wonder they had any brain cells left. They played their music too loud and they dressed like buffoons, and the girls—nine out of ten of them—got pregnant. "Free love," one cop snorted. "Nothing free about having a baby. And no respect for authority." He looked pointedly at Charlotte.

"I'm not a lemming," Charlotte said. She was in a plain black T-shirt and blue jeans. She had a headband in her hair, which was cut to her neck, making her just about the only girl beside Lucy in the whole high school who didn't have long hair. Charlotte might have a joint wrapped in strawberry paper in her sock drawer, but that didn't make her a head. "I'm going to Brandeis in the fall."

"Okay, so not you, then," said one of the cops. "Every other kid in the world but you." He studied Charlotte. "Does she have a boyfriend?" the police asked. "A girlfriend she might have left with?"

Charlotte stared at the cop. He actually had an angry zit on his chin. "I don't know."

"Of course she doesn't have a boyfriend," said Iris. "I'd know about that."

"We'll keep this," the cop said, tucking Lucy's note in his hand. "We have to wait twenty-four hours, then we can start looking."

"But where is she?" Iris cried. "A lot can happen in twenty-four hours! What does this look like to you?"

The cop put one hand on her shoulder. "It looks like she's alive and safe. And it looks like she wants you to know it."

Chapter 3

William and Lucy were in Pennsylvania, after nearly six hours of driving. The traffic had been terrible and they had stopped overnight at a small motel, where the man at the desk had thought William was her dad. It was the first time she saw William angry, and the next morning, on their last stop, William had gone into a drugstore and bought her a tiny fake gold band. He slid it on her ring finger. "There. Now people should have no confusion," he said. "Soon there'll be a real one."

"I can't wait to get to our home," Lucy said.

Home, what a funny word. But this would really be her home. She could find work and help with the bills. She and William would decorate, make it cozy. She'd be the lady of the house.

William told her that he had always wanted to have a little farm with food he could grow himself, to see nothing in the distance but sky and trees. He couldn't stand the Boston area, all its hum and noise, the bureaucracy of the school system, the way money seemed to rule everything and everyone.

She loved William, but the deeper they got into the country, the more she felt doubt fluttering around her edges. When he had first mentioned Pennsylvania, she hadn't realized how rural a place it really was. "The cities are dying," he told her. "Going back to the land is the only thing that makes sense." The only time she had ever really lived outside the city was when Iris put both her and Charlotte in overnight camp one summer. It was just two weeks, and Lucy had hated it—the bugs, the mosquitoes, the terrible silence at night. "There's nowhere to walk," she had said to Iris, but Iris had pointed out the miles of fields humming with grasshoppers, and Lucy had looked at her as if she were crazy. She got bitten alive on the nature walks. She was told to love the scenery, but the trees all looked the same. She didn't even get to see or be with Charlotte because they were on opposite sides of the camp, and it was only later that she learned that Charlotte had been as unhappy as Lucy.

You could take the country and throw it into the lake, she thought. She was a girl who walked from Warwick Avenue to Belmont to catch the bus to Harvard Square, where she could cruise the streets and go in and out of every shop or sit in the Common listening to music, her face lifted to the sun.

Well, William was wonderful and he had happened to her. And maybe being in the country would be different when you were with the person you loved. It wouldn't matter where you were, anywhere would be paradise. It was a new experience she could write about. And she would be lying if she didn't think that William might grow tired of the solitude, too, that maybe they could stay here until she was eighteen and then move to San Francisco or Los Angeles. "Think about what you want to see five years from now," William said, "and I will make it happen," and Lucy always thought of the two of them in a small, bright apartment, a glittering city spread below them like a banquet.

"Wait until you see the house."

He told her how he had found it. One day he was sitting at a diner, and he had overheard the waitress talking about renting out her house with an option to buy, because she had had enough of the chilly weather. She was moving to California, where she was going to bread herself in beach sand and work on her tan. "Could I see the house?" he asked, and she turned, her hand on her hip, a smile spreading across her face. She drove him over after her shift, just another half hour. "This is it," she said, and as soon as he saw it, a neat little Cape Cod with a yard and trees and a porch, he wanted it. The inside was even better. He loved the snug little bedroom, the way the light slanted into the dining room, and the kitchen was so big he could imagine cooking feasts. It felt like fate. He immediately signed the lease, and his fake name gained new importance, because now he knew he'd ask Lucy to come with him.

"It's cozy, set off from the road," he told Lucy now. He talked about all the things he wouldn't miss: Boston traffic, the crappy Waltham school system, the crowded Green Line subway. "Think about waking up hearing mockingbirds outside instead of honking cars," he told Lucy. He stroked a rope of her hair. "I'll teach you to drive," he said.

She brightened. She'd like that, learning to drive. She could go places, explore the towns nearby. Lucy gazed at the countryside stretching out on either side of the road. They seemed to be driving for miles down a road without any other houses. She was used to seeing people walking around, or at least hitching, but there were hardly any cars on the road, just thickets of trees. "Look, a deer!" William said, pointing, but all Lucy saw was the bob of its tail before it vanished. They passed a house with boarded-up windows, another with a mangy-looking goat tethered to a stick in the front yard. The goat raised its head and bleated. She could see its ribs poking through its hair. "Are we lost?" Lucy asked, gripping the armrest, craning her neck until the goat was gone from sight.

"Not at all."

Lucy sank lower into her seat. White trash. That was what

people who lived in such a place were called, and now it was where Lucy lived.

William finally turned down a dirt road. There at the end was a one-story brown clapboard house, with a walk surrounded by yellow flowers. She liked the flowers, like little bobbing suns, and there was a big maple tree in the front. But all around the house were woods. She sat up straighter. "It's nice, right?" William said. "Didn't I tell you?" He looked so hopeful she didn't dare say no.

She got out of the car, her legs stiff as glass straws. William shut his door and took her hand. But the closer she got to the house, the worse it looked, and her hope faded. The paint was chipping along one side, the windows were cracked in places. She stumbled across the dry, patchy lawn. "We can fix it up," William told her. He waved his hands, pointing out the wood shutters, which actually worked, the fireplace ("Imagine how comfy we'll be in the winter!" he said), all the land in the back that they could use to plant a garden. He partitioned it out with his fingers. "This soil's great for vegetables," he promised. "Wait until you see how self-sufficient we can be."

Every direction she looked, there was nothing but land. Not even neighbors.

She heard clucking and then what sounded like a scream from a pterodactyl. "What the heck is that?" she said, and William laughed. "You'll see," he said. "It's a surprise for you. You're going to love it." He took her hand and led her around to the back. Then she saw the wire chicken coop, the little open wood henhouse with rafters, and three chickens, black, red, and orange, pecking at the dirt. A rooster strutted in front of them. "We have chickens?" she said.

"The owner left them for us. She had someone else feeding them until we got here. Isn't it great? We can have eggs. Real eggs, not the junk you buy in the supermarket." He pointed to each hen. "Let me see if I remember. Dorothy. Lisa. Mabel. And the rooster is George." Lucy felt the rooster staring her down, his eyes like BB pellets. "Shoo," she said weakly, waving her hands, and George flew up against the coop, his wings flapping, his feet like spurs angled in front of him. He banged against the wire of the coop, making it thwang, and Lucy jumped back. The black chicken—Dorothy, was that her name?—made a sad, mournful sound, as if she were beseeching Lucy.

"Jesus, do we need him?" She pointed to the rooster, who was back on the ground again, kicking fiercely at the dirt.

"Of course we do. And he's just being protective of the hens. He'll get used to you." William put an arm around Lucy. "Come on. Let me show you our house." He led her away, but she took one look back. The rooster was standing perfectly still, glaring at her.

THEY WENT IN through the front door. He had to be kidding, Lucy thought. The inside didn't look much better than the outside. The kitchen had chipped, yellowing linoleum and an old-fashioned stove. The bedroom was so tiny the bed barely fit in it. "We can paint everything white and it will look larger," William told her. He grabbed her hand and led her into the bathroom, all black tile and peach walls, but then she saw the stain in the bathtub, like the piece of a map, and when she tried to flush the toilet, it kept running. William waved his hand. "It's nothing. I can get it to work. You'll see." She tried to feel hopeful, to count the good things about the house, ticking them off on her fingers. The floors were wide-plank oak, the ceilings were high, and there were tall windows in every room. The kitchen was large enough to eat in, and best of all, there was a skylight in the bedroom so she could look up at night and see the stars.

"We'll buy furniture cheap at yard sales," William said. "We can really make this our home, Lucy."

"The TV could go here," Lucy said, pointing to the far wall of the living room.

"Do we really need a TV? Then you don't read as much."

"We read a lot."

"You'll read more without it. And anyway, we have a radio and my stereo system," he said. "What more do we need?"

"We could watch movies together. Cuddle up, drink some wine."

"Can you be happy here?" he asked her. "Are you telling me this isn't a good idea, what I planned for us? Because if you are, well, I'll figure something else out. I want you to be happy."

She walked over to him and rested her head along his chest. She could feel the thunk of his heart. "I'm with you," she said. "Of course I can be happy." She tucked the idea of a TV back in her mind. She could convince him later, or maybe she could find a cheap little black-and-white set and just surprise him with it. She'd turn on a movie and he'd see how easy it was to get caught up in someone else's story.

THE NEAREST GROCERY store was a forty-five-minute drive (she timed it) on a long, empty road. But when they pulled into the crowded parking lot of the Giant Eagle Market, she felt instantly better. There were people milling around their cars, packing grocery bags into trunks, tending to misbehaving children. Civilization, Lucy thought.

Inside was even better, with more people. Anyone looking at them would think they were a married couple, she bet. She smiled at everyone who met her eyes, the girl in the plaid dress, the young woman with a blond baby on her hip, and when they smiled back, she felt a flush of warmth. She could meet people, make friends. Maybe it wouldn't be so bad. Within ten minutes, she decided she loved everything about the Giant Eagle. She bounced to the loud Muzak, a syrupy rendition of "Yummy, Yummy, Yummy." Lucy felt so grown up walking with William, her arm looped in his, deciding on laundry soap, macaroni, and fruit, even though she had no real idea what to get. The only time she felt sure was in the toiletries aisle, where she bought shampoo, conditioner, and soap and a new toothbrush and toothpaste. But when she reached for a small package of hamburgers, William took it out of her hands and put it back in the case.

"No, no, honey, we're vegetarians," he said.

"We are?" She remembered all the lunches they had shared at school, the late nights at the diner. He had eaten meat. Both of them had taken bites from a roast beef sandwich, and she still could remember how sexy and intimate she had thought it was. "Since when?"

"Since lately. Did you ever see a slaughterhouse? Do you know lobsters have nuclear families? Why shouldn't they be allowed to live out their lives the same as we do?"

"But I like burgers."

"Honey, we'll have burgers. Buckwheat burgers. Wait until you taste how delicious they are, how great you'll feel after you eat them." He wheeled the cart away from the meat section. "Anyway, it's really bad karma to eat meat," he said. He tapped her nose gently. "And you and I, we need all the good karma we can get right now." She glanced back at the burgers. For a moment, thinking about them, her mouth watered. "But we have chickens," she said finally.

"We're not eating them. We're just eating the eggs. That's different."

"But what will we eat?" She knew only one vegetarian at school, a girl who had lived in a commune with her parents and then moved to Waltham, and every day she brought the same sad-looking packed lunch to school, brown rice and broccoli in a plastic tub. No one wanted to eat with her.

"You'll see. We'll eat well."

Lucy reached for a pint of chocolate ice cream and then looked at William. "This meet with your approval?" she said.

"Come on, don't be like that," he said. "Of course we can have ice cream, but it's a long drive. It'll melt. " He took the pint and put it back on the freezer shelf. "We'll learn to make our own," he said. "It'll be fun." She wheeled the cart to the checkout line.

The whole market was so crowded it seemed to hum. She wanted to just stay here, wandering up and down the aisles, looking at all the different kinds of cookies, the cheeses and candies. All this choice. She smiled happily at William.

"Soon we won't have to come here so much," he said. "We'll have our own eggs, our own vegetables. We'll be growing all our own meals."

Lucy leaned against him. You couldn't grow ice cream, you couldn't grow every single vegetable. They'd still have to come to the market.

They set their food on the conveyer alongside the register. A girl about Lucy's age, with long blond hair, bangs brushing her eyes, was pushing the food through, and she smiled at Lucy and made circles in the air, like twirls. "I like your hair," the girl said, and Lucy looked at her name tag. Freda. "I like yours better, Freda," Lucy said. "Especially your bangs."

Freda laughed. "I razor-cut them myself."

"Do you live near here?" Lucy asked, and then William nudged her and looked at her meaningfully.

"We can help you out and bag this quickly," he said, and he began plucking up items and stuffing them into brown paper bags. "We need to get a move on," he said to Freda, and then he handed a bag to Lucy.

Lucy waited until they were outside. "How come I couldn't talk to her? She doesn't know anyone in Waltham. How is she a danger to us?"

William opened the car door. "You never know," he said. "That's the thing. You never know. Besides, you can do better than a checkout girl for a friend."

She felt stung, but he drove to another store, with dresses and blue jeans in the window, and she looked at him curiously. "You didn't bring very much," he said. "Let's get you what you need."

He bought her two pairs of bell-bottoms and six T-shirts that were on sale, underwear, socks, and a dress, pale blue with a flounce on the bottom. "For when we hit the town," William said, and Lucy twirled around and hugged him.

WILLIAM'S NEW JOB started immediately. Spirit Free School, just half an hour away, was a year-round school because, as the slogan said, "We are all lifelong learners." When he had come down before to scope out jobs, this was the first place William had found, and he had instantly loved the vibes. The walls were festooned with colorful drawings and displayed fanciful essays the kids had written about what Robin Hood would do in retirement (William's favorite was that Robin would open a muffin store). A special room had been set up just for clay, and another for blocks, with a big sign that said BLOCKS BUILD IMAGINATION. To William's surprise, the principal didn't ask for his credentials or want references but instead told him he'd like to watch him teach a class, spur of the moment. A class could have five-year-olds and ten-year-olds, because age had nothing to do with learning. Pictures books were set beside volumes of Shakespeare. William walked into this one big room. "No desk!" he said. "Not one in sight!" Instead there were comfortable old couches and pillows, armchairs and rugs, and kids were wandering all over the room, picking up books and musical instruments, talking to one another. William was fast on his feet, and he made all the kids stand up and then he taught them how to do the Charleston, all the while talking about the 1920s and the Jazz Age and throwing in something about F. Scott Fitzgerald and Hemingway. Just like that, the principal decided he was hired.

The school was founded with a focus on living in the natural world. Every kindergartner would learn to make and play a recorder out of wood gathered from the local forest. Students would learn to paint, sew aprons, plant gardens, and cook a few simple dishes like baked apples or mashed potatoes. Girls could learn woodworking, and boys could learn needlepoint, because nothing was assigned by gender. He had free rein to do whatever he wanted. When William came home at night, he couldn't stop talking about the kids: Rain and Flower and Jacobean, little sponges who would just soak up knowledge. "It's busy and noisy and wonderful," he said. Students were not subordinate to teachers, and everyone would go by their first names because the philosophy was that there needn't be a hierarchy. "They all call me Billy," William said. "No more Mr. this or Mr. that." William could wear whatever he wanted, including T-shirts and jeans, and no one cared how long his hair was. When Lucy looked at him, she swore he had lopped off years from his age. And forget report cards. Instead, teachers were encouraged to write narratives about each child, telling the story of a student's progress. Sure, there were sometimes tests, but kids could do them collaboratively, figuring it out together.

"Isn't that cheating?" Lucy said, and William shook his head.

"Tests are to frighten you into studying things you may not

want to study. You should learn what you want to learn, what's practical for you. And who better to know that than you?"

"Oh," Lucy said doubtfully. "Do little kids always know what they need to learn?"

"Jesus, Lucy. Of course they do."

She tried to think what had been useful to her in school, and all she could come up with was the Home Ec class all the girls had to take. She had loved making Hamburger Helper, frying it in a little metal pan, and wolfing it down when it was done. Still, now hamburgers were off the menu, so a whole lot of good that class was. And William would probably ban Hamburger Helper anyway.

William was in charge of eight kids, all different ages (there were only forty students in the whole school), which William said was a plus because it meant he could really get to know each child.

"What about the other teachers?" She hoped there weren't any pretty young women. She couldn't imagine anyone not falling in love with William.

"Two other guys, one woman. They seem nice."

"What's the woman like?"

William sighed. "Lucy, she's married and she's pregnant."

"Can I come see the school?"

"Let's wait a bit. We want to be careful."

"What about my GED?" Lucy said. "When can I start that? And I should get a job, too. Help out."

"Luce, we have all the time in the world," he said.

WILLIAM LEFT THE house every morning by six, since parents could drop off their kids anytime between seven and nine. He slid out of bed, trying not to wake her, but Lucy always bolted up because she felt greedy for time with him. She poured them both juice. She scrambled eggs, which she had also learned from Home Ec class, and when they came out fluffy and golden, she wished she had a camera so she could snap a picture of them. She thought, I'm the lady of the house. "Who knew I could cook so great?" she beamed, and William laughed, kissed her, and then was gone.

Their house. How she loved saying that. Maybe it wasn't much, maybe it was rundown and rural, but it was hers. Theirs. The whole world was spread out in front of them. Maybe they had to stay hidden here for a while, but this little place could be their oasis. She rearranged the furniture so the bookshelves were in the sunny part of the room. She found a can of paint out back and a brush, and she painted the bathroom deep blue. And she loved him. Oh, how she loved him. When she was eighteen, maybe they could even get married here. Then she could invite Iris and Charlotte to come see her. She could cook something delicious for them. She could show off how wonderful her life had turned out.

When William came home, when he saw the painted room, his mouth dropped open. "Lucy, what you've done!" He told her everything about his day, the two of them sitting on the porch in the cooling evening, and then he took her hand. "It's such a relief to have someone to talk to like this, isn't it?" William said.

Lucy thought of all the things she had ached to say when she was at home with Iris and Charlotte, how lonely she was, how scared that she'd never amount to anything. She looked at William, how handsome he was, his hair long and loose around his shoulders, that straight nose that she loved to kiss. Away from school, he looked younger to her, almost like a kid, and she leaned over and started unbuttoning his plaid shirt, tumbling him to the porch floor until he kissed her.

One day she cleaned the kitchen from top to bottom, scrubbing the stove with steel wool, washing the floor by hand. The following week she dug a garden in the backyard, the sun beating on her back. It was hard work and she was exhausted by the time William came home, happy to sit on the porch with him. But by the third week, she was running out of things to do. William had surprised her with a pad of paper, brushes, and a box of watercolors in little tubes. She had grasped the box in her hands, pleased. "You have all this time to write now," William had told her. She grabbed her blue journal and a pen and settled by the kitchen table and wrote a story about a young woman who goes to live on a farm and grows apples, but after a few hours, Lucy set the pen down. She had no idea where to take the story. She heard the house ticking around her.

They got a phone with an unlisted number, using the same fake name he'd given the school. The phone rang only once a day, and Lucy rushed for it. They had agreed she wouldn't speak until she heard his voice, and when she did, she relaxed, braceleting the cord around her wrist. "I miss you like crazy," she whispered.

"I'm kissing you," he said quietly. "I'm imagining your gorgeous face and counting every freckle on your shoulders."

"Come home, I'm lonely."

"Soon," he told her. She heard someone shouting his name, and then there was a rush of his breath. "I got to go," he said. She could hear kids yelling in the background, and then he hung up and there was the dial tone. She always felt better after he called, but she wished that his calls would last longer, that the feeling she got from his voice wouldn't fade so quickly.

Lucy roamed around the yard, but the only sounds she heard were the cry of a heron and the twittering of the chickens. No matter where she stood, when she turned around, all she saw was sky and land and bugs. She thought of the cashier at the Giant Eagle, but that was forty-five minutes away by car. And William took the car every day. And Lucy didn't know how to drive yet, though William still promised to teach her. It would be hours to walk, and even then, how could she know the girl would even be there? William wouldn't be home until around four or five, which was at least three hours away. She came back inside and fiddled with the radio, finding a rock station. "Good Morning Starshine" came on and she danced a little, lost in the music, swaying, and then she stopped. If they had a TV, she could watch movies at least. It didn't have to be stupid game shows or the soaps that Iris was so addicted to. There were educational shows on TV. She could make that case to William.

Every week he came home with cash. "This is for us," he told her, but she never knew where he put it, and when she asked him, he teased her and said, "Now who's the banker around here? If you need money, just ask me." She searched the house anyway, but she couldn't find it. Well, it was their money. If she needed some, she was sure he'd give it to her.

She wandered around the house, looking at William's books. He had a macrobiotic cookbook, *You Are All Sanpaku*. What the heck was *sanpaku*? She leafed through the book until she found the definition: if the whites of your eyes showed below your pupils, you were in danger both physically and spiritually. She stood in front of a mirror and stared at herself. Holy hell, she was *sanpaku*. The book was filled with curing recipes. Rice and seaweed. Rice and broccoli. Rice and raisins. They sounded worse than being *sanpaku*. She shoved that book aside and picked up *The Ten Talents*, but when she opened it up, she saw it was from the Seventh-Day Adventists. God's original diet for humans, it said. The recipes were complicated. You had to mix and match vegetables with grains to get whole proteins, and she didn't like the tone of the authors, who seemed a little bossy to her. What was wrong with a piece of fish? She thought of Iris's baked chicken and sweet potato casserole, the crunch of the skin, the creamy marshmallow bonnet. The skirt steaks Iris would sizzle up in a pan, smothering them in gravy. Then she thought of Iris's concern about her grades, Charlotte's obsession with college. No, she was lucky to be here with William.

IT WAS SUPPOSED to be her job to feed the chickens, but she hated doing it, having to get into the henhouse with all the hens, the rooster with them, like a little martinet. He was always watching the hens. It looked as if he was swaying in a dance, and as soon as he noticed her, he would stop and crow at the hens, as if he were warning them about her. She quickly set down fresh water, scattered feed, and hightailed it out of there.

But most of the time the hens were outside, waiting for her. As soon as she came near them, they got manic. All she had to do was reach out her hand, feed clenched in her fist, and they would poke and prod one another out of the way, jockeying for position. When she scattered the feed, as far away from her as she could, they pecked noisily to get at it. But it wasn't just food that excited them. Sometimes something as simple as a squirrel running past their pen would set them off on a twenty-minute fusillade of squawks and ruffling feathers. Knowing the birds were penned up was the only thing that made her feel safe.

One day she walked into the little house where the hens were sitting. All the chickens were accounted for. She looked around for George and finally saw him lazing in a spot of sun, ignoring her. Good. Good. She'd be in and out of the coop as fast as she could. Lucy wanted to check to see whether there were any eggs, but the thought of putting her hands under the hens' bodies scared her. The hens, bobbing their heads, watching Lucy suspiciously, weren't making it any easier.

Lucy didn't even like eggs that much, and she didn't taste

any difference between these and store bought, though William shut his eyes and practically swooned. Why couldn't William collect the eggs instead of her if he liked them so much? William had told her to reach in quickly with her hand facing down, so that if a hen got nippy, she was more prone to snip at the back of your hand. But Lucy just poked a finger under Mabel, who bit Lucy's thumb, a sharp pinch that made her wince. "Hey!" She put the thumb in her mouth, wondering about what diseases chickens carried. The other chickens began screaming, which brought George running toward her. He lunged, beating with his wings, making her jump. She slid her hand under Dorothy, feeling the weight of the hen on top of it, then quickly grabbed for the egg and removed her hand before the hen could attack her. Dorothy bobbed her head and squawked. Lisa was easier. Lucy gathered the eggs, just three of them, warm and speckled in her hands, feeling the strange glittering eyes of the hens on her, the heated stare of the rooster.

Already she was dirty. She'd have to do laundry, but she didn't really know how. It was something William had been doing for them. She was tired of her T-shirts, of her bell-bottoms. She wanted cutoff shorts and a halter top.

She put the eggs in a blue bowl on the kitchen table, like a vase of flowers. She had to admit they looked pretty, like a still-life painting. Then she went to get the watercolors and paper that William had bought for her. She'd capture the eggs while she waiting for him to come home to her again.

THE SOUND OF the door woke her. She had been sleeping on the bed, a book beside her. "Hello!" William called, and she wandered out into the living room. She was cranky from having just woken up, but as soon as she saw him, her whole body felt lighter. The air seemed to glow. "You can't believe what a great day I had!" he told her. In the morning, he said, a nurse came in and all the kids had their fingers pricked so she could tell what blood type they were. "Dig it, I'm B Positive," he said, showing her the card. He said that later one of the kids was interested in studying the lake, and then all the kids were, so they spent the whole day swimming in their clothes, using math to calculate how long it would take to swim out to the float, how long it might take for their clothes to dry. "You went swimming?" Lucy said wistfully. She thought about how hot it had been that day, how she had wanted someone to wring her out.

"It was educational. I'm starving," William said. "What's for dinner?"

Lucy blinked at him. She hadn't had lunch, hadn't even thought of eating.

"You didn't cook us dinner?" He looked around the house as if there must be some mistake. "Honey, we have all this food."

"I didn't think—you usually do the cooking—"

"I'm exhausted, Lucy. I had a really hard day. What did you do all day?"

She showed him the painting. "Wow, that's pretty," he said, but he was headed into the kitchen, and she followed. William took out some noodles, which would be quick, some canned sauce. There was a green pepper in the refrigerator.

"Could you start teaching me to drive?" she said. "Then I could drive you and pick you up from school. I could have the car all day so I could go places."

"That won't work. I never know when school will be out. We go until the kids decide they want to stop."

"Well, I could hang out. I could watch you—"

"No, no," he said. "It might be disruptive to the kids. They think of themselves as this self-sufficient community."

The world seemed to stretch out in front of her like a hard pane of glass.

He noticed her deep frown and wrapped one arm around her, drawing her close. "I'll take you exploring, Lucy. But you know, I like knowing where you are, knowing that you're safe."

"I'd be safer if I was with you," she said.

ON HIS WAY out the door the following morning, William reminded Lucy that there was brown rice in the cupboard, tahini, fruits, and vegetables. He left the *Ten Talents* cookbook pointedly on the counter. There was more than enough to make them dinner, and no, it didn't matter that she didn't know what time he would be coming home, because the beauty of vegetarian food was that it was quick. "You can spend your time going through the cookbooks, finding us something great to eat. Just get all the prep work done, and then when I come home, it'll take you just ten minutes at most. Surprise me." Prep work. She had no idea what that even meant. He promised that soon he would take her into town. They'd find a great GED program for her, or even a job, which would be helpful because William's salary barely covered their expenses and they couldn't save a thing. Even if the transportation might be tricky, they'd work it out. "You'll be a great driver," he told her.

BUT JUNE TURNED into July and then August, and Lucy was still at home doing not much of anything. In another month, school would start up and she wouldn't be there, and what would all the kids back home say about her being missing? She tried to imagine it, to hear their voices. She thought of Charlotte off at Brandeis, of Iris living alone in the house, and she swelled with longing. Soon, she told herself. Soon she could make contact, when her adult life was in place.

One morning, as soon as William left, she turned on the radio just to hear other human voices. She wasn't used to being so alone. She liked noise all around her. Even at Iris's, she liked hearing Charlotte thumping around or Iris singing along to the

radio. The quiet dug into her bones. The announcer was talking about a murder, some actress she'd never heard of, Sharon
Tate, and a bunch of other people, brutally killed right in their
own home, the word *pig* scrawled on the door. *Helter skelter.*
But misspelled in blood, *healter*, and somehow that made it all
the more terrifying to Lucy. Sharon Tate had been pregnant,
and when Lucy heard who she was married to, she gasped, because Roman Polanski was one of the filmmakers William used
to talk about in his class. No one knew who did it. Her mouth
went dry and she switched off the set. It was in California. It
wasn't here.

She went outside, feeling funny, because here she was, and
the best company available to her was chickens, who were no
company at all. She grabbed some feed from the big bag by
the coop and scattered it. The hens squawked and Lisa pecked
Dorothy out of the way. "Cut that out," Lucy ordered. She
put some feed in her hand, crouched down, holding out her
palm for Dorothy, lifting it up and away when Mabel tried to
get near. "This is Dorothy's," she said. Dorothy pecked at her
palm, her beak like tiny little scissors. She made an odd purr-
ing sound.

When all the feed was gone, the chickens headed for the
henhouse, pushing Dorothy out of the way so they could go
into the coop first, picking out their favorite places. Dorothy
went in last, but she settled farthest from the door, in a patch
of sun. "At least you have some warmth," Lucy told Dorothy.

Lucy went back inside and, because there was really nothing else to do, fell asleep on the bed, dreaming that someone
was talking to her, telling her something important, but she
couldn't make out the sound. Something bit her, and she woke
up. Dorothy was on the bed, her head cocked, murmuring.
Lucy didn't move, and Dorothy then settled down, her eyes
shutting, the steady buk-buk-buk winding down. William had .

told her that chickens could be smart, that they could figure out ways to escape if they really wanted. Or maybe she had just left the door open. "You smarty-pants," she whispered. Lucy reached out a finger and stroked the hen's side, the feathers smooth and glossy, but Dorothy kept sleeping, and then Lucy yawned, and the two of them napped in the summer heat.

Chapter 4

After twenty-four hours, then seventy-two hours, then days, weeks, a month, the police still seemed to have no leads in Lucy's disappearance, and Iris was beside herself. "She'll come home," Iris insisted some days, and then on others Charlotte would find her sobbing by the window. "Where is she?" Iris cried. "Why would she do such a thing?" Iris called the police every day, but there was never any news, and after a while the cops seemed to be tired of talking to her. They assured her that they were working on it, that they had feelers out and one of their best detectives was on the case, but they kept telling Iris how unworried they were. "Teenagers run away all the time," they told her. "She'll be back." Iris called Lucy's friends Heather and Sable, but neither girl knew a thing, and Sable was furious because Lucy had been supposed to come to a party the day she left, and Lucy hadn't told her anything about not showing up. "I thought she was my best friend," Sable said. "I thought we told each other everything."

Iris put ads in *Boston After Dark* and some of the San Francisco papers. *Lucy. Come home.* She even hired a private detective, but he never seemed to turn up any information. "Sometimes people don't want to be found," the detective told her, which made her so angry she fired him.

Charlotte was floored. Of course she worried about and missed her sister, of course she was terrified, but she was angry, too. Lucy had planned this. She had goddamned planned this. Why couldn't Lucy just call Iris and let her hear for herself that she was fine? Why couldn't she give an address? Lucy had done what she wanted without even thinking of anyone else. Look at Lucy, out in the world somewhere, acting like a grown-up without having the responsibilities that would really make her one.

Still, Charlotte's fear for Lucy kept gnawing at her, and she couldn't share it with Iris. No, she had to keep calming her down. "What if she's hurt? What if she's in trouble?" Iris kept crying.

"She's fine, I just know it," Charlotte lied. She told herself that, over and over, as if it were a mantra. Because it had to be true.

There were memories, like splinters. How when Charlotte went off every day to kindergarten, Lucy would be waiting for her to come home, leaping up from her front-step perch and running out to hug her. Once, Charlotte was in a play in seventh grade, and she hadn't been very good—she knew that—but Lucy made a big deal of her. They were walking out and Charlotte overheard a girl behind her say, "I never realized Charlotte's not that ugly." Charlotte wanted to die, to sink into herself. Lucy whipped around, glaring. The girls were all bigger than Lucy, but Lucy didn't care. "My sister was asked to be in *Ingenue* magazine," she lied. "Did they ask you?" And for the next month, until they forgot, the girls were nicer to her, more respectful. Just the year before, when Charlotte had been huddled over her college essay, crumpling up yet another piece of paper, Lucy had walked by her and impulsively hugged her, as if she had known exactly what Charlotte needed. Why hadn't Charlotte known what Lucy needed? Had she been so absorbed in her own life that she had lost sight of her sister?

Charlotte did her own detective work. She scoured Lucy's

room, trying to figure out where she had gone. She couldn't even open Lucy's top drawer without giving it a yank, and then it spilled open, filled with stretchy orange-and-red love beads. She tugged open another drawer crammed with concert tickets. When had Lucy ever gone to see the Who? Who knew she even liked them? There were tickets to Tom Rush and a napkin from Club 47, which didn't even let you in if you weren't eighteen, something Charlotte knew because she had tried to go there herself with her friend Birdie and had been turned away.

"Did you find anything?"

Charlotte saw the way Iris was hovering there, as if she wanted something. "We'll find her," Charlotte insisted. "She'll come back to us."

BUT LUCY DIDN'T. Every time Charlotte heard a noise in the house, she leaped up, sure it was Lucy, but it was always the burner kicking on. When the phone rang, her breath stopped, but it was someone wanting to sell her a magazine subscription or get her to donate to one cause or another. She told herself there were things she could do, like make sure that Lucy's bedroom window was open every night so that if Lucy came home, she could easily climb back in. She went to the head shop in Harvard Square, way to the back room where the magic stuff was—spells, candles, and potions. "I need to find someone," she said to the salesgirl, who sold her a small blue rayon bag that smelled like an old feather duster. "This will do it," the salesgirl insisted. "Put it where you want the person to be."

"How long does it take?"

The girl sighed. "You think you can hurry magic?" she said.

Charlotte put the bag in Lucy's room, tucked under the blanket. Every day she came into the room and handled the bag, as if her yearning would make the magic more powerful.

BY THE TIME September came and Charlotte needed to move to school, the window sills in Lucy's room were mottled from the rain. How could she leave when Lucy wasn't here? How would Iris do living alone?

Charlotte went to find Iris, who was in the backyard, under a big gardening hat, digging up weeds. "Do you want me to live at home and commute?" Charlotte blurted out, and Iris sat up, taking off her gardening gloves. Charlotte felt sick with guilt. She'd spent so much time thinking about what it would be like to be on her own, to be at college, but Lucy's vanishing had never been part of the scenario.

"I want you to live at school, to have the experience," Iris told her. "And don't look at me like that. I have plenty to do here."

The last thing Charlotte did before she left the house, her suitcases already packed and in the car, was to place her hand on the pane in Lucy's room, thinking, Come back. Come back. It's not supposed to be this way.

IRIS DROVE HER to the campus, which was crowded with kids and parents. Iris parked by Charlotte's dorm, North A, and helped her bring her stuff upstairs, neither of them talking until Charlotte was in her room, putting her suitcases on one of the small beds jutting from the wall. She was on the second floor, too high up for Lucy to climb and find her.

"Well, this is lovely," Iris said finally.

Iris put some of Charlotte's books on the shelves. She reached for clothes to smooth into dresser drawers. When everything was put away, Iris's hand fluttered as if she were trying to grab onto something. "I'll come home on holidays," Charlotte blurted out. "I can make it away on some weekends."

"That will be wonderful," Iris said.

"I'll still be looking for her," Charlotte said. "I can put up posters, or ads—"

"I'll do that. You just study."

Iris didn't stay long. "Your roommate will be here soon," she said, gathering her things. She walked out into the hall, which was filled with girls and parents and steamer trunks, and then she turned and stroked Charlotte's hair. "I'm not saying good-bye because I'm going to see you soon," Iris said. "Just give me a hug and kiss now."

Iris held her so close that Charlotte couldn't catch her breath. Charlotte watched the older woman climbing down the stairs, her hands clasping the railing. There was the shriek of girls racing up and down, a fog of cigarette smoke, and, somewhere, the sharp tang of dope. Everyone looked cooler than Charlotte did, in tie-dyed shirts and embroidered jeans, while Charlotte's shirt was plain black and her jeans were just denim. These girls had long riots of hair and big, complicated earrings. Watching them, Charlotte pulled off her headband and roughed up her hair. And then the bottom door opened and closed again, and Iris was gone, leaving Charlotte in her new life.

Chapter 5

That night, alone in her house, Iris sat up in the living room in her nightgown and slippers. The hours ticked by. There was nothing but the occasional sound of a car's engine or a dog barking. There was no Lucy. Iris wouldn't let herself call Charlotte, not yet. She hoped that girl was busy with her roommate, getting to know people, having fun, and if Iris yearned for her, well, that was just the way the heart worked.

Once again, Iris thought, here she was, undone by love and mad with grief because of it. She had seen that poster in Lucy's room, that ridiculous sentiment that you don't belong to me, and I don't belong to you, but if we find each other, it's beautiful. What a stupid thing to say! Of course people belonged to each other. Love owned you. It kept you captive.

For Iris, it had been that way since 1917, when she first fell in love herself. She was twenty-seven back then, a Jewish girl with marigold hair, which she wore pinned up in a loose chignon, and a bowed red mouth she carefully painted, kissing a tissue to blot away most of the color, because nice girls didn't wear makeup. The four years she had been in Boston, she had lived in a room in a boardinghouse in a marginal Dorchester neighborhood. She had to share the bath and shower with four other women, but at least her room had a view.

That year, Boston was a city of women waiting for their

men to return from World War I. There wasn't money to spend on clothes or the theater or meals in fancy restaurants with real silverware on the table. Women worked swing shifts and used ration stamps. The married ones with families either stayed home knotted with worry or rushed from their jobs to feed their children after claiming them from babysitters they couldn't afford, the kids roaring like fighter planes.

The single women, like Iris, might hate the war, but still—though Iris wouldn't say this out loud—you couldn't help seeing it as an opportunity. Suddenly it didn't seem to matter how plain you might be or how you might have the personality of a kitchen sponge, or even, like Iris, how close to being a spinster you were. Love threw itself at your feet. It became a question you just had to answer. Iris could go out every evening if she wanted, having her pick of the handful of boys who had stayed home, the ones with flat feet or bad backs, the ones she'd never looked at before. They were suddenly gleaming like jewels simply because they were available, and if they were boring or too fast, or resentful because they were at home, at least it was company for an evening.

But what Iris really loved was when the soldiers came home on leave. Every magazine she read told her that all you had to do was give a little encouragement and bring a soldier home for dinner, and then maybe when he left, you'd have a diamond on your finger. A man would have to stay alive so he could get back to you. He'd fight harder because he had someone special to fight for. But even though girls at work popped up with rings on their fingers, Iris's hand stayed bare. None of the soldiers she had made spaghetti for had wanted anything more from her than a kiss. Not even the one, a marine named Tommy Ruffalo, who had convinced Iris to take her shirtwaist off, "just for a moment," so he could remember her beauty. He had never even written to her. When would it happen for her?

All that summer the neighborhood women hung pictures of President Wilson in the windows of their brick apartments. They planted food gardens in bright-colored, cheery window boxes because no one had any sort of backyard, but the city light was so transient, so thick with soot, that Iris's boxes usually yielded nothing more than a scrubby carrot or two. It didn't matter. The rampant patriotism made her dizzy with hope that things could be different, that they could change.

Iris was a girl with few skills, but it was wartime, and she had managed to land a job as a welder in a shipyard, working for a burly guy named Jackson Marks. Jackson had a tattoo of an American flag on his forearm, and he made sure to remind everyone that if he hadn't had asthma, he would have been on the front lines. He told Iris that he hadn't been the one to hire her, that his boss had, and personally he thought it was a mistake. "You people," he said, "started this war." Iris knew that he meant Jews and that like most people he was suspicious of anyone who wasn't what he called purebred. Just last week, in her neighborhood, people had actually burned German books, because didn't everyone hate and fear the Huns? Horrified, Iris had stayed in her apartment.

The hours at the shipyard were long. Iris welded braces and vertical plates, lying flat on her belly, so hot and unsteady she knew that any moment she could faint. The fumes drove her crazy. The noise hammered inside her head. In the quiet of her bedroom, she still heard the sound.

But Iris was proud of her work; as she welded heavy steel doors and braces for ships, she thought about all the handsome soldiers who might sail off to battle on the decks she was helping to build.

Saturdays were the highlight of her life, when the public dance halls were open. Every Friday, Iris would go to Boylston Street as early as she could to rent an outfit. For three dollars,

Iris could twirl around in a satin party dress. For a dollar, she could fit into shoes a hundred other women had probably danced and dreamed in, but for one glorious night, they would be no one's but Iris's.

The night she went crazy was in the middle of July. It was nearly one hundred degrees outside. Just that morning she had found the perfect dress at the store. Red-and-white polka-dot with a fitted waist. Red patent leather shoes to match, with only a tiny scuff at the heel.

The dance hall used to be an Elks Lodge. The walls were wood-paneled and decorated with crepe paper and American flags, and the floor was glossy with shine. Two mothy-looking elks' heads, their mouths gaping open, lined up along the top of the paneling and stared down at the dancers.

Iris didn't care that inside was a steam bath, that the music came from a three-piece band and a singer who looked old enough to be her grandfather. She wanted to dance. She wouldn't mind marrying a soldier or a sailor. It sounded so romantic, and she wouldn't be stupid like her mother, marrying her high school sweetheart right after graduation, a man who left her when Iris was only eight. Some father. Some husband. Her father was tall and silent, and he left the house every morning at seven, just as she was getting up, and he would kiss her on the head before he left. When he arrived home at eight at night, he wanted dinner and peace and quiet. Weekends weren't much better. He wasn't the type of father to take her to the zoo or the circus, though he did drive her to the library a few times. Still, he was her father. She felt he belonged to her. And then he came home one day, his face grave. "Sit down," he told them, and Iris sat down beside her mother.

"What happened? Were you fired?" Iris's mother asked, and he told them that he was leaving, that he was in love with someone else, a waitress he had met at the diner where he always had lunch. They were going to move to Colorado so they could ski all year round. "But you don't ski," Iris's mother pleaded. "You hate the outdoors."

"I like it now," he said. He left Iris and her mother the house and said he'd send money, but it never came. Iris's mother couldn't afford a lawyer to sue him for it. Plus, there was the disgrace. "Tell people your father's away on business," she told Iris, even after the divorce came through. Iris's mother had to get a job cleaning houses, leaving Iris with a neighbor until she was old enough to come home from school and stay in the apartment by herself.

Iris saw how her mother suffered, how her sadness seeped through the walls, held there like a stain. "He'll be back," her mother said. Every week, she still went to the beauty parlor because she wanted to look her best for when he came back. She wore makeup and dresses and cooked elaborate roasts, because any night could be the night he was coming back, and wouldn't he want something delicious to eat? Every day when Iris got home from school, her mother was at the kitchen table, looking at the society pages, and Iris never knew why until the day she came home and found her mother crying and then saw the photo of the young, pretty bride in a white gown, and her father standing behind her. Iris saw how young the bride was: twenty-three. Ten years younger than Iris's mother. "Mom," Iris said, putting one hand on her mother's back, but her mother put the paper down and went into her room, and Iris heard the door close, and after that, they began eating macaroni for dinner. Her mother set her own hair and stopped fussing with lipstick. She still checked the papers, picked up bits and pieces of news from people who used to be mutual friends, and when she heard he was divorced again, she laughed out loud. "He's coming back to us," she insisted. "You wait and see." She saved Iris's A papers, her drawings, the medals she won, all this bounty, but all Iris could think was, Screw him.

One day, Iris came home to find her mother weeping at the kitchen table, a letter in her hand.

"What happened?" Iris asked, alarmed, and her mother shook her head.

"It's from your father."

"It is?"

"He's remarrying again, a woman—a girl—twenty-nine years old, Jewish and religious, and he can't marry her unless I have a get. A Jewish divorce."

Iris stared at her mother, who was tearing the letter into confetti, her mouth set. "I'm not getting one. One divorce was enough. What does it matter? He'll marry her anyway," she said. She pointed a finger at Iris. "Take my advice. Never fall in love."

Her mother was wrong, Iris decided. Her father might have been a jerk, but her life was going to be different. She wouldn't settle for a silent man who could leave his family—his child—as he might his old socks. And she would give herself all the things he hadn't given her—love, attention, respect.

Now, Iris strode over to the punch table. She liked to be early enough to have her pick of the men, but not so early that she seemed desperate, and she was happy to see a large group was already milling around. She recognized lots of the girls from the shipyard: Debby and Eileen and Mary, who came every week, the same as Iris. Their hair was pin curled, their cheeks flush with rouge. They nodded at her and waved and showed off their outfits, bright as hard candies.

Everyone was dancing, clapping, and stomping their feet to "Oh Johnny, Oh Johnny, Oh!" And then "Always Treat Her

Like a Baby" came on and the mood changed and she swayed to the music and let her hair dip over one eye and wondered whether she really looked a little like Theda Bara the way all the boys told her, and for a minute she didn't think about her tiny apartment or the rationing tickets she had already used up or how tired she was. Instead she scanned the crowd hopefully and tapped her toes on the linoleum.

She was pouring herself some of the watery red punch when she felt someone staring.

"Excuse me, but I think you need to dance with me."

Iris swiveled to find a tall, striking man in an army uniform. He had eyes so black she couldn't see the pupils. He smiled and bowed deep from the waist with a flourish, making her smile.

He took her hand and led her onto the floor as if he had always known her. He had a loose, rangy build and he held her close when they danced to "You're a Dangerous Girl." He hummed the melody, swaying her, suddenly clearing his throat.

"Doug. Some of the guys don't give real names, but I swear to you, that's mine."

Jewish. He was Jewish. She felt the heat rise in her face. "Iris," she said.

"Iris," he said, as if he were chewing on her name. "You and me. We're the same tribe." Iris nodded.

He told her he was from Paris, Texas, where he was also based, and he was in Boston for just one week before he had to go back. "They're shipping me to France." He gave her a blinding smile. "Don't you worry. Those Huns don't stand a chance," he said. He dipped her and she let her eyes shut, just for a second, almost like a swoon.

"You know, I always wanted to see Boston," he said. "The streets are kind of noisy, but I guess I like it."

"You guess?"

"Well, I like it now."

Iris smiled and moved in closer. When the dance was over, she waited, but he didn't leave her side.

They danced every dance together, and all the while he whispered jokes against her hair, he tapped his fingers along her back. She couldn't stop laughing. She didn't know what was wrong with her. It was as if something had happened to her senses, as if the air suddenly had a taste, thick and sweet as cream. She leaned against his shoulder and didn't care that nice girls kept their distance. She wanted to be close and she pressed herself against him. She needed to hear him sigh again. Just like that. Just like music.

When the hall emptied out, couples paired off. She and Doug walked toward the park. The city streets were lit, casting her shadow against Doug's, which she thought was a good sign. She commented on the old, beautiful brownstones, the cobbled streets, but he kept looking down at her, warming her with his interest. "Let me tell you the story of our life," he said.

"Our life?' said Iris, amused. "We don't even know each other."

"Oh yes, we do. And this is important, so pay attention."

He told her about the house they would build from scratch, a blue-and-yellow clapboard with a bright red door. And in their sunny, flower-strewn backyard, there would be a tiny replica of the house for their devoted dog.

"Rex," Doug decided. "We always feed him scraps from our dinner even though we know we shouldn't." He paused. "That's okay for a dog's name, isn't it? Rex? It means 'king.' It's got dignity to it. It's noble."

"We sometimes let Rex sleep on our bed."

"Only when our cat Grace isn't there."

She laughed. "And a pool. I love to swim."

"Olympic size, with fish painted along the bottom."

He walked her all the way back to her boardinghouse, and

every detail he spilled out made Iris glow. Imagine having a life like that. Just imagine. At her door, Iris tensed, waiting for him to ask to use her bathroom, to get a drink of water, even though the landlady had strict rules against male visitors. Instead he merely tapped her nose with his fingers. "Tomorrow," he told her. "I'll meet you here. I'll take you to dinner."

Iris blinked at him. "Really?"

"You don't eat dinner? You don't get hungry? Come on, you love steak. You can't wait for chocolate cake. You always eat your portion and mine, too, and you stay small as a button."

Iris smiled. "I'm a fool for sweets," she said.

DOUG COURTED HER PROPERLY. Although he had danced with her close, he treated her with so much polite respect it made her crazy for his touch. In the movies, she leaned toward him, waiting, every rustle of his clothing amplified in the dark. She kept her hand on the armrest so he could easily find it and wouldn't have to grope for it in the dark, and finally, when he folded her fingers into his palm, she couldn't keep a sigh from escaping.

He talked to her all through dinner, telling her about his parents, who ran a greengrocer back in Texas, about his married sister in Topeka. Iris could barely concentrate on what he was saying, because all she wanted to do was lean across the table and kiss his mouth. Love, she thought, was a chemical reaction, one person igniting another, like the hot sparks she made when she welded.

But he didn't come up to her apartment that day or the next. He didn't do more than tilt her chin up and kiss her. His lips were dry, barely brushing hers. She didn't know whether he kept his eyes open because she shut hers. She told herself he was being polite, a real gentleman. He surely knew the same stories she did, about soldiers who got girls pregnant and then left and never returned, and all the girl had to show for it was a fatherless child.

Every day, she looked at the calendar and pretended that Doug wasn't leaving, that her life might go on and on just like this. Now she understood why every day at five, before her father came home, her mother would spritz perfume on her pulse points. She'd dress up and rush to the door, waiting. Love made you crazy. "You be careful," Iris's mother said when Iris told her she was in love, but to Iris, love was like a flame, and she wanted to burn. Every time Iris passed another storefront with an American flag in the window, she felt both a pulse of patriotism and a rage because the war was taking Doug from her. She stopped reading the newspapers because the war was growing more terrifying. The only other Jewish girl at the shipyard kept finding terrible things in her locker: a dead rat, a chicken bone. She slammed into the break room holding the bone in her hand, flinging it at their feet. "I don't have to take this. I quit," she said.

That night at dinner, as Doug was pointing out the dessert selections to her, Iris burst into tears. "Oh my God," she said, swiping at her eyes. "I'm so sorry—I'm such a big dummy."

"What's going on?" he said. He put down the menu and scooted his chair closer to hers.

"It's just that I'm going to miss you so much."

He was quiet for a moment. "Who says you're not going to see me again? Did I say that?"

She shrugged, wrapping her arms tightly around her body. "I'm so stupid." She waited for the lecture she knew was coming. We hardly know each other. Things can change. If it's love, it will keep until I get back.

He reached for her hand, but she tugged it away and wiped her damp eyes.

"Well," he said finally, "then I guess there's nothing to do about this but get hitched."

TWO DAYS LATER, Iris stood in a new white dress beside Doug, the girls from the shipyard around her, her mother beaming at her side. It was such short notice that Doug's parents couldn't make it, but they called, promising to visit.

"I hope this works out," Iris's mother said, and Iris hugged her and then became Mrs. Douglas Gold.

THAT NIGHT, THE honeymoon was a placeholder, too, a night at a nice hotel. "We'll go to Bali. To Hawaii. Or Paris," Doug told her. "You wait and see." While Doug went into the bathroom, Iris left the lights blazing. She peeled off her clothing, sliding out of her chemise, letting it pool on the floor. She took off her new white hat and set it on the dresser and then stood in the middle of the room, pale and naked, like a beam of moonlight. She wasn't afraid. She didn't believe the stories her mother had insisted on telling her. How sex was terrible but you had to do it when you got married. It could hurt and humiliate you in ways you couldn't imagine. How it turned rational men, God's finest creations, into mindless animals. "Sex is only for procreation," her mother told her. A decent woman could think of something else. "It's meant to be mortifying," her mother had whispered to Iris. "Otherwise, why would it be in the same place where you go to the bathroom?" She told Iris all kinds of facts that she knew for certain. Without pubic hair, couples would electrocute each other during sex. That you could keep from getting pregnant by having sex on the first night of the full moon. "Always keep a towel nearby," she told Iris. "Tamp it tightly to you. And immediately go to your own bed. If too much of the vital fluids leak out, you could get sick and die." Yet Iris couldn't bring herself to believe her.

"Fine. Laugh. See what happens," her mother said. "I think I know better than you about these things."

Doug came out with a towel wrapped around his waist.

When he saw her naked in front of him, he started. "Cover yourself," he said, his voice hoarse.

"What for?" Iris moved to him, her bare feet against the cool floor.

"It's sexier," he insisted.

"I'll cover you, instead." She draped herself around him, kissing him, pulling him down onto the floor right there.

"The lights," Doug whispered, but Iris tugged him closer to her. "I want to see everything," she whispered back.

Doug kissed her. "Is this all right?" he said. "You just tell me no and I'll stop." And at that, Iris kissed him, her mouth deep and soft against his. She pulled back. His eyes were wide open, filling up with her. "Good. You're looking at me," she said.

"Don't be afraid," he said, and Iris felt him shivering.

"Afraid? I've been waiting for this forever," she told him.

It was all fast, all elbows and knees bumping, and when she tried to look at his face, he turned away from her. She felt as if she were somehow outside her body, watching herself slide and tumble, and then after a while she stopped thinking altogether. She could have used her clothing for the vital fluids, just in case, but instead she kicked her dress far away from her. If she was going to die, it'd be in Doug's arms, not separated from him with a bolt of cloth held between her thighs. He skimmed her body with his.

"My God," Doug said when they were finished. "How did you know how to do that?"

"Do what?" Iris edged herself up along his body. She bit his shoulder. "You taste like potato," she said. She licked his ear. "You taste like apples." She touched the damp hair growing up toward his belly. "I like this hair," she told him.

"Okay, settle down and rest," he told her. He pulled the bedspread off the bed and covered them.

"We weren't electrocuted," she told him.

"Electrocuted?" said Doug. "What are you talking about?"

She rolled closer toward him. "Oh, nothing," she said.

He hugged her tightly. Her long hair fanned around her shoulders. "My funny wife," he said.

THE NEXT DAY, they pretended everything was normal, but Iris knew it wasn't. In two hours, Doug was leaving for the base and then for Europe, leaving her behind. The room was in ruins, but rather than clean it, Doug left the maid a huge tip, five dollars smoothed out and held in place by a glass. They dressed in their rumpled clothes and went to Teddy's Inn down the block and ordered pancakes drenched in butter and syrup, though neither one of them ate more than a bite. Iris pinched her thighs under the table to keep from grabbing his hand and begging him not to go. She imagined all sorts of things. They could get on a train and flee to Mexico and be free in a hot, sweaty little town. They could go to Canada, where moose could wander in their backyard. She glanced out the flyspecked window. There was a car in the lot, the motor still humming. It would take less than ten steps to get to the door, to rap on the window and ask the driver where he was headed, to make up a story and persuade him to take them both. She bet the car was comfortable. She bet it was fast.

"Doug," Iris said, and he looked at her and then at his watch. "I have to go now."

Iris walked Doug to the bus stop. They held hands, and she could hear his breathing, deep and stretched out. Don't die, she wanted to plead, but she kept her lips buttoned. "Pretend it's an ordinary day," he told her. "Tonight at six I'll come home to our house and you'll have supper ready." She nodded, not daring to cry.

"We have red curtains in the dining room and tonight we're having my favorite meal."

She hesitated. "Steak and green beans," she guessed.

"Veal chops. Mashed potatoes with gravy."

"And afterward we'll go to a picture."

Iris couldn't stand it. Her eyes pooled with tears. She felt her body shaking.

"We'll go roller skating," he said. "We'll—"

She stopped his mouth. She kissed him hard.

He pulled away, his face suddenly drawn. "Until tonight, baby girl."

There were other people gathering around the bus, watching her. Fathers and mothers, kids, and girls with sweethearts. She wrapped her arms tightly around him.

He got on the bus, stopping as he got to the top step. "See ya tonight, honey," he said. She watched him taking a seat, by the window, where he rapped on the glass and waved.

"Don't go," she said, but she knew he couldn't hear her. He looked straight ahead. His image was clouded by the smeary glass. "Don't go," said Iris, louder. Her voice cracked with tears.

"Don't make him feel worse than he already does," a woman standing beside Iris murmured, and Iris swallowed, pasting a big, stupid grin on her face. She kept waving until the bus pulled away from the curb.

She stood watching the bus leave, and even after it had disappeared, she couldn't move. The other people left, in pairs, in groups, talking. The woman who had chastised her was gone, too. Iris kept standing there, alone, and anyone who passed by might just have thought, Now, there's a pretty girl waiting. Iris wrapped her arms around herself. She turned and started walking away from the bus stop.

That night, she roamed around town. She ended up back at Teddy's. She wasn't hungry, but she sat in a booth and ordered the most expensive thing on the menu, because she thought that was what a new bride should have. It took the waitress only ten minutes to bring her lobster, mashed potatoes in a well of brown gravy, and green peas so overcooked they had turned dingy gray. She pushed them around her plate and ordered chocolate pie, and by the time the pie came, she was in tears. Everyone politely ignored her except for the waitress, who quietly crumpled the bill. "On the house," she whispered.

SHE WAS A WIFE without a husband. At work, they all knew that she was married, that she would quit as soon as Doug got home, so they treated her differently. With a kind of respect, in fact. They didn't invite her to join them in the break room or to go out after work, and Friday nights she couldn't go to the dances anymore, because what was the point? She was spoken for. So she stayed home reading magazines and novels, waiting for Doug to come home. The magazines urged girls not to make their men unhappy. Make him proud that he's fighting for you. Make him glad to be a soldier. Don't think of yourself or your problems, because they're nothing compared to what he's going through. Write him letters. Send him gifts. Work for the war effort.

Iris wrote a mad flurry of letters to Doug, pouring out how much she missed him, retelling him the story of how they met, and once deliberately dropping a pinch of water on a word so it would smear and he would think she had been crying, which nine times out of ten wasn't so far from the truth. She never told him how difficult it was at work now, how skimpy the rations had become. How terrified she was by the war. When he didn't write back, she told herself her letters must have gotten lost.

The whole time Doug was gone, Iris saved money, going without lunches, eating cornflakes for dinner, and darning all her stockings. She began to grow her hair even longer, and when it was long enough, she braided it in a ring around her head. When she had enough money for a month's rent, she began to search for a house that she and Doug could afford.

Boston was too expensive, but she could manage in Waltham, which was just a half hour away on the bus line. She found a small house to rent in a wooded neighborhood on Warwick Avenue, and when she told them her husband was at war, they didn't ask for a male cosigner. "You thank your husband for us for the job he's doing for our country," the real estate agent said. Although Iris didn't own a thing except a bed, she moved in. By the time Doug came back, it would be a home.

NEWS OF THE WAR'S end reached Iris a year later, in November 1918, when she was delivering a batch of invoices to the shipyard. The women all whooped and hugged, but Iris felt a clutch of fear. The jobs would be ending, the men would be coming home, and though she was thrilled the war was over, thinking about Doug made her uneasy. "You can stay until your husband gets home," her boss told her. She wouldn't be the only one who had to leave. All the women would be replaced by men.

That night, she cleaned her little rented house. She was used to living alone, she could do what she wanted. She had almost mastered the welding tool and she liked going to work. What was she supposed to do all day? She shut her eyes and tried to imagine Doug's face, but the outlines stayed blurry.

Two days later, Iris was asleep on the couch after work when she heard the door knocker. She jumped up, her dress rumpled, and went to the door. It was probably the neighbor's boy, a rangy kid with a face like a rat, wanting to do chores in exchange for money she didn't have. She never said yes to him, and maybe today she'd even scold him. She was in that kind of mood.

Instead a skinny man in an army uniform stood there, smiling at her, a duffle bag looped over his shoulder. An angry red scar mapped his face. "Hey," he said, and then she burst into tears and flung herself at him, kissing his mouth, warm as a bowlful of honey.

She pulled him inside, not wanting to take her hands off him. He didn't talk much, but she told herself that was all right, she wasn't really talking either. He looked around the house and then yawned. "I'm so sorry," he said. "I'm tired."

"Me, too," she lied, though every cell was switched on.

They went into the bedroom, and Doug immediately flopped onto one of the twin beds. She didn't know what to do, so she undressed, naked, and slipped under the covers next to him. "Doug," she said, and then he moved to her, and if the sex was too quick for Iris, too hurried, she told herself, well, it had been a long time. Her mother had told her that men had needs that had to be satisfied or else they could get sick. She curled up against him and he got up. "Bed's so small," he said, and he moved to the other bed. She stretched out her arm to touch him, but he was already turned the other way, his back to her. Well, she told herself. He's used to sleeping alone. That's all it is.

She stopped working the next day, but already half the women had left the shipyard. "Keep in touch!" everyone said, but Iris knew they wouldn't. She packed up her things, left her welding tools, and came home to her husband.

Doug got a job working in the shipping department of a metal manufacturer in Watertown. He would leave at six in the morning and come home at seven at night. "I wish I could talk to you during the day," she told him. "I miss you."

"There's nothing going on," he said. "What am I supposed to tell you? That I shipped ten boxes to Minnesota?" He came home so tired all he wanted was to eat dinner and then go to sleep. Iris always felt him staring at her as if he didn't know who she was, and when she turned toward him, he would quickly look away.

"Tell me about what you did. Tell me about what it was like for you. What you thought. What you felt," she asked.

Doug looked alarmed. "I don't ever want to talk about it," he said.

"I know what went on over there," she said. "I read the papers. Maybe if you talk—"

"I said no." His voice was like the snap on her clip purse.

She could hear the kitchen clock ticking. "Tell me about how you feel now. What you think about. What you want in life."

"Honeybunch, I'm tired," he said. "I just want to relax." For Doug, relaxing meant sitting in his chair and reading a book, though he usually fell asleep after a few chapters, snoring, and even though she was right beside him, sprawled on the couch, Iris had never felt more alone.

She tried. You got married, you had kids, and maybe that was what was missing for them. At least with a child she'd be busy, she'd have someone who would crave her company. But nothing took for them. The doctor she went to shrugged and said he couldn't find anything wrong, as if he blamed her. When Iris suggested adoption, Doug looked at her as if she had six heads. "I don't want a child who isn't mine," he told her. "I'd just feel funny about it."

She tried to enliven their social life, arranging dinner parties, going to films with couples she knew, but Doug just talked to the men and ignored the women, which embarrassed Iris. When she called her mother, crying, her mother sighed. "He doesn't cheat. He doesn't drink. You're lucky he's not chatting up the women," her mother said. "You just need to get used to it. You have more than some people do and you should be thankful." Iris knew what her mother meant: You have more than I ever had.

Did Iris ever get used to it? Maybe she didn't have to, because she and her husband led such separate lives. During the day she played cards with some of the neighborhood girls and shopped and took herself out for lunch. All the other women mocked their husbands. This one tried to make roasted chicken for dinner and forgot to defrost the bird. Another did the dishes without using soap. They were fools and dolts. No one had it better than she did. Dorothy's husband gambled. Eliza's husband had a temper and smashed things. At least Doug was steady.

She bobbed her hair, sitting astonished in the chair in the beauty parlor, the hair a carpet by her feet. Her head looked so big now, her features so tiny. "You look smashing," the hairdresser said, but Iris wasn't so sure. She came home and Doug touched her cap of hair. "It's wonderful, honey," he said, and she felt a little better, until that night, when he still didn't reach for her.

One day, an accountant named Rick moved in next door. He was a little younger than Doug, with a thatch of black hair that kept falling in his eyes. He was long and lanky and he seemed pleasant enough, but to Iris's surprise, Doug really liked him and spent hours in Rick's backyard playing badminton. Iris heard the thwack of the rackets. She could see the men running back and forth across the grassy lawns, laughing, Doug with his head thrown back, Rick lithe as a greyhound, both of them soaked with sweat. They played for hours and then sat out on wicker chairs in Rick's backyard, talking, but when Iris appeared with glasses of lemonade for them, they grew quiet, or they made small talk with Iris, not picking up their conversation until she walked away. "What do you talk about with Rick?" Iris asked, jealous, but Doug just shrugged. "This and that," he said. Evenings, when it was too dark to play badminton, Doug began to go over to Rick's to play poker and have a few beers, not coming back until Iris was already in bed.

Iris was getting tired of it. "Maybe I could learn to play poker," she said.

"Honey, we're both near champion players. You'd be lost playing with us."

"We could fix Rick up with one of my friends," she said. "We could double-date or something."

Doug laughed. "Rick has plenty of girls," he said. "Leave the man alone."

"Really? He has girls? I never see them at the house."

"Iris—please. It's not our business."

One night she woke up at three in the morning and Doug wasn't there. She had had enough. She got dressed and combed her hair. She was going to go over there and bring her husband home. She stepped on the wet grass and headed to Rick's front door. She was on the side of the house, and she glanced up, and there she saw the two of them, standing together, almost like a seam. Rick moved closer and then he kissed Doug. And then Doug was unbuttoning Rick's shirt, his hands greedy in a way they had never been with Iris, his mouth on Rick's neck, his shoulder, his open lips.

Iris turned around, her heart rocketing. She grabbed onto the hedges to stop the dizziness, the pain. She wished that she were blind.

She went home and sat in the living room, giving herself over to heaving sobs. Everything about Doug made sense now. He wasn't incapable of love or tenderness. He just wasn't capable of it with her or with any woman. Instead of making things better, it made it all worse. What would she do now? Where would she go? Nobody divorced, and she certainly couldn't tell anyone the truth. They'd be run out of town, and then what? How would she live? Would Doug even be able to get a job if people knew about him? Doug didn't make enough money to support her in a separate household, and the only jobs she could get would be waitress or receptionist, and she knew those didn't pay very much. She could confront him, but then, with the truth out, he might leave her. He might move away with Rick, and she would be here alone again. But would that be so bad? Hadn't she been fairly content before Doug came home?

The door creaked open and she sprang to her feet. When Doug saw her, he started. "What are you doing up, honey?" he said. As soon as she saw him, so relaxed, she wanted to scream, What about you? What are you doing?

"Couldn't sleep," she said, and he bent to peck her cheek.

SHE HATED HERSELF for it, but she didn't bring it up. She stopped trying to get Doug into her bed, and he never asked. She told herself, as she lay awake at night, that at least she had a home. Doug had bought the house, and she didn't have to worry about money, and maybe that was the best that life was going to give her. Every time Doug went over to Rick's, she felt a frost sweeping through her. Every time she saw Rick playing badminton with her husband, her heart seemed to puddle in her chest. When she saw Rick going to work or coming home, she smiled curtly and then turned away. She had nothing to say to him. When Rick called the house to ask whether Doug was around, she barked, "No," even though Doug was really right there, and then she abruptly hung up, feeling both ashamed of herself and triumphant.

But Doug never asked her why she didn't like Rick, and when she brought him up, wanting to know why he didn't seem to have other friends at his house, Doug changed the subject.

One day, a few months later, she walked into the house to find Doug crying. "What's wrong?" she asked, sitting beside him, and he shook his head. "Allergies," he said, but two days later she saw the FOR SALE sign on Rick's house. She heard his company was transferring him to London. That night, when Doug came home, she put one hand on Doug's shoulder, waiting, but he still didn't tell her the truth.

There were no letters from Rick. No calls. She couldn't help feeling hurt for Doug. He sat on the couch, staring into space. "Let's play Scrabble," she said impulsively. "I'll let you beat me." He got up and they played for hours. She saw that funny tightness in his mouth loosen. Every day, she tried to think of something they could do together—a movie and ice cream afterward, or a free dance lesson at Arthur Murray. To her surprise, not only was he willing to go with her, but she had fun with him. She liked his company, and he seemed to like hers, the way she could make him laugh by imagining what people were thinking ("That guy in those awful, loud plaid pants is thinking, I know these pants look sharp on me"). She never asked for more. She wasn't even sure she wanted it anymore. Instead of cuddling on the couch, they played Scrabble for hours. Then they each lay in their separate beds and talked across the space about their childhoods, their day, the best meal they had ever had. He told her jokes and made her laugh, and then she thought up a few, too. It wasn't perfect, but whose marriage was?

One night, a few months later, Doug went out on his own. "Poker game," he said, but she saw how anxious he was, how he checked his hair in the mirror, straightening his tie. She knew what he was probably doing, but she knew, too, that she loved him, that part of him was better than none. When he came back home, before midnight, and saw her waiting for him, he looked distraught. Was this really how it was going to be for them now, Doug hiding his secret, and Iris helping him do it? She saw how pained he was, and she knew he needed to talk, and the person he talked to most now was her.

"Want a late night snack?" she asked, and he nodded.

They ate in the kitchen, toast and eggs, and she felt how wary he was. She had been growing out her hair, and it tickled the back of her neck. "We need to talk about this," she said quietly.

"Talk about what?"

"Doug, it's okay," she said slowly. Her hands faintly shook.

His fork stopped in midair. "What are you talking about? What's okay?"

She reached over and put one hand over his. "I saw you with Rick one night at his house. I should have told you, but I didn't know how."

He stared at her, shocked, bumping up from his chair, but she kept hold of his hand. "You don't have to leave. You don't have to do anything—or not do anything. We have a routine. We have a life."

Slowly he sat back down.

"I *know*, Doug. And I don't want to lose you."

"Iris—" He put his head in his hands.

"I'm telling you, it's all right. We can deal with this."

He looked up at her. "How?"

"Well, you can keep going out—" She swallowed hard. "And always, you come back to me."

When he started to cry, she scooted over closer to him, resting her head on his shoulders. "I do love you," Doug said. "In my way."

"I love you in my way, too," Iris told him.

THEY STAYED TOGETHER. He signed them up for tango dancing, and her hair was now so long she could flip it while she danced. They took a painting class and made funny bets on who was going to do the worst that evening. The loser had to belt out a song on the subway. The winner got to eat the rest of the ice cream. Every night, when he came home from work, he had a new, silly joke for her ("What do cows like to do in their free time? They go to the mooo-vies"). He remembered her birthday and their anniversary and brought her windup toys just for fun. He went out sometimes, all spiffy in a new shirt and tie. He never told her where he was going and she didn't ask.

Sometimes he came home in a great mood, his smile wide. Other times, he was quieter. "Come on, let's go get pancakes," he said, and they would drive to the all-night diner and order tall, syrupy stacks.

When Doug began to tell her about his relationships, Iris was surprised how little she minded, how this talk seemed more intimate and important to her than any caress. She was moved by how much he trusted her, by how open he was with her. "We're best friends," Iris said to him.

And then, one day, she turned fifty, which amazed her, and then sixty. Her mother died, and then Doug's parents, and time rushed by so fast she wanted to shout at it to stop. Her hair had grayed and then turned white already, and she wore it braided now, pinned to her head. Nineteen fifty-six, and she and Doug were still best buddies. They had weathered two wars (his high blood pressure kept him out of World War II) and gone to Europe together and were now such expert dancers they could have won contests if they had wanted.

One afternoon, she went outside to hang clothes up on the line, thinking about making meat loaf for dinner. She saw Doug watering the garden, taking good care of the plants, something they both liked to do. Maybe after dinner they could take a drive to Walden Pond and walk around the lake.

He turned to her, splashing her skirt with the hose. "Hey!" she said, laughing. "Who said we were having a water fight?" She tried to get out of the way of the spray, but it was making the blue cloth of her dress navy. "You'll be sorry because I'm going to fill the big pot from the kitchen," she warned, gathering up the skirt of her dress. The water was cool and lovely, but when she looked at him, his face was blank. "Doug!" she called. The water shot down onto the grass, sprinkling her ankles cold. "Doug!" she called, but Doug crumpled gracelessly onto the lawn, and by the time she got to him, he was dead.

SHE SAT SHIVAH for him, and the neighbors came over with casseroles and plates of food that Iris would politely take and put in the kitchen, lacking the appetite to eat. They told stories about Doug, how funny he was, how smart. "He was devoted to you," Mary Curtis, from down the block, said, and Iris started to cry. "Yes, he was," she sobbed.

Widow. She didn't like saying it out loud because of the way people looked at her. The sad eyes. The pity. "I know how you feel," people said, but how could they? Doug had left her the house, and his insurance policy gave her enough money that she'd never have to work.

She missed him. She couldn't seem to get it into her head that he was really gone. She kept expecting him to turn up, the way he always did, to tell her that it was a mistake, that the hospital had revived him. She heard his voice in every room, calling her to come play cards or go out bowling, and at night she dreamed about him, the two of them salsa dancing, being so good everyone else in the ballroom stopped to watch them, to applaud. She woke up, her face streaked with tears.

AFTER A WHILE, the neighbors stopped coming over. She repainted the whole inside of the house, every room a bright color, and she bought herself a whole new wardrobe, too, but none of it eased the wound inside her. She went out almost every night, with her friends Eliza and Dorothy, to the movies, the theater. But after a few months, she found she'd show up at a dinner and her friends would have an extra man there for her, nudging the two of them together.

Iris was always polite, but the men left her cold, like second helpings after a meal, when your appetite was gone. She had stopped yearning for romance a long time ago. And anyway, none of these men were as funny, tender, and bighearted as her dead gay husband.

"I'm too old for this," Iris said.

"Oh, that's such baloney," Eliza said, after Iris turned down a date from an architect. "What was wrong with the banker I introduced you to? What was so bad about the dentist? You could be happy, you know, if you let yourself."

"Who says I'm not happy?" Iris said.

One day, Iris was in downtown Waltham, browsing the windows of the shops, on her way to get an iced coffee, when she passed Fly Away, a travel agency. The whole front window was one big poster of a woman in a bathing suit standing under a waterfall, her dark hair sluiced back, the water so blue it was like a chip of sky. Iris walked inside, something prickling along her spine. Ten minutes later, she had a ticket to Paris for a two-week stay. It wasn't even that expensive. She had enough savings that she could go someplace every few months if she wanted to. She didn't have to decide on anything now. *Voulez-vous*. It was the high school French she remembered. Do you want? Yes. *Oui*. Yes, she did want.

She got a passport and guidebooks and began planning more of her trip. She saw herself walking the Louvre, sitting in the cafés, sunning herself in an outdoor garden, pleased as a cat. She bought a little tape recorder, and every night she listened to a perky female voice repeating phrases to her, waiting while she parroted them back.

"You're going alone?" Eliza said. "Don't you even want

to take a tour? At least you'll be with other people." Iris just laughed. "Well," Eliza said doubtfully, "I hear the French like older women. Maybe you'll meet someone."

"All I want from cafés are chocolate croissants."

Two days before leaving, Iris was already thinking about her next trip. A week in Spain. After that, maybe Istanbul. The whole world was opening for her. She didn't want to take her sensible clothing with her, so she had gone shopping for all-new outfits. Instead of her usual shirtwaist dresses, she bought silky sheaths. She tossed aside her comfortable tie shoes for a pair with slim little buckles, and she had even found the perfect coat, slim fitting, in an almost scandalous acid green. As she packed, she repeated to herself phrases she had learned. *Où se trouvent les toilettes? Combien, s'il vous plaît?* When the phone rang, she scooped it up.

"Iris Gold?"

Since Doug had died, she got calls every day from insurance companies, from brokers, from anyone wanting to take her money, to convince her that they could take care of it—and her—better than she could. But this voice said, "I'm the lawyer for your father," and then she straightened up. "Excuse me?" she said. "My father?"

"I'm so very sorry."

Iris sat down, the phone still in her hand. She looked around her kitchen. There was the red clock, the white fridge, everything real and familiar, and all she had to do was reach out and touch it. She hadn't heard from her father in years, not since she was a little girl. She hadn't even known whether he was alive. "He's dead," she said in wonder.

"He and his wife."

"His wife," Iris said. She pressed the receiver against her forehead. "How did it happen?"

"A club fire."

A club. Her father would be an old man now, in his early eighties. She couldn't imagine him at a club. "How old was his wife?" Iris asked.

"Excuse me?"

"His wife. How old was she?"

There was a funny silence, a rustle of paper, and then the attorney cleared his throat. "Forty," he said.

Of course, Iris thought bitterly. Oh, of course. He must have kept marrying younger women, trading them in when they didn't work out. She knew he had had two other wives besides her mother. He must have married again, and who knew whether this wife had been his fourth wife, or even his fifth or sixth? She felt dizzy just thinking about it. But what could a younger woman see in an old man unless he was rich? She wondered whether he was one of those men who wore toupees and dyed the gray out of their hair.

"Where was this?"

"Phoenix," the lawyer said. Iris wrapped the phone cord around her wrist. Her father had hated heat.

"I don't need his money, if that's what this is about." If there was a funeral, she wouldn't go. A gravestone, she'd never visit.

"This isn't about money," the lawyer said. "There is some, but that's not the point. It's about his two little girls."

Iris could hear something hissing through the wires. Her father hadn't been interested enough in Iris to keep in touch with her. He had wanted young wives, not kids. But here it was. Little girls. Her father was an old man and he had young children. Had the wife talked him into it? Did he think children would keep him young?

"Were there other children? From other wives?" she asked.

"No others," the lawyer said, which made Iris wonder even more. How could someone that old have kids? He must have had Charlotte and Lucy in his seventies. She knew it was possible. She had even known another couple like that, the aged father, the young wife, the young kids. But what kind of a thing was that to do to children, to bring them into the world just as you were headed out of it? Iris had half sisters she didn't even know about and they were young enough to be her granddaughters. How could that be possible? Iris swallowed.

"Six and a half and five," the lawyer said. "There's no other family. Which is why I'm calling you. You don't have to adopt them. They just need a home."

Iris looked over at the table where her travel books were. She thought of her father, how little he had known about her, how little he had cared. These little girls were strangers, and she was old now, too. She doubted he had told them anything about her. What was she supposed to do with them? How could anyone ask this of her, especially now? "I'm sixty-seven," she said.

"All right," he said. "I'll tell foster care to take them in."

Foster care. Living with a family who took money to care for you, who didn't love you. But would she love them? Was she even equipped to take in children? They were so far away. If she didn't take them in, she'd never see them.

"If you change your mind, give me a call," he said, and he barked out a phone number, and then the dial tone rang in her ear. Iris jotted down the number on a slip of paper, folding it up into a tiny square, sliding it into the bottom of her sock drawer.

She needed air. Grabbing her cardigan, Iris headed out for a walk. But halfway down her block, she began to feel as if there were some kind of conspiracy going on. Before, she had never noticed mothers with kids. Today, she spotted them everywhere. A woman tugging a little boy by the hand while the boy neighed as if he were a horse, scuffing his heels against the sidewalk, hurling his body backward. A woman wheeling a crying baby in a carriage, her own face soft as pudding; the woman bent down and whispered something, and the infant sneezed and stopped wailing. She observed these other mothers as if they were some experiment. She remembered how she had yearned for her own child, how disappointed she had been when it didn't happen, and how Doug hadn't wanted to adopt.

What did her father's little girls look like? she wondered. Did they have her father's eyes, large and lashy, just like her own? She wondered what power those girls had that she didn't, the thing that made her father love them. Or had he loved them? Maybe he had just doted on their mother and had agreed to have kids to keep her. Iris was ashamed that the thought made her feel better. There was no use thinking about this, she told herself, and she turned to head home.

Back at the house, she settled down at the dining room table with the schedule for her Paris trip. She liked things organized, so she knew what she would be doing every day. Monday she'd visit the Bastille. On Tuesday she'd go all the way to the top of the Eiffel Tower.

But she couldn't shake thoughts of the little girls. She turned over her schedule, and on the blank side of the page she wrote, *Noise. Dirty hands on everything. Runny noses.* She put the pen down.

She tried again to imagine them. How tall would they be? Was their hair straight or curly? Brown or blond? Did they look alike?

No, they weren't her responsibility, these little girls. Her father's young wife probably hadn't even known Iris existed. Iris tried to remember a single good time with her father, and then a memory rose to the surface. She was just four, settled in his lap, her cheek against the rough tweed of his jacket. He was warm and thrumming, singing something to her, his voice vibrating in his chest like a purr. *I went to the animal fair, / The birds and the beasts were there.* He sang it over and over until she had learned the words and could sing it first with him, right up to the line *and what became of the monk*. "That's my girl," he said. He smelled like tobacco and she clung to him and then he popped her off his lap, laughing. Dark eyes, dark hair, smelling of the cigarettes he loved. It wasn't so very much to remember about a person. And now there were girls that he had left her by accident, and somehow they were a part of her.

TWO DAYS LATER, she called the lawyer. "I'd like to have the girls," she said. "But I'd rather not tell them I'm their half sister. Please tell them I'm an aunt." As soon as she hung up, she called the travel agent and canceled her trip.

The lawyer had told Iris that a social worker had to check her out first, and as soon as that was done, if everything seemed fine, the girls would be put on a plane and then brought to her. Iris cleaned out her old sewing room and painted it pale pink. She bought two little twin beds, lavender bedspreads, and two wooden dressers, each with its own mirror, because didn't little girls like to admire themselves?

Almost immediately, Iris didn't like the social worker. Mrs. Cutler was a young woman in a red suit, her hair in dry-looking curls. She asked Iris all sorts of foolish questions about what she cooked, whether she went to church, whether she had friends. "These little girls are my father's daughters," Iris said. She saw the way the social worker was looking at the two beds. "When they're older they can have their own rooms," Iris said. "I just thought that for now they might like to be together."

Iris felt as inspected as the room. She hated the scratch of Mrs. Cutler's pencil on the pad, the scribble of notes, but eventually the woman drew herself up. "I have what I need," she said, and she held out her clammy hand for Iris to shake.

A week later, there was paperwork to sign, and then a week after that, Mrs. Cutler brought the girls to Iris, both of them in identical blue dotted swiss party dresses, clinging to each other. Each one carried a suitcase. Lucy looked like a little dandelion, a stranger, but Charlotte had her father's strong nose, his full mouth, and thick, choppy dark hair, and when she gazed at Iris her eyes narrowed, and Iris felt their father standing there, judging her, just the way he used to. Now, this was familiar. She reached for Charlotte, but Charlotte stepped deliberately away from her, leaving Iris's hand floating in the air. It was Lucy who grabbed at Iris's charm bracelet, smiling when it jangled. "Can I have this?" she said. Her voice was like a splash of dimes. Her frizzy gold hair sprouted around her head like a halo. What in the world would Iris ever do with such hair? Iris took off her bracelet and gave it to the little girl.

"I'll let you all get acquainted now," said Mrs. Cutler, though Iris wanted to grab her, to call out, Wait, wait, don't leave me alone with these children. Instead she turned to the girls, who stood in her living room, holding hands and staring at Iris. "Well," Iris said, "in times like these, I always think ice cream is the answer. Do you agree?"

SHE TOOK THEM to the Brigham's down the street, driving like a chauffeur, with both girls sitting silently in the back. Unsettled, she switched on the radio. She sang along, but she was the only one. Every time she checked on them in the rearview mirror, Charlotte stared back at her with dark and accusing eyes, as if Iris had already done something wrong.

Brigham's was bright with light, and she settled them into a booth, letting them each order hot fudge sundaes with a cherry on top. She ordered one for herself, too, though she wasn't that hungry. "Is there anything you want to ask me?" she said. She thought they'd want to know about her being their aunt, why they had never heard of her. But Charlotte just dug her spoon deep into the dish and sighed heavily. Lucy studied her. "You don't want to ask anything?" Iris said.

"Do you have any pets?" Lucy finally said. When Iris shook her head, Lucy asked, "Can we get one?"

"Allergic, honey," Iris said, and Lucy frowned.

"What about a turtle?" she said. "Or fish?"

"Maybe fish," Iris said, and Lucy brightened.

"I get to name them," Lucy said. "Banana and Ha Ha."

Iris promised herself she wouldn't lie to these girls, so she told only the facts she herself knew. "There's a nice school you can walk to," she said. "Northeast Elementary. It's right behind our house." She told them there was a bowling alley and roller skating right at the Wal-Lex, with duckpins and tiny little bowling balls that weren't heavy at all. There were paths to ride bikes, and the neighborhood was full of kids.

"We didn't bring our bikes," Charlotte said.

"I only have a trike," Lucy said. "But I want a big-girl bike."

"Well, then we'll have to find you one," Iris said.

They were outside when she realized she had forgotten her purse. "One second—" she said, and she went inside, and when she came back out, the girls were pressed against the wall of the store, their faces pale, clutching hands. Charlotte spotted her and waved her arms wildly. "You left us!" Charlotte cried.

Iris crouched down so her face was level to them. "I didn't leave you," she said. "I went to get my purse. Why didn't you call for me?"

"We did. We yelled, 'Lady, lady,' but you didn't come," Lucy said.

Iris stared. "You called me 'lady'?"

"What are we supposed to call you?" Lucy said.

"You're not our mother," Charlotte said.

Iris was silent. How could she tell them that their father was her father, too?

"What are you, then?" Lucy said.

Iris crouched down so that her face was at the same level as Lucy's. "I'm Iris," she said quietly. "And that's what you can call me."

Chapter 6

L ife in the country was failing to grow on Lucy. They could pick up only five stations on the radio—two were Christian talk shows and one was scratchy progressive jazz that she couldn't listen to. The postman came at odd times and almost always when she was in the bathroom or in the kitchen, so she couldn't have a conversation with him, and she learned that she could read one full book a day, but it gave her a headache.

She had learned, too, that chickens had moods, and not all of them were bad. She could feed Dorothy table scraps from the kitchen, but the other hens avoided her, and if she left the kitchen door open, Dorothy would come and keep her company, settling down by the table. She glanced at the pile of cookbooks. She could figure out dinner, but how long would that take? And what would she do after that? She envied William, out in the world, teaching, being around people, having fun. Only rarely did they go out, and then it was to a movie or occasionally to a restaurant out of town, where no one would recognize them.

She was surprised by how much she missed Iris and Charlotte. She wondered how they were doing and whether they missed her. She remembered odd things, like how comfortable her bed had been, with all the extra pillows she piled on. And how much she loved being able to bike into Harvard Square and hang out. She yearned for Sable, Heather, her friends. Girls she could talk to.

And then she thought of how eager Charlotte had been to go to college, the way Iris wanted to travel to France and Spain and Italy, once the girls were out of the house. They could have found her by now if they had really wanted to. Lucy's heart knotted into a fist. What if it was a relief that she was gone? Her Waltham world closed like the spring lid of a jar.

By November, she felt utterly housebound. How could it be snowing when it wasn't officially winter? The flakes fell hard and fast and then the snow was so deep it was difficult to walk beyond their front gate, and the wind chapped her skin. She rearranged all the books on the shelves, she sat with her blue journal and tried to write, and when she glanced at the clock, she was dismayed to see that only an hour had passed. The house never felt warm enough, so she wore two of William's flannel shirts, one on top of the other, but it wasn't the same as having him there beside her. She had to brave the cold to give the chickens warm water twice a day and cover their pen with extra straw. All of them, even Dorothy, were leaning against one another by the coop light. "I know, I don't like the weather, either," she told them.

William began coming home in a bad mood, but when she tried to comfort him, he just brushed her off. He used to be filled with stories about school, but now when she asked him about his day at dinner, he would only mumble. "I'm just tired," he said.

She knew it wasn't possible, but sometimes, when William was at work, she felt watched. Once, she heard footsteps from the kitchen and she ran to the back of the house and saw shoe prints in the snow, but when she opened the door and called, "William?" all she heard was the icy wind bearing down on her, pummeling her face. "Who's there?" she cried, her eyes searching the snowy woods. She went back inside. At least she had the radio. She went to get her journal, to work on her stories, spreading everything across the table, riffling the pages until she came to the story she had just finished. But then she saw William's handwriting in the margins. He had crossed out one of her scenes and rewritten it, putting in a Groucho Marx joke. When had he done this? Why hadn't he told her, and why had he thought it was all right to do? She pressed the journal to her chest.

When she asked him about it later, he shrugged. "I looked at it last night when you were sleeping. It needed some humor, honey," he said.

"It's mine. It's my writing."

He rubbed at his eyes, as if he were teasing a headache out. "Don't you want me to help you?" he said. "Isn't that what we do for each other?" He looked so unhappy she put one hand against his cheek.

"Is work okay?" she asked.

"Everything's fine," he said. "Why do you ask?"

"I think maybe it's not," she said. She took his arm and felt him stiffen. "Why can't you tell me what's going on? Don't you think I'd understand?"

He pulled his arm from her. "Of course you'd understand," he said. "You understand everything about me. There's nothing wrong." He glanced at the calendar they had pinned to the door, twelve different photos of the Pennsylvania woods, and then he brightened. "Look at that big red X," he said, pointing to the fifteenth. "We've got to do something special for your birthday. Seventeen. It's a biggie for us."

"One more year after this one," Lucy said. "Just one more year." And then William leaned over and kissed her, and everything seemed all right.

• • •

BECAUSE IT WAS a special occasion, they drove an hour to a pancake house, all black chrome and vintage fixtures, and when they were finished eating, William slid a box wrapped in foil paper across the table to her. She laughed and tore it open, and when she saw what was inside, a tiny heart on a thin gold chain, she held her breath.

She slid it over her head, admiring how it gleamed in the light. She wanted to show it off, to tell everyone, but whom could she tell? "I need to look at myself in the ladies' room mirror," she told him. "Be right back."

She walked past the shiny main counter and saw a small rack of postcards, all of them with the same cowboy waving a lasso. She lifted up one of the postcards to see what was on the back, and to her surprise, it was already stamped. She thought about Iris and Charlotte, how the year before for her birthday they had taken her to Anthony's Pier 4 and let her order wine. Iris had given her a gold bangle bracelet from Kitty Haas, the expensive shop in Harvard Square, and Charlotte had bought her a hand-embroidered peasant blouse. She had loved that night, had loved them, too. She felt a pang. One more year, and she could have them back in her life again. All of a sudden it didn't seem so far away. She reached into her purse and took out an eyebrow pencil and scribbled down her old home address. On the left side she wrote, *I am fine. I am happy. I love you. Please don't worry. Lucy.* William would be furious if he knew she was writing home, leaving tracks, but they were an hour away from their house. How could anyone find them? She left the postcard on the counter, stamp side up. Someone would find it and mail it. She could imagine how happy Iris and Charlotte would be to get it. How surprised.

Chapter 7

When the girls first arrived, Iris approached parenthood the way she did most things in life: systematically and pragmatically. That first night, she let them watch TV, turning the channels until she found something that looked like a cartoon. At eight o'clock she told them, "Time for bed." She showed them the toothbrushes she had bought for them, one red, one green, and let each girl pick her color. She got them into their nightgowns and into bed, and then she bent and quickly kissed their foreheads before they could stop her. The next morning, she woke them up at seven, and though she always had just coffee and a piece of dry toast, she made eggs for everyone and she even ate some herself so that they would, too.

She bought a book about raising children and decided that hers would be a home of schedules, proper bedtimes, decent food, routine. She watched the other mothers in the neighborhood as if she were doing research. Elaine down the block sometimes spit on her fingers to wash her son's face. Martina let her kids run through the sprinkler on her front lawn, but when one of them took off her bathing suit, Martina swatted her on the bottom. Iris noted what worked and what seemed less effective.

But she quickly began to realize that something was wrong. She had bought them separate beds so they would feel they had something of their own, yet they always curled up in the same one, Charlotte's arm hooped around Lucy, the two of them like puppies piled together. "Us against the world," she heard Charlotte whispering to Lucy. "Say it back to me." And then Lucy did. They wore only the dresses they had unpacked, not the new ones Iris had purchased at Filene's. Iris wondered who had packed those bags for them, who had thought to tuck in a small photo album hidden at the bottom. When the girls were asleep, Iris had looked through it, her hands shaking. There was her father, hugging a woman so young she could have passed for a college coed, the girls laughing beside them. Iris touched the photo with her finger. Riffling through the pages, she noticed how many of the pictures were of Lucy alone: Lucy playing the piano in a party dress. Lucy standing in front of an easel painting something. Lucy sitting on both her parents' laps at the same time. Iris turned the page, and there was Charlotte, standing with her family, who were all hugging, but she was on the outer edge, like an afterthought. Her father was beaming down at Lucy. He had one arm around his wife.

She put the album down. Her father hadn't changed. No wonder Charlotte seemed suspicious of her, and Lucy so warm.

But when she tried to take their hands crossing the street, Charlotte took Lucy's and refused to take Iris's. When she tried to interest them in a board game after dinner, proclaiming that Charlotte could even be the scorekeeper, Charlotte wanted to play only with Lucy. One night when Lucy wasn't feeling well, she curled into Iris's lap, and Iris sat there, overwhelmed. She rested one hand on Lucy's yellow hair. She leaned down and breathed her in, this warm, sleepy child, and then Charlotte came into the room and jerked Lucy awake, pulling at her arm.

"Hey, hey—" Iris said, but Charlotte was tugging Lucy into the other room. "She's my sister, not yours," Charlotte said.

"Give them time," the social worker had counseled when

Iris called, near tears, to tell her she wasn't sure how things were working out.

One night she heard Charlotte crying, but when she went into the room, Charlotte burrowed under the covers, turning her back. Iris touched the girl's shoulders, her sweaty pajamas, but Charlotte kept still. "Charlotte," Iris said. "Honey, I know it hurts." Charlotte didn't move, and Iris left the room.

SHE DIDN'T THINK the girls would ever love her, but her own feelings came as a surprise. At first, it was a smell—clean hair and baby powder, and maybe youth—and she couldn't get enough of it. She grew to love the sound of their voices in the morning, like bells. When she watched them, she couldn't help thinking how amazing it was, that here she was, with two little girls in her home. Every time she did something right—cutting the crusts off their sandwiches before they asked, serving Kool-Aid in a pitcher she'd drawn a smiley face on, so that the kids laughed—she felt a flood of joy. They were all things she had imagined doing when she had wanted to have children with Doug, and every time she did them for the girls, she couldn't help thinking, I could have been so good at this. And then she would think, I'm good at this now. I can get even better. She saw it, and maybe one day the girls would, too.

Falling in love with children was different from giving your heart to an adult. Oh, it was so much better! She remembered the way she had fallen for Doug, how she couldn't sleep because she kept thinking about him, how when she saw him she wanted to kiss him. Later she felt deep comfort that he was around. But it was love with edges and complications. Loving the girls brought her deep peace, something she could sink into like a blanket.

She found her mind crowding with ways to make the girls

happy. When they started school, she bought them enough pretty dresses so that they could each go two weeks without repeating one. She stocked the house with games they could play together, like Go to the Head of the Class or Sorry! She laid the bounty out on the bed so that it would be the first thing they'd see when they got home from school. She would stand at the door, watching them fingering the fabrics or eagerly tearing plastic from the games. Lucy always ran to her and hugged her, but Charlotte remained aloof.

One day, Iris showed up at the elementary school to walk both girls home. Lucy broke free from her first-grade class and ran to her, as usual, her arms wrapping tight around Iris's waist. Iris laughed out loud and ruffled Lucy's hair, and then Charlotte's third-grade class appeared and Charlotte ran over, too. Iris noticed another mother glancing at her, smiling. The other mother must have been in her late twenties, in dungarees and a tight top. "Your granddaughters?" the other woman said, and Iris stiffened. She felt Charlotte watching her, but what she was supposed to say, that these girls were her half sisters?

"They're my daughters," she burst out, and the other woman looked startled and then shuffled away. Iris was annoyed with herself for reacting, for taking it so personally. The girls' father had been older, too. How was this different? But then she felt a small hand, a starfish, grasping hers. She looked down, and there was Charlotte, her eyes clear and shining, holding on to Iris's fingers.

At school, on the bulletin board, kids had written the ages of their parents. My Daddy's 22! My mom's 28! My mom is 19! (That one made Iris do a double take.) And there in the corner was Charlotte's handwriting. Iris is 103! Everyone thought it was funny, but Iris felt her face flame, and when no one was looking, she took the piece of paper down.

Still, she couldn't deny that she was older. In a sea of blonds and russets, her hair was frosty white. At the playground, her knees buckled when she tried to hoist Lucy up the ladder for the slide, and her back hurt pushing both girls on the swings. She could hardly throw a ball, and the one time she did, it hurtled out into a street full of cars. The girls always ran ahead of her, stopping short at the street when she called to them.

During the day, she missed them, but she couldn't nap. There was too much to do. Laundry piled up. She had to go food shopping, because she was trying to find foods they liked, and so far it was only spaghetti, fried eggs, and peanut butter and jelly sandwiches. At night, when the girls were asleep, she was exhausted, but when she sat down to try to read, her mind crowded. They were so small, so young. How could she possibly protect them?

She rented a little cottage in Falmouth for two weeks in the summer so they could go to the beach every day, and the only time she didn't worry was when they were in the backseat of the car, in their pajamas, watching drive-in movies until they fell asleep. Iris never paid attention to the movie but instead listened to their soft breathing, watching their peaceful, sweet faces in her rearview mirror. When they went to the beach, she made sure to stake a spot close to the lifeguard before slathering the girls with sunscreen. When they wanted to go in the water, Iris went with them, her eyes glued to their small bodies. Charlotte cautiously picked at shells and refused to go into the water deeper than her hips. "There's jellyfish," she insisted. "I see sharks." Lucy, though, was like wildfire. She wouldn't wait after eating her hard-boiled egg, her cheese sandwich with the crusts cut off, but ran into the water until it was up to her neck, ignoring Iris's frantic waving and the whistle of the lifeguard. She stayed in so long her lips turned blue.

Iris read the papers. She knew how dangerous the world was. Children were run over by cars. They were struck by lightning.

They drowned. She had to watch the girls every second, and yet she began to notice that her eyes weren't as good as they used to be. One day, she and the girls were at the beach, and Charlotte and Lucy had run down to the waves. "Stay where I can see you," Iris said, following them, but she had to squint to keep track. The lines blurred. And then she saw a pair of kicking legs, Charlotte diving into the water and pulling Lucy out. Lucy bent over, bracing her hands on her knees, coughing water. Iris's heart tumbled. She ran down to the water. "Are you all right?" she asked, panting. When she touched Lucy, the girl's skin was clammy and pale.

"Charlotte saved me!" Lucy said. Charlotte was busy brushing off Lucy, her hair wet pinpoints on her collarbone. "Charlotte," Iris said, and the girl looked up at her, blinking.

"Thank you. Dear God, thank you," Iris said. She hugged Charlotte tightly, and this time, Charlotte let her. Iris could feel the girl's heart pounding under her skin, and suddenly she knew just what to do, and it would help both of them.

Iris waited until they were home, all three of them in the park, Lucy swinging, Charlotte beside her. "You know honey, you were a big help to me at the beach with Lucy," Iris told her.

"I was?" Charlotte looked cautiously over at Iris.

"Lucy's far too young, but you—well, how would you like to be my big-girl helper for everything?"

"Really? You would let me do that?" Charlotte twisted around excitedly.

"Of course. I count on you, honey," Iris said.

SLOWLY, GRADUALLY, CHARLOTTE began to open up to Iris. When she helped Iris set the table, she told her about how her teacher always wore silver bobby pins, how she had told the class she liked to square dance, and how she smelled like old shoes. At the park, instead of hanging out with her own friends, Charlotte sat beside Iris to watch Lucy run around like a colt. Charlotte helped Lucy dress and pick up her toys. And when Charlotte grew a little older, she began to help Iris with dinner, to help cleaning up.

Iris loved them. Oh God, she loved them so much. But when Lucy skinned her knees, the first person she ran to was her sister, not Iris. She realized they didn't belong to her, even though she belonged to them. She would do anything for those girls.

But one night, a year later, when Iris was out at a PTA meeting, leaving the girls with a sitter, she came home to find the babysitter running around outside after the girls, who were carrying their suitcases. "Charlotte! Lucy!" Iris called, and the girls skidded to a stop. Charlotte's mouth opened.

"You came home—" Charlotte said.

"Well, of course I did. I told you I was going to the PTA—"

"No, you didn't! You didn't!" Lucy cried.

She paid the sitter and took the girls inside and sat them down. "Don't you know that I'm not going anywhere? That I love you?" Iris said.

Charlotte looked doubtful, and Lucy shrugged.

"I have plans for us," Iris said. "We're going to go to the mountains in the spring, and next summer, maybe we'll go to Maine."

The children were so still Iris could hear their breathing. "Don't you know we're a family?" she asked.

"We have different last names," Charlotte said. "That's not really a family."

Iris hesitated. "Would you like to have the same last name?"

"What do you mean?" Lucy asked.

"Well, I could adopt you," she said. "If you wanted me to." Neither of the girls moved, and for a moment Iris thought she had made a terrible mistake. Maybe they wouldn't want that at all. Who was she to adopt them? They had had parents, and they might think she was threatening that tie.

"For real?" Charlotte said.

IRIS MADE A big deal of it. She bought both girls new dresses and something special for herself, a slim-fitting blue jersey sheath, and they all stood before the judge, who solemnly shook Charlotte and Lucy's hands when the process was done. "You see?" Iris told them. "No one's going anywhere. We're family now. We're all Golds."

It made a difference, that adoption. Lucy loved saying her new name, over and over: "Gold, Gold, Gold," she proudly told everyone. And Charlotte's face gradually lost that pinched, worried look. "You can call me Mom, if you like," Iris offered, and she told herself it didn't matter that neither girl ever did, because look at what love was in her house now. Look at her family.

BUT THEN THE girls became teenagers, all arms and legs and curves, and shockingly lovely. Though every time she told them that, they looked at her as if she were insane. She gave them each their own room, their own door to shut, and the only way she knew they were inside was by the music that blared behind the walls. When they left for school, she would sometimes find herself in their rooms, standing in the center of the teenage debris. She lifted up a T-shirt and examined it and put it back exactly where she'd found it. She tried on a ring or a bracelet and put it back, too. It was as if these were all clues that would help her understand who they had become.

She lifted up a strip of photo-booth shots. Lucy's hair was wild and yellow as butter, and though Iris bought her brush rollers and magazines that had diagrams for hairdos, Lucy just let it go free. When Iris tried to suggest they visit Clip and Curl, Lucy's face darkened, and she smoothed her hair with her hands, over and over, until Iris let it go. At thirteen, Lucy could walk down the street with Iris, and men stared at her, with Lucy none the wiser, continuing to chatter about school to Iris. Charlotte also had no idea how lovely she was, but it concerned Iris that Charlotte always looked so worried, especially when she had such a beautiful smile.

As Charlotte and Lucy grew up, they grew away from Iris, and she felt her hands helplessly grasping at air. The girls didn't care that she had experience in life, that she might know something that could help them. Iris had known girls like Lucy, who came to rely on the attention of boys. And she herself knew what it felt like to worry over everything, the way Charlotte did. But when she tried to help, to encourage Lucy to study, Lucy just sighed and went to wash her hair. When Iris told Charlotte to take a break from studying, to come with her to check out the sale at Filene's, Charlotte shook her head. "I can't," she insisted.

The girls didn't seek her out as much, which she understood. They needed space. They were becoming young adults, and this separation was supposed to happen. The only problem with it was that she hadn't realized it would hurt. She began to notice that something had changed between the sisters, too. It saddened her. Lucy did her homework on her own, whereas before, Charlotte would always help her. Now, when Charlotte drifted by, college catalogs bunched to her chest, Lucy covered her papers with her hand. They had their own friends, their own secrets and problems, and they no longer even watched the same TV programs or played a game of Scrabble together. Their once close relationship seemed to be shut out by the doors they each kept closing.

One day, Iris caught sight of her reflection in the mirror. Her face was wrinkled as a dishcloth. Her eyes bleary. Her hair, wrapped around her head in a corona of braids, had thinned with the years. She cupped one hand to her face. She was in her seventies. Imagine that. Seventies. How could such a thing be possible? She couldn't pretend anymore that she was just an older-looking mother.

What really broke her heart was that the girls would be going soon. Charlotte was so smart she had gotten into Brandeis, her first choice, on a full merit scholarship, too, even though Iris had put aside money for her. Brandeis was just ten minutes away by car, but Charlotte wanted to live on campus, and Iris wanted that experience for her, too.

Lucy, though, was another story. How would that girl manage out in the world? Lucy brought home failing report cards. "She could do better," Lucy's teachers told Iris, but when Iris tried to talk to Lucy about it, Lucy threw up her hands and said, "I'm not Charlotte!" Lucy would have to get a job, but when Iris suggested the Katie Gibbs secretarial school, Lucy looked at her as if she had told Lucy they were going to adopt a pet python.

The girls would be gone. And how she would now spend her days was completely beyond her. Some mornings she lay in bed, trying to catch her breath, her head spinning. She knew it was just depression, the mind altering the body, and she would have to rally her strength to put a stop to it.

Iris found herself in town, shopping for towels for Charlotte to take to Brandeis with her, when she passed the old travel agency. It wasn't Fly Away anymore but was now renamed We Give You the World, which she thought was a terrible name. She pushed open the door, and a young man in a suit beamed at her. "Paris, am I right?" he said. "Or maybe a beach." He tapped the air. "I'm thinking a tour for you, right?"

"Solo," she said, and he nodded as if solo were his idea and not hers.

The last time she had done this, she had been so happy. Just touching the brochures had made her heart skip. She couldn't wait to roam the cobblestone streets of the Marais, to see the curve of the Seine, the majesty of Notre-Dame. But now what she yearned for was Lucy curling into her lap, or Charlotte sitting beside her on a park bench talking about her day in detail. Well, life went on. You had to fill the spaces as best you could.

Ten minutes later, her purse was overflowing with brochures about Paris, London, and Rome. Already her step felt more lively. Iris *would* go somewhere when Lucy was settled. She'd stay in a little hotel on the Left Bank. She'd walk around and visit museums and sit in the cafés and eat éclairs until she burst.

Inspired, Iris took herself to Grover Cronin and bought two new bathing suits, both with skirts, and cover-ups. She bought a pair of raspberry-red slacks with a zipper on the side and stirrups, and some cotton sweaters, and then a new suitcase in a rich fake leather. Goodness, it felt as if she hadn't shopped for herself in years.

Two weeks later, Lucy had vanished, Charlotte was living at Brandeis, and Iris wasn't going anywhere.

Chapter 8

It was November, and Charlotte sat in the dorm lounge, cramming for a chem exam. She was curled in one of the orange plastic chairs, eating leftover Halloween candy corn from two weeks earlier, and panicking because nothing she read was making any sense. How was it possible that she had been the best student at Waltham High, racking up As, and here at Brandeis she was struggling to hold her own in almost every class? She had thought that college would be exciting, that she would ace all her tough classes, but instead she was drowning.

Most of the other students were like another species. They came from prep or private schools, and they kept talking about novels Charlotte had never heard of and theories she had never learned. Charlotte knew that Waltham High was a terrible high school, that only 10 percent of the kids went on to college, the rest marrying young or joining the service, but she hadn't realized until now how much the school hadn't taught her. She floundered in biology class. The other kids in her French class seemed fluent, and the professor was constantly correcting her accent. She had always thought she was so smart, but now she wasn't sure. The other students bantered with the professors as if they were old friends, while Charlotte couldn't bring herself to raise her hand for fear of asking something stupid.

Charlotte flipped a page of her text, hoping the next page

might make some sort of sense, but instead it was worse. She had barely passed her first few chem exams with Cs and had been so upset she had tried to talk to the professor. But he just referred her to the TA, Tim, a tall, lanky redhead who was rumored to be sleeping with some of the students. Tim spent ten minutes going over what she got wrong and then stopped. "You look like you aren't understanding. Why did you take this class if you didn't have a solid foundation in math?" he said. He scratched his arm, not even looking at her.

"If you could just explain again—" she said, staring down at her squiggle of notes.

"I can't babysit here. You're just going to have to study and listen harder," he said.

But how could she do that? She studied every spare minute, and in her free time she worked at the information desk at the Usdan Student Center, looking up phone numbers (it was easy to tell who was popular just by how many times someone asked for a number) and directing people to the bathrooms. She had thought this would be a great way to meet people, but students tended to walk right by as if she were furniture. One day she even put a big piece of masking tape across her mouth to see if anyone would notice and laugh and come over, but no one did. After a while, she gave the job up. She had saved some money, but she wasn't making friends the way she thought she would.

Even the campus wasn't what she expected. She had thought a small college would be a cozy place where it was easy to meet people and feel at home. Instead she felt cloistered. She sat on the grassy lawn by the chapels and watched people playing Frisbee and hated herself for being too shy to ask if she could play, too. She walked around the campus, which didn't take very long, hoping she would bump into someone and could start a conversation, but that never happened.

Charlotte had believed that college would bring her the parties and people she had never had time for in high school. Instead she had never felt more alone. Her roommate, who she thought might be her best friend, arrived in a Porsche. She unpacked cashmere sweaters and ten different pairs of corduroy bell-bottoms. "You can borrow anything," she said, but two days later she moved in with a guy she'd met her first day, and she never even bothered to say good-bye to Charlotte.

She'd have to try harder. She'd have to find a way to make this be her new life, to separate into being an adult. Maybe she could go home a little less. Maybe she could join a club and meet more people that way, feel a part of something.

She still called Iris every Sunday and had dinner with her at different restaurants every few weeks. She didn't have the heart to tell Iris she was unhappy, so she made things up, assuring Iris how much she loved school, how well she was doing. After dinner on Moody Street, near the college, she walked Iris back to her car, pointing out the signs she had posted about Lucy. "I put an ad in some papers, too," she assured her, and Iris quieted. "I call the police every week," Iris said. Charlotte looked back at one of the flyers, at her sister's face. How could she not feel as though there weren't a hole punched in the world?

CHARLOTTE FINALLY MANAGED to make a few friends. Sandy, who sat beside her in history class and wore a T-shirt with the letter N on it ("For *nihilism, nothingness*," Sandy said cheerfully), could always be talked into hitching into Boston to see movies every once in a while. Charlotte hung out sometimes with her old high school friend Birdie, who was going to Emerson. But more often than not, Charlotte had to cancel plans in order to study, to catch up, and Birdie was getting annoyed. Sex at Brandeis was as plentiful and casual as the acid that was readily available, but Charlotte got neither.

She wasn't interested in drugs, and she had never been good at dating. Lucy was the one who always got attention from boys, including the ones Charlotte wanted. All junior year of high school, she had been in love with Bobby Morton, who sat opposite her in study hall every day, always wearing the same fringed suede boots, his long, dark hair falling to his shoulders. He was like a fever that raged through her body. He was always friendly to her, but one day Lucy came home with him, and Charlotte retreated to her room and closed the door. Lucy didn't see him or talk about him after that day, but Charlotte couldn't even look at him after that.

Charlotte tried as best she could. She trailed after boys from class, making herself strike up conversations that never went anywhere. She went to a few Brandeis dances and ended up leaning against a wall, until one day a blond, lanky boy from California named Teddy Roth took her hand and danced with her. When the dance was over, he tapped her nose. "I'm premed and I have just the prescription for you—dinner with me," he said. When he said "dinner," she thought he meant Kutz Hall and the disgusting chicken livers and rice they kept serving, but instead he had a car and he drove them into Boston to Legal Sea Foods and insisted they both have lobster and wine.

She fell in love quickly. She and Teddy spent all their time together. He unlocked her math and science classes for her, helping her bring up her grades. They walked around campus holding hands. In the middle of the cafeteria, he tilted her face up and put his lips to hers. Nights, they studied some more in his room and went to movies. She loved that he called her when he said he would, that he showed up when he was supposed to, and that he didn't push her into having sex. At night he just held her, stroking her hair, while they talked. When she told him about Lucy and Iris, his face was grave, and then he told her about his four younger brothers in Los Angeles, all of them runners. "You'll meet them," he said, and Charlotte felt a thrill. She rested her head on his shoulder.

The first time they made love, Teddy made it an event, with candles in his dorm room, one of the few singles on the floor, and a bottle of real wine, not the Ripple stuff or the cheap Mateus everyone was drinking. He undressed her quietly, kissing her shoulder, the small of her back. She shut her eyes and sighed. "I love you," she said, and he held her closer.

But in the morning, he prodded her up. "Wakey, wakey," he said. He picked up his shirt and threw it on. She stood up and reached to kiss him, and he gave her a loose smile. "Later, you," he said, kissing her. She didn't think anything of it until right before dinner, when she saw him making out with another girl in front of Kutz Hall. She waited for the girl to leave and then stumbled toward him.

"You kissed that girl," she said, dumbfounded.

He laughed. "Come on, Charlotte. It's nothing."

She leaned forward. "It's something. I thought—"

He smiled. "Charlotte, you need to lighten up."

"I told you I loved you last night."

"Of course you did. Everyone says that during sex."

She pulled back as if he had struck her.

"Charlotte, don't be like that," he said. "Come on. It's not the nineteen fifties anymore. You don't have to marry everyone you sleep with. I don't own you. You don't own me. We're here to have fun."

She blinked at him. "What we had was fun?"

"Well, wasn't it?" he said. "Come on, I dare you to say it wasn't." When she didn't answer, he sighed. "Okay, I'll catch you later, then," he said, leaning forward and kissing her.

She waited one day, and then two, but he never called her or came by. Well, she had studying to worry about. Love could come later.

TWO NIGHTS LATER, she was cramming for an exam when the phone down the hall rang, startling her, and then she heard her name being called out. Maybe it was Teddy. Maybe he had changed his mind. She ran outside to the pay phone in the hall, and a girl handed her the receiver. "Hello," she said.

"Can you shoot home with your key? I locked myself out of the house," Iris said.

"How did you do that?" Charlotte asked.

"I thought I heard something, and then when I went out, the door slammed shut on me. Please, honey, I'd drive to you to get the keys, but the car keys are locked in the house. Please just take a cab, and I'll pay for it both ways. I'm so embarrassed."

Charlotte glanced at her watch, her mind racing. She had five more chapters to get through. She worried about this class, but she worried about Iris, too.

"Be right there," she said.

AS SOON AS the cab dropped Charlotte off, she saw Iris on the porch in her nightgown and bathrobe and fuzzy slippers. Her hair was sloppily braided, wisps falling out. She stood up slowly, grabbing the banister for support. "Are you OK?" Charlotte asked, and Iris nodded.

"Why didn't you stay inside a neighbor's house until I got here?" She rubbed her hands along Iris's arms, trying to warm her up.

"I didn't want to be a bother. And I figured you'd be here soon."

"Well, I'm here," Charlotte said, hugging Iris. She had seen her just two weeks ago, but Iris suddenly looked older. When had her hair thinned so that a line of pink scalp showed through?

Charlotte fit her key into the lock and opened the door, and as soon as she stepped into the house, something felt wrong.

Newspapers were spread on the couch. There was laundry piled on a chair. The house smelled funny, like something was spoiling in one of the rooms. "Iris—" she said. "I'll get to it," Iris said.

Charlotte saw a silver package, tied with a bow, sitting on a table in the foyer. "Today's Lucy's birthday," Iris said quietly. "It's a silver locket."

Charlotte was quiet for a moment. When she had got up that morning, she had known it was Lucy's birthday, but it hurt to think about it, so she had pushed it away. "But Lucy's not here."

"I thought she might come home for her birthday. Or at least call. There's still no news from the police. How can that be?" Iris sighed. "I didn't want her to think we forgot."

"Let me take care of all this mess for you," Charlotte said, gathering up newspapers. She glanced at her watch. She had so much more to read tonight.

Charlotte did two loads of laundry. She did the dishes and vacuumed the living room. When she came back into the kitchen, Iris was making a cheese omelet. Two cups with tea bags in them were sitting on the table. "Eat with me, honey," Iris said. "Tell me about your week before you go." Charlotte hesitated. "Come on, I made it with that sharp cheddar you like," Iris said. "And the tea is decaf."

Charlotte sat. All through school, whenever she couldn't sleep, Iris had always made tea and sat up with her. Charlotte didn't even like tea that much, but she had always loved the way the warmth of the cup spread through her hands, the way Iris would intently listen to whatever Charlotte would tell her about. As soon as the eggs were in front of her, her stomach roiled with hunger. She had been studying so hard she had forgotten to eat. She wolfed down a bite, and Iris sat beside her, smiling. "I knew you'd be hungry," she said.

They talked about Charlotte's classes, about a book Iris was reading. After they finished eating, Charlotte called a cab. "I'll see you soon," Iris said. When she walked Charlotte to the door, she stumbled, and Charlotte grabbed her arm to steady her, alarmed. "Are you okay?" Charlotte asked. "I'm worried about you."

"I'm fine," Iris said, peering out the window. "Oh, there's your cab!"

Chapter 9

By March, Lucy's cabin fever was more like a never-ending flu. All that winter, the snow had been so heavy she sometimes couldn't open the front door. William would have to heat up water and splash it out the window, gradually making a path. Everything seemed eerily quiet, as if the world had been erased, turned white, brown, and the washed-out blue of the sky. The insects and the birds were gone. Just making her way to check on the chickens took her an hour, the air so frigid it made her gasp, the high snow soaking her jeans, getting into her boots. But she didn't mind so much, because at least it ate up part of her day.

The first day that the snow really cleared, she grabbed the house keys and set out on a walk down the road.

The world was desolate. The only sound was the skip of her breathing. She suddenly thought, what if something happened to William? What if he crashed the car and died and she was left here all alone?

She began to run, her legs pumping through the melting slush. She was coming alive with speed. She thought of all the stories Iris had told her when she first found out that Lucy hitched everywhere. Men carried shears and they would cut off your nipples and keep them in a jam jar like a souvenir. Iris told stories about girls who were captured and put into white slavery. There had been rapes, broken bodies left by the side of the road. Lucy had laughed back then, but she didn't feel like laughing now.

Lucy heard a car coming and felt a pull of fear, but the car whizzed past her.

She kept walking. Soon, she told herself, there'd be a house or at least a store, but all that happened was the road curved.

She had been walking for an hour and had nearly given up. The weather wasn't as warm as she thought it would be, and she was shivering a little. This had been a mistake. She was tired and she felt like crying, because now she had to get it together to make the long walk back. She'd have to figure out something in time for dinner. And what if William came home and she wasn't there? He'd be so worried. And then he'd be mad because they had agreed that she'd stay home during the day.

She swallowed. She was just walking. She had a right to do that, didn't she? No one knew who she was. There was no danger. And she'd make it home before William, the way she always did.

She made another turn, and there were more cars on the road, and a gas station.

And a pay phone.

She hadn't called home yet. William had told her to wait and certainly not to call home on their phone because even though it was unlisted, it could be traced. But the other night she had woken up to hear him on the phone, and when she got up and padded to the door, she heard him talking. "It's wonderful out here, Mom," he said, which confused her. Why could he call his mother if she couldn't call Iris? Weren't they supposed to be invisible for a while? She walked out into the living room, and William, lean and handsome in just his pajama bottoms, beckoned her over. He wrapped an arm around her. "Me, too," William said, and he hung up the phone. "She won't tell anyone where we are."

"Does she know I'm here?"

William kissed the top of her head, then her forehead, then her mouth. "Of course she doesn't."

Lucy knew that William was the child of a broken home. Diana had divorced when William was ten, and William's father cut all contact, barely paying child support. "You have no idea how much she loved me and needed me," he told Lucy. Lucy remembered seeing Diana once. Lucy had snuck out to surprise William, but Diana was outside his building, talking to him, her voice like water pouring. "You don't think, William," Diana had said, but then she had given him a hug.

"If you can call your mom, why can't I call Iris and Charlotte?"

"I'm not a minor like you are, Lucy. We could get into big trouble here."

"But you told your mother where you are. What if she just shows up?"

"Do we have to talk about my mother?" William switched on the radio. Gary Puckett was singing "Young Girl," a song Lucy always liked, but William was frowning. "Jesus." He turned the radio off.

"What? I like that song," she said.

"Are you hearing the words? Do you realize what it's about? He's telling this young girl that his love for her is way out of line, that she's a baby under her makeup. Then he tells her she'd better run because he can't control himself."

"It's just about desire," she said. She leaned against William, tracing a hand along his back, but he pushed her away.

"No, no, it's not." His mouth tightened.

Another evening, William had asked her to iron a shirt for him because the next day the parents were coming to watch the kids at school. He looked so distraught that she didn't want to tell him she had never ironed before. She got the board out and the iron and did the best she could, but then she smelled something burning, and when she looked down, there was a scorch mark on the sleeve. Horrified, she touched it. "William!"

He walked over. "Lucy!" He looked at the shirt, dismayed. "How did this happen?"

She hung her head. "I've never ironed before."

"What?"

"Charlotte or Iris always did it."

She waited for the flicker in his cheek that signaled he was mad, but instead he was just deflated. "Of course you don't know how to iron. How could I expect you to?" he said, but he wasn't looking at her. "I'll wear another shirt." He shoved his hands into his pockets and was quiet for the rest of the evening.

Now, she hesitated in front of the pay phone, remembering William's words: *Minor.* That meant big trouble with a capital *T.* No, she couldn't call her family. Not now. Not yet. She turned and then began the long walk home.

AS THE DAYS dragged on, Lucy began to take longer and longer walks. She would leave earlier in the day, right after breakfast, so she would be back before William would get home. "What did you do today?" he asked, and when she said she took a walk, he frowned.

"You did what?" He wanted to know where she walked, who she saw, and who saw her. "Lucy," he said, "when you're eighteen, you can walk the world."

"OK, I'll stay put."

But the next day, after reading a bit, writing, and trying to figure out how to make a buckwheat burger, she felt stir-crazy again. She didn't want to lie to William—they never lied to each other—but she would just not mention it. She would tell him everything else. She grabbed her jacket and headed outside.

She began taking walks more and more. She felt her legs

growing stronger. She saw a slight muscle building in her calves, hard under her touch. She loved seeing the stark trees taking on green leaves and filling up the sky, the shy poke of a wildflower along the road. Even the cars that passed her seemed more cheerful, and sometimes a window was even opened, and she could hear a smear of music. When she got home, she fed the chickens, and even they seemed livelier, happier to see her. "It's a great day, isn't it?" she said to Dorothy, who pecked at her feet.

IT WAS THE beginning of May, and Lucy picked up the newspaper William had brought home the night before. There was a big photo, a girl with a bandanna tied around her neck, screaming over a dead body. Lucy held the paper closer to her face. Kent State. Four killed, nine injured, in a riot over Nixon's invasion of Cambodia. The National Guard was shooting kids. Lucy dropped the paper, her hands flying to her mouth. Kids at New York University hung out a banner proclaiming, THEY CAN'T KILL US ALL. Lucy started to cry. She grabbed at her arms, her legs, making sure she was all there. She had to get out of the house.

She did what she always did: she walked, only this time she half ran, trying to chase the fear and tension out of her legs. The greenery was sprouting everywhere. Tiger lilies and Queen Anne's lace dotted the road.

She tried a new route today, heading down a road budding with crops. Eventually she saw a sign for a farm stand, which meant people. She quickened her pace. The stand blazed with color; indoors, it seemed filled with fruits and vegetables. Behind it stretched a long greenhouse. Even from here she could see how huge and lush the tulips were, how flashy the pansies. She could hear the chatter of the people, the laughter. There were a few men, but older men, probably retired, trailing after women who must be their wives. The only man under fifty was at the register. He had long hair and dark sunglasses and wore a black T-shirt with black jeans. Who did he think he was, Johnny Cash? He was ringing up jars of some kind of jam, talking with customers. He squinted at Lucy as if he were sizing her up, and she looked away. She strolled down the aisles of produce and let one hand drift along a row of fiddlehead ferns, parsnips, and pea greens. Then she felt a grip handcuffing her wrist. It was the man from the cash register, his eyes on her like a laser.

"What do you think you're doing?" he said.

"Nothing. I'm just looking."

He let go of her wrist. She stepped back from him, her breath narrowing.

"Where do you live?" he asked.

"Why do you want to know that?"

"I was just trying to figure out what you're doing here, touching all my fruits and vegetables."

"I won't do it again. They were just so pretty—"

"How old are you?" he asked.

She chewed her lip. "Twenty."

"Right. More like sixteen."

"I just turned eighteen. I look young. How old are you, thirty?"

"Twenty-nine, though what difference does that make?"

She looked around the farm stand, seeing the people. "You could make your displays prettier," she said.

"Oh, I could, could I?"

"And those plants over there are drooping. They need water. People notice things like that."

"I was just about to do it."

"If you hired me, part-time, I could do it." She felt her body shaking. What was she thinking? William would be so pissed.

But she couldn't stop herself from imagining what it might be like to actually be around people and activity again. To have money of her own. And William didn't have to know. "I'm a really good worker. And spring is just starting up. I bet you're going to need help. Why not try me out?"

"I already have a crew."

"But you might need more."

"I don't know—"

"How about just for today? Then you can decide."

She gave him her best smile, saw him loosen.

"What's your name?" he asked.

"Lucy," she said, and she knew she was hired.

HE WOULDN'T LET her work the cash register, but she could stock the shelves and arrange displays. She could go in the greenhouse, which was so warm she shucked her jacket off. She watered the cold-hardy geraniums and the leeks, chard, and spinach, the year-round crops, and harvested some to sell. Out at the stand, she sorted through the fruit and vegetable bins, taking out the produce that was going bad and restocking it from the root cellar.

While Patrick showed her what to do, Lucy gave him bits and pieces of information about herself, but not necessarily the truth. She told him she lived by herself in Ryserstone, where there was nothing all around her, just a small house and some chickens that had taken forever to like her.

"Rysterstone? I don't believe I know where that is," Patrick said.

"It's a nice walk from here to there."

"It's not so safe out there. You don't know what's on those roads."

"Sure, I do." She rearranged an errant carrot. "I'm on leave from college."

"What college?"

"Brandeis." She looked away from him. "I'm going to be a vet."

"Pretty far from school, aren't you?"

"I told you. Leave of absence. I'll go back."

She kept working the rest of the day, loving the way it felt to be busy and full of purpose. Sometimes customers asked her things, and she was happy when she could answer them. At the end of the day, she walked over to Patrick. "So, can I come back?" she said.

He was quiet for a minute, making her a little scared. And then he smiled. "Sure. Come back tomorrow around nine."

Chapter 10

It was April when Iris received a postcard from Lucy, a cowboy with a ten-gallon hat and a lasso. There was a circle of red on it, as if someone had used it as a coaster. On the back was the shock of Lucy's handwriting. The postcard trembled in her hand. Her eyes flooded. *I am fine. I am happy. I love you. Please don't worry. Lucy.*

Iris pressed the card to her forehead. Then she turned the postcard over in her hands, rereading the message again and then once more. There was no return address, so she looked for a postmark. November. This was mailed in November, so why had it taken all these months to get here? She looked at the address again. The zip code was wrong by one number, Lucy's handwriting was illegible, and it looked as if the card had even been sent to two different states—Pennsylvania and Ohio—before it got here.

How could that be? She called information and got the number of the local post office, but the person on the phone was no help at all. "This is a rural area, ma'am," the woman on the phone said. "You can't track someone down here." But Iris didn't give up. She called the police and then the private detective again, but they all told her the same thing. Impossible. It was impossible.

She wouldn't believe that. She wouldn't give up. There had to be a way.

Iris called Charlotte, who came right over, a denim jacket thrown over her dress. When she saw the postcard, she rolled it over in her hands so many times that Iris wanted to take it from her. "It took so long to get here—" Iris said.

"She can't call?" Charlotte said quietly. "She can't give us a phone number or an address?"

"She's alive, that's what matters. She'll call us eventually. I know she will—and she says she's happy—"

"Happy? Happy doing what? Being where? It's so irresponsible. So cruel. It's not like her—" Charlotte began to pace.

"Stop. Stop this. This is good news," Iris said. "I'm sure it's just the beginning, and she's let us know she's all right! Why are you so angry?" She held out a hand. "Please stop moving around like that. It's making me dizzy."

Charlotte abruptly slapped the postcard on the table and sat down. "Aren't you mad, too? Even a little? Why is this all right for her to do to you?" Charlotte asked. "To us?"

"Why are you raising your voice to me?"

"Because my sister is so selfish I can't stand it! I love her and I'm glad she's okay, but doesn't she think that we're still going to worry? That we'd like to know where she is? How she's living? Doesn't she know how worried we are? This postcard— it's all on her terms. She can reach out to us, but we can't reach out to her? Is that right? Is that fair?"

"Oh, honey, she's the baby of the family—she doesn't realize—"

"She's not a baby. She's grown up enough to make decisions that hurt others."

"I'm not excusing anything, I'm just relieved she's all right." Iris couldn't bear the way Charlotte was looking at her, and she tried to speak and coughed, and then she couldn't keep her breath and she had to sit down. She felt Charlotte hovering over her, her hands moving across Iris's back as if she were trying to read a secret message.

"Honey, I'm all right," Iris said.

"Are you sure?" Charlotte said quietly, and Iris nodded.

"I'm sorry. I'll get you water. Make you tea," Charlotte said, but when she started to get up, Iris took her arm.

"Stay here," Iris said. "I'm sorry, too."

"I have to go back and study," Charlotte said.

"You always ace every test," Iris said.

"No," Charlotte said, sighing. "I don't. Not anymore. College is harder than high school."

Iris was quiet for a moment. "Do you know how proud I am of you?" she said quietly.

"For failing? For not finding Lucy, for screwing up college?" Charlotte's skin began to blotch under her right eye, the way it always did when she was upset.

"You haven't failed. You got into a fantastic school and you'll do better. It just takes time." Iris cupped Charlotte's face until Charlotte closed her eyes. "Go home, honey," Iris said.

As soon as Charlotte left, Iris felt troubled. What could she really do to help Charlotte? She couldn't study for her, and when she had offered a tutor, Charlotte had just shaken her head. Charlotte had accused her of being soft on Lucy, and maybe she was—but wasn't that what love was all about?

It hurt her to see Charlotte so lonely, but what could she do? When the girls were little, Iris had taken them both around the neighborhood, looking for children playing. Then she would call out, "This is Charlotte and Lucy, and they're new to the neighborhood. How would you like to play with them?" The kids were always welcoming, and when Iris came back later to retrieve the girls, both their faces were shining.

But Charlotte was grown now. Iris couldn't make friends for her anymore, couldn't make sure she ate. There was supposed to be a separation in college. You were supposed to let kids try on their new lives, their fresh independence, and if it made Iris lonely, so what? This was the way it was supposed to be, and she would have to let Charlotte go, let her face her struggles.

When Lucy had first vanished, the neighbors had been helpful. Betty Hunter down the block had put up missing posters around the Star Market and the Wal-Lex. Bob Farragher had driven her to the police station more than a few times because she was too upset to drive herself. Now they were back in their old routines.

Well, maybe she could work harder at finding Lucy. She got out a pad and pencil and began to write things down. *Call all Lucy's old friends and see if they remember anything.* Her pencil stopped. She had forgotten what else she was going to write down. She couldn't remember the names of Lucy's friends. She rubbed at her temples. It had been happening more and more lately. Last night, she hadn't been able to find the TV remote and had almost given up on watching a show, until she opened her purse and there it was. The day before she had put a roast in the oven and had forgotten to turn the oven on. It was stress, she told herself. It was nothing. She did get winded more often, but there was a solution for that, too. She could hire people to do the things she needed to get done. When the grass grew too long, she hired two neighborhood boys to mow it. After a while, the boys began showing up at her door every other Sunday, sheepish, knocking into one another, all knees and elbows, asking her, "What else can we do for you?" She sent them out with a grocery list. They washed her car. For five dollars they would do pretty much anything she asked.

One afternoon, a beautiful April day, Iris went down to the basement to do a wash. The basement had been a real selling point to the house. The real estate agent had told her she could always make it over into another small apartment, but she never gave it a thought. She had loved having something subterranean, but the girls had been so afraid of the basement when they were growing up. Lucy used to tell Iris that she was sure there was a family of wolves living down there, that they dressed in overalls, and that she could hear them howling at night. "There are no wolves," Iris had told her, but the girls still cowered by the door, giggling with the pleasure of being scared, and sometimes Iris thought they just made up the wolves to get out of doing the laundry.

She put a load in the dryer and was heading for the stairs when her right knee locked. Her hands flew to her leg, rubbing at the jolt of pain. Her left arm hurt, too, and her breath seemed squeezed, but that was probably just panic. She couldn't lift her leg to make the stairs. Iris stared up at the steps. Fourteen of them. But each one now seemed as insurmountable as the Empire State Building. "Help," she said experimentally. Outside, the Browns' collie Winston barked hysterically.

She rubbed at her kneecap. It was just swelling, and that would go down. She tired again to go up the stairs, but there was a flare of pain, like a comet. She settled herself down on a pile of towels. All she had to do was wait it out. The soreness would go away and then she could go back upstairs.

IN THE MORNING, she tried to move, but her knee had stiffened, locking her leg in place. She tried to drag herself up the stairs, the way the girls had done when they were little, but she missed a step and tumbled back down. She was getting hungry. She had a neighbor, a Mormon, who kept a year's supply of food in her basement, in case of flood or disaster. At the time, Iris had thought, What a great waste. But now she wished for a can of tuna, some cling peaches or chips.

Plus, she had to pee.

She could crawl, and she made it to the bucket she used to wash the floor. It was humiliating, but what else could she do? All that day, she watched the basement windows. She saw the children running by. "Help!" she screamed, but they ran past. A large gray tabby leaned against the pane, falling asleep and blocking her view and most of the sun for hours, until it finally woke and left.

She didn't start to panic until the world turned dark again. Her chest felt stitched up, as if a hand were cupping her heart, squeezing it. She stumbled over to the washing machine and ran it cold, cupping her hands, sipping the water. But how long could she go without food? Upstairs, she heard the phone ringing. Four times, then six, and then it stopped. "Wait!" she cried.

The house ticked around her. She saw a mouse in one of the corners, and then it scampered away. She heard someone's car pulling in. She went back to the stairs and sat. Her knee throbbed. Her chest felt heavy and she couldn't seem to breathe. Her eyes shut.

HANDS WERE PULLING her up. Her eyes fluttered open. Charlotte hovered over her, her face pale. "How long have you been down here?" Charlotte asked. Iris could hear the silence. The dog and the kids were gone.

She stretched and stood. "I'm so hungry," she said. When she stood up, the room moved in waves. She saw the wash bucket full of urine and was embarrassed. She didn't want Charlotte to see it, too.

Charlotte helped her upstairs and got Iris's car keys and drove her to an ER and sat with her until a doctor told her that she had sprained her knee and, more alarming, that her heart was weak. "What?" Iris said. Charlotte sank against the wall.

"You can't be serious," Iris said.

"It's minor," he said. "You just want to take care of yourself." He gave her a sheaf of papers about what to eat, how to exercise, the words all swimming in front of her, and then Charlotte drove her home.

"Well, that was lucky," Iris said.

"Your heart is weak. How is that lucky?"

"The doctor wasn't that concerned."

"Yes, yes, he was. And what if I hadn't come by? Who would have known you were down there?"

"But you did come by." Iris thought of being down in the basement, unable to get up, the humiliating bucket of urine in a corner. She rested one hand on her chest. The doctor had said it wouldn't happen again, but what if it did?

"Your knees aren't great. How much longer can you walk up and down these stairs? And what if your heart gets weaker? You can't live like this anymore." Charlotte looked the same way she had when she was ten years old and had been playing submarine in the bathtub, dunking her head underwater, and broke her front tooth. She was scared, Iris knew that, and maybe Iris was a little frightened, too. She was never short of breath. Her heart never galloped enough to wake her at night. She used to swim for miles. She used to travel. She used to do the crossword puzzle in ink and parade around Crane Beach in a daring maillot. Sure, she needed some help now for some things, but so what? And what was the alternative?

She had friends who lived with their adult children, but Charlotte was a college student. Her life was just getting started. How could Iris ask her to rewind? She knew a woman who had someone come in and check on her every day, but Iris kept thinking how annoying that would be, as if you were a child and couldn't be trusted in your own home. Plus, that would get expensive fast.

Charlotte hesitated. "Maybe . . . maybe you could move into one of those new retirement communities."

"Are you crazy? Why would I want to do that?"

"You'd be safe there. There would be other people, too."

"No. Absolutely not. I'm not leaving my house. And what if Lucy comes home and she finds the house empty?"

"If she does, she's smart enough to ask the neighbors. And she knows I'm at Brandeis. She can find me there. We'll make sure they all know where you are."

"And where will that be?"

"Are you listening to me?" Charlotte said. "You can't live like this. It scares me."

A WEEK LATER, Charlotte showed up with brochures for special housing for the elderly. Charlotte had made appointments for them to go and look at three establishments. "Excuse me, housing for old people?" Iris said. Iris had heard of the communities springing up in Florida. She had seen the photos, a bunch of white-haired folks lining a pool, the women wearing bathing caps with flowers blooming on them, the men kicking their legs in the water. There were photos of old people dancing the samba with their hips cocked like weapons and sitting around a dining room table with forks raised in approval over what looked like steak on their plates. But it seemed so silly to her, so ridiculous. What would she have in common with these people?

"We'll go visit. We'll just check it out," Charlotte told her.

"What about you?" Iris asked. "What about holidays and summers? Where will you live?"

"I'll find a sublet near school. I already heard of one place." Iris stiffened. "What?' she said. "What?"

"I saved money from my job, the one I used to have," Charlotte said. "Enough for three months—"

"I'll pay for it—" Iris said, but Charlotte shook her head.

"No, I've got it," Charlotte said, and she didn't seem to see just
how bereft, how useless, that made Iris feel.

IRIS WENT WITH Charlotte to the appointments. All
three places made Iris feel physically ill.

The names were so wretched: Luxury Acres, Beaumont
Fields. Couldn't they have thought of something better than
that? The first one, Luxury Acres, looked like a brick apartment building, with a doorman who smiled too much and a
lobby full of people. At first it seemed fine to her, until she
saw how some of the people just sat there, their mouths open
like mail slots. Others stumbled when they walked, and a few
stared at Iris and Charlotte hungrily, as if they never had company. "This place has a smell," she whispered to Charlotte.
"Like baked ham."

"Not like you at all," Charlotte said. "You smell like honey.
Except for that time you stepped in vomit on the street. You
didn't smell so great then."

Iris laughed. "Then I guess ham is an improvement."

The second place, in Belmont, was a little nicer, with light
streaming through the big picture windows. A pleasant young
man who introduced himself as Ron took them around, pat-
tering a commentary. Each of the five floors had a community
room with a TV and music, and there was a big, noisy dining room. The people didn't look so terribly old to her. There
wasn't that ham smell. In one of the rooms, a klatch of women
were laughing over a game of cards. "You play?" one woman
called out to Iris. In another room a man was playing pool,
and he winked when he saw Iris. "You see?" Ron said to Iris.
"You're already making an impression."

"This is nice, right?" Charlotte said, but Iris wasn't so sure.
There was something disquieting about being in a place that
shouted, This is the last place you will ever live. What was it

someone had said to her once? Bloom where you're planted. But what if the soil was depleted?

"Let's go," she said to Charlotte.

Ron held out his hand for her to shake. "I hope you'll join us here," he told her.

In the car, on the way home, Charlotte chattered about what a nice place it was, how if Iris sold her house, she could afford to live in any of the places and would even have money to spare.

Iris didn't know what to do; all she knew was that she didn't want things to change. She wanted to adapt, the way she always had—when Doug returned home a stranger, when the girls came to live with her.

The following week, Charlotte showed up with a man, and at first Iris thought it was a boyfriend and she quickly straightened up the living room. Finally, she thought. But then Charlotte introduced him as Bob Blanker, a real estate agent, and Iris realized the greedy look in his eye was not for Charlotte but for the house. "We could do really well," he told Iris. "Especially with a full basement. A backyard. This great neighborhood with a school right behind the house."

"Maybe in the fall," Iris said. "This is happening a bit too fast for me." But he shook his head. "You don't realize how long this whole process takes," he said. "It could take six months to sell your house. Or even longer. It's better we start now." He patted her hand.

MAYBE HER PROBLEM was that she never actually thought any of it was going to happen. Look at her house, how old it was. Falling apart just like she was. She didn't have a new kitchen or a new bathroom. There was that leaky basement, and the house could stand a paint job. Who would want it but her? She'd let people see it just to appease Charlotte, but she had no intention of leaving. Not really. Maybe she'd have to hire someone to come in, a visiting nurse who could help her out once a week.

Some nights, she sat in Lucy's room, on the bed, holding one of Lucy's old stuffed animals. If Lucy were home, none of this would be happening. She felt a flare of anger. "Some people just don't want to be found," a cop had said to her, but why wouldn't Lucy? Maybe Charlotte was right, and Lucy was selfish. Why hadn't Lucy called or sent another postcard? Why couldn't she come home? How was Iris supposed to know that Lucy was all right, that she wasn't on drugs like the hippies Iris read about, or living on the street?

Iris's heart beat faster. Not now, she thought. Not now. She took low, even, deep breaths until she calmed down. What if she had a heart attack? She wouldn't be well enough to go into one of those places. She'd have to go into a nursing home, and everyone knew you went there to die. She put both her hands on her chest. Please, she thought. Please.

Two days later, Bob called to say he had an offer on her house. "It's a good number and they're solid buyers, a nice young couple," he told Iris.

The word "young" stung Iris. She didn't want these people living in her house. But when she told Charlotte, Charlotte shook her head.

"Think of the winter, how hard it is," Charlotte told her. Iris remembered the door getting snowed in. The way the basement flooded. "Think of those stairs," Charlotte said, and Iris's chest tightened. She didn't want to do this, but maybe she had to.

"Don't think of it as your house anymore," Bob told her. "You're on to bigger and better things."

She was to move to the place in Belmont in May, the same month as her eightieth birthday. Now her house felt different to her, as if it were spiraling away. These young people would change it, would tear down everything she had built. She wondered whether all her memories would crumble with the remodeled rooms. How long could you hold on to your memories once your familiar places were gone?

She spent the night going through the rooms, taking pictures with the Swinger camera the girls had gotten her for one birthday. She took a shot of the inside of her closet, which she had painted blue because she thought it would be cheerful. She snapped the kitchen, because Iris felt it was homier than the formal dining room. She photographed the girls' rooms, and the bedroom, where she had spent so much time talking with Doug.

Then she got to work, room by room. She took down pictures, leaving white squares on the walls. She dismantled shelves, put books into boxes. She took the most time with Lucy's room, because there was so much Lucy had left behind, so much she didn't know the meaning of. A frayed blue ribbon Lucy had saved deep in her underwear drawer. A bracelet made out of moonstones tucked in a shoe. All of it could mean something, and she couldn't throw any of it out, because maybe one day Lucy would solve the mysteries. Iris took the birthday present she had bought for Lucy, tucking it under one arm. She'd take these pieces of Lucy with her.

In the end she boiled her whole life down to four suitcases, six boxes, and some furniture. The rest she let go. She paid one of the kids to drag the bags out front. She left her new address with the neighbors so that if Lucy returned, she could find her, and she tucked Lucy's birthday locket into a suitcase. She signed the car over to Charlotte, telling herself it wasn't because she couldn't drive but because Charlotte could really use the car. "You got a great price for your house," Bob had told her. "That money'll make your years *extremely* golden ones."

She didn't understand how this could be her life, golden or not.

Chapter 11

When Patrick first saw Lucy, he thought, Here comes trouble. She had a wild corona of blond hair and she was skinny as a whippet. Jeans, sneakers, big, complicated earrings. He knew the type. When he was at the commune, whenever they couldn't grow enough of their own food, a few of the members would go out to a stand to steal fruits and vegetables. Just a little, because they didn't want to ruin anyone's business. Just enough so they could eat. They always sent the younger members because they thought it was less likely that kids would be caught, and if they were, the kids were instructed to cry, to act terrified, and usually they were just let go with a warning never to come back.

He didn't really expect Lucy back the next day. Still, all morning he kept looking toward the entrance. Maybe it was the early morning rain that had kept her from walking all this way. He switched on the radio and heard the Kinks and then the news. The superintendent of schools had resigned. It was going to be warmer again tomorrow.

He worked all morning in the greenhouse, getting the plants ready to bring outside: lettuce, spinach, leeks, chard, and the easily stored root veggies. His crew had arrived in April, plowing the fields, starting to plant his onions and parsley, which could take the lingering cold. Here it was May, and everything was now in full swing, the farm stand hopping, and it would stay that way until October and maybe even until December, when he brought in Christmas trees and decorations, and then he'd shut down for a few months, choosing seeds, setting up a schedule, tending the greenhouse. He was bringing in a crate of carrots, the earth still clinging to them, when he saw her standing by the cash register, looking around for him. She was wearing a red dress and cowboy boots, a gold clip in her hair. "Lucy," he said, and she gave him a smile.

He walked over to her, setting the carrots back down. She shifted her weight from foot to foot, her face bright with hope. "Where do I start?" she said.

Every few minutes he watched her. She picked up a broom, curving herself around it, sweeping the floor. She talked to the customers, and at one point he looked up and she was laughing as a man with a baby strapped to his back like a papoose clearly flirted with her, dipping his head to say something that made her blush. Well, she was a pretty girl. He couldn't blame the guy. But she was also really young, no matter what she said.

He made her take a break, telling one of his crew to take charge of things. "Let's get a snack."

"I'm not hungry."

She was so skinny he could have threaded a needle with her. He couldn't imagine what she was eating at home or even what her home was. He'd already decided that when she left for the day, he'd give her some carrots, a few pears. "Come on. I'll make something for us both to nosh on."

He hadn't really planned on taking a break with her. He had his routines. A cheese sandwich and soup. An apple. Some quiet time with a book in his kitchen or sitting out on the porch swing. A few times he had actually yearned for company. He would drive into town and grab a beer or two with his friend

Sal, who supplied his restaurant with Patrick's produce. Or he'd go to Sal's house, where Sal's wife, Becky, would fuss over him and try to talk up her female friends to him in hopes of piquing his interest. "I'm not ready," he said, cutting her off in midstream.

"Well," she said, "who ever is?"

So usually he just kept to himself, sometimes sipping wine to get through the rest of the day.

Lucy finally agreed and followed him into his house. He hadn't had company for a while. He had slept in the living room the night before so he could see the stars from the main window, and now he suddenly felt a little embarrassed that there was a pillow and blanket on his sofa. When he and Lucy went into the kitchen, he was relieved that he had done all the dishes that morning and put them away. He had even scrubbed the stove and the countertops. "Tea?" he asked, reaching for the kettle. "Some cake?"

"I never eat cake. All that sugar."

"What? Sugar is one of the great pleasures of life." He took out a chocolate cake and cut them both thick slices. She leaned down to the plate and inhaled deeply. Then she picked up her fork and took a bite, her eyes closing with pleasure. "What did I tell you?" he said.

Lucy talked nonstop, about how she was from Boston and she hadn't seen her family for a while and, though she missed them terribly, she sometimes wondered whether they missed her. It sounded like a true story to Patrick.

"Why wouldn't they miss you?" he asked.

"It's complicated," she said. "So do you have family?"

He thought of his parents, now retired and living in a beachfront condo in Florida that was hilariously called Pelican Heights. As soon as his parents had moved in, they both took up golf and cards, and his mother did scrapbooking with a group of women. Every Sunday they called him, wanting him to visit more often, his father trying to talk him into moving down there so they could all be together. But Florida to Patrick was the land of the white shoes, the place where you went to be bored to death. The few times he had managed to visit, he couldn't bear the sticky heat, the way everything was washed out in pastels. The beaches were crowded and noisy, and everything hummed with air-conditioning that was so cold he ended up wearing his jacket. He hated the way his parents fussed over him, their concern like a scratchy wool blanket he was desperate to throw off. His parents never mentioned his past. Instead, everything was about what was next. "What would you have to do to finish your degree?" his father had asked him the last time they were together. "Whatever it is, we'll pay for it."

"Go back to school," his mother urged. "Get back to life."

But when Patrick thought about taking exams, getting his botany degree, he didn't think of it as getting back to life. It just reminded him of what he had lost. "I have a life," he told his parents. "I'm perfectly content."

"Really," his mother said. "A college-educated man running a farm stand in the middle of nowhere."

"I make a living."

"Talk to me when you use the word 'happy,'" she said.

The one time his parents had visited, his father had walked around the farm stand without saying a word. His mother picked up the apples and put them down. She studied the jars of honey he sold from another farmer who kept bees, the delicate hand-painted labels, but then she put the honey back and didn't reach for her wallet. When Patrick showed them the house, the vintage couch that had a tiny rip on the arm, the chipped wooden desk he kept, the kitchen floor that needed to be retiled, his mother's face crumpled. At night, they all sat out on his porch, and when a shooting star appeared, his mother shut her eyes. "There, I made a wish for you," she said. He didn't have to ask her what it was. He knew.

Now, he looked at Lucy. Welcome to the fucked-up families of the world, he thought. "My family situation's complicated, too," he told Lucy. Then he busied himself clearing plates.

"What's your story?" Lucy said.

"I don't really have one."

"Sure, you do. Everyone does."

"I lived in a commune for a while. How's that?"

"You did? Was it like a cult?"

"Nope. It was sometimes wonderful. For a little while, anyway. But it wasn't for me."

"I don't know. It sounds good to me. Always having people around you and all. It gets lonely, you know?" She bent her head into her hands.

"What's wrong?" he said, and she waved her hand, swiping at her eyes. "It's nothing. I just sometimes get sad." She stood up. "We should probably get back to work. Do you have a bathroom I could use?"

He pointed down the hall. While she was gone, he did the dishes. He had a quick glass of wine and then called her, but there was no answer. "Lucy?" he called again, and then he went down the hall, past the empty bathroom to his bedroom, and there was Lucy, staring at the photo he had on his dresser. He and Vera at Cape Cod in the fall, both of them laughing and windblown, holding on to each other on the sand. "Who's this?" Lucy said. "She's beautiful."

Patrick carefully took the photo out of her hands and put it in his dresser drawer.

"Why'd you do that?" Lucy asked.

"It's time to go back to work," he told her.

AT THE END of the day, Patrick gave Lucy her pay, minimum wage, a total of five dollars. "No, no," she said, waving her hands. He took the bills and fit them into her hands.

"You did a great job. You deserve this money."

She hesitated, and then she tucked the bills into her back pocket.

"I'm driving you home," he said. "Just let me grab my keys."

"No, no. You don't have to do that."

"I need to pick up some things in town."

"I like to walk," she said. She hesitated. "Can I come back? To work, I mean?"

He nodded yes as he ducked inside the house, grabbing the keys from the green hook in his kitchen, but when he came outside, she was gone.

THAT NIGHT, AFTER he closed the stand, covering the produce, shutting the door to the inside market, Patrick sat alone on his porch swing, slowly rocking back and forth. Stars speckled the sky, and he could hear a dog howling in the distance. He thought about Lucy. The girl was like an ellipsis, a sentence with something left out. Who knew what her life was really like? He couldn't even figure out his own. He went back inside, back into his room, and opened his top drawer. There was the photo of Vera that Lucy had noticed. He picked it up.

Patrick had fallen in love with Vera when they were both fifteen and living twenty minutes away from each other in Cleveland. She was the new girl in school, with big, cartoony eyes, curly black hair that seemed to be running away from her head, and bright orange basketball sneakers. She was always reading. He had never seen anyone like her. She felt his stare. "Come to my house after school," she said, socking him playfully in the arm. They spent the afternoon talking, making cookies, and kissing. After that, they were together all the time.

Patrick knew his parents thought that it was just puppy love, that it would fall apart when he and Vera went to college, but Patrick knew different. "We love Vera, but can't you find a nice Catholic Vera?" his mother asked him, and when Patrick told Vera, laughing, she sighed. "My parents want to hire a Jewish matchmaker for me," she said. He and Vera applied to the same schools: Boston University, Berkeley, the University of Michigan. They both got into the University of Michigan at Ann Arbor, and it wasn't long before Vera moved into his dorm room, and then they moved into an apartment, and their parents gave up trying to split them apart.

One day, Vera took Patrick to see a psychic. "Really?" he said. "This is really what we're going to do?"

"Maybe she can tell us where we'll end up working," Vera said. "Come on, it'll be fun."

Patrick believed in God, but he also believed in science, in the things that he could see and feel or that could be proved. You couldn't convince him that a woman in a turban would know what was going to happen. "Come on, this is silly," he said, but Vera just grinned. She believed in all manner of things. She had to tap the light four times before leaving a room because it was good luck. She couldn't start a flight of stairs on her left foot; it always had to be her right. She wore lucky earrings, an old cheap pair of red glass danglers, and she insisted that every time she wore them, something good happened. And she loved going to psychics because she said it gave her life a framework. "Don't be so closed-minded," Vera said. "Doesn't science say that the world is stranger than we can imagine? Scientists say there's really no such thing as time, that the past, present, and future are happening all at once, and maybe that's just what psychics are tapping into."

He still thought it was nuts, but he went with her anyway. The woman in the shop didn't have a turban but was wearing a floral shirt with blue buttons, her frowsy white hair held up with a chopstick, which somehow made it even funnier to him. "I'm Madame Celeste," she said, and Patrick gave Vera a look, wanting her to smile with him, but Vera's face was serious. Vera handed Madame Celeste twenty dollars and sat in the chair opposite her. Patrick took the seat next to Vera. Madame Celeste spoke in a bored drone and said the usual things. Vera would travel. She would have a good job. Money would not be a problem. "You will move to a new house," Madame Celeste said, which was hilarious, since they could hardly afford their apartment right now, let alone a house.

Then Madame Celeste leaned forward and looked from Vera to Patrick and back again. She sat up straighter. "Marry him fast," she said quietly.

Vera smiled. "Really? Fast?"

"Don't wait," Madame Celeste said. Her mouth closed like an envelope and then she shook her head. "That's enough for today," she said.

Patrick followed Vera outside. He felt giddy. It had been a silly thing to do, but he looked over at Vera, and her cheeks were flushed, and she had a faraway look in her eyes, as if she were in another zone. He grabbed her hand until she met his eyes.

"Please," he said. "Marry me fast."

THE DAY AFTER they graduated, they married in Vera's backyard in Cleveland. It was a Mexican-themed outdoor wedding that Vera's mother, Ellen, had planned, with a mariachi band, three kinds of make-your-own tacos, bowls of guacamole, and a chocolate wedding cake. They had both a Catholic priest and a Jewish rabbi, which seemed to satisfy all the parents.

Patrick's parents came in from Florida tanned as leather

and bearing the gift of a sizable check and two big boxes of oranges. Ellen and her husband, Tom, Vera's father, clapped Patrick on the back and told him that he was now officially the son they never had. "Not that you weren't that way before," Tom said. Ellen wrapped both arms around him. "Anything you need, you just ask us," she told him.

"By the time you have kids, maybe you'll decide on one religion," Vera's mother said. "Being both is so confusing to a child, don't you think?"

"We just got married," Vera said. "And now you want me pregnant?"

"You know what I mean," her mother said, and then she leaned over and told Vera that all she had had to do was look at Tom and she got pregnant. "We're a fertile lot," she said.

MARRIED LIFE WAS WONDERFUL. They moved into a new apartment in Ann Arbor on East William Street, with a kitchen so small there wasn't enough room for more than one person at a time. The walls were so thin they could hear the guy walking upstairs and the married couple below them arguing. Ann Arbor was filled with movie theaters and museums and restaurants, and there was the Arb, where they went to picnic, sometimes throwing stones into the brook.

Their days were crammed. Vera studied library science part-time, squeezing in a waitressing job, while Patrick managed Flower Child, a florist shop, and pursued his master's in botany with a full-ride scholarship from the university.

He felt like an adult. He had friends who were still dating, crashing into breakups, and then going out again and were not very happy about it. But Patrick was in a state of bliss. He loved studying botany. Plants made sense to him. He loved his job at the flower shop, too, tending the showy blooms, watching over the refrigerated compartment where the more fragile flowers were kept. He got to know the customers who came into the shop. His favorite was the man who bought a bouquet of lilies every Friday for his wife because that was her name. Every flower was symbolic of something, he knew that, but what he really appreciated was that flowers took on the meaning you wanted them to. If you disliked roses, then who's to say that giving a rose wasn't the worst gift you could give someone? If daisies made you yearn, then that was the message you sent by giving them to someone. He filled the apartment with Vera's favorites: dahlias, poppies, zinnias, anything bright and splashy.

The only thing he loved more than being married was her. They cooked makeshift dinners—noodles and beef, spaghetti and broccoli. Whatever was cheap and healthy and could be dreamed up in a pan. They went out to the movies, always sitting in the first row because Vera liked the film to be right in her face, and at night they sat out on their front stoop eating ice pops and talking. They didn't have a lot of money, but they both had stipends at school. They could make do.

His last year of school, Vera began to notice babies. Even though Ann Arbor was a college town, people loved it so much they stayed. They built families and businesses. Vera and Patrick couldn't go out to a restaurant without Vera's homing in on whatever little one was wedged into a booster seat or seated on a lap. She waggled her fingers, smiled, and played peekaboo, and if a pregnant woman was there, Vera congratulated her, asked how many months pregnant she was, how she felt, and whether she wanted a boy or a girl or didn't care. When Vera turned her attention back to him, he saw the longing in her eyes. "What do you think, should we get one of our own?" she said, leaning toward him.

He loved her, but they were so young yet. There was so much he wanted to do with her. Go scuba diving in Bermuda and ride camels in Morocco. Camp out under the stars and see the

Great Wall of China. He loved kids. Of course he did. But it felt too soon. Was it wrong that he wanted more time with his wife? He loved being able to just pile into a car together and go upstate, to sit up all night watching movies or talking. You couldn't do that with a baby. "It's just—I don't know, right now? Neither of us have graduated yet. We both are going to need to find jobs. Can't we wait a bit?"

"I don't know if we can," she said. He thought of all those times they had had sex in high school and the condoms had broken and she had never gotten pregnant. Maybe it would take a long time, and by then he'd probably be ready to start a family. She punched him gently in his arm. "Think of the fun we'll have trying," she said. "Come on, say yes," she said. "You know you can't say no to me."

He kissed her mouth. "You got that right," he said.

VERA DIDN'T GET PREGNANT. Every time she had her period, Patrick felt relieved. "Next time," he told her, and she echoed it back, and then she'd go take a shower and Patrick would hear her crying under the rush of water.

Vera's unhappiness began to seep into him. Was this his fault somehow, because he didn't really want it? Because he didn't feel ready? Because maybe part of him wondered why his love wasn't enough. One day he brought her a bouquet of perfect lilacs, and she accepted them so sadly that he couldn't bear it anymore. "Let's go to bed and make a baby," he said.

He focused on her face, her lovely eyes, but the sex felt more like a job than something erotic, and when they were finished, she lay on her back, staring at the ceiling.

A month later she saw a specialist who did a round of tests and told her everything was fine. Patrick went to have his sperm tested, whacking off into a cup in a little air-conditioned room with magazines like *Big Bottom Girls* on a shelf by a

TV. He thought of Vera and splashed into the cup. His sperm were plentiful and strong swimmers, and somehow that made it worse, because if there was no one and nothing to blame, how were you supposed to proceed?

Vera began to look faded and get tired earlier, and her back began hurting her. "The body will heal itself if you let it," she declared, and she began making macrobiotic dishes, brown rice and seaweeds, which she barely touched. He'd come home and find her asleep in a chair, a book on her lap. She couldn't stay up past dinnertime and would collapse on the couch. "Just for a minute," she said, and then she was dozing. She complained of indigestion that came and went, and she began going on these crazy diets, popping Tums and drinking baking soda in water, but nothing seemed to help. When he reached for her, she gently pushed him away. "I just can't tonight."

"Come here, then," he said, curling around her, wrapping her in his arms. She sighed and then fell asleep against him.

One night he woke up to find Vera standing in the middle of their bedroom, her hands tucked into her armpits. "Can't sleep, that's all," she said. He touched her forehead, glowing with heat. "Are you okay?" he said. "You feel feverish."

She shook her head. "It's just hot in here," she said, and then her mouth moved in a funny way, as if she didn't want to say the next words. "Do you think we can't have kids?"

"Of course we can," he told her.

But Vera began to look more and more haggard. "Things taste funny," she complained, perking up only when he told her he had read that was sometimes a sign of pregnancy. She pounded her fist on her chest. "I wish. I think in my case it's heartburn."

She gave up on macrobiotics, but she still ate lightly, so that the two of them often had different dinners. One night, he caught her studying herself in the mirror. "I look like shit," she said. "My color's really awful. Should I go to another doctor? Maybe get completely checked out?"

He thought of all the bills they had. They were barely making their rent, and the last time he had looked in their bank account, there was only three hundred dollars. Even with the crappy health insurance they had, it would still cost a fortune just to have a checkup. "Honey," he said, "you're just stressed out. All you need to do is relax."

"Yeah, you're probably right," she said.

It was her idea to stop trying to have a baby, to give it a break. She dropped out of school for a semester but kept working because they needed the money. "I'll go back to school," she told him. "You don't have to worry." She began going to the local YMCA to take a yoga class and meditate, but as far as he could see, she didn't seem more serene, and it worried him. But then he was in the middle of his finals, and he had to concentrate. He had to study. But the more he studied, the more he realized he hadn't paid enough attention in class, he hadn't taken good enough notes, because he had been worrying about Vera. What was he thinking? Why hadn't he done both? He called his other classmates to borrow their notes, he tried to set up study groups, but it all made him more exhausted and confused.

He began staying up until three, cramming on the dining room table, while Vera slept on the couch, keeping him company. He carried his books everywhere with him, reading at breakfast and on the bus. He began to worry: What if he didn't pass? What if he didn't get his degree? As it was, they were barely managing on Vera's meager waitressing salary and his at the shop. How would they live? He watched his wife reading on the couch and felt a stab of irritation. The last time he had asked her, "When do you think you might want to go back to school and finish?" she had shrugged. She got to just read and work part-time and sleep. When was the last time he had been able to sleep? He had to work and go to school, and he felt as if it was all on his shoulders now. How would they ever afford a child?

The week before his finals, he had fallen asleep on the living room couch, still in his jeans and T-shirt, his sneakers on, his textbook spilled across his chest. He woke up startled to see Vera, fully dressed, standing in the middle of the room. "I know, I know," he said. "I'll come to bed." They had always had a pact: no going to bed alone. He'd go to bed and lie there until she was asleep and then he'd get up and study some more.

But Vera didn't look right. She was blinking hard as if she had just realized something important. She took a step and stumbled and her hands flew to her head. "I think I need to go to the hospital," she said.

"What's wrong?" he said, and then Vera's eyes fluttered and she crumpled to the floor.

He jumped up. Three steps to get to her, to gather her up in his arms. A sound rumbled from her, like song. "Vera!" he shouted. "Vera!" He had to call someone, he had to get help, but the phone was in the other room. He could see it from where he was huddled over her, but he couldn't reach it, and to get there he'd have to leave Vera, and how could he do that? "Help!" he screamed through their thin walls. "Help!" Her eyes rolled in their sockets, and he let go of her and leaped for the phone, dialing the operator, yelling out the address for an ambulance. "Tell them to come now!" he shouted. He flung the receiver from him, running back to her, cradling her, stroking her hair, and then, finally, finally, there was the banging on the door, and his door opened as if it were being broken in, and two paramedics in blue uniforms took Vera from him. "She's

CARITONE LEAVITT

still warm," one of the guys said, his hand flat against Vera's shoulder. He leaned closer to Vera, and the paramedic looked at him.

"What are you doing?" Patrick said, panicked. But then they were carrying her out, down to the ambulance, to a hospital, and he rushed to follow.

HE WAITED FOR NEWS, one person in a sea of orange plastic chairs, until a doctor came out in green scrubs. As soon as Patrick saw the doctor's face, he knew. He stumbled back until he hit the wall.

The doctor told him that she had an enlarged heart, that she might have had it since birth, that some people never even had symptoms.

"What symptoms?"

"Indigestion, extreme fatigue, sweating—" the doctor said.

Patrick tried to swallow. "If I had known—if I had seen— could this have been treated?" he asked.

"There are medications," the doctor said, and then he put one hand gently on Patrick's shoulder. "I'm so sorry," he said.

It was five in the morning. A social worker had come and given him the name of a funeral home. He had to fill out papers. Afterward he stood in the corridor, holding one of his hands with the other. "Is there someone who can come get you?" the social worker had asked, but the only person he wanted to be with was Vera. He kept expecting her to round the corner, laughing at the fuss made over her. She'd calm him down. She'd hold his hand. Can you believe this? she'd ask him.

No. He couldn't.

He couldn't leave her. Not yet. He walked to a pay phone and called Vera's parents, making them both get on the phone at the same time. When he told them, his voice tight, a woman walking by brushed past him, and then Vera's mother screamed so loudly Patrick let the receiver clatter against the wall, hanging, and then he walked away, his hands clapped to his ears, as if even a mile away he would still hear her.

HIS PARENTS FLEW up from Florida. Vera's parents were there, too, from Cleveland. So were his friends. But he didn't remember much of anything. Everyone crammed into their apartment, someone put food in front of him, crackers, cheese, and grapes, but he couldn't eat. Everything hurt him. Her face creams in the bathroom. The hairbrush with her hairs threaded through it. He found, hidden under the bed, where he had never looked, a small blue box, and when he opened it, there was a tiny red taffeta party dress, a funny pair of baby suspenders with dogs on them. He put the clothes to his face and wept.

It felt as if someone had ripped off a layer of life, something that had kept him from seeing what was really there, and now he could never go back to the way things were, to the way he had felt. He could sleep only if he downed four glasses of wine or took a pill, and his dreams, when he did sleep, were thick and heavy with her. In his dreams, she was serene, and smiling at him. How come you aren't calling me? she asked him, and then she handed him a piece of paper and leaned over and kissed him. But where are you going? he asked, and she laughed, like a line of jazz, and then she was gone, and when he opened the paper, the numbers she wrote were smeared and he couldn't make them out. Wait! he called. Wait!

A MONTH AFTER the funeral, he stopped going to work. He stayed at home and he talked to his wife as if she were still there. Why did you leave? Why didn't you tell me? Do you hate me for not knowing how sick you were? Because I sure as fuck hate myself. The house ticked around him. He bolted up in the middle of the night, sure he heard a rustling in the kitchen. "Vera—" he said, and he went into the kitchen and turned on the lights, and a mouse scooted under the stove.

"Marry him fast," was what that psychic had said. He couldn't stop thinking about it. What if he could have done something?

His boss sent over a huge bouquet of flowers with a note that said, *Come back whenever you're ready.* But he knew he'd never be ready. He let the bills pile up on the side table, even though there was the surprise of money from Vera's life insurance, a policy he hadn't even known she had. A check for $100,000 arrived in a nondescript white envelope. Why hadn't she ever told him about that? he wondered. It was typical Vera, taking care of details, taking care of him. Well, what did he care about money now? There was also a letter from the college, saying that they acknowledged his situation and that even though he hadn't taken his finals, he could still do so. He could still graduate, but he had to let them know, he had to make arrangements. He thought about how much he had wanted this degree, how much it had meant to him, and how it would have changed his life and Vera's. He crumpled the paper in his hands. Dreams. All of it dreams, and now he had woken up.

At night he lay on Vera's side of the bed. Come back. Come back.

Mostly he thought about how he should have insisted she go to a doctor the first day she said she wasn't feeling well. He could have paid more attention. Not been so cheap. He should have known something was amiss. What was wrong with him? She might have lived.

His parents called often. And then one night, when he was staring at the TV, Vera's mother, Ellen, called him. Her voice was soggy with tears, and she asked him how he was doing, whether he was working or eating, and he lied and said he was.

"Was Vera sick? Was there any sign?" Ellen said. He heard her swallow. "I know what the doctor said, but I just wondered . . ." Her voice trailed off like a ribbon.

He put his head in his hands. Here they were. All the questions he had been asking himself every night. Why didn't you see? Why didn't you do something? She had *told* him. She had described symptoms, and he had told her it was too expensive to see a doctor. If he told Vera's mother the truth, she would be as haunted as he was, always wondering what might have happened if he had taken action, wondering whether Vera might still be alive. She would hate him, and he would deserve it.

"She was fine," he lied, and he hated himself even more.

"Was there anything you noticed about her? Anything at all?"

"Why are you asking me this?" he said quietly.

"You were the last person to see her. I'm her mother—"

"And I'm her husband."

"When she was a little girl, all she had to do was cough and I'd take her to the doctor. I'd make sure she stayed in bed," Ellen said. "You love someone, you notice everything about them, you take care of them. That's all I'm saying."

Anger beat like a pulse inside him. He pressed the receiver against his forehead.

"Are you listening to me?" Ellen said.

"The doctors told me it was something in her heart. That she might have always had it," Patrick said.

"But you never noticed anything?"

"Neither did you."

There was a clip of silence, and then he heard her quietly weeping, and instantly he was ashamed of himself. "I didn't mean that," he said, but she hung up, and then he missed Vera so much he couldn't breathe.

The college phoned Patrick, asking him point-blank whether he was going to make up his finals, warning him he wouldn't graduate if he didn't act soon. His friends began slipping him the names of grief therapists. He quit his job. He quit school. He kept walking around the city, going in and out of stores, because he couldn't manage to stay in one place without thinking of how Vera might like those soaps or how she might like that brand of chocolate. Was he doomed to see the world through the eyes of his dead wife? Would life never stop reminding him that she was gone?

He went home and packed up his things and shipped them to his parents. He paid all his bills and then he called the landlord and said he was giving up the apartment. And then he got in the car and drove.

HE DIDN'T WANT to be alone, so he stayed at a commune for a year, learning to grow and tend vegetables and fruits. He worked the plow and planted seedlings in their greenhouse. In winter he pored over the seed catalogs with everyone else, and later he helped with the harvests. At first he loved the sense of order, the people all around him, the way he was so busy he didn't have a moment to think about anything other than what he was doing. He slept in a big white house, in a high-ceilinged room with six other people, mattresses spread on the floor. He chose his clothes from a communal closet and he ate meals at a round table. He never had to leave the commune for anything, and he felt safe and cocooned. "Love you, man," people kept saying to him, and even though he knew it wasn't really true, the phrase wrapped around him like a blanket. But then they instituted a community meeting every week. Everyone sat around a small campfire, and one of the guys held up a piece of wood decorated with blue paint. "This is our talking stick," he said. "Whoever holds it can speak his or her mind." They passed the stick around. One girl talked about how she was mad at her boyfriend, Bill, for sleeping with someone else, even though she knew there was no ownership. A man mentioned that he was really hungry at night, and he wanted to keep food in his sleeping room. Everyone talked, until they got to Patrick, and then he said, "Pass."

At first they let it go, but gradually, when Patrick hadn't spoken for weeks, people started pressing him. He looked sad, even when he was happy, they said. He seemed as if he was hiding something. "You're supposed to open up. To share. We're here for you," one girl said. He looked at her open, eager face, her hippie braids and paisley dress. She had painted a daisy on her cheek and she had rings on most of her toes. "*I'm* here for you," she said in a low voice. She trailed a finger down his chest. He realized he had to leave.

This time he ended up on the other side of Pennsylvania, in Tioga, which was just as isolated and green as the commune but seemed to have fewer people. When he saw a small farm stand that was for sale—a big wooden building with rows of tables, a greenhouse, and a small porched cottage attached to it—it was an easy decision. He bought the property, kept the crew that was already there to help him, and got busy building a business. He would wake up at five to start working. He tended the plants he grew, widening his garden, growing organically, the way they had at the commune, and he began to get a reputation for having the best produce around. By nine o'clock each night, he was exhausted. It was the same as living on the commune except he was on his own and no one asked him to talk about his feelings. In 1969, he got his draft notice, but his lottery number was 315, and part of him was too numb to be glad about it.

He habitually had a glass of wine at dinner to take the edge off. To dim the panic. And then he started having two. It was easy to begin having wine at lunch. He was proud of the fact that he made it to eleven thirty before having his first drink. He told himself it was really like a happy hour, because after all, he had been up since five. He told himself he wasn't tearing up the house. He looked at himself in the mirror and he didn't look drunk. And what did it matter anyway?

At night he watched movies on TV until he fell asleep, all those other lives flickering in black and white in front of him. Well, that was what his life was like now, black and white. He had just turned twenty-eight. He knew he wasn't fooling himself. It wasn't a good life, but at least it was something.

Chapter 12

Working at the farm stand turned out to be Lucy's salvation. She got up earlier than William did, making them both cups of strong tea and oatmeal. "Thank you, love," he said, patting her hair, and she felt torn and guilty because she was lying to him. "You're awfully chipper today," William said once, and for a moment she debated telling him: I have a job. I was good enough to be hired! But would he be proud of her, or, as with everything else, would he just be suspicious and protective? She'd have to risk it. At least for now.

Every day, before she arrived at work, she tucked her fake wedding band into her pocket. She had told Patrick she was a student. She had already lied about that, and she couldn't risk telling him about William.

Patrick began teaching her the cash register, how to bang it open because the drawer always stuck. He trusted her enough that he would go into the house while she worked the register. Sometimes she got confused, like the time a man gave her a twenty, and the bill was $15.45, and she was counting out the change in her head when he dug in his pocket and gave her a nickel. "That'll make it easier," he said, and she suddenly couldn't calculate the change. The man waited and then sighed, exasperated, and came behind the counter and was picking out his own change just as Patrick came out and saw what was happening. But Patrick wasn't angry at all. "Takes time to learn," he said.

"What should I do next?" she kept asking. Once, when he came upon her sitting on the porch swing, under his macramé wall hanging, her face lifted to the sun, she scrambled to her feet. "I'm sorry!" she cried. "It won't happen again! I'll get busy—"

"Lucy, relax," he told her. "It's okay to take a break. You work hard here. And you're doing great."

"I am? I really am?"

"Of course you are."

She felt as if her whole body had filled with light.

"Plenty of people watching the stand and in the fields," he told her. "I feel like I need to play a game of gin, don't you?"

Her shoulders relaxed. "I bet I can beat you," she said.

On Friday, before she left, Patrick handed her a twenty. "What's this?" she said, and he laughed.

"Your pay."

She turned it over in her hands and thought, Look what I did.

When she got home, she ran upstairs and hid the twenty in an old sneaker at the back of the closet. William had their money stashed away, but this was hers alone. Twenty dollars didn't seem like very much, but she'd keep working. Soon, maybe she could walk to the Giant Eagle and buy the things William wouldn't keep in the house—deli meat, sugar cookies, and soda—and eat them by the side of the road before she got home.

LUCY LIKED WORKING for Patrick. He felt more like a friend than a boss. They would hang out at lunch and talk. He was so nice, so easygoing, and so sad. One day, at the beginning of June, after she had been working for him a month, she was boxing up apples for a customer when she heard his front door slap. Sunlight splashed across his hair. She had never noticed before how green his eyes were or how shiny his hair was. "Everything okay?" he said when he came toward her. He patted her shoulder, and she felt a jolt of heat. Her cheeks flamed. "Everything's cool," she said, but her voice was shaking.

"Sit," he told her, leading her to his porch. "Have some tea with me."

He brought out the tea in blue cups and sat beside her, telling her about his plans for the future. Most farmers took other jobs to make ends meet in the off-season, driving a bus, teaching a class. But he hadn't had to. In fact, he was thinking of expanding his storage areas, making an insulated shed. That way he could start a delivery program, with boxes of winter squash, potatoes, carrots, beets, herbs, and greens from the greenhouses. And he was going to advertise. "And one of these days, I'm taking you out for a proper lunch," he said.

He leaned over the porch railing and plucked a dandelion and handed it to her. "Sometimes the wildest things are the most beautiful," he said. She tucked the flower in the back of her jeans. Later, if she looped one hand around to her back pocket, she could still find it.

That day, before she left, Patrick called her over. He was holding an old bike, the chrome a little rusty. "Now you can ride home," he said.

Lucy lit up. A bike! A real bike! "I'll take such good care of it," she said, her words rushing. "I'll return it the way I found it—"

"Whoa, whoa—" He pushed the bike closer to her. "This is yours. I've had it around for years and never did anything with it." He smiled, and she got on the bike, so excited she wasn't sure she could work the pedals.

• • •

THE BIKE WAS BLISS. The trees flew by her, and she saw two deer peering at her from the woods. Never had she felt this exhilarated. She rode fast and hard, as if she were trying to burn away this stirring, this new feeling she had for Patrick.

When she got home, the drive was empty, as she knew it would be. She knew, too, that she couldn't tell William she had a bike. He'd want to know where she got it, and why she needed it. So as soon as she pulled up to the house, she took the bike and hid it in the woods.

Then she flew into the house. She grabbed her blue journal and wrote about the bike, about Patrick, about how they might grow closer, and even though none of it had ever happened, it still might. But she couldn't risk William finding out. She got up and wedged the journal behind the bookcase where William would never think to look. He'd badger her about seeing her work, but she could use loose leaf paper for that, writing about things she didn't care about as much, things she didn't mind William seeing.

She began boiling water for noodles, opening a can of white beans, pulling the ring back on her finger. When William came home, he narrowed his eyes at her. "Spaghetti again for dinner?" he said. "I gave you all these cookbooks. You have to be more creative here. We keep having the same three dishes all the time."

He sat at the table. "What did you do today, Lucy?"

"Nothing. I read."

"What did you read?"

She looked past him at the bookcase. "*Oliver Twist*," she lied.

"What was the last scene you read?"

She panicked. She had read the book, but she couldn't think of a single scene now, not with the way he was staring at her. "Why are you giving me the third degree? What about your day?" she asked. "What did you do?"

"I don't want to talk about work. We're talking about you," he said.

William had been having more and more off days. She could always measure how work went for him by how full an account he wanted of her time. What did she do all day? Where did she go? Whom did she see? She knew those were trick questions, and she always lied, which made her feel guilty, but she also felt as if she didn't really have a choice. There was no way he would let her keep working at the farm stand, and there was no way she was giving it up.

She used to tell William everything. That was the best part of their relationship, the way she could say anything and he would listen. He would never make her feel small. He used to know her better than anyone did. But lately, whenever she tried to tell him how she really felt—how lonely she got—he would go silent.

"You're not blaming me, are you?" he said quietly, and then she felt so terrible that she always said no, of course she wasn't. She had thought that hiding out with him would be exciting and romantic, that it would bring them closer. Us against the world. Just the way it used to be with Charlotte. But it didn't feel like that anymore with William. Now the one person she wanted to talk to was Patrick.

William began marking off the days on the calendar to her eighteenth birthday with a huge red *X*, but every *X* made her feel uneasy. Would he really relax when she was eighteen, or would he be just as possessive, just as paranoid? She felt her feelings for him chipping away more and more every day, and it scared her, because without their love, what did she have?

That night, she woke up to find William sitting up in bed, staring at her. "Just watching you sleep," he said, but it unsettled her. Sometimes when she was feeding the chickens, she swore she saw him behind the kitchen curtains, watching her, and then he would vanish. One day, she'd come home early from Patrick's and was reading the newspaper from the night before. The movie ads made her wistful, but so did the articles about what was going on in the world. The colleges and universities were striking because of Kent State, because of the war. The student strike headquarters were at Brandeis, and she felt a pang of yearning. If she were there, she'd be helping out in any way she could; maybe she would even be working beside Charlotte. She turned a page, and there was a photo of the three beautiful Manson girls at the preliminary hearing, smiling, holding hands. The article said that the young women had already been interviewed so often they were on a first-name basis with the reporters. Susan Atkins even defended Charlie, claiming that the murders were nothing, that you had to have a real love in your heart to do such a thing to people. To kill them was to kill part of yourself, a kind of gift of freedom. She said even though they were separated from Charlie now, Charlie was still watching over all his girls. He always knew what they were doing and thinking. Lucy felt chilled. She put down the paper. It reminded her of William.

Chapter 13

Iris had been in her new apartment for a month, and she hated it. Still, she tried to make the best of things. She had her walls painted a deep, soothing blue, and Charlotte took her shopping to buy a new bedspread in a rich, deep russet, like a bite of plum. She also bought a new stereo and a television. She didn't want to have to answer questions, to have her grief out there shimmering in front of her, but she kept photographs of the girls in her nightstand, and every night, she looked at them.

But when she left her room, she felt the world crashing down around her. The halls were filled with people struggling with walkers or, even worse, being pushed in wheelchairs. Most people dressed nicely, but there was a woman at the end of the hall who wore nothing but the same black dress day after day, as if she were at her own funeral.

It was the beginning of June now, and warm enough to sit outside, but then what? Was she supposed to just stare at the driveway?

Meals were the worst. All those people sitting at the tables, waiting like patient children, and the food was like that mystery meat the girls used to joke about being served up at their school cafeteria. Everything was starchy or from a can, bonneted with cheese, and though she had never been a cook, she did have a sense of taste. She looked around her table, at the six other people, and one woman was shoveling in the food. "This food is terrible," Iris said out loud on her first night, and everyone looked at her.

"You get used to it," a man said to her.

"What are you talking about? I think this spaghetti is tremendous," a woman said.

"Why should I get used to it?" Iris put her fork down. She had a can of tuna and macaroni and green peas in her apartment. A stove that worked. She stood up and walked out of the room and went back to her apartment, where she made herself a meal. She put Frank Sinatra on her stereo, but when the food was ready and she put it on her plate and sat down at the table, she burst into tears, her appetite gone. She stood up and dumped the food into the trash.

She'd never get used to it.

CHARLOTTE CALLED HER a few times a week and came to visit every Sunday, and Iris tried not to complain, because Charlotte seemed to have a new lightness about her and Iris wanted that to last.

Every floor had a TV room, a game room with a pool table, and a sitting room with couches, and there was always someone to keep you company. Iris played pool. She watched programs she didn't really want to watch—nature shows about wild seals, or courtroom dramas.

One day she was reading the newspaper when she saw an advertisement for a special exhibit at the local museum. She wanted to go, and then she realized there was no one stopping her. She could really come and go as she pleased. There was no one she had to even tell. Her heart began to beat faster, and she dressed up, putting on a favorite blue dress and her best shoes, and then she walked outside, past the concierge, out to the street, to the pay phone, where she called a taxi. No one stopped her. No one gave her a second look when she went to the museum and bought her ticket.

By the time she cabbed home, it was dark. When she came inside, everything looked different again. The people sitting at the chairs didn't look as old as she had thought they were before. The man laughing didn't seem crazy anymore. One of the women stood up when she passed. "I like your outfit," she said, and Iris felt herself glow. She didn't feel helpless any longer.

Back in her room, Iris opened up her top dresser drawer, and there, under her nighties, was the postcard from Lucy. She took it out and stuck it on the mirror of her vanity.

She had so much she wanted to tell Lucy. She wished Lucy knew where she was, how she was doing, so that they could share it. She wanted to tell her, Do you remember the time we made brownies and we both ate the batter before it cooked? Do you remember when you told me there was a contest going on at the gas station and I could win fifty dollars if I just said, "Yabba dabba doo," like in *The Flintstones*, and I did, and you laughed so hard at me, and then I laughed with you?

There had been no more postcards from Lucy. Iris kept wondering, what had she done to make Lucy leave? How could she make amends to her if she didn't know?

The other residents talked about their kids all the time, but she never mentioned Lucy, because what would she say? My other daughter's living a life I know nothing about and I don't know why?

Well, she was still strong, still active. And she had to admit that living here had eased a lot of her burdens. She didn't have to worry about the grass being mowed, or the basement leaking. She had time now for more things. Tomorrow she would call the police and ask them if they had any more leads. She would take out another ad in more newspapers, and this time, she'd put in a photo of Lucy.

Chapter 14

Patrick had to admit he liked Lucy's company. She was now comfortable enough to ask whether she could go into his house to get some water or make a sandwich or read one of his books. He always left his door open, and when he came back inside, he found traces of her. A barrette on the couch, a glass washed and stacked in the kitchen by the sink. It made him feel good, taking care of her, as if he had a connection to the world.

He began to think that maybe she was telling the truth. Yes, she did seem spooked. He caught her staring at him, as if she wanted to tell him something. Her gaze was a little too intense, and he always looked away. A few times she told him she had to leave early, and she bolted away on her bike. But maybe she really was eighteen and a Brandeis student taking time off. No one came by asking about Lucy. No cop. No social worker. No parent. He glanced in the notices in the local papers, but there was never any mention of a missing girl. Maybe she wasn't lying. And if she was, he figured she would tell him the truth when she trusted him enough.

She worked hard and was helpful. It was almost July when she came in one day with a little farm newsletter she had neatly written up, talking about the fruits that were in season, including recipes. He liked her writing, how it fancied up his fruit.

Peaches are like the first blush of summer. "You could make copies and then hand them out for free, right by the cash register," she said shyly. "If you wanted to, I mean."

"Lucy, this is a great idea. I can have the copy shop put it on really pretty paper, too."

She shone when she smiled.

"And I want you to put your name on this."

"Really? My name?"

"This is great stuff, and I want you to have the credit."

The next piece she turned in, about fresh figs, was signed "Lucy Smith." "Smith?" he said, and she shrugged. "Lots of people have that name, including me," she said.

Customers began to look forward to her newsletter, to comment on the recipes. In one day, the peaches sold out because everyone wanted to try the cobbler recipe Lucy had included. "You," he told her, "are a goddess."

She flushed. When she walked past him, he felt her fingers brush against his. He stepped back to give her room.

ONE AFTERNOON, PATRICK felt overwhelmingly tired. He couldn't concentrate. It took him three times to understand that a customer was asking for Gala apples. He walked over to Lucy. "I'm going to go lie down," he told her. "I'll set my alarm and be back in an hour." She was wrapping up a jar of homemade jam for a customer, and she nodded.

He poured himself one glass of wine, then two, and then another. Just to drown out the distractions. He shut the blinds and the door. Outside, a car backfired. A woman shouted, "Jason, I told you no!" He jammed the pillow over his head, but it didn't muffle enough. A fly was buzzing in the room, and he began to doze fitfully, moving in and out of dreams where he was biking into the ocean, or having lunch with a shark that kept eyeing his right leg. He tumbled back into sleep, turning, trying to get comfortable. And then he felt someone watching him. His eyes flew open.

Vera stood at the foot of his bed.

She was in jeans and an old sweater. Her lips were moving, saying something to him, something important, he just knew it, but her voice was mangled, a record being played backward. He tried to get up, to touch her, to talk to her, but his arms and legs were cemented to the sheets. The only sound in the room was the whir and click of his fan.

She crawled into bed, curling against him, and there was the shock of her, and his body trembled. Her silky warmth. Her vanilla smell. Her head resting on his back. He wanted to beg her to stay. He wanted to touch her and talk to her and do everything with her. Sleep, Vera whispered, and his lids glued shut, even though he tried to wrench them open. But he could still hear her—the rasp of her breathing, the Vera-ness of her—and he clung to it as long as he could.

HE WOKE WITH a start. The fan was still going, but now it was blowing dust around. He felt a weight in the bed behind him. She was still there. Vera was there. For a moment he felt so ridiculously happy, so buoyant with hope.

He tried to move, first his fingers, then his legs, and when they worked, he kicked off the sheets so he could move toward her. "Vera," he said.

Lucy was sleeping beside him, her mouth faintly open.

He jolted out of bed, a roaring in his ears, bracing his arms on the wall. There was his dresser, his closet, his shoes on the floor. There was Lucy.

Lucy was fully clothed, her rainbow socks winking in the light. "Lucy," he said, and her eyes fluttered open. She propped herself up on her elbow. "What are you doing here?" he asked.

His voice sounded funny to him, like someone scraping rust off steel.

She climbed out of the bed, and he felt his anger rising like a tide.

Lucy was standing too close to him, and then she moved even nearer. There was something in the air that he didn't like, poking him in the ribs just like a finger. The way she was looking at him. She looked so small and lost he almost felt sorry for her. Her face looked as if it were collapsing.

"What were you doing?" he asked.

"I was just tired," she said. "I thought we were friends." She bent, shoved her feet into her sneakers, and rushed out of the room.

FOR THE REST of the day, they worked together in silence. She was at the cash register ringing up customers, and then he went out to the fields to see what was ready to pick. He didn't have to look at her at all. He didn't have to think how he had thought she was Vera. He could concentrate on pulling carrots, inspecting the corn, pinching the basil back so it would grow more lush. He felt the sunburn glazing over him. His nose would be clown red, most likely, but he kept working. He was glad when the afternoon was upon them. He had picked two big buckets of carrots, some peppers, and a little bucket of red leaf lettuce and was washing them with the garden hose when he saw her leaving, walking her bike to the road, her head bent down, anger still coming off her in waves.

He almost hoped she wouldn't come back.

THAT NIGHT HE was at the grocery store, looking for paper towels, when he heard a man arguing. "Because I told you," the man said. When Patrick looked up and followed the sound to the frozen-food section, he saw the back of a tall guy in a tight T-shirt and bleached jeans, his hair shaggy to his shoulders, arguing with someone, jabbing his finger in the air. Patrick rounded the corner, curious, and then he saw the guy's face. And then he moved closer and saw Lucy, staring at the ground, her arms tightly folded.

Lucy lifted her hand, and he saw a wedding band. He felt a flare of heat. It wasn't that he had feelings for her—he didn't—but somehow the fact that she was married and he hadn't known it made him feel as if he'd been taken.

For a moment he thought her husband couldn't possibly be this guy, who looked as if he was at least thirty, but then she balanced on her tiptoes and kissed him on the mouth.

What else had she lied to him about? Was she playing him, somehow, and if so, for what?

He walked over. "Hello." His voice sounded like a bark. The color drained from Lucy's face.

"Hi," her husband said, furrowing his brow. "I'm sorry—have we met? You know my wife?" He looked at Patrick as if he were memorizing him, then looked at Lucy, saw her eyes trained on the floor. "You know this guy, Luce?"

Something wasn't right.

"Luce?" her husband repeated.

Lucy shook her head and wouldn't meet Patrick's eyes.

Patrick thrust his hand out to her husband. "I run the farm stand," he said. Lucy's husband slowly shook Patrick's hand but kept his gaze on Lucy.

"What farm stand?" Lucy said, her voice wavering. "Is there a farm stand near here?"

Up close, Patrick could see that Lucy's husband was much older than she was, maybe older than Patrick, too, which made things even stranger. Lines fanned out from his eyes, and there were a few wires of gray threaded in his hair.

"Hey, man, I think you're mistaken," Lucy's husband said.

"I thought I knew you, but I guess I don't," Patrick said. Lucy raised her eyes to look at him, but Patrick turned and walked away.

He knew now that she had lied, but instead of being angry, he felt concerned. He hadn't liked Lucy's husband. Well, so what? he told himself. It was none of his business. They were having an argument, a bad time. The world was filled with rotten relationships. He saw it all the time at the farm market. Husbands yelled at their wives for dragging them there when they wanted to be watching the game on TV. Wives complained that their husbands couldn't pick out a properly ripe tomato. Nobody held hands or put a tender arm around anyone's back. He wanted to shake them. If you were lucky enough to have love, shouldn't you protect it while you could?

Chapter 15

What was up with that guy? Do you think he was high?" William said when they were driving home. He studied her. "You didn't really know him, did you, Lucy?"

"No way." Lucy hunkered down in her seat, her arms wrapped around her, feeling sick. William would be furious if she told him she had a job at the farm stand. He'd be even more angry about the lying, and now she was stuck and she couldn't say a word. She had seen, too, the way Patrick looked at her. She was sure that he would fire her if she returned to the stand.

Lucy wanted to cry. He had been her only friend. And maybe she had wished that he was more than that, too. And then she had blown it.

She opened a window, the cool air flooding her face. "You hot, honey?" William said, rolling down his window, too. He reached over and tapped her leg the way he always did. Love taps, he called them, but sometimes they hurt. She stared at his hand, confused and miserable, and drew her leg away. She shut her eyes, pretending to sleep.

She thought how, at Patrick's, she liked to snoop around his house. She had seen the photographs of him with that woman. The way they looked at each other, she knew it was some sort of huge, majestic love. Something had happened there. A mystery. Maybe the woman had left him, and he was hoping she would come back. Maybe she had cheated on him and he had left her. Lucy had stood in his closet, breathing in the smell of his leather jacket, resting her cheek against the sleeve. You have no idea how I feel, she thought. And she could never tell him. Especially not after the way he had acted when she had fallen asleep beside him, one of the biggest mistakes of her life.

WILLIAM PARKED THE CAR, and Lucy scooted ahead of him into the house. As soon as the door closed behind them, she wanted to go curl up in bed, but William took her hand, burying his head against her shoulder, kissing her neck. Not now. Oh no, not now. He kissed her neck, her shoulders. He tugged her dress off her body, and she let him, because she didn't know what else to do. "Wait, wait," he said, and then he rushed to the table and lit the candles so that shadows flickered along the walls. He lowered her to the ground, taking off his clothes. He touched her breasts and she shut her eyes, and then she put her hand on him. He was too soft. He'd never get inside her, but he was hovering over her, trying, one time and then two. "Just a little more," he whispered, but she could tell it wasn't working. His face shut and then he rolled off her and the two of them lay on the floor, staring up at the ceiling, and Lucy thought of the curve of Patrick's back, the way he had felt when she slept against him. She had felt so safe. She'd do anything to feel that way again.

She shut her eyes, but that didn't stop the tears from streaming down her cheeks. "What's wrong? Tell me, please tell me," he said.

She didn't know what to say, how to make sense of her confusion. "I hate being so alone all the time."

"But you're not alone. You have me. Don't you know I'm with you every second even when I'm not?"

"Don't say that. What does that even mean, what you just said?"

"It means we have a connection, like we're part of each other."

She felt as if she were skating on a frozen lake, the ice crackling under her feet.

"I'm afraid of Charlie Manson," she blurted out, and William laughed. "What?" he said. "He can't hurt you. He's locked up a million miles away. He's on trial now and he'll never get out of prison."

"But his family's still out there—some of those girls—"

"They'll get locked up, too. You'll see."

"The world is so crazy now," she said. "We live in the middle of nowhere. I'm alone all day. Anyone could come here and I wouldn't be able to stop them." She thought of Charlotte living in Waltham, getting on a subway, surrounded by people and noise and cars. She could go anywhere she wanted, do anything she wanted. "Maybe a city would be safer," Lucy said. "It doesn't have to be Boston. We could go to LA. Or Chicago. Or Santa Fe." You could vanish in a city, she thought.

"A city? God, no," he said. "I'll never live in a city again."

"I miss skyscrapers," she said quietly. "And all-night diners. I miss subways."

"No. You don't mean that. You're just missing me because I'm gone all day," he said. "But I like that you miss me. It makes me feel good." He kissed her hair. "Let's just lie like this," he told her, one leg thrown over her hip, pinning her in place. Lucy's eyes were open, her mind roaring like a train.

"You know, you could get another teaching job," she said quietly.

He looked at her as if she understood nothing.

"Really. I mean it. Why couldn't you?"

"Lucy, no—" He held up one hand. "We can't."

"Why not? What's holding us back? We could go to a new place. I could get my GED. You're a great teacher. You could get a better job—"

"Lucy, I can't."

"But I don't get it. Why can't you?"

"Because I was fired in Waltham. "

She sat up and blinked hard at him. "What?"

"I was fired. I was refused a recommendation."

She started. "You were fired? You told me you quit."

"I would never have quit. I had benefits and vacation. I was tenure track. I was fired because I wouldn't follow the curriculum. Because of the handouts. Parents complained. The principal didn't like me. And now no place reputable will hire me."

He was looking straight ahead. Lucy's bones filled with glass. If she moved, she might shatter. "But you're doing okay at this school, right?" she asked.

"Not really," he said. He was so still she wanted to shake him.

"What does that mean, 'not really'?"

"It means it's hard. No one wants to learn anything, and you can't insist. I can't adjust to their methods. I might as well just sit and smoke a jay with the teenagers because I'm sure as hell not doing any teaching. You know what the senior kids are reading? Picture books. The teacher tells me they can learn so much by keeping things simple. She says, 'Why should a kid who can't read be made to feel inferior to those who can?'"

"Why didn't you tell me?" she said.

He was quiet for a moment. "I didn't want to worry you," he said. "I didn't want you to know that things weren't working out here as I'd planned."

"I miss my family," she said. "I miss my home. If you hate

it here so much and I hate it, why can't we go back? Why can't we go home?"

He shook his head. "Go back to what? To sneaking around? To no job?"

"To my family—"

"Your family? I'd be arrested, Lucy. And anyway, do you think if they really cared about you, they wouldn't have found you by now?"

She swallowed. "How come you can call your mother and I can't call Iris or Charlotte?"

"We've had this conversation before. You know why. It's different."

"Maybe my family *is* looking for me."

"If they were, I'm sure they would have found us." He looked at her with great pity, and she felt a wash of horror. He was right. Charlotte and Iris didn't care. They really didn't. She had kept expecting them to show up. She had sent a post-card, and no one came for her. Charlotte was at Brandeis. Iris was traveling.

He took her hand in his free hand and held it for a moment. "Baby, I know you aren't happy, but things are going to be better. As soon as you're eighteen, we can go anywhere we want. We can stop hiding. We can get married. And in the meantime, you have all this time to write. Isn't that what you want?"

She didn't tell him that she hid her blue journal now and that her stories were all about a runaway girl who gets a job at a farm stand and doesn't tell her boyfriend and is rescued by the guy who runs the farm stand. She didn't tell William that he could go out anywhere he wanted, but she had to be hidden, like Rapunzel.

"I'm the only family you've got now," he told her.

Lucy waited until he was sleeping, then gently squirmed out

from under his embrace. She got up and went to the hall closet to count the money she had made. Eighty dollars. But how far would that get her?

She went into the bathroom, peed, and then stared at herself in the mirror, at the hollows in her cheeks. She took off the fake wedding ring he had bought for her and put it in the toilet and then flushed.

BY JULY, LUCY hadn't been back to the farm stand in almost a month. She was too ashamed, or maybe too afraid of what Patrick thought of her now. Instead she rode her bike up and down the roads until she was too tired to think about all the things she had done wrong.

One night, William brought home a small black-and-white TV and settled it on the end table. Lucy's mouth flew open. William hated television, but he was grinning, switching it on. A weather girl swam up into view, windmilling her long bare arms at a map, tapping a sun icon, her smile blooming, and Lucy felt the world ignite. "Thank you, thank you, thank you!" she cried. "Thank you for changing your mind."

"The school didn't need it anymore," William said. "It would have just been landfill if I left it, so I was really doing everyone a favor. And hey, I guess a little TV is fine. But why don't you do some writing now first?"

She looked at him, annoyed. "I will," she said, just to appease him. But why wasn't he doing any writing? The plan was always for William to finally have time to finish his novel. "When I get published, it'll be easier for us to get you published," he told her. When he talked about his plans, he got so excited his eyes lit up. But she had seen him writing only once, typing pages on his old turquoise Smith Corona manual, tearing them out, and throwing them into the trash. She fished the pages out the next day. One page was a grocery list: *tomatoes, spinach, bread*. But the other page was just a paragraph, about a fisherman who was after a marlin, and all she could think about was *The Old Man and the Sea*, and wasn't this too similar? He didn't really write like Hemingway, though. He used strings of adjectives, and she thought you weren't supposed to do that. *The wide, teeming, frothy sea. The biting, gentle cold.* How could the cold be gentle and biting at the same time? She pushed the paper back into the trash can. He threw these pages out, so he must have known they were bad. Besides, he complained how the school took all his energy, so that he couldn't write anything really meaningful. But sometimes he told her that even though it looked as if he wasn't writing, he was crafting his novel in his head. He pointed to his temple. "I'm mapping out the scenes, fleshing out the characters. There's still work going on," he had told her.

"Don't you want to show me?" she had asked.

"I will when it's ready," he had told her.

Now he flicked off the set. "Come on, let's work," he said.

She used to love his critiques of her work. She had felt that she couldn't do it on her own, that she wasn't smart enough. When he helped her, he noticed things for her that she'd never have thought about herself: A character who wasn't revealing himself by his actions. A line of dialogue that sounded tinny. Working with William had felt as if she had caught the tail end of a comet, all that brightness catapulting her forward. But now she just got annoyed when he read her stories. None of his comments made sense. He wanted her to make a story about a drowning funnier. "You need more moral complexity," he told her. "You're swimming in the shallows here." But he never really pointed out what he meant by that or how she could fix it.

She went to the desk drawer and brought out some loose leaf pages she didn't think would upset William and spread them on the table. William sat down, so close their shoulders were touching, making her want to move, but he was smiling at her. "This is what I always dreamed of," he told her. "The two of us, working side by side."

She showed him a story she was working on, about a young woman on a train with an older man, anxious that he like it. He read it silently, and then he looked at her, pained. "You're writing about a girl and a grown man?" he said. "Really?"

"Well, yeah."

"It's a little close to home, isn't it?"

"You told me to write about what I know."

He told her the story might work if she changed it, if she made them an older couple living in Alaska. Or Detroit—now, that would be even better. She listened, numb, as he picked apart her story, the wrong storyline, the bad dialogue, the lack of emotion. "I'll look at it after you rewrite," he said.

Later that night, when William was asleep, Lucy got up and went into the dining room and pulled out her blue journal, the one she now hid behind the bookshelf. She sat up all that night, writing. She wrote about a girl whose boyfriend took her way out into the country, and the girl fell out of love with him and deep in love with someone who ran a farm stand. Patrick. She used his real name, then crossed it out and wrote "Jason." She wrote about a young girl's wanting to break up with her older boyfriend, who controlled everything in her life. She embellished it so that the man wouldn't even let her eat, watching her every bite. "Look at that little belly," the boyfriend said. "Now we know what you'll look like when you're pregnant." It felt true to her. Real. The boyfriend had William's eyes. It was as if William had said those words to her. She felt her characters getting stronger, but what good was it if the only person who saw them was her? *This will all change.* She wrote it across one page, like a promise to herself. Here it was, the thing she was finally good at, but she had no idea where you sent out stories or how you did it, and if she asked William, would he actually help her? She needed a plan. More money. Maybe she could get another job, earn some money so she could get to California. Just enough so she wouldn't have to sleep on the streets. She wished she knew where William kept the cash he made from the school.

Meanwhile she was still only seventeen. She had seen how scared that made William. She could walk into any police station and tell them how she and William had run away, but then what would happen? She'd get to go home, but they'd put William in prison. And as much as she wanted to be away from him, did she really want that?

Maybe Patrick would even change his mind about her when he saw how famous she was going to be. Maybe she could get a huge book deal. She was lost in thinking about it, how she might end up in New York City walking into a big publishing house. How she might get to be on TV, talking about her influences. How there might be parties and she would be glittering as tinsel, moving through the crowd in a spangly party dress. And then the lights dimmed on her fantasy and she was back in the farmhouse again. It was just she and William.

She shut the journal and hid it. Then she went back to bed, trying to will sleep to come, though stories still flew around in her head.

THE NEXT EVENING, William came in with paint spattered all over his good shirt, frowning. "What happened?" she said.

"Art class didn't go as planned." He sighed. "It never goes as planned."

"What do you mean?"

"Nothing." He looked over at the TV and then at the burgers. "Buckwheat burgers again?"

She opened up the cupboards. "What else do you see for me to cook?"

"We have chickens, honey. We could have omelets. Or fondue."

"What's fondue?"

William got that look again, the one she hated, his mouth opening as though he were remembering something painful.

She didn't tell him that she hated to take the eggs from the hens, especially Dorothy, who always gave her a brooding sort of cluck. She let the hens sit on the eggs as long as they wanted, because what else did they have that was their own? But despite the hens' efforts, and hers, none of the eggs turned into chicks. Instead the eggs began to rot, and then pop, the smell forcing her out of the henhouse.

She got the spatula, the sounds of the TV a backdrop. A newscaster on the local news was talking about a man who had robbed a store with a gun, killing an eighteen-year-old kid who was working the register as his after-school job. "Local residents have been told not to open their doors and to be cautious. This man is thought to be armed and dangerous," the newscaster said.

Lucy stood still. Most of the Manson Family was locked up in California, which had made her feel at least a little safe, but they weren't sentenced yet, and what if they went free? She had seen a photo of Charlie Manson, his eyes wide and crazy, so much white showing above the pupils. She braced one hand on the wall. That book of William's, *You Are All Sanpaku*, had said if you had too much white below your pupils, like she did, you were in danger. But if you showed too much white above, you were the one causing the mayhem. She felt nauseated. Both of those things were true. She had seen that photo of the dead body at Kent State, the girl wailing over it. And this gunman was right here. William turned up the sound. The newscaster said they thought that the gunman was hiding in the woods, that he was emerging to steal eggs from the local farms, or carrots. One of the guys they interviewed, a man in a hunting cap, said he was sure this guy had taken one of his rabbits. Lucy turned off the burners and came into the other room.

"I think the news is scary and I don't want to be here anymore. I want to be in a city," Lucy blurted out. "With people. And police."

"This again?" William said. "My job is here. Our home. And anyway, what makes you think a city is any safer? The worst sorts of crazies live there." He shook his head. "Don't you think I can keep you safe?"

"Of course I do," Lucy said doubtfully. "But keeping me out of sight isn't being safe. What if he comes to the house and you aren't here? What do I do then? I'm scared, William. I'm really scared."

"We're not moving to a city," he said. "I'll figure something out." He turned off the set, the picture growing smaller and smaller until it blinked and went dark.

Two days later, William walked into the house looking like he had a secret he wanted her to know.

"Look, I know you don't like it out here. I know you're afraid, especially with that crazy person on the loose," William said. "But look." He reached into his pocket and pulled out something slim and shining, and it took her a moment to realize it was a gun.

She recoiled. "Oh my God, is that real?"

"Of course it's real," he said. He ran his thumb over the barrel. "It's sort of beautiful, isn't it?"

She put up her hands. "Are you crazy? A gun?"

"You said you were scared."

She had fallen in love with William because he was a pacifist. He had his conscientious objector status. He didn't believe in the death penalty, had never even been in a fight.

He carefully set the gun on the table, pointed toward the window. "Relax," he said. "I know how to use it. And I think if you know how to use it, too, you'll feel better about being out here alone so much of the time."

"Where did you get it?"

"I asked around and then bought it from a store." He admired the gun. "Thirty-eight Special. Smith and Wesson."

"How do you know how to use it?" Her mouth was dry.

"Some of the kids were talking about guns at the school, about what it would feel like to shoot, about responsibility. We all went to take lessons at a shooting range."

She drew back, astonished. "You taught those kids how to shoot a gun? I can't believe you'd do that."

"We don't censor curiosity," he said. "We looked up a gun range, they gave us a deal, and a bunch of us went on a field trip and learned how to shoot, including me. There were housewives there. All sorts of people. All perfectly safe and legal."

She stared. "This is crazy."

"I told you, the kids wanted to learn. How could we stifle that, especially if we had a safe environment to do it in? The principal himself was on board. And the parents don't dictate the kids' education. The kids do. That's the whole philosophy of the school. We took the kids there all week and they learned something, and so did I, and now we're doing organic farming."

"Well, I don't want it here."

"Come on," he said. "I'll teach you how to use it. Knowledge is power, right?"

"I don't want to," she said.

"What if that guy the news was talking about shows up here?" he said quietly. "You said you were worried. What would you do?"

"No one shows up here. Ever."

"But what would you do if he did and I wasn't here?"

"I'd run out the door. I'd run into the woods and hide. I'd kick him in the balls. I'd—"

He looked at her with great pity. "You think you're faster than a grown man? Stronger? You need to be able to protect yourself," he said. "I want you not to worry and I want to not worry about you."

He picked up the gun again in one hand and with great tenderness took her arm with the other. "Come on," he said.

THEY WENT TO the backyard, William carrying five empty cans. They walked past the chickens, who clucked in their path. William set up the cans, perching them on the edge of the fence. He showed her how to aim the gun, how it wasn't like the movies, where you just pointed and you hit the target all the time. It took practice and skill. "Always point it in a safe direction," he said. He handed her the gun, a weight in her hands, and then he lowered her hand so that the gun was pointing at the ground. "Keep your finger off the trigger and the guard until you make a conscious decision to shoot," he said.

She put one hand on the gun, and he brought up her other hand. "Two hands. It'll give you more leverage and help with recoil," he said.

He stood behind her. "Think of the gun as part of you. Like an extension of your whole body."

Lucy thought of how she and Charlotte used to play Wild West when they were little, using their water pistols, soaking each other until they were drenched. Lucy had loved those games, had loved being the sole playmate of her sister.

He helped her place her hands around the gun, with her thumb pointing forward where the slide met the frame. Her hands fit together like puzzle pieces. William touched her hips. "Bend those knees. Stand with your legs apart and stretch those arms out. Now aim."

"I don't want to do this."

"Aim."

Lucy squinted at the cans, shutting her left eye, trying to focus. How on earth would she ever hit anything? She was nearsighted and the cans blurred in front of her. And if she didn't hit the cans, where would the bullet go? If she shot a bird or an animal, she would never forgive herself. Her hand shook. "Now, you don't want to pull the trigger. You're going to squeeze it gently. Otherwise you'll fuck up your sight," William said.

She squinted harder.

"Open your eyes," William told her. "Don't squinch them shut like that. You have to see what you're doing. And be careful. It's got a bit of a hair trigger, so you don't need much pressure at all."

She took a breath, like a sharp little pant, and pulled the trigger. The gun roared. There were fireworks in her ears, a vibration that shoved her back like a fist. The shell of the bullet flew out, burning her wrist, so she yelped, dropping the gun into the grass. The air smelled like iron. She could hear the chickens clamoring. She had black ash on her hands, and her whole body was trembling. William was saying something to her, but she couldn't hear him over the ringing in her ears. His voice was muffled as if he were underwater. "My ears!" she said, alarmed. She clapped her ears. He said something to her and she still couldn't hear him, which made her panic even more.

"I can't hear!" she cried. "I can't hear!"

He nodded at her and took her back inside. She thought he'd get her a doctor, but instead he got a warm washcloth and gently cupped it around her ears. The water dripped into her collar and down the front of her shirt. He wrote down on a piece of paper: *It will come back. I promise. I should have had you wear ear protection.*

All that evening he wrote her notes. *Is it better?* She always shook her head. She tried to read, but she kept worrying. What if her hearing didn't come back? How would she live? "Maybe I should go to a doctor," she said, and he wrote down: *We will go tomorrow if it isn't better, but I know it will be.*

That evening, he poured out two glasses of wine for her. "It'll help you sleep," he said, and she read his lips. She tilted her head back and drank the wine.

In the morning the chickens woke her, the clucks like the tap of typewriter keys. She sprang out of bed, kicking back the covers, going to find William, who was in the kitchen. She could hear him before she even saw him, his low humming along with the music from the radio. He had been right, and now every sound was amplified: the creaking of the wood floors as she strode across them, the sound the refrigerator door made. She was so happy she could hear she wanted to cry, but when she went into the kitchen and saw William, her joy soured. *He* did this to her.

"Your ears back?" he said, and she nodded and sat at the table.

"Didn't I tell you?" He beamed at her. He was cooking, something he almost never did. He flipped a pancake in the pan.

"I'm never doing that again," she said.

"You're being silly. It's like writing. You have to practice if you want to get good."

"I don't want to get good at shooting a gun. And having it in the house scares me more than not having it. Can't we sell it? We could use the money."

"I worry about you, I want you to be protected." He bent toward her, murmuring in her ear. "The gun is in the drawer by my side of the bed, a box of bullets right next to it."

La-la-la, she wanted to say. I'm not listening. I can't hear you.

"I don't want to live here anymore," she said, and he straightened, and for the first time she couldn't read what was in his eyes. He put both hands on her shoulders and said quietly, "You listen to me now. Because this is what is going to happen. You are going to stay with me and we are going to live here. Do you understand? This is how it's going to be. And I don't want to have this discussion again."

He lifted his hands and smiled at her. "Now let's eat," he said.

She picked at the pancakes, her appetite gone.

Chapter 16

When Brandeis had shut down for the student strike in May, Charlotte hadn't known what to do. Suddenly there were kids thronging the campus with black armbands, handing out leaflets and working the phones at the national strike center, organizing teach-ins, and recruiting volunteers. The Black Panthers were supposedly on campus now, and, it was rumored, the FBI, and the whole campus felt tense.

Though Charlotte hated the war as much as anyone, she was also terrified about her finals. When would they happen? Were they canceled, too? No one seemed to know, though everyone had theories. Some kids, the ones who weren't political at all, had simply gone home. Others were paying to stay in the dorms. Of course she wanted to help with the strike, but she had to keep up her grades or she'd lose her scholarship. Plus, she hadn't counted on school shutting down early. The woman she had sublet her summer apartment from said it was fine for Charlotte to move in in May. Charlotte had saved enough from her job at the information desk for three month's rent, which meant she'd need money for August. She'd have to find something fast.

There were all sorts of rumors. Kids could either take the grade they had when the strike began, or they could wait until fall and take the final exam then. It was case by case, someone told Charlotte, and it was completely up to the professors, some of whom were already working at the strike center themselves.

Charlotte went to talk to all her professors. A few lifted up their hands and told her they didn't know and not to worry about it. "You won't get kicked out of school," her math professor told her. But her professor in Zoology, the one course she was most worried about, was different.

"I've been studying so hard . . ." Her voice faltered.

He leaned back in his seat. "Well, do you want to take your exam now?"

"Could I take it in the fall? I can study more—" Charlotte said, and then she felt him looking at her.

"I know that you've worked hard this semester," he said. "I've been watching you. You come in early to class. You're always taking notes when everyone else is staring into space." He shuffled some papers. "I wasn't going to get to this until later, but now's as good a time as any. Do you have plans for the summer? Are you working for the strike center?"

She didn't know what to say, what he might think was the right answer.

"I've got an internship, if you want it," he said. "It's perfect for you because it's with Fur Friends, the veterinary office off Moody Street."

She stared at him. An internship like that would be amazing. It would look great on her application to vet school and, of course, give her real experience. She had to have a paying job. She didn't want to put off her professor, but there was no way she could do this. "I—I have to work . . ." she said.

"This one pays," he said. "Pretty decently, too. I pulled some strings to get them to offer this. And if you do a great job, I'll count it toward your final."

"It's paid?"

"That's right." He smiled at her. "Pretty cool, right? Not often something like this comes along."

"Why are you doing this for me?" she asked.

He glanced out his office window, at the students milling around. "Because sometimes, in crazy times, it helps to do something nice for someone," he told her.

TWO DAYS LATER, Charlotte moved into her sublet on Moody Street. It was furnished, so she didn't have to buy anything, and if the couch was a little ratty, the table unbalanced, it didn't matter because she'd spend most of her time working.

In June she started her job. The doctor running the place was named Martin Bronstein. He was tall, thin, and bald, with blue wire-rimmed glasses, and he didn't smile very much, not until he said, "We'll work you hard here," and Charlotte said, "Well, I hope so. That's what I want." He was about forty, and he wore a wedding band, and when she went into his office, it was filled with photographs of animals, each one signed as if the pet could write. *Thank you for saving my leg! Love, Muffin. I hated the dog cone collar, but I loved the liver treats you gave me! Love, Annabel.* What a softie, she thought. It made her like him.

First he gave her the tour: the waiting room for the patients and their pets, the two examining rooms, the surgical area, and the recovery area in the back, where another woman in a white coat was busy feeding a tortoise lettuce. She looked up at Charlotte. "He won't eat unless I wiggle it and make it seem like live food," she said. Then she stuck out her hand to shake Charlotte's. "Priscilla," she said. "The tortoise's name. I'm Jo."

Dr. Bronstein took Charlotte to the closet and handed her a white lab coat. "We'll get you a name tag later," he said. As soon as she put it on, she felt special. Important. She put her hands deep in her pockets and beamed. "Let's get started," he said, handing her a list of everything he wanted her to do: greet the patients, call in the animals and calm them, help him with some simple procedures, and make sure everyone— including the staff—was fed and watered. Charlotte laughed at that. "And always call people in by their pet's name," he said. "Give the animals that dignity."

She didn't mind that he was crabby, that when he wanted her in an examining room, he wouldn't come out to look for her but would simply shout, "Charlotte!" so loudly that everyone in the waiting room could hear. He was a stickler for doing things right, but that was fine because she was just learning. By the end of the first week, she could give a dog a shot and administer its medication, and she could pull thorns out of a cat's paw. Dr. Bronstein never praised her, but he gave her more and more challenges, and Charlotte met every one.

Most of the time that first month, she worked through lunch, but sometimes she had a sandwich at a local deli with Annie, the receptionist, who gossiped about Dr. Bronstein. "His wife is a knockout," Annie said, "And they have about six dogs at home." Sometimes, too, Charlotte put up flyers about Lucy, right next to the ones at the Brandeis strike center about a teach-in to stop the war.

When the day was over, Charlotte, exhausted, would go home to her sublet. Sometimes she tried to study. Sometimes she read or called Iris. She always told Iris that everything was under control, that she was working hard, that her grades were going to be stellar, that she was getting closer to finding Lucy. "I'm sure all my posters will get someone's attention," she said. Charlotte knew she was lying. She heard the ticking clock of Iris's health, and it propelled her. She had to find her sister before Iris died or was too sick to know. But she had a feeling Iris was lying to her, too, assuring Charlotte that she felt great even when she was coughing into the phone, fibbing about her blood pressure numbers, when all Charlotte had to do was call Iris's doctor to get the real results.

But most nights she was too tired to do anything other than shrug off her lab coat and eat a quick dinner. Then she would stretch out on her bed and fall into a deep sleep.

Chapter 17

The gun seemed to be giving off vibrations from the drawer, actual heat Lucy felt when she walked by. She kept checking on it from time to time, hoping the gun might be gone, but it was always in the same place, the box of shells beside it.

She began biking the roads again. Sometimes she walked. She couldn't bear to be inside the house all day, especially with the gun there. She could no longer go to Patrick's, though she had conversations with him in her head. She was always apologizing, but he told her that it didn't matter, that people sometimes did things you couldn't understand, but that it didn't mean you didn't still love them. She wrote in her blue journal, a fantasy about running into him one day, and he would see her and there would be that fierce connection between them and he'd realize his mistake. He'd know that she was his next great love.

The roads seemed even quieter than usual today. She could hear every footstep she took. Maybe she'd go to the supermarket, she thought, just to be among people.

She had been walking for a little while when a car slowed and pulled up beside her. A woman with a riot of gray ringlets peered out at her. "Are you lost or hurt?" she called, and Lucy shook her head. "Then what are you doing on the road by yourself?"

"Just walking," Lucy said, and the woman frowned.

"I'm going into Scranton. Can I drive you there?"

Scranton. Lucy had heard William talk about it. It was a real town, a pretty big one. He had promised they would drive there some night, go out to dinner, walk around, maybe even see a movie, but of course they never had. "I'm happy to take you," the woman said. "I have a daughter myself."

Lucy looked inside the car. Every door had a handle. The backseat was clean and empty, the front seat, too. Scranton, she thought, and she got inside.

The woman kept up a patter the whole ride, and Lucy soon realized she was fishing for information. How old was Lucy? Because she looked fifteen, if you wanted to know the truth. Where were her parents? Because if her daughter were out there, she would want to know how to help her. "This is for me, not you," the woman said, and so, because Lucy sort of liked her, she told her what she wanted to hear. "My parents are cool," Lucy said. "I'm not in any trouble."

The trees began to give way to buildings. The deserted roads suddenly had shops and people, and everyone seemed to be moving in fast-forward. Brightening, she sat up straighter, craning her neck, wanting to see everything. The world was like a cold glass of water when you were thirsty. "It's so lively," she said, and the woman looked at her and pulled over.

She dug in her purse and handed Lucy a card: NELL WILSON, REAL ESTATE. "You can always call if you need help," she said. "What can I say? I'm a mother." She peered at Lucy. "You promise, you'll call if you need to?"

"Yes," Lucy said, taking the card. She stepped out onto the city street. She waited for the woman to keep driving, rolling the card over in her fingers. She started to put it in her pocket and then she took the card to the nearest trash can and popped it in. She didn't want to risk having William find it.

Everything around her seemed to be jittering with color and noise and scents. Restaurants she passed smelled amazing, like garlic and curry, and once she caught a whiff of melted chocolate and her mouth filled with saliva. Oh, how she had missed all this! The last time she had had chocolate was in school, when she used to buy three Snickers bars from the vending machine and pull off bits while she was in class. She had forgotten how wonderful real life was. A big kiosk fluttered with bills and posters, and she studied it. People were looking for roommates. Bright, sunny room. Shared kitchen. Wouldn't that be something, to be able to live with other people and come and go as you pleased and not have to answer to anyone? There was an advertisement for a show, with two bands, Washing Machine and Dead to You. She used to go to shows at the Boston Tea Party, getting in with a fake ID. She had seen Nazz there, and the Velvet Underground, stepping on the lit floor, dancing by herself, lost in the music.

For the first half hour, all she did was wander in and out of stores. She stopped in front of a Realtor's window. She could imagine herself in that little studio with the natural light. Or what about that one-bedroom with the wood floors? But even the tiniest apartments were way too expensive, plus they wanted the first and last months' rent and a safety deposit. She didn't even have a job.

She kept walking and spied a local high school. Maybe she could get her GED there, and with that she might get a real job, and with that she could get a place to live. Imagine being able to come here every week to study, get to know the local cafés, and maybe even make some friends.

Maybe the school had summer classes and was still open. She strode to the door, grinning when it opened, and as soon as she got inside, she laughed, because it had that school smell: old bologna sandwiches and sour milk.

Everyone was in classes, but she could see inside the rooms, through the windows in the doors. Kids were sprawled at their desks, taking notes, whispering to one another, and all Lucy wanted to do was slide into one of the desks beside someone. She remembered the fun parts of school. The kids. The parties. Imagine sitting in a classroom and doing experiments. Imagine getting to hang out with kids her own age again. All the things she had hated about school—writing reports, taking tests, even going to summer school—she now felt hungry for. If she could just have this chance, she'd do everything right this time.

The bell rang and the doors flew open and kids sprang like colts into the corridor. Lucy walked among them. Kids lined the walls. She saw two girls laughing. A boy passed a note to a girl. A girl opened her locker, and plastered on the door was a photo of James Taylor. Everything Lucy had thought was childish and stupid before now seemed like nirvana. She ran her hand along the wall.

She rounded a corner and found the office. "Do you have GED classes?" she asked, and the woman handed her a pamphlet without even looking at her.

When Lucy went outside, the sky was already dusky, and yellow buses lined one side of the school. Kids began spilling out of the front door, couples holding hands, a boy taking out a cigarette, girls with their arms linked, carelessly laughing. Any of those girls could be her friend, someone to go to the movies with, to shop, to make plans that didn't include making dinner and keeping house and trying to look and be older. She couldn't stop watching them, the girls. She looked at the way they were dressed, in flowing paisley pants and tops with little embroidered mirrors in them and skirts so short the girls were constantly reaching down and tugging at the hems. She yearned for their white fishnet stockings, or the windowpanes one girl was wearing. Two girls walked past, and they looked alike, and Lucy thought maybe they were sisters, and for a moment she missed Charlotte so much she had to lean against the wall. Take me with you, she thought.

She walked back toward the stores, where the cars might be more plentiful, hoping to catch a ride. She wished she had kept that real estate agent's card, because she could have called her if she was desperate. She glanced at her watch. Four. She still had time to get home before William, but she'd have to hustle. She stood at the corner, jabbing out her thumb. There was traffic. Surely someone would stop. But cars drove right past by her. No one was stopping.

By five thirty, Lucy began to panic. What if she couldn't get a ride? She could never walk this far. What if William got home before she did? He'd go look for her in the woods, and he'd be furious that she hadn't stayed closed to home. He might find her bike, and that would make him angry, too.

Tears stung behind her lids, and then finally a car slowed. A guy wearing a suit and tie. His hair was clean and there was no trash piled in his backseat. All the doors had handles. It was against her rules to get into a car driven by a man, but it was also now five thirty, and she didn't know what else to do. "Where you headed?" the man said. She saw a flash of gold on his finger. He was married. There was a photo of a little girl attached to his visor. His daughter, maybe. She got in.

He drove without speaking, without glancing at her, which unnerved her a little, but he took her all the way to the lip of her road. And then she jumped out, thanking him, and he was gone, and she turned around and there was William, planted in front of her, his face unreadable. "William," she said, and he took two steps toward her and then he hit her in the face.

Her hands flew to the hard flash of pain. She stumbled, falling into the dirt, skittering back from him, like a crab. "Who was that man?" he shouted. "Are you seeing that man? Do you know how worried I was when you weren't home? And then you show up with some guy? What are you doing, Lucy?"

She scrambled away from him, drawing her legs up against her chest. Something was trickling down her face, and she touched it and drew her fingers away and saw that it was blood. "I hitched into town!" she cried. "I hitched back! He was my ride and that's all!"

"How do I know that's the truth? Is he calling the cops now? Is that what's happening?"

She pulled out the GED paperwork and thrust it at him. The paper shook in the air, and he grabbed it, staring at it and then at her as if he didn't know her.

"You went to the high school?" His breathing slowed. "This is all to get your GED?"

She nodded. He folded the paper and put it in his pocket, and then he crouched toward her. As soon as he touched her, she winced and drew back. He grabbed for her hand and pulled her up. "Why didn't you tell me? I would have taken you," he said.

"You hit me," she said, stumbling farther away from him. "You hit me."

He reached to touch her face and then drew his hands back. He started to tremble. "I didn't mean to." He swiped at his eyes. "I swear, when I saw that guy, I went crazy. I thought I'd lost you. I thought he was the authorities. Forgive me. You have to forgive me."

She kept silent. The pain rolled over her and she couldn't meet his eyes.

"I didn't know what I was doing, but it will never, ever happen again. Let's go inside the house," he said. "We'll put some ice on that eye. We'll talk about your GED. I promise things will get better. I'm just under so much pressure. We're just both on edge." He began to guide her back toward the house, his arm around her, a weight. "Soon we can be out in the world together," he said. "Together forever." He tightened his grip and walked her inside.

HE SAT WITH her in the kitchen, watching her put the ice to her eye. He put on music, the Doors album she liked, and for the first time since Waltham, he cooked her dinner, her favorite, spaghetti with sauce he made himself, mashing up tomatoes in a pan with fresh garlic and basil. Her appetite was gone, but she moved the food around to make it look as if she had at least nibbled. "I'll do the dishes," he said. "I'll clean up. You just relax."

He washed the dishes and put things away while she sat at the table. When they went to bed, he held her, spooning against her, a vise. When he lifted his hand, she tensed. "Want to know how I know we're perfect together?" he said. He moved closer to her. "Because we fit together. Just like this."

Like silverware, she thought. Like inanimate objects made of metal. She stayed still, waiting for him to go to sleep, hoping he wouldn't want to have sex. Her eye throbbed, but she couldn't risk waking him to go get ice.

She knew it now. Falling in love with William had been a terrible mistake. She had felt so grown up when it had all happened, and now she felt clueless as a child. And worse, trapped. What had she been thinking? *We did what he said. He was Jesus.* Wasn't that was what the Manson girls had said? And look what happened to them.

AFTER THAT, LUCY could tell that William no longer trusted her. Every day he came home and he sniffed around the house as if he were checking whether anything was amiss. Once again, when he was working and she was alone, she heard footsteps outside. "William?" she called. There was no answer, but in the backyard, where they didn't mow, some of the grass was newly mashed down, as if someone had stepped on it. Another afternoon, William came home unexpectedly, and she saw the relief washing over him when he saw she was there. "I forgot something," he said, but she knew it was a lie, because he turned around and got in the car and went back to the school. That night, while he was sleeping, she got up and wrote a story about a girl who leaves her boyfriend after he hits her, and then her life opens like a blossom. She bore down on the pen so hard it tore the page.

She shut the journal, her heart jackrabbiting in her chest. The only difference between her and the girl in her story was that the story girl had money, a cache from being a waitress. The money Lucy had from working at Patrick's was nothing. She thought about calling the police, but could she trust the cops? Everyone called them pigs. What if they didn't believe her? Could she be sent to prison for running away? And wasn't she culpable, too? She hadn't been kidnapped or coerced by anything but love. And that love was gone.

She hid the journal again, pacing as quietly as she could so William wouldn't wake and want to know what she was up to. She thought of the Realtor woman again, Nell Wilson, how motherly she was. And then she thought of Iris. Maybe she could call her. Iris might scold and maybe even yell, but that would be so much easier than dealing with William. She could go back to school and have friends. She could see Charlotte. If Iris questioned her black eye, she'd tell Iris someone had attacked her while she was hitching. Feeling better, as if she had a plan, she went back to sleep.

The next morning, she was silent at breakfast. "I ate already," she told him. She felt his breath on her neck when he leaned down to kiss her, and she made herself into stone,

thinking, Go. Please go. As soon as she heard the engine sput-
tering, she went into the bathroom and saw her face, black
and blue and yellow around her eye, the tissues so swollen that
when she touched her skin she winced. She had a little bit of
makeup left and she daubed it on, but it made things worse. She
went to get sunglasses so she wouldn't have to look at herself.

She dialed, her hands shaking. It was seven in the morning,
and Iris would probably be in the kitchen now, making breakfast. Lucy pressed the receiver to her ear, and then there was a
strange click. "The number you dialed is no longer in service,"
a voice said.

Lucy stared at the phone. She must have dialed wrong. She
tried again, and this time when the same recording came on,
she called information, but the operator told her the number
was no longer valid and there was no forwarding number.
"There has to be!" she cried, and the operator hung up, and
Lucy dropped the receiver, so that it clattered against the counter. There had to be an explanation for this. Something simple.
Nothing could have happened to Iris. She just knew it. She
called the operator again, this time asking for the number of
Brandeis University. At least she could find Charlotte.

After she got the general number, she dialed and was then
connected to Charlotte's dorm. The phone rang two times and
then three, and then she was sobbing so hard she wasn't sure
she would be able to speak. A young-sounding girl answered.
"Oh, yeah, I know Char," she said, and she gave Lucy a number. But when she called it, no one answered, so she called
Brandeis back again, panicked. The same girl answered. "Let
me think," she said. "Wait. I know. She's working someplace—
I can get you the name—"

"No, no!" Lucy cried. "Can you get me the number, too?"

There was a beat of silence. "Sure, why not," the girl said.

As soon as Lucy had the number, she dialed. She pinched her thigh, the way Charlotte had taught her to do, to distract herself. A bored female voice got on the line. "Fur Friends," she said, and Lucy sobbed Charlotte's name. "Hang on," the voice said. Lucy twisted the cord around her wrist, and then she heard Charlotte's voice.

"Charlotte! It's me! It's Lucy!"

At first there was no sound at all, and Lucy was terrified that Charlotte had hung up on her. "Charlotte!" she said again.

"Lucy?" Charlotte's voice was a train speeding. "Oh my God, Lucy." Lucy could hear Charlotte crying, which made her cry, too. "Are you okay? Are you hurt? Where are you?" Charlotte asked.

"I called the house and no one was there! There was no forwarding number—"

"Wait—you called the house? They didn't give you a for-warding number? Where are you?"

Lucy wrapped the phone cord around her wrist. What was the point of lying anymore? "I'm in Pennsylvania with William."

"William? William who? Lucy, I don't understand."

"The teacher. William the teacher. From the high school. I'm leaving him—"

There was a moment of silence. "What? Lucy, no—tell me this isn't true. It has to be a joke. You're with William?"

"Can you come get me? Right away?"

"Lucy, I—"

"Please, you have to! Right away!" She recited her address. Maybe Charlotte could even get there before William came home. He couldn't stop her from leaving. He knew what he had done, and he wouldn't want to be arrested.

"Do you realize how terrified we were? How worried?" Charlotte said. Her voice was rising now, changing, and Lucy pulled the phone away from her ear. "How could you do such a thing?"

"You're angry with me. You have a right to be—I know it—"

"We were so scared. Why didn't you call? Why didn't you let us know where you were? Do you know what's been going on here? What happened to Iris? Do you even care?"

"I did let you know! I sent a postcard. Charlotte, please come now. Please—I need you—"

"A postcard!" Charlotte said. "We didn't get it until April!"

"What? How can that be?" Lucy remembered setting it on the counter the day of her birthday. Maybe it had gotten lost or hidden. Maybe someone had taken a while to mail it, but at least it had gotten there.

"You think a postcard is enough? What about a phone call?" And then the line went dead, and Lucy stared at the phone. She called Charlotte again, but the line was busy. Maybe Charlotte was calling to rent a car, or to borrow Iris's. Charlotte couldn't get Lucy's number because it was unlisted, but she had the address. Lucy knew her; Charlotte would have written it down. And what had happened to Iris? Lucy couldn't bear the thought that something was wrong. She tried to call the two numbers she'd been given, but no one answered. She had to rush to get things ready. She'd find out everything soon enough. Her sister would come for her.

Lucy figured Charlotte would be there in five hours, at the latest, and that would still be a few hours before William got home. Lucy felt a flush of emotion. She couldn't wait to see her sister—and Iris. She wanted Iris to hold her, to stroke her hair, to breathe against her, to find the words to forgive her for all she had done.

She dug out her old knapsack, the same one she had taken

to run away with William, and stuffed it with a few things, her mind rolling. A pair of jeans. A sweater. Underwear. Socks.

By twelve, Charlotte still wasn't there, and when Lucy called her, there was no answer. By two, Lucy began to think that she wasn't coming. That this silence was a message, crashing against her. Charlotte didn't believe Lucy, or maybe she was just fed up.

Lucy walked through the house, her arms wrapped around her chest. What would she do now? How could she manage? Had Charlotte called the police? Were they on their way here? She went and found all the money she had saved from working. Surely eighty dollars was enough for a bus ticket home. But what if it wasn't? Then what would she do?

There was only one other person who might help her. She grabbed her pack and got her bike from the woods and started to pedal.

PATRICK WAS AT the register, counting change, talking to a customer, a middle-aged woman with her hair in a wide headband. Lucy bided her time, waiting for him to see her, walking her bike toward him. When he finally looked up, his face was unreadable. She took her sunglasses off, and he flinched. She knew what she looked like, the bruising still splashed across her face, as if someone had thrown a pot of paints at her. He called someone else in to work the register and then came over to her. "Park your bike and come with me," he said, nodding to the side of the house, and then he led her into his kitchen and sat her down.

"You might want to tell me the truth," he said. "About your eye. About everything."

"I'm seventeen," she said, but he didn't react.

"Go on," he said.

She told him that she wasn't married, that she had run away

from home with William, who was her high school teacher, and everything had turned out wrong.

"Did William do that?" he said, and she nodded. Then she told him everything—about Charlotte and Iris, her loneliness, the chickens—and when she got to the part about the gun, Patrick frowned. "Lucy—"

"I know I lied to you. But I'm not lying now." She grabbed for his arm again. "You have to help me, Patrick. Please. I want to take a bus home. I have some money but I don't know if it's enough. If you can loan me money, I can get a bus ticket to somewhere. I can get a job and I'll pay you back. I promise."

"Listen to me. This is serious stuff. I think we need to go to the cops."

Her panic was wild, beating against her like wings. The police. She could just imagine it, coming into the station with her black eye, trying to tell them about William. What if they didn't believe her? "Please. You have to help me get home."

"Lucy, you're a minor. I think you really want the authorities to handle this," he said.

"I have to go to the bathroom," she said, and she flew into the other room.

She knew Patrick kept a strongbox with extra money in the kitchen. She could just borrow something. She could pay him back with interest. She found the box, and to her surprise, it was unlocked. She opened it and began stuffing money into her jeans.

"Hey!"

She turned and Patrick was standing there. "What are you doing?" he said. "You don't have to steal from me!"

She clenched the money in her hand. She heard herself panting.

He moved toward her, and she didn't know what else to do, so she grabbed the rest of the money, jamming it into her pockets. "You won't help me!" she cried. Then she ran out to her bike and started pedaling furiously.

She couldn't tell whether he was following her, so she pumped the pedals faster, skimming the road, not stopping until she hit a patch with no cars. Then she pulled over, dug the money out, and counted it. Ninety bucks. Definitely enough to get home now. Then she noticed her blue journal was missing. It had her best stories in it, plus the start of her novel. She glanced at her watch. She still had time before William came back. She could run home, grab it, and go.

BACK AT THE HOUSE, she grabbed her journal and was stuffing it into her pack when she heard the door open. She froze. It was too early for William. She had timed everything perfectly. But then she heard a stamping of feet and William's whistling, and she was about to fly out the back when William came around the corner and spotted her. For a moment they just looked at each other. "I know I'm home early." He had wildflowers in his hand. His eyes slid over her knapsack. "Where are you going?" he said quietly, and she swallowed.

"Luce?" he said. He took a step closer to her and she stepped back. She couldn't outrun him, and he could chase her in the car.

"I'm leaving you," she said. Her voice hung in the air.

He put the flowers down. "No," he said. "No, you're not. That will never happen." He stood there, between her and the front door.

"Are you listening to me?" Lucy cried. "I'm leaving. You can't stop me."

He was faster than she was and stronger. If she turned and ran to the back door, he'd still be able to grab her. And then what would she do? There was no air left in her lungs, but she took a step forward. He grabbed her by the wrist and she scratched him, drawing blood.

"I'll put the bag away," she said, as if she were staying. She went into the bedroom, deliberately slowing her movements, as if she were defeated, and dropped the pack on the ground with a thud loud enough for him to hear. Her hands were shaking and she had trouble opening the drawer. There was the gun. It was never loaded. She had made William promise her that it never would be, but he didn't have to know that she hadn't slid bullets in.

She plucked up her pack and then strode out, holding the gun the way he had taught her, forming her stance, staring down the sight, remembering every detail. She motioned with the gun. "Get away from the door," she said. "It's loaded." He wouldn't risk not believing her. She'd brandish the gun and he'd get out of the way, and when she got to the bus station she'd toss it into a trash can and never think of it or him again. He'd know what she was capable of. He'd never come after her after this.

He didn't move. "Lucy," he said. His voice sounded funny, as if it were burbling underwater. "I love you. You know that. I love you. I love you so fucking much. I don't know how to be in the world without you."

And then he took a step toward her and she lifted the gun.

Chapter 18

As soon as Charlotte hung up on Lucy, her whole body began shaking. Lucy had called her. Lucy was coming home. Charlotte wiped her eyes, torn with grief, gratitude, and anger, too. Lucy had demanded that Charlotte pick her up, as if it were a done deal, as if Charlotte would just drop everything to come and get her, make things right the way she always had. Lucy hadn't asked about Iris, and Charlotte had gotten so agitated she had slammed down the phone, and as soon as she did, she was horrified.

Of course she tried to call back, but she didn't have the number. She called the operator, who told her there was no listing for Lucy or for William. "Charlotte, please don't use the office phone for personal calls," Dr. Bronstein said as he whisked past her, carrying an iguana in both hands. Charlotte hung up the phone. Lucy would call back. And in any case, Charlotte had scribbled down the address. She would go as soon as she could.

She glanced at her watch. She thought about calling Iris and telling her but then decided against it. Better to just bring Lucy home, the prodigal daughter, the happy surprise.

She couldn't leave early—they were short staffed that day. She had already seen Dr. Bronstein fire someone because he came in half an hour late. He was not a man who tolerated excuses. She couldn't risk losing her internship, not after her professor had pulled strings for her, not when her grade depended on her doing a good job, not when it was her income. She told herself that it was only a matter of a few hours before she could drive to get Lucy. Lucy could wait just a few more hours.

WHEN THE DAY was over, after watching an operation on a dog who had swallowed six pairs of socks and a whistle, she rushed out and got into the car, glancing at herself if the rearview mirror. Her eyes were red rimmed, her clothes rumpled, and her bangs had grown out now, so that she had to tuck them behind her ears to keep them out of her eyes. She knew she'd be driving all night, but at least it was Friday and she didn't work weekends, so she'd have time to recuperate. Pennsylvania was the last place she'd ever expected to find her sister. Who would want to live there? She had figured Lucy had run off to San Francisco, seduced by all that Summer of Love stuff. Instead, Lucy was with William. A teacher. What was she thinking? And what was he?

Oh, she remembered him. Everyone at Waltham High used to talk about William. How he was the coolest teacher on the planet. You could learn things that were really important from him, things other teachers wouldn't tell you. How to make yourself grilled cheese by wrapping the sandwich in aluminum foil and ironing it. How the boys could resist the draft by burning their draft cards. Plus, even though he was old, there was still something sexy about him. The way he strode the corridors, his sleeves pushed up, his hair falling nearly to his collar. The way he looked at you when you asked him a question, moving closer to you, making you feel that there was no one else in the world at that moment but you.

Charlotte had been so thrilled when she had gotten into his advanced class. She sat in the front, like all the other swoony girls. Every day, he wore a tie that was like a painting, a shirt that was drenched in color. Sometimes he wore a purple T-shirt that poked out under his collar. "I'm here to challenge you," he said, and her heart did a shimmy. One day, when the principal came in to tell William he couldn't show a film on the war, Charlotte had blurted out, "Why not? Isn't there such a thing as free speech?" The principal had stopped talking and turned to her. "Your name is?" he said.

"Charlotte Gold."

"I see," he said. He walked out without answering her, but Charlotte had felt William looking at her, and when she looked up, he was smiling at her. "Ladies and gentlemen," he said to the class, "a shining example from Miss Charlotte Gold of civil disobedience and free speech." Charlotte's cheeks flushed. She was so happy she couldn't even concentrate on the movie he showed.

After that, William made a point to talk to her either before or after class. She liked that, at first. He wanted to know what she was reading, what movies she liked. He agreed with her that Truffaut was a master of French New Wave cinema, that Simon and Garfunkel were poets as well as songwriters. He gave her a list of other films she should see, Godard and Bresson, and music she should listen to, especially jazz.

She definitely had a crush on him. She saw him at the supermarket buying ice cream and she was too nervous to go talk to him. She spotted him coming out of the movies, but she was rooted in place. Whenever he appeared, she weakened with desire. She told no one how she felt, but in class she'd daydream about how it would feel to walk up to him and kiss him. How his hand might feel on her waist, her breast.

She was a junior then and terrified about the SATs. She had to do well in order to get into college, to get a scholarship. She was sure William would help her; maybe he'd sit with her after class and go over those tricky analogies. She imagined the two of them, their heads tipped together. She could bring in a thermos of cocoa. Or coffee—that would be more adult.

But when she went to ask him, he just gave her a mild smile. "Why do you want help with analogies?"

"Well, not just analogies. I want to learn more vocabulary, too. And I think my writing could use some work."

"You get your vocabulary from reading. Just read more. You want to learn to write great essays? Read them."

"But I could use some help. Analogies are hard."

"That's the trouble with our educational system. When are you ever going to need to know how to do an analogy in life? Do you think anyone is ever going to come up to you and say, *Book* is to *school* as *needle* is to what?"

"The SAT will," she said, and he scoffed. "So that's it," he said. "The SAT. I don't believe in the SAT, Charlotte. How does that tell how smart a student is? How well he or she will do in the world? I'm surprised at you."

Because it does matter, she thought, because how can I make it in the world if I can't get into college? But he was fired up now, waving his hands as he talked, and while she used to love that, now it made her feel as if she were standing on the edge of the building, two stories up, with no railing, and he was about to give her a push. She said nothing, but she was angry and more than a little disappointed. He didn't seem so cute to her anymore, and her desire began to fade.

She ended up buying a vocabulary book, *What You Need to Know for the SATs*, and began studying nights on her own. When she realized how much of it he wasn't teaching, she studied harder, assigning herself five pages a night, and then six, staying up until she was bleary-eyed.

She still sat in the front row of William's class, but he didn't look at her anymore. One day, when they were talking about the changes that went on when books became films, Charlotte raised her hand because she wanted to talk about how disappointed she had been in the film of *Jane Eyre*. He looked past her. She turned around to see what he was looking at, who he would call on ahead of her. No one else had their hand up except for her, and he was ignoring her. She stretched her hand up higher. The other kids in the class stared at her.

She left his class unsettled, but when it happened the next day, she went to the office and requested a transfer into the other accelerated English class, because this one wasn't rigorous enough for her. Because she was an honors student, they made the change. The first day she was in her new class, when they had to pull out their vocabulary books, she was the only one who didn't groan. She looked at the list of all those words in her Manter Hall book as if she were a starving person reading an all-you-can-eat menu.

A week after she left the class, she saw William standing in the hallway. She had never told him she was leaving, she had just vanished one day, and she figured he would get the paperwork. He barely looked at her. She walked right past him without saying a word.

A year later, Lucy was in one of his classes, but Lucy never talked about him. But then, she never talked about anything to Charlotte anymore. Still, how was it possible Charlotte didn't know that William and Lucy were together? How did Charlotte know so little about her sister? When had they stopped telling each other everything? Was Lucy having sex already? She must be—William was an adult. But had Charlotte known, she would have told Iris, the principal, the police. And Lucy would have known that she would have. Charlotte exhaled. Of course, that's why Lucy stopped confiding in her.

• • •

CHARLOTTE STOPPED AT a pay phone to check in on Iris. She wouldn't tell her about going to get Lucy, not until she knew how things were going to play out.

Iris talked about the tuna casserole for lunch, about the two women who didn't think she knew Yiddish and called her a shiksa until Iris said in Yiddish that she wasn't.

"So you became friends then?" Charlotte said hopefully.

"Not this time," Iris said.

"It will get better," Charlotte said. "Maybe you can go to one of the activities today. Or maybe someone new and unexpected will show up. Sooner than you think, too."

"Well, that would be so nice," Iris said.

Charlotte hung up the phone, shaking her head. Wait until Iris saw Lucy. Charlotte felt her eyes pooling with tears. She'd missed her, her crazy diamond of a baby sister. Lucy was an irresponsible pain in the ass, but her absence could still make Charlotte ache like nothing else.

SHE DROVE FOR HOURS. The city gave way to country. The light to dusk. She stopped at a rest area and slept in the car. Just for an hour, she told herself, but when she woke up it was already dawn. Well, Lucy was probably sleeping, too.

Tioga. What a name for a town, she thought, and what a place, so deep in the woods she felt like looking over her shoulder. Still, she was surprised how pretty it was. The trees were lush, the grass was this vivid green. You could hear birds, and she even saw a deer leaping across the road. She had written out directions to the town, but she had no real idea how to get to Lucy's, so she stopped at a gas station to ask, scribbling it all down on a piece of paper.

Every once in a while, she would see a farmhouse. A couple sitting on the porch. Children riding their bikes. It all made her think of how she had felt Iris's house was home, how some days she couldn't wait to run through the door and see Iris. Charlotte hadn't thought she would care when the house was sold, but the day she had moved Iris out, she had stood on the edge of the lawn, biting back tears.

Maybe Lucy would move in with her when they got back. How strange and wonderful that would be. She'd be the big sister again, helping Lucy get back into school. And thank God she had that little sublet, and some money and a job. Maybe she could work something out so she could rent something bigger during the next year. Maybe Lucy could get a part-time job to keep herself out of trouble. Maybe Lucy could help Iris out, do some of her shopping. Or they could do it together.

Charlotte turned down a dirt road. There were no houses here, no people. How could Lucy be living here? She wondered whether Lucy would look different. God, she'd better not see William. Just thinking about him made her want to throttle him, to see him behind bars. The only reason she hadn't called the cops yet was that she wanted to come get Lucy herself.

There it was. A little brown clapboard that needed a paint job, surrounded by trees. There were chickens running around a pen, scratching at the dirt, a big red rooster strutting around them. Imagine. Lucy had chickens? The grass wasn't really cut, and there were dandelions dotting the lawn, an overgrown hydrangea bush by the front steps.

She glanced at her watch. Six in the morning. A little early, but Lucy had wanted her to come as soon as she could, and here she was. No one answered the bell, so she knocked loudly. "Lucy!" she called, but there was no answer. Charlotte felt a ripple of irritation. She tried the door, and to her surprise it opened.

"Lucy," she called, "I'm here." She glanced at her watch. It was a long drive back. Maybe they could stop for dinner.

"Lucy." The house smelled funny. Not mustiness, but something else. She rounded the corner from the foyer, and then she saw her.

Lucy was sprawled in a pool of blood on the floor, her face turned to the side. There was a dime-size hole in her temple, a bigger chunk punched out from the back of her head. Her skin was blueish and blotchy on her face, her bare arms, as if she were bruised, and it grew paler farther away from the floor. Her eyes were open, but the whites were gray, glazed over, and her shirt was riding up. There was a ring of what looked like soot burned onto one of her hands.

A lamp was shattered on the floor. A cup and plate were overturned and the cup had rolled to a corner. The upper wall behind her was spattered with blood, darker in color, almost brown, leading to the high ceiling, where it fanned out.

Charlotte started screaming.

HANDS SHAKING, SHE called the operator. She was sobbing so hard the woman on the line had to ask her to repeat herself, but how could Charlotte say again that Lucy was dead? She stammered out the address and, trembling, went outside to wait. The world felt like shards of glass.

Can you come get me? That's what Lucy had said. *I'm leaving him. Come get me. Come get me.* Lucy had been in trouble and Charlotte hadn't gotten there fast enough to save her sister. Charlotte jerked to her knees, vomiting onto the ground. She fell back against the porch, dizzy, wiping her mouth. Had William done this? And where was he? And what if he hadn't done this? What if he didn't even know? And if he hadn't done this, who had? And why?

She heard sirens, and two police cruisers pulled up. She waited for the cops to get out, three of them, older, puffy faced.

She saw how they had their hands on their holsters, how they were watching her. "I'm Charlotte—I called—" she blurted out. "My sister was shot!"

"Let's slow down here. Who are you?"

"I called, I told you. I'm her sister—Charlotte Gold." She looked toward the house.

"And she is?"

"Lucy Gold—"

"Where is she?"

"In the living room—"

"Is there anyone else inside?" one cop asked, nodding at the house.

"I don't think so—but her boyfriend also lives here—"

"Go sit in the cruiser. Ed will stay with you."

One of the cops drew his gun and went inside. The other headed for the back of the house, his hand on his holster. She sat in the front seat beside Ed, who smelled like cigar smoke and gum. "Who is she?" Ed asked. He wanted to know Lucy's full name and their relationship, he asked Lucy's age, and when Charlotte said seventeen, he stopped writing. "Seventeen? What was she doing here?" he asked. She told him how Lucy had run away from Boston but no one knew where or why or with whom, since she'd left only a vague note. How they had filed a missing persons bulletin on her. How Lucy had sent only one postcard, but it was from a vast rural area and made it hard to trace her. And then Lucy had finally called and asked Charlotte to come get her.

"What's the boyfriend's name?"

"William Lallo. He was her high school teacher."

He paused and studied her. "Where does he work?"

"I don't know."

Another car pulled up, followed by an ambulance, which

made her flinch. Two plainclothes detectives got out and glanced her way before walking into the house.

"When's the last time you saw Lallo?" Ed asked. He kept asking her questions, all of them simple, but he didn't seem happy with any of her answers. He kept frowning or shaking his head, and then after a while the door opened again, and one of the detectives came out and walked over to her. "You her sister?" he said, and when she nodded, he said, "Detective Harry Mosser. Could you step out of the car, please?" She got out.

"What did you see?" he asked. He made her describe it. She heard the scratch of his pen on the paper, but she couldn't see what he was writing.

"What did you do then?"

"I called you."

He asked the same questions Ed had. He wanted to know when the call from Lucy had come and what time Charlotte had gotten here. Where had she been before, and could she prove it?

Charlotte looked at him as if he were speaking a foreign language she didn't understand. Her mouth felt full of metal. She looked at the house, and it felt as if her eyes were covered by thorns. "I had to work," she said. "Call Fur Friends in Waltham. They have Saturday hours. My boss will tell you."

He raised one brow at the name, but he wrote it down. She heard a noise, and two paramedics came out carrying Lucy's body, wrapped in a white cloth, paper bags over her hands and feet. Charlotte looked down at her own hands, her fingers knotted so tightly they were white. She wrapped her arms around her body to stop herself from shaking.

"Did you bump into anything in the room?" he asked. She thought of the smashed lamp, the cup rolled into a corner. She shook her head.

"Did you see or hear any cars when you got here?" he asked.

"No cars. No people."

"What do you know about the box of shells?"

"What shells?" she said.

"There's a box in the bedroom, in one of the drawers."

"I didn't go in the bedroom."

"Did you see a gun in the house?"

The room flashed in her mind. The cup on its side. The bloody walls. Her sister.

"There was no gun. Maybe he took it with him—"

"What was their relationship like?" the detective asked. "Had she seemed unhappy?"

"I didn't even know they were together. I hadn't talked to Lucy for over a year—since they ran off."

He wanted to know more about William, whether he was violent, whether he ever hit Lucy or raised his voice. "I don't know anything. But she wanted to leave in a hurry," Charlotte said.

"Did he have any friends around here? Did your sister? Did she work?"

"I don't know," she said. "To all of it. I don't know."

"What time did she call?"

Charlotte remembered how she had felt, called to the phone at work. "I came as soon as I could." But was that really true? She hadn't even tried to ask Dr. Bronstein whether she could leave early.

He wrote something down. Someone came out of the house. Another car arrived, and a man jumped out with a camera. She heard one of the officers say to him, "Look, I'll give you something later. I can't talk to you now. We'll get to you when we get to you."

"Is that a reporter?"

Harry shrugged. "Small town. There's always someone

whose job is just to sit listening to the police radio. You might want to get out of here before they realize who you are."

Charlotte felt her legs turning to water, her air siphoning from her. As she fell, she grabbed onto the jacket of the detective. A button popped loose in her hand, and her fingers curled around it. He scooped her up by her elbows. "I've got you," he said, and for the first time his voice was sympathetic.

"We'll call the vet's office, corroborate your story," he said. "We'll look for this guy. Stick around town until we tell you otherwise. You have a place to stay?"

She shook her head, and he mentioned a hotel, and then he nodded toward the guy with the camera, the flash of his camera. "Do us all a favor and don't talk to the press."

THAT NIGHT, CHARLOTTE got a cheap room in the hotel. She knew she had to tell Iris now. She had wanted to surprise her with news of Lucy's return. Instead, all she could tell her was this. How would she even find the words? She glanced at her watch. Ten at night. Iris might be asleep. But Charlotte couldn't put this off. She reached for the phone, took a breath, and dialed.

"Hello?" Iris's voice was full of sleep, and Charlotte began crying again.

"Honey, what's wrong?" Iris said.

Charlotte wished that she could rest her head against Iris's. She wished Iris would hold her and rock her the way she sometimes had when Charlotte was little. She wanted Iris to stroke her hair, to tell her everything was going to be all right. She drew herself up.

"Lucy—" Her voice cracked. "Lucy—" She swallowed. "I'm in Pennsylvania."

"What about Lucy? And you're in Pennsylvania? Why?"

She tried to keep it as spare as possible, but she felt as if she were standing outside herself, listening to this other person explaining something so horrific that it couldn't possibly be true. As soon as she said that Lucy was dead, Iris began to scream. Charlotte held the receiver away from her. "Lucy! My Lucy!" Iris cried. "What kind of person would do this? What kind of monster?" Charlotte shuddered.

"Why didn't you tell me she had called? Why didn't you tell me you were going down there? Did you know she was with that man?" Iris shouted.

Charlotte looked out her window, across the parking lot. There wasn't a person in sight. The road was silent and empty. "I was going to bring her home today," she said.

"Why didn't she call me?" Iris wept. "Why didn't she let me know she was all right?"

"She did call you. At the Waltham house, but that line was disconnected."

"Thank God she found you!"

Charlotte explained that the police wanted her to stay in town, that she'd call Iris in the morning. She'd tell her what the police said, what new information there was. "My poor baby," Iris said. "My poor Lucy."

"I love you," Charlotte said, but Iris was sobbing so hard Charlotte couldn't tell whether Iris had heard her.

"I'm coming down there," Iris said. "I need to be there with you, with Lucy—I'll figure out a way to come."

"No, no, please—stay where you are. I'll call you tomorrow," Charlotte said. "I promise." She hung up the phone and stared out at the sky and thought of all the ways she would never be all right.

IN THE MORNING, Charlotte called her boss and told him what had happened, digging her fingers into her thigh so she wouldn't sob. She heard the silence on the line, and then he cleared his throat.

"You take as long as you need," he said, and Charlotte started to cry.

She called Iris to tell her that she'd call her later that evening. "I'll be here," Iris told her. When Charlotte hung up, she drove to the police station. She hadn't slept and she was in the same clothes, her T-shirt and jeans. The world seemed to have changed, the air felt rough against her skin. Colors seemed bleached. She didn't see many people, but the ones she spotted, driving, walking, seemed to be sleepwalking, staring into space, their movements robotic.

She walked into the station and saw Harry talking to two officers. She could tell by the way he was looking at her, his head tilted as if he was listening for something, waiting for her, that something had happened.

"The bullet matched the rest of them in Lallo's drawer," he said.

She braced a hand along his desk. Her legs were like shoelaces. She thought of the first day she had walked into William's class, the way he had smiled at her. She remembered how all the girls scribbled his name on their notebooks. "Where is he?" Her mouth dried. Her hands shook. She wanted to claw him apart with her hands.

"Sit down," the detective told her. She didn't move. "Sit," he ordered, pointing to a wood bench, and then she did.

"We found Lallo's car parked by the Ben Franklin Bridge near Philly. The keys in it. There was blood on the seat, a match for Lucy's. And a different blood type, same as the type we found listed on a blood donor card in Lallo's house."

She stared at him, waiting.

"A couple was on the bridge last night, looking at the water.

They saw a man standing on the edge of the bridge. The girl yelled to him to be careful, and then she said they heard a splash. The description they gave matches."

"They found him?"

He shook his head. "It's the Delaware River. It feeds into the ocean. We're not going to find anything."

Charlotte thought she was crying. She was sure of it because of the way her chest was heaving, the way her air seemed funneled into a tight band. But when she lifted up her hand, her cheeks were dry.

"What happens now?"

"Without the body, we still have to keep the case open. Maybe there was an accomplice. Maybe someone else did it, and Lallo was so upset about it that he jumped."

Charlotte's whole body began to shake. "You know someone else didn't do it."

"The Boston police contacted his old school. They're talking to his mother. They'll watch her house, her phone records for a while."

"His mother?" Charlotte couldn't picture William having a mother.

"She's by herself in a house in Belmont. His father passed away years ago."

"What about his things?"

"What things? You saw the place. There was just about nothing there. And frankly, sometimes it's easier for family just not to come look."

"I want my sister's things."

"You can go get them. The scene's been processed." He handed her a card from a local funeral home. She stared at it. Brown and Sons.

"We're releasing your sister's body from the morgue. You'll want to call them." He hesitated. "You may want to wait until someone's cleaned the place. Your sister's name wasn't on the lease, so you aren't responsible for that. But Lallo's name was. Misspelled, too. His mother will have to call a special cleaning service to take care of it. Sometimes funeral homes can send someone. Sometimes local butchers do it."

Charlotte looked at him, stunned. She tried to imagine a cleaning service washing away her sister's blood, handling her clothes, her books, the things she had loved. None of this would have happened if she had gotten there earlier. Her boss had been kind when she called him. Why hadn't she thought to tell him the truth when Lucy first called? Why hadn't she put her sister first? Lucy was murdered, and she had had a hand in it. "No, I'll do it," she said.

"You? Are you sure?" When she nodded, he sighed and put his hands in his pockets. "It's a nasty business. You want to think twice about this. It's not your responsibility."

"Yes, it is."

She had heard about Sharon Tate's father cleaning up Cielo Drive after the Manson murders. She thought of how people used to wash the bodies of their dead, hand-sewing them into shrouds. "I want to do it myself," she said.

He shrugged and then reached for a sheet of paper and drew a little map. "Make sure you wear gloves," he said. "Get the really thick kind. And get lots of bleach." He handed the paper to her, and she saw the store, the arrows pointing her there. "Thrift-T-Mart. They'll have what you need," he told her. "Mops, pails. The works." Then he handed her his card and told her that if anything occurred to her, any new information, she should call him. "If we find anything out, we'll call you," he said. "And if you change your mind about the cleaning, no one will think less of you."

When Charlotte left the station, it was hot out again, the sun nearly blinding. She turned the funeral home card over in her hand. She tried to think what to do, but her mind was roiling. Lucy would never want to be buried. Neither of them had ever even been to the cemetery where their parents were. "It won't be them in the ground," Lucy had said, but Charlotte knew it was because Lucy was afraid. Charlotte would cremate her sister and keep the ashes until she figured out what to do with them.

She got into the car and went to the supermarket. Muzak was playing "Grazing in the Grass." A woman was bopping as she wheeled her cart, tapping her manicured fingernails on the handle. Families were wandering around. A couple was smooching by the ice cream. Charlotte wanted to shake all of them. She shoved items into her cart, everything the detective had told her to buy: Bleach, sponges, rubber gloves, a bucket, and a mop. A box of heavy-duty trash bags. A face mask. She also found a package of T-shirts and underwear, which would get her through a few days, and a pair of black sweatpants. When she got to the checkout, the girl, wearing a brown smock, smiled ruefully. "Spring cleaning, huh?" she said. The cashier's face was open and friendly when Charlotte handed over her credit card, the one Iris had insisted she have "for emergencies." She gave Charlotte the once-over. "You painting?" the girl said.

"No," Charlotte said.

The girl looked at her funny, then kept quiet while ringing up Charlotte's remaining items.

When she got to the house, the crime tape was gone. The chickens screeched, as if they knew what had happened. What was she supposed to do with them? She hadn't seen any neighbors for miles around and she couldn't just let them go free.

She stood outside and tried to take a step forward, but she couldn't breathe. The pounding in her head grew louder. The house seemed farther and farther away. She never thought of turning around, getting back in her car, and letting William's mother take care of all of this.

She inched her way up the stairs, and the screaming of the chickens seemed to fill her head, and then she pushed open the door and she was inside.

The house looked ransacked. Every drawer was open, contents scattered everywhere. Muddy boot prints crisscrossed the floor. Lucy's body was gone, but her blood was still there, pooled and sticky, and when Charlotte looked at it she felt her stomach rising. She walked through the house. All the clothes from the closet were flung on the floor, the drawers were open, the sheets pulled back. Folders were spread across the floor, containing bills, it looked like, receipts, papers. In the kitchen, the cops had even emptied a box of cereal, as if they expected something might be hidden, leaving the whole mess on the table. The ants had already found it.

She started in the living room. She put on the mask, the protective glasses so that the bleach wouldn't sting her eyes, and the gloves. Shaking, she mixed bleach in water and began to scrub the floor, pressing down, breathing hard and fast. She would have cleaned a thousand houses like this if it would bring Lucy back. Death was too easy for a fucking scumbag like him, slipping under the water, not having to face what he did. She wanted him in jail, stripped of everything, afraid for his life. She wanted him never paroled. Never forgiven.

Just as she would never forgive herself.

Blood had seeped into the wood, into the joints, but she got it out of the surface, taking away the finish, leaving a lighter area that looked like a map. The bleach freckled her jeans white.

The walls were the hardest, spattered with blood. Some of it was still wet, and that came off easily, but a lot of it was now rusty and hard. She scrubbed with a brush, but the blood didn't want to come out. She took a kitchen knife to the dried blood and scraped. The trick was not to think about what you were doing, to simply do it.

By the time she had finished, it was dark, only a few fingers of light ascending on the floor. She had gone through three packages of garbage bags and four pairs of gloves. She still had to go through Lucy's things. She moved automatically from room to room. This is where her sister had lived. This is where Lucy had been alive. She could be breathing in the same air Lucy had breathed.

Whatever she touched felt like a burning ember. When she got to the bedroom, she found a contract for William to teach at some school, the name Billy Lalo on it.

She didn't start crying again until she saw Lucy's clothes, thrown on the floor. Lucy used to wear a riot of color. Tiny tube tops and skirts so short she could grip the hems with her fingers, but here were faded, drab T-shirts and jeans. There were William's clothes, his jackets, his shirts. There, in the corner, was a paisley minidress. She pulled it out and put it to her face. This had been Lucy's "grown up" dress in Boston, the thing she wore when Iris took them out to a nice place for dinner. She pulled the dress off the hanger and threw it over her arm, and then she noticed her own red silk scarf, hanging on a hook.

She had spent a whole month's allowance on this, buying it at Truc in Harvard Square. It had been her lucky scarf, and she had worn it every day, until one day she reached for it and it was gone. Frantic, she had combed her whole room for it, had gone everywhere in school where she might have left it, but it had never turned up.

But Lucy had taken it, something of Charlotte's. Hands trembling, she wrapped the scarf around her shoulders.

She left the room and was heading around to the front again

when she noticed something blue poking out under a shelf, as if someone had thrown it there. She pulled out a notebook and opened it and saw her sister's scrawl. *I have to leave.* Lucy had written this, maybe in this room. It was another part of her sister that was here. She found a spot on the floor that wasn't wet and slid down.

She opened the journal to the first page, dated two weeks before Lucy had vanished, and as soon as she saw the tiny heart Lucy had drawn in the margins, Charlotte felt sick.

I am the only one up, as usual. It's just my same crummy room, but tonight it feels like everything is made of silver. One hour ago, William kissed my eyelids and told me we see the world through each other's eyes. We are the same person. Falling in love is like being cotton candy, pink, light, and sweet. Sometimes when I'm with him, I feel sad, because Iris never had this. I know she didn't or her mouth couldn't circle shut like a change purse and she wouldn't always be worried about the future instead of today. And Charlotte, does she ever even have a date? Everything with her is tangled up with grades, her school, her future, like life is a blank check and she can fill in any number she wants. If I tried to tell either of them about this, they wouldn't get it at all. Oh, I love them. But I'm talking about Love, with a capital L, how I feel just when I say his name in my head.

Charlotte turned the page, and there was a scribbled list, like the ones Charlotte herself made all the time. *Me in two years:*

I will have a job I love. (A writer!)
I will be with a person I love. (William!)
I will be living in a place I love. (A big city!)
I will love myself (finally).

All that night, Charlotte read Lucy's journal, her sister's life rising from the page, her voice sounding on Charlotte's tongue as if she herself were saying the words. The journal was jubilant in the beginning, all about how Lucy and William had fallen in love, how they were going to go and make their own brave new world. Lucy had been happy, really happy, at least for a while. *He's my oxygen. I breathe in and he breathes out.*

But then, halfway in, the writing began to change. The funny drawings Lucy made in the margins stopped altogether. Charlotte read about how Lucy began to hide her journal in a small space behind a bookshelf, how the freedom they were supposed to have in Pennsylvania had ended up being so isolating she thought she was losing her mind. She wrote about the empty, dark skies, about her fear of the Manson girls, and then she wrote about William's teaching her to shoot, making her do it. *I'm not in love with him anymore. I don't know what he wants from me.* Charlotte turned a page, chilled, and then a new name popped up.

Patrick really listens. He's so kind. I think I love him. Who was Patrick? She turned another page, and Lucy wrote about how she worked at his farm stand, keeping it secret from William. How she had finally told Patrick everything because she knew he'd help her. *I slept with him. Sort of.* Charlotte suddenly felt dizzy. What did that mean? How did you sort of sleep with someone? *He's so beautiful that it hurts.*

It was still all so confusing. She had thought her sister was living this wild and happy life, and instead she was miserable and alone and scared and in love with some farmer. She had thought Lucy wasn't really good at anything, and maybe she had even thought her sister wasn't that smart. She had worried over her, but the writing in the journal was raw and touching.

Wednesday, May 18. William and I eat the same thing just about every night, but Patrick serves me a dazzle of flavors. Cheese with peppercorns and mustard in it. And homemade rhubarb ice cream. "Cooking for guests is supposed to be a blessing," he says, and all I can think about is how William never wants people over, not for dinner or any other reason, how he'd probably put me under a veil if he could. The first time I ate a piece of chocolate cake at Patrick's, I thought, William will know. William says he can tell who eats sugar just by their skin tone or the smell of their breath. "Live a little," Patrick said, giving me a plate, and I lived a lot because I had seconds, and when I got home, William didn't notice a thing. But Patrick has a secret, too. I found a photo of this woman in his house. A beautiful young woman in a white dress laughing at the camera, but he wouldn't tell me about her, and that was okay because God knows there are things I don't talk about either. So we both have secrets. So we are both the same, and isn't that what binds people together? Yesterday, Patrick had a motorcycle he borrowed from a friend and I asked if I could have a ride. He said yes. He always says yes to me. I sat behind him, my hands around his waist, the wind whipping against us, the smell of exhaust and oil and the leather of his jacket so strong I leaned forward and put my mouth to it like I'm kissing him through it and all I could think was, Keep going. Don't stop. Take me into a whole other world with you and we will never look back.

Charlotte blinked hard, the words swimming on the page. The police hadn't mentioned Patrick to her. Had William found out, and was that why he had killed her? She took a spare piece of paper from the table beside the couch and wrote down, *Patrick.*

She'd ask the police tomorrow about him. She riffled the pages
back to the beginning to see if there was more.

*Monday, June 15. It was so hot and we have no air-
conditioning, no fan, nothing but windows, and when we
open them, it just lets in the flies and the dust and the
mosquitoes. I'm jeweled with itchy bites. I was so miserable that William suggested we go to whatever movie was
playing, just so we could sit in the air-conditioning, but it
wasn't enough for me. "Can we go to a lake?" I said, and
William grimaced, but I begged him and he finally said all
right. We drove, and the lake was big and beautiful, and
no one else was there for some reason, but as soon as he
got out of the car, William began to act weird. Dragging
back. Not even looking at the water. "I'm not going in," he
said. "Then why did we come?" I said, and he said, "For
you." He wouldn't even get into a bathing suit, wouldn't
even look at the water, how pretty it was, how shining.
There I was, stripped down to my bikini, and William was
in a T-shirt and shorts and sneakers, sitting on the grass,
looking worried. "Why don't you come in and cool off?
Why can't you wade?" I kept asking him and asking him,
and he said, "I don't want to."*

*"We don't have secrets," I said, even though of course
we did, including Patrick, and of course this journal is my
biggest secret of all. His face softened when he heard me
say that, and he moved closer to me. "All right, I'll tell
you," he said. He said when he was little, just four, his
dad tried to teach him to swim. He didn't think William
needed lessons. He was sure he could do it himself. His
father took him to the penny pool on a day when it wasn't
crowded, and William was all excited, all feeling like he
was a big boy or something. Plus, he was so proud to be*

with his big, strapping dad, so surprised to have time with him because his father usually just ignored him. And then his dad lifted him up and carried him to the deep end, William's legs keeping time to a song he had in his head. He thought his dad would set him down, that maybe he would get to use one of those big inner tubes the pool had, or water wings. But instead, William's father threw him into the middle of the deep end, into a shock of cold. William went under, his mouth and nose filling with water, everything tasting like chlorine. Every time he came up, gulping at the air, grabbing for something solid that might help him, he saw his father waving his arms. "Swim!" his father shouted to him. "Move your arms! Kick those legs! What's the matter with you? Are you stupid?" William tried to shout help, he was drowning, help, he was going under, help, but when he opened his mouth, the water flooded in, and he was going under again, deeper and deeper, his feet brushing the bottom. The world went blue and cool, humming around him, narrowing into a cone. Then hands found him. Hands pulled him up. Daddy. He would be mad, but he had saved him. Hands placed him on the cement around the pool, and he looked up, wanting to see that his father wasn't angry, but instead there was a stranger's face peering down into his. A man with inky black hair and eyes like raisins, who was pushing on William's chest, until a flood of water poured out and the full choking feeling was gone. William coughed and sat up, startled that he was breathing air instead of water. "You're all right then," the man said, and he got up and walked over to William's father, who was shaking his head in disgust, and that strange man punched him in the face. "You don't deserve to have a son," he said, and he stalked off. William didn't know what to do, so he sat there, and then his father, one hand cradling his face, looked at him. "Get up," his father said. "I'm ashamed of you." And William stood, and they walked to the car, not talking. His father took him home after that, and when his mother asked, "How did it go?" they both said, "Fine." William's father grew a black eye the next day, which he told everyone came from walking into a door. He never tried to teach William to swim again or do anything again. That was it. He lost interest. William's one chance. From that day forward, William was terrified of both his father and the water. He wouldn't go near either, especially water. Wouldn't even sit in a bath or a hot tub. Just looking at water bothered him. "It's a little bit like dying again," he said to me. And I knew what he meant: I will do this because I want you to be happy.

"You go in," he said to me. "I'll watch you." So I did, swimming out, so that he was a dot in the distance, and I couldn't help it, I kept thinking, All I have to do is keep swimming and he won't be able to come after me. He won't be able to find me. I made my strokes longer. I covered ground. I don't know why I came back. Maybe because of the way he was standing, pacing on the grass. For a minute he looked like the old William. Like he needed me to save him. Like I was really worth something. I could have kept swimming. I could have swum all the way to another town, found a job and a new life, but instead I felt that tug of love, like a rope around my ankles as if I was a fish, caught on his line. I swam back. I took his arm and I could see he was trembling. "Come on, honey, let's go home," I said. "You don't have to prove anything to me." I told myself, and then him, that I'd never ask him to take me to water again. I'd never do that to him.

"Well, now that's a relief," he said.

And sometimes, too, I told myself: I know his weak spot now. Besides me, I mean.

Charlotte felt something prickling along her spine. William was afraid of water. If he was so terrified, how could he have jumped into the river even if he wanted to die? Why hadn't he just killed himself with the gun after he murdered Lucy?

She went back to the journal, feeling sicker and sicker. Lucy was biking the roads now, trying to find rescue. Charlotte turned to the last page. *I am so lost.* She closed the journal and held it to her chest.

There was still so much night left. She needed to get back to the motel. The house was now dark, except for the lamp she had turned on to read, and she began to feel frightened.

She packaged everything up—the rags, the brushes, the mop—and put it into bags. She went into the bathroom and ran the shower as hot as she could and scrubbed her hands, her face. She bent so the water ran over her hair. Then she changed into the clothes she had bought and threw her old ones into another bag. She brought all the bags outside, setting them by the side of the house.

She came back inside. One last time. She left the lamp on, as if her sister might need it. Then she left the house, all the while thinking, Oh, Lucy. I'm so lost, too.

Chapter 19

Earlier that day, Patrick was working the register, thinking about Lucy and hoping she had made it to the bus and gone back to Waltham okay. He thought she might call him, but then again, she had taken money from him, and he had fucked up by overreacting. She was just a kid. She was scared. He had yelled at her when all she did was take the petty cash he would have willingly given her if she had asked.

But what if she hadn't made the bus? Then he needed to find her, to get her away from William. Patrick could help Lucy get back to her family. He would put her on a train or drive her home himself. It was the right thing to do, maybe the only thing. He imagined her writing him letters from Boston as if he were a mentor, telling him about her day, about her studies, and he'd write back like a wise old sage. It made him feel good to think there was something right that he could do. But first he had to find her. He had to hope she'd come back here to the farm stand, the way she always did, because he didn't have a clue where she and that jerk lived. He didn't even know his last name.

That night, he went into his house, turning on the TV for company while he ate his supper. There, flashing on the screen, was a photo of Lucy. Underneath was the legend: LUCY GOLD, 17-YEAR-OLD MURDER VICTIM.

She had been shot, her body found by her sister the morning before.

Patrick stumbled down onto a chair, his heart pounding. Then a newscaster came on, a man standing out on a bridge by the highway, the wind whipping the sleeves of his jacket. His face was blank. "We're standing here at the Ben Franklin Bridge in Philadelphia, where late last night, William Lallo, thirty-one, a teacher recently fired from the Spirit Free School in Tioga, allegedly jumped to his death after the murder of his girlfriend, seventeen-year-old Lucy Gold."

Patrick began crying, so that the TV screen began to blur.

"Our story begins two days ago, at two a.m., when a couple reported seeing a man jump into the Delaware River from the Ben Franklin Bridge near Philadelphia. Police went to investigate and found Lallo's abandoned car parked nearby."

The camera flashed to two young kids, both with long bangs like sheepdogs, being interviewed by another reporter. "We just wanted to look at the water," the girl said. "It's a romantic spot when no one else is around." She looked anxiously at her boyfriend. "We saw him jump," she said. "We heard a splash."

The reporter mentioned a sister, who had gotten a call and come out, only to find Lucy dead. Patrick shut off the set.

He should have put Lucy on a bus himself, never mind going to the cops. If he had, she'd be alive now.

He thought of Vera's mother, asking him over and over, "Why didn't you do something?"

There was something he could do now. He got in his car to go to the police. He knew about William a little, things Lucy had told him. They might be helpful.

When he got to the station and said he had been friends with Lucy Gold, a detective squinted at him. He asked Patrick where he'd been the day before and whether he could prove it, and when Patrick told him and said he could, the cop lost interest.

"I just thought—maybe some information I have—I'd like to give it to you," Patrick said.

The detective considered him. "Okay," he said. He led Patrick into a back room, taking along a yellow pad. Patrick told him everything. How Lucy had shown up, how he had given her a job, the awkward time at the grocery store when he had run into both of them, and then her coming to him with a black eye. None of it seemed helpful, and halfway through he began to feel the way he had at confession when he was little, the priest always seeming not to believe him or even like him. Patrick looked up. The cop wasn't even writing anything down. Instead, he was tapping the pen against the table, scraping it along its side.

The detective leaned forward. "What was your relationship with this girl again?"

Patrick swallowed. "We were friends."

The detective stood up. "Terrible thing," he said, and then he led Patrick to the door. Patrick had no idea what to do, no idea where to go. He didn't know whether Lucy had other friends or where her sister might be right now so he could talk to her. He got into his car and put his head on the wheel, his ears roaring.

Chapter 20

It took Charlotte until the end of July to look at the newspapers, to stop sobbing long enough to see Lucy's story splashed on the front page, a photo of her (where had they gotten it?) in a floral minidress, her hair wild, a daisy poking out behind one ear. VIXEN FLOWER CHILD AND TEACHER-LOVER IN GRISLY MURDER SUICIDE. Her hands were shaking so much that she couldn't see the print at first. They were blaming Lucy as if she were a seductress who had done William wrong. They called Lucy a high school dropout, which was what she was, but the way they said it made it sound so much worse, as if she had been stupid, one of those kids hanging around, looking for trouble, making nothing more of their lives than working as a cashier at Woolworth's candy counter. There was a photo of William, too, the one they used in the yearbook for all the teachers. He was sitting at his desk, writing something, his pen tipped between his fingers, wearing a jacket and a shirt and tie. You couldn't see his eyes. Underneath was the caption: FAVORITE TEACHER A SUICIDE.

Whose favorite teacher? He let kids do whatever they wanted, pretending it was relevant, acting as if he were one of them, and that was why they liked him. He taught them nothing, and he couldn't be trusted at all. She scanned the pages, but there was no quote from the Waltham school, nothing about how they had fired him. Instead, on the next page, there was a story about William's mother, Diana. How had Diana been able to talk to these vultures without screaming? Why would she do this? "I'll never believe my son is guilty," Diana insisted. She knew he was in Pennsylvania, but it was for a job, and he had gone there alone, as far as she knew. She had never visited him because she didn't drive, and how would she get there? You couldn't expect someone her age to take the train or, God forbid, the bus. "He called me every Sunday," she said. He came to visit her in Waltham one month, just for two days, and they had lunch together and caught up, and he never mentioned a girl.

Even though there was no body, Diana had bought him a plot and a gravestone, etched with his name, and the newspaper ran a photo of her standing in front of it, her face haunted. Charlotte wished she knew where that grave of William's was so she could go chisel *murderer!* into the stone.

She finished the paper and shoved it into the trash. How long before a reporter found her or Iris?

WORK WAS CHARLOTTE'S salvation. She got to the office early, left as late as she could, and kept busy. Dr. Bronstein never asked her about Lucy, but he brought her a cup of coffee some days and she felt him watching her, his gaze deep with concern. He kept telling her to take time off if she needed, but she liked being among the animals. It helped her—holding cats in her arms, taking away a dog's pain with a shot or a pill. The pet owners thanked her, sometimes spontaneously hugging her, so for a moment she felt human contact.

It didn't seem real. Lucy dead. She had called the police to tell them about the journal entry, about how William was afraid of the water. But they hadn't seemed interested. "A bunch of stories don't prove anything," an officer told her. "It's not hard evidence. Plus we have witnesses to his jumping. We have a description."

Defeated, she had collected Lucy's ashes from the funeral home and returned to Waltham. She brought the urn to Iris, who cried and then put it by the window. "She always loved the sun," Iris said. It hurt Charlotte to see Iris's sad face, the slow shuffle of her steps. Charlotte called her every day. She visited almost as often. But how much grief could an old person take?

One day, Charlotte came home from work, and as soon as she got in her apartment, her watch fell off her wrist. She had gotten so skinny because she couldn't manage to eat very much. She had to wear a belt to keep her jeans up. She swam in her shirts. She stared at her reflection in the mirror. She'd never had her hair this long, almost to her clavicle. She'd never not had bangs. Her color was paler than usual, and when she rummaged in her purse for a bit of blush and brushed it on, it looked startlingly unreal, and she rubbed it off. She thought she looked sick, but what did it matter? She felt hopeless. She got the phone book and leafed through it. There it was. Diana Lallo. William's mother. 1401 Lincoln Street. Belmont. That wasn't far from here. She could go see her and then swing by and see Iris in the evening.

She got in the car and drove to William's mother's house, a little white ranch surrounded by a picket fence, right by the bus stop. There were daisies sprouting by the walkway, blue curtains in the windows, even a big tabby cat prowling in the yard, probably looking for birds or a patch of sun, but Charlotte couldn't get out of the car. What was she doing here? Why did she think this was a good idea? It had taken her only ten minutes to drive here, but she sat in front of the house in silence for half an hour, her heart knocking in her chest.

Finally she made her way up the walk and pressed her finger against the doorbell.

She could hear footsteps. The door opened and there was a woman, maybe in her fifties. She was buttoning the top of a green dress that looked one size too small, smoothing her hair, which was dyed a bright shade of yellow. She looked at Charlotte, her face welcoming until Charlotte said her name, and then she stiffened. "What do you mean coming here?" she said. "What do you want from me?"

Charlotte swallowed. "No one will talk to me. Not the cops, not the detectives. The only people who want to talk are reporters, and I hang up on them."

Diana's jaw softened. "You and me both," she said. "I gave one interview and now they keep wanting more. They're like sand flies."

"Please. I just want to talk. Maybe we can help each other make sense of this."

Diana studied her for a moment, then opened the door wider, peering at her. "You're so young," she said, and she let Charlotte in.

She led Charlotte into the living room, its deep blue walls covered in photos, including a picture of a little boy holding a ball. The boy had William's smile, his blue eyes. Charlotte had an urge to knock the picture from the wall, but instead she followed Diana toward a plaid couch and sat.

"Do you want tea?" she said, and Charlotte shook her head. From here, she could see out the window, her car parked in the road.

"Every time the phone rings, I think it's going to be him," Diana said. "When the mail comes, I'm sure it's from him, too. He liked to send me postcards."

"Lucy wrote to us, too." Once, she thought.

Diana straightened in her chair. "I didn't know anything about her," she said. "When he lived here, William had lots of girlfriends. But grown women. Professionals. He'd bring them over to dinner and some of them seemed serious and I never knew why they fizzled apart. They just did and I didn't think I should pry about it. All I knew was what William told me, which was that he was unhappy here in his job and then he got a great opportunity in Pennsylvania. He loved that new job. He loved Pennsylvania. He never mentioned your sister." She picked up one of the cushions and hugged it. "Maybe none of us will ever know the true story," Diana said.

"He was afraid of the water," Charlotte said.

Diana frowned. "What? William?"

"William was afraid of the water. I read it in my sister's journal. She said William told her that his father threw him in the water when he was little, nearly drowned him, that someone else had to save his life. After that, he never went in the water. If he was so terrified, well, maybe he didn't jump into that river."

"You think I don't wish that were true?" Diana said. She got up and pulled out an album from one of the end tables and opened it up. She pointed to a page. A young boy was in the ocean beside his father, laughing. She pointed to another shot of William, soaking wet, slick as a seal, a beach towel wrapped around him. "I admit his father was nasty. He had a temper, but he was never abusive toward William. Never hit him. And William loved the water. We couldn't keep him out of it. As soon as summer started, he'd beg us to go to the beach." She shut the album, tracing one hand over the cover.

Diana studied Charlotte for a moment. "Why did you come here? You lost your sister, but I lost my son. Even though we don't know their story—and we never will know—we're both going to have to find a way to live with that." Diana headed for the front door.

In the light, Charlotte saw the fine lines mapping Diana's face, the gray hair poking out among the brassy strands of blond. Diana pulled open the door. "Please don't come back here," she said. "Not ever again."

When Charlotte stepped outside, the light was so bright she shielded her eyes with the flat of her palm. The trees seemed to be shimmering. Down the street, two girls were jumping rope, singing, *Fire, fire, false alarm. Rosie fell in the fireman's arms.* She and Lucy used to sing that when they were little, playing on the patio in the back, Iris watching them from a lawn chair. Charlotte heard the door shut. She imagined Diana inside, taking out the album again, looking at the photos of her son, tracing his face. She got into the car and drove and tried to think about what she would do next.

She reread the journal. She wouldn't stop asking questions. She'd find the truth about her sister's life—and her death.

CHARLOTTE DROVE OVER to see Iris. She was surprised to see that Iris's color was better, that she was eating a sandwich at her table. "*Password* is on," Iris said. "We can pretend it's educational." She turned on the set. "Come and watch with me." Charlotte couldn't really concentrate. She kept getting up to bring things for Iris.

"You don't have to babysit me," Iris said. "I need to get up, to exercise."

"I'm just trying to help you. I worry about you."

Iris stood up. "It isn't healthy, your being here all the time. You need to have a life that isn't just me." She took Charlotte's hand. "Don't you think I worry about you, too?"

"Is it any better here for you?" Charlotte asked.

Iris shrugged. "It is what it is. I'm getting used to it."

Liar, Charlotte thought. She could see how lonely Iris seemed, and sometimes it scared her, the way Iris would ask her what things of hers Charlotte might want, as if this were the last stop and Iris were preparing for the end of her life. She yearned to tell Iris about Diana, about what she had learned, but why make Iris more unhappy?

"You can go on home, honey," Iris said. "I'm getting really tired." She lifted her arms, stretching them into her yawn.

THE MORE CHARLOTTE came over, the more other women from the complex approached her. Charlotte always said hello and made small talk, but she was surprised just how much the other women knew about Iris. One woman could rattle off Iris's medications and when she should take them and how those medications differed from the ones they were taking. Another stopped Charlotte to ask how Iris had liked the roast beef sandwich she had brought over. And when Charlotte was leaving, one woman in a floral pantsuit took her arm.

"She's a tough old bird, your mother," the woman said. "I'm Bess. I know you don't know me."

Bess grasped Charlotte's shoulders for a moment. "I'm so sorry about your sister," she said.

"You know about Lucy?"

Bess shrugged. "You think we don't read the papers or listen to the news? You think no one here recognizes pain? A bunch of us knew, and we waited for her to say something, but she never did. Then one night I walked by her room and heard her crying, and I stayed there knocking and knocking until your mom let me in. As soon as I saw her, I hugged her and then let her cry. I told her that my daughter Melanie died when she was fourteen from an asthma attack, right in my arms while I begged her to breathe. And that's how we started to talk about Lucy, over and over, as much as she needed."

"She doesn't talk about Lucy that much to me," Charlotte said.

"Well, of course not," Bess said. "You're her daughter. She wants to protect you." Bess leaned closer. "And you should let her think she can."

CHARLOTTE CAME HOME to her apartment and turned on the lights. It was just a tiny space, but she loved the smooth wood floors, the high ceiling. She turned on the stereo and put on James Taylor, singing about having seen fire and rain, gliding into a love song. Charlotte poured herself a glass of wine. She took out a chicken breast and some vegetables and put it all in the oven to roast. The first sip of wine relaxed her, but the next two were even better.

She listen to James singing about love, and then, as always, she thought about her sister, about that man she had been in love with. Patrick was still in Pennsylvania. He was another part of Lucy she didn't know that much about. Charlotte thought of all the unfamiliar places and people that Lucy had mentioned in her journal. There was an ice cream joint Lucy liked because they made all these desserts by hand. There were people like the cashier whom Lucy had befriended. Maybe someone might know something. Or maybe Charlotte was kidding herself, trying to keep Lucy alive for a little bit longer.

She went to one of her albums and looked through it until she found a photo of Lucy. Her sister was standing by a tree in their old backyard, wearing a pink psychedelic minidress. One hand was on her hip, and she was smiling.

Charlotte downed the rest of her wine. She could smell the chicken roasting. Iris had told her to take care of herself. Well, tonight she would. She'd eat this delicious dinner she had made, maybe pour another glass of wine. Tomorrow was Friday, the start of a three-day weekend because Dr. Bronstein was going to a convention. In the morning, she'd get in the car and see who she could find.

THE FARTHER SHE DROVE, the lonelier everything seemed. Jesus. She had driven this road before and had thought it looked pretty and peaceful, but now it seemed like a no-man's-land. All she could see was farm after farm, cows dotting the fields, a spotted horse grazing. She knew people at Brandeis who went on and on about the glories of the country, how they wanted to live on a farm, get away from the cities and get back to the land, how the country was cleaner, purer, the people more genuine. One guy she knew actually took his tuition money and made a down payment on a small piece of land in Maine, and he and his girlfriend, a scrawny blond art major, were going to farm it. They'd dig a swimming hole, an irrigation system. They'd get back to basics. "Really?" she had said. "You know how to farm? How to irrigate crops?" He had laughed at her. "I will," he said. The last she had heard, they were still out there, but the farm was a struggle. Their crops wouldn't grow, at least not enough to make any money or to feed themselves. He was working as a carpenter, and his girlfriend was waitressing in town at a diner.

She followed the map, and there it was. PATRICK'S FARM, like an image swimming up from a dream, a hand-painted sign in bright blue letters. It was small. Tables of fruits and vegetables, bins of flowers, an outside and inside market, filled with people milling around. The usual plaid flannel shirts and blue jeans, hippies with long hair, little kids in sneakers, and women in granny dresses. She parked the car and got out, not sure whom she was looking for, what Patrick might look like, or even how old he was. Lucy hadn't said much about how he looked except hyperbole: *He has eyes like green grapes.* Just because he owned the place didn't mean he would be here. She squinted at an older man in a sweatshirt. She started toward him until a child ran up and hugged his waist. Charlotte walked in the other direction, past the bins of apples and carrots, the bursts of different colorful lettuces, purple and green and red. She turned another corner, and there was a guy at a cash register. Maybe that was him. And if it wasn't, at least he'd know where to find Patrick.

The guy could have been a Brandeis student with that straight black hair, eyes hidden behind shades. He was rangy like a greyhound, and he had on a T-shirt the color of a purple grape. She waited while he finished counting out money to a customer, and then he looked up and saw her.

"Hi," she said. She thought of him making Lucy lunch every day, sitting beside her and talking to her, and she was suddenly jealous of all that time he had had with her sister. He closed the register. "Are you Patrick?" she asked.

"I sure am. Can I help you find something?"

"Thank you, no," she said. He studied her. "You're not from around here," he said. "I can always tell."

She swallowed. She knew so much about him from Lucy's journal. She knew that he loved french fries dipped in tomato sauce, that he loved old movies and would deliberately let Lucy beat him at Scrabble. She knew he had a secret, or at least Lucy had thought so.

"I'm Lucy Gold's sister. Charlotte."

He took off his glasses and studied her, and then she saw his eyes, his lashes long as palm fronds, startling her. No wonder Lucy had fallen for him.

"Charlotte," he said finally. He put one hand over his eyes for a moment, as if it hurt to look at her. "We should talk," he said. He scanned the stand and then he called out, "Ray," and a young woman appeared, two blond braids snaking over her red overalls, a smile full of teeth.

"Can you take over for a bit?" he said, and Ray stepped in front of the register, and then Patrick turned back to Charlotte. "It's more private inside the house," he said, and she followed him.

His house was directly in the back, more of a cottage, small but clean, and he led her to the kitchen, to a red Formica table. On top of it was a bowl filled with fruit. "Let me just pour us some coffee," he said. "I always have some going." He brought down two mugs and filled them and set them on the table. He brought out sugar and cream and then he pulled out a chair for her, a politeness that startled her.

"I'm so sorry," he said.

"Me, too," she said.

"What exactly happened? I know only what the cops told me. And the news."

"I don't know much, either. But I want to find out." She swallowed. "I have her journal. She said that William was terrified of the water, and I don't see how he would have jumped off that bridge." She watched his face.

"People do a lot of things to themselves when they're in pain."

"She mentioned different people, different places. I need to see what she saw, to know what she knew . . ."

"That makes sense."

She took a sip of the coffee and frowned. "Sorry, it's chicory," he said. "I should have warned you."

"She wrote a lot about you," Charlotte said. She watched the way his mouth tightened, and wondered what that meant. "She wanted to be a writer. She wrote about your farm stand. That's how I found you." Charlotte stirred cream into her cup. "She said she loved you."

"She was a kid. There was nothing between us."

"She said there was. She said she slept with you."

He drew back. "Jesus! That's not true!"

"She said it happened."

"She crawled into bed when I was napping, and I booted her out. Both of us were fully clothed. Look, I gave her a job. I tried to help her, to be her friend. That's all it was."

Charlotte frowned. "But she wrote—"

"I'm telling you it's not true. Did she used to make things up? You're her sister, you'd know that better than I would."

That used to be true but hadn't been for a long time. Charlotte remembered when they were younger, how she and Lucy told each other everything. She remembered, too, how abruptly it had stopped, how secretive Lucy became, and if Charlotte dared to ask, Lucy would go blank. Charlotte felt a stab of longing.

"Did you know how young she was?" Charlotte asked.

"Not at first. And lots of people look young. She had told me she was in college, at Brandeis, studying to be a vet."

Charlotte blinked. "That's my life," she said quietly. "Lucy never wanted that." She pushed the coffee away. "Did you know William?"

"No. I saw him and Lucy at a grocery. Lucy pretended she didn't know me, and I didn't like the way he was talking to her. Plus, he acted like a dick to me. He made it clear that he didn't want anyone intruding on them. When she finally told me that things were bad, I told her to go to the cops. That was the only thing to do, that's what anyone would say, but she was so frantic. It was like she couldn't listen to anything." He took both their cups and put them in the sink and then sat back down again. "You don't know what you're seeing sometimes, when you see it," he said. "You don't know how bad it can get."

"I hate him for jumping," Charlotte said. "I wanted him punished in prison."

"It won't bring her back, coming out here," he said. "It won't change anything. And chances are you're not going to find out any more than the police have."

"You don't know that."

"Could I read her journal? Would that be possible?"

"I don't want to let it out of my hands—"

"You can watch me read it. How's that?"

She nodded. "All right," she said, but she didn't really want to let him. It seemed too private, too personal. Maybe he'd forget about it. Or she'd leave here and she wouldn't see him again. Outside, the sky was darkening, as if someone had smudged it. It was getting late, and she yawned.

"I think I'm going to have to find a hotel and call it a day. I'm only here for the long weekend."

"You think that's a good idea?"

"I just want to talk to people she might have known. Go to places in her journal. She was *here*—I need to be here, too."

He considered her. "I have a spare room. You can stay here, if you want."

"I can't do that. I mean, won't that be weird for you?"

"Oh, probably. Will it be weird for you?"

"Probably a little. Why would you do that, though? Let me stay?"

"Because you're Lucy's sister."

Of course. She was always Lucy's sister.

HER ROOM WAS tiny, just a bed covered with a hand-made quilt and a bookcase, and when she opened the closet, there was the leather jacket Lucy had said she kissed. Charlotte ran her hands over it and then drew it to her face, inhaling, but it didn't smell like anything. She let the jacket fall back and then she moved from the closet to his books. Ken Kesey. Typical. But he also had *The Great Gatsby*, her favorite novel. And some botany books. And there were also medical textbooks. Why did he have those? Some of the pages were underlined. Thoracic embolism. Mitral valve prolapse. So he was smart. That counted for something.

She opened one of the drawers, and there was the photograph Lucy had written about, Patrick standing with a beautiful woman, the two of them radiantly happy, a photo Lucy said he refused to talk about. Maybe he'd tell her or maybe he wouldn't. Maybe it was none of her business. She shut the drawer.

She could hear him outside the door, so she got into bed and shut her eyes, but she couldn't stop thinking about Lucy.

WHEN CHARLOTTE WOKE in the morning and came into the kitchen, there was a note. *At work. Make yourself at home. You don't need a key because the door is always open. If there's anything you need, come and find me.* He had left her a fruit salad, some bread for toast, and a jar of homemade peach jam. Each thing she did—washing her plate, putting the jam back in the refrigerator, which was stocked with produce—she wondered whether Lucy had done.

She walked outside. There he was, piling apples onto a table, joking with the girl with the braids. She could walk over there and say good-bye, tell him where she was going, or she could just take the car and go.

He didn't look up. She kept walking.

SHE WASN'T SURE where to start, so she drove back to Lucy's old house. Maybe she'd notice something new. It hadn't been that long, but maybe someone had rented it and had found something she had missed. The closer she got, the more she remembered. The cackle of the hens as they skittered in the dirt. The blood splashed on the floor. The way Lucy's legs were splayed, as if they had been kicked from under her. The smell, like rusted metal. She pulled the car over and put her head to her knees. It's okay, it's okay, she told herself. It's okay. But she knew better. It would never be okay.

The first thing she noticed was that the house looked different. Someone had painted the outside yellow, and there were new flowers by the walkway. The henhouse was gone. She walked up the path, and when she knocked on the door, a woman carrying a baby answered. "Yes?" the woman said. The baby, sunny and fat, yawned. Charlotte could see inside. The living room was gold now, and even though there was wall-to-wall carpeting, Charlotte still knew exactly where the bloody floorboards had been. Charlotte braced one hand along the door.

"Are you lost or selling something?" the woman said. The baby burbled and the woman laughed. The woman peered at Charlotte again. "You don't look so well. Are you okay? Should I call someone for you?"

"My sister used to live here," Charlotte said, and the woman tightened her grip around the baby, but Charlotte kept going. "I just wanted to know if when you moved here—if you found anything."

"This again?" the woman said. "How many times do I have to call the cops? This is a private home. It's not a tour. I live here now with my family, and none of us know anything about her or want to know anything about her. I've had enough gawkers here."

"I'm not a gawker. I'm her sister. And any information you could give me, anything you found, anyone coming by—"

"No one came by, and we found nothing. I'm very sorry for your loss, but this is a private home," the woman said. She closed the door, and there was the click of a lock, leaving Charlotte alone out on the porch.

THE NEXT MORNING, Charlotte went through Lucy's journal like a map, determined to go to all the places her sister had written about, trying to imagine what Lucy must have felt, to find someone else who might have known her. She drove to William's free school and spent half an hour looking for any adult who might know something. Kids were running wild, hurling paper airplanes, and when she stopped one little girl to ask where the principal was, the girl laughed, jutted up her third finger, and ran away. When Charlotte finally found the head of the school, he didn't want to speak to her.

"We fired him. We knew there was something wrong," he said defensively. Fired, Charlotte thought. Lucy hadn't written that in her journal. He told her Lucy had never come to the school. He said he had never seen or heard of Lucy before this, and then two kids slammed into the room, and he excused himself. "Good-bye, now," he told her.

She got back into her car and drove to a dress shop Lucy had mentioned, then a bar. There was a high school where she had gotten her GED information. Charlotte brought out Lucy's photo, and no one ever knew anything about her, except sometimes they recognized that she was that girl, the one who had been murdered. And then they started asking Charlotte questions, and she didn't want to talk to them anymore.

She came back home tired. She didn't want to bother Patrick, so she ate quietly and then retreated to her room.

The next morning, just as she was leaving for an ice cream shop Lucy had written about, Patrick came outside. "Where you off to?"

"I'm just going to this ice cream place. Sweet Stuff," she said.

"Come on. Let's go together," he said. "I know the place." She stayed still, considering.

"I have to go into town anyway," he told her. "I need to pick up some things at the hardware store."

"You don't have to do this, you know," she said.

"Do what? I need nails. And I like ice cream."

"Okay," she said finally. "As long as you're going anyway."

It felt funny to be a passenger in someone else's car. Patrick rolled down the window and put his elbow out, and when she put on the radio, he took out his sunglasses and put them on, hiding his eyes.

"It's around here," he said, and then he turned down a road, and there it was, a small white building with a FOR SALE sign on it. The front door was boarded up, and a few kids in jeans and sweatshirts were hanging around, smoking cigarettes. They looked up expectantly when they saw the car and then looked away when they saw who was in it. Charlotte felt herself deflating.

"I'm sorry. You drove me here for nothing," Charlotte said.

"It's not for nothing. Now I know I can't get ice cream here anymore."

He drove to the hardware store, and she came in with him, studying the nails, watching him banter with the owner. When they got back in the car, he began talking quietly to her, telling her about a dog he had as a kid, until she realized he was trying to make her feel better.

THAT NIGHT, CHARLOTTE saw Patrick sitting on the porch, drinking a glass of wine, and she came out. "Did you want to be alone?" she said, and when he shook his head, she sat beside him.

"Want some wine? I can get you a glass."

She shook her head. The sky was thick with stars, each one more brilliant that the other. She hoped for a shooting star, so she could wish on it. She looked at the huge coleus he had growing in a pot and, beside it, an even bigger pot of basil. "Those are amazing," she said, nodding at the plants.

"The coleus is Fred. I grew him from seed, so I named him. The basil just grows and grows."

"I like Fred," she said. She glanced around and pointed at the macramé hanging, twisting knots of blue twine. It wasn't very pretty, but he obviously thought enough of it to hang it up. "I like that, too," she said politely.

He laughed. "I was at a commune and some girl tried to

teach me to do macramé, and as you can see, I'm no expert. Still, I like to see it hanging up there. It's a big mess, but I like anything imperfect. It's got its own sort of beauty."

"It does at that."

"So tell me about your work, Charlotte Gold. Why'd you decide to be a vet?"

"I never had pets. I always wanted one, but Iris was allergic. This way I get to baby all of them." She told him about a snake who had a cataract operation, about a woman who came in with a baby owl with a broken wing. The animals she loved the most were the unique ones: A tortoise with orange-ringed eyes and an overgrown beak because his owner hadn't known it had to be trimmed. A dog with mottled red fur that had the sweetest blue eyes. "Animals talk to you in ways you can't imagine," she said. "They just look at you and it feels like they're reading your mind."

"My folks had a cat named Elvis," he said, and Charlotte laughed, which made Patrick laugh, too. "He used to bop me on the head every morning at five because he wanted to play. He'd race around the furniture. I swear he was half-human."

Patrick drained his glass. "You leaving tomorrow?" he asked, and she nodded.

"Did you find everything you were looking for?"

"I didn't have enough time . . ."

He was quiet for a moment and then he glanced over at her. "Maybe you should come back," he said.

Chapter 21

Patrick liked Charlotte. He had liked Lucy, too, but Charlotte was different, quieter, more thoughtful, and when she listened she gave her full attention. He had meant it when he invited her to come back, but when she actually called at the beginning of August and mentioned returning another weekend, saying she wanted to find another teacher who had worked with William, he felt nervous. What was it she really wanted?

As soon as she got out of the car, his mouth went dry. Her hair was a little longer, her skin had a little color, and she was in a summer dress that showed off her long legs. "Hi," she said shyly.

That night she sat out on the porch swing, looking at the stars. When he came out with glasses of lemonade, the ice clinking, she scooted over and made room for him, but instead he took one of the chairs. She didn't seem to mind. "You have the best stars here," she said.

He was happy to sit out in the dark with her. Nights could get lonely, and it was nice to have the company, to hear the gentle rock of the swing. He liked listening to Charlotte, too, the cadence of her voice, raspy like wild grasses, filling in the blanks of Lucy's life for him, unfolding how Charlotte had brought her up, how she had watched over her. How she had failed her.

"You didn't fail her. You drove out here to rescue her."

Charlotte slid the glass of lemonade around in her hand and said nothing.

Talking about himself was another matter. "Where did you grow up?" Charlotte asked him, and that segued into what his parents had been like, and where he'd gone to school, and it veered close to his having to talk about Vera, which he didn't want to do. He answered her politely, telling her just the outline of his life, but she kept probing. Her hair, like a wing, spread against her cheek. He felt like an orange she was unpeeling.

"Why didn't you love her?" Charlotte asked quietly.

"What?"

"I mean really, why didn't you? Lucy was young. She was beautiful. She loved you. Why didn't you love her back?"

"No one knows why anyone loves anyone," he said. He looked at her, pained.

"Tell me about the woman in the photograph," she said. "Lucy wrote about her."

He stiffened. He had always been able to deflect Lucy when she had asked about Vera, changing the subject or having her do a chore. Lucy was a hummingbird, always off to the next thing, but Charlotte was different.

"I can't," he said.

"What was her name?"

He didn't answer, but he felt her quietly waiting, giving him space. What did it matter if he told her? She wasn't going to be here much longer.

"Vera." There was that dull ache, that pain. Well, he had said this much, he might as well say the rest. "She was my wife."

"What happened to her?" Charlotte asked.

"She died."

Charlotte set her glass of lemonade down, tilting her head toward him. He waited for her shock, her discomfort, but she stayed still and calm.

He told her, just to get it out, to get it over with. That they had been happy. That they had been trying to have a child. That one moment she was perfectly healthy and the next moment he was in the waiting room of the ER, the only person in there because it was the middle of the night, and a doctor had come out and hadn't said a word, and Patrick had known. He told her how he had left school, how he had joined a commune, trying to outrun his grief. And then he had wound up here.

As soon as he told her, he wished that he hadn't, because he knew what would happen. She would tell him what everyone else did, that things would get better, that he should remember the good times. That things happened for a reason or, even worse, that Vera was in heaven looking down on him, making sure he was okay. When one door closes, another one opens. All that shit. He would kill to believe any of that, but he couldn't. He shifted in his seat. "So now you know," he said, and Charlotte reached across and took his hand, and he felt a jolt of heat before she let it go. "I'm so sorry," she said.

She didn't say another word, and neither did he. She simply sat there beside him, and Patrick was surprised at how soothing that felt. How less alone.

Charlotte didn't move until he finally got up, and then she stretched. "I'm going to sit out here a bit longer," she said, and he nodded and went inside.

He tried to go to sleep, but he kept thinking of her sitting out there alone on his porch. He didn't relax until he heard her footsteps back in the house, her bedroom door opening and closing.

He was embarrassed after that, but she didn't bring up Vera again.

THE NEXT MORNING he woke to find Charlotte sitting at his kitchen table, scribbling lists and then tossing them into his wastebasket. Later he dug one out. She had categories: "Find

Lucy's Friends." "Lucy's Work." "Find William's Friends." Patrick didn't think Lucy had friends, but he couldn't know that for sure, and he couldn't imagine anyone palling around with William. "Visit William's School" was crossed out. And then he saw his own name, Patrick, with a question mark after it. Again he wondered, what did she really want from him? She never asked him for help. He thought it must be hard for her, but she never talked about where she had been or whom she had talked to.

That night he heard her crying in her room. The sound reverberated in his bones, and he walked to her door, and the closer he got, the louder it became. He lifted his hand to knock but then hesitated and walked back into the kitchen instead. He banged the teakettle onto the stove. He ran the water as hard as he could. She'd hear him. If she needed him, she'd know he was there.

But she didn't come out. He went and got a bottle of wine. He always kept a spare juice glass on the table so he could pour himself a glass, and he filled this one to the rim.

When Lucy was around, he never drank in front of her. She was a kid and no happier than he was, but he didn't want her to think that alcohol was the answer. And he didn't want her to think he was an alcoholic, either. He wasn't. No one ever found him lying on the side of a road. He didn't sway when he walked or slur his words or otherwise act like an asshole. And he never drank anything harder than wine.

Before Vera died, he never used to drink. He and Vera liked juice or seltzer with a squirt of lemon in it. Sometimes he'd have a glass at the commune if someone made it, but the homemade wine was always made from dandelions and it tasted like crabgrass, and he drank it just to be polite. No, his drinking habit had started at the farm, the long nights when he was tired of reading and there were no movies on TV, the darkness crowding around him, the crickets deafening. Wine muddied the edges.

He started to pour another glass and realized he had finished the bottle. Something was knocking in his head. He tilted his head and listened. Charlotte had stopped crying. Maybe she had cried herself to sleep. Or maybe she was lying in bed, staring at the ceiling, wishing she could go backward in her life and do things differently, the same way he did. Maybe they were alike in that. He listened harder, but the house was silent.

Chapter 22

The next morning, the day she was supposed to go home, Charlotte's coughing woke her. She tried to sit up, but the room began to spin, so she flopped back down. She never got sick, because she couldn't afford to. Her entire time at Brandeis, she swallowed vitamins every morning, because missing a class would be a disaster for her and she couldn't count on anyone else's scribbled notes to save her. She'd never go to the student health clinic, either, because they made you wait for hours and then the strongest thing they gave you was aspirin. She ran a hand along her forehead. Hot.

She dragged herself out of bed, and the whole room seemed to be wobbling. Make yourself well, she told herself. How many times had she been in bed feeling sick when she knew she had to get up and go to class? She had splashed cold water on her face and slid on a dress and shoes, and she had managed to hold it together until she could come back to her dorm room and sleep it off.

She pulled on her jeans and a T-shirt, sweating. She would get juice. Coffee. She stumbled out into the kitchen, and as soon as she saw Patrick cleaning the dishes in the sink, she felt embarrassed. Who wanted someone sick in your house, spreading germs everywhere? She reached up a hand to smooth back her hair, and her legs noodled under her. She gripped the edge of the wall, and Patrick turned at the noise and saw her.

"Hey," Patrick said. "Hey, hey."

"I'm fine," she insisted, and then she took a step toward him, and the world blurred into a white cone.

SHE FLOATED, HALLUCINATING in fever, burning up the bed, so that the sheets were soaked in sweat. She didn't always feel her body, which seemed to glide away from her and then return with a sickening bump.

She felt someone sitting beside her, but she couldn't open her eyes. She strained until she caught a voice. Patrick. He was telling her about how when he was a little boy, he had begged his father for a baseball uniform, but it was too expensive. "I need it," he kept saying, and finally his dad bought it for him. He couldn't wait to wear it to school, to show it off, but when the big day came, the other kids snickered at him. They made fun, and one kid deliberately kicked Patrick so he fell in the mud. He never wanted to wear the uniform after that, but he had to pretend that he did because his father had spent so much money on it.

She wanted to laugh, to tell him how sorry she was, but she couldn't get her mouth to move. Her eyes seemed glued shut. She struggled to speak. "What day is this? My job . . . ," she rasped.

"It's Sunday. August sixteenth. You've been sick with the flu for two weeks. Tell me the name. I'll call them. You're not going anywhere."

She gave him the number and he called right from her bed. "That's so kind of you," he said, and he hung up.

"Am I fired?" she whispered.

"He's a good guy. He said to take all the time you need."

She fell back on the pillow. "Please. Talk more," she said.

He told her about this guy Dylan from the commune where he had lived, and how he did nothing but crochet these god-awful ponchos in rainbow yarn, but no one wanted to hurt his feelings, so they all wore them. He told her about the first time he saw Lucy, how he had thought she might be a runaway. And then he told her more about Vera. How it had been his fault.

Patrick, she said, it wasn't your fault. But no sound came out of her mouth.

"I had a friend who's a doctor come to see you."

What doctor? she thought. She couldn't remember anything.

She felt thinner, more compact under the covers, and her hand found her ribs. She tried to get up again, and the room lost focus.

"Lie back down," he told her. "Sleep this thing off a few more days. Just because there's no fever doesn't mean you can get up."

When he left her room, he kept the door slightly open, which she found reassuring. She sank down under the comforter, her eyes rolling shut. Patrick. She wanted to call to him to stay beside her. Patrick.

The whole time she was sick, she'd wake and see signs that he had been there. A tray of tomato soup and Goldfish crackers sat on the end table. There was ginger ale with ice clinking in the glass. An extra blanket put over her. Clean sheets. And most miraculously, she was always in dry, clean nightclothes—tie-dyed shirts and sweatpants—which meant he must have gotten her into them, which made her feel more relief than embarrassment. She vaguely remembered a doctor, a man hovering over her, saying something, and then she fell into a swamp of dreams again. She was a bird flying, landing on a boat in the middle of the ocean, her feathers falling from her. She was running in a field, calling for Lucy. She was at Brandeis, her hair in an Afro, her fist raised, taking over a building. Her fever blazed through her. Patrick's voice wound around her. She remembered only bits of what he said. Something about riding a horse up a mountain, and the horse started to tumble over the edge. Something about learning to ride a motorcycle, so vivid she felt the air rushing past her. It didn't matter what he said, really. She just liked his voice, like a life raft she could hold on to. She didn't have to do anything or be anything but here, getting well. When she felt him leaving the room, a breeze floated past her. The air seemed to dim.

THIS TIME WHEN she woke, her inner furnace was gone. The sheets felt cool and dry, and so did she. She was in a purple T-shirt and a pair of drawstring pajama pants—not her own clothing. Patrick must have changed her again. He must have seen her naked, and she felt suddenly strange and unmoored.

She found she could hoop her legs out of the bed and stand, wobbling a little, like a colt. The room was clean, a window open so that the summer air came in. She could hear bees outside, and she changed into her own T-shirt and jeans, which now hung at her hips because she had lost weight. The ring she wore fell off her finger onto the floor, and she scooped it back up. Ah, the fever diet, she thought.

She wandered into the kitchen. Patrick was shucking green beans, the light coming in through the window like a halo around his head. He looked at her and beamed, which made her suddenly shy.

"Thank you," she said. "For taking care of me." She swallowed. "What day is it today?"

"Wednesday."

"My job—"

"I took care of it. I called your boss back and gave him an update. He said, don't come back and get the animals sicker than they already are. And he laughed when he said it."

"He made a joke? He never makes jokes."

"Well, he did this time."

"Iris—I need to call Iris. She must be frantic."

"I hope you don't mind, but I looked in your purse for an address book. I called her and told her you were getting over a flu."

"You called Iris?" Charlotte tried to imagine it, what Iris must have thought about her staying with a man.

"She was happy for the update."

"I'll do a laundry. I'll clean up. Make it up to you."

"Don't be silly. There's nothing to make up," he said.

"I'll do it anyway," she said. "Then I'll head home."

She stripped the bed, but there wasn't anything else to do. He had washed her clothes and put them in a neat pile on the chair. She picked up Lucy's journal and leafed through it to the end, to the blank pages. Every place Lucy had mentioned, Charlotte had already visited. There was only one more place to go, and it wasn't in these pages. It wasn't even a place where Lucy had been, and Charlotte didn't think she had the courage. There was nowhere else to go. Nothing more to find. At least not here.

"Wait out the weekend," Patrick said. "Take it easy. Your job will be there, and so will Iris." He was looking at her strangely, and it felt different between them.

She agreed to stay, just for a couple of days. She got used to being back on her feet. She hung out at the stand and watched Patrick work. He got down on his knees and hand-weeded with his crew, his hair held back in a ponytail, and she could hear them all laughing. Once, he gave free apples to all the little kids. Another time, a man was short five dollars, and Patrick waved his hand and said, "Oh, you can pay me next time, don't worry about it."

A woman in a minidress, her red hair spilling over her shoulders, strode over to Patrick and said something to him that made him laugh. He dipped his head toward the woman. Her smile matched his, and Charlotte dropped a few of the peaches she was arranging and bent to grab them up. He had taken care of her when she was sick. It didn't mean anything, and it was stupid of her to even imagine that it did. If she was the kind of person who took every kindness to mean something other than that someone was just being nice to her, then she was really in trouble. Besides, was she feeling this about him just because Lucy had? Did she want him because Lucy hadn't been able to get him? She looked up again, and the woman in the minidress was scribbling something on a piece of paper and handing it to Patrick, who folded his fingers over it and smiled.

Well. There you had it. And why shouldn't he take someone's number? She swallowed her jealousy. Patrick suddenly looked up and saw her, and she couldn't read what was in his face, so she abruptly turned and went back into the house to call Iris, to tell her she was coming home in a few days.

This time, Iris's line rang and rang. She glanced at her watch. It was two in the afternoon. Where could she be? Lunch was over, and dinner wasn't served until five. It was the third time in a week that this had happened. She hung up and called the front desk. "I'm worried about my mother, Iris," she said. "She hasn't been answering her phone. It's not like her."

"Why, she's probably busy," the woman at the desk said. "You should be so happy about it."

"Please, can you just check on her? See if she's in her room? Room two thirty-four?" Charlotte imagined Iris slumped on the couch. Or, good God, what if she had fallen in the shower? Women Iris's age had heart attacks. They had strokes. Or sometimes they simply died. "I need to know she's all right." Charlotte heard her voice quicken.

"Okay, honey. Hang on a sec."

Music blared in her ears, and five minutes later the woman

came back. "She's not in her room," she said. "But I'm sure she's fine."

"Can you leave her a message that I called?" Charlotte said. "And wait—can you tell her I love her?"

"Sure, I will, honey."

"And can you check on her again this evening? See if she's in her room?"

Charlotte heard the woman sigh, but she didn't care. Iris was paying a small fortune to be in this place. They could check on her.

Charlotte hung up the phone and went to look for Patrick. She found him by the basil plants, pruning the leaves.

"My mother's not answering her phone, and I'm worried."

He nodded. "So you have to go home?"

He stood up. He was so close she could see the shadows his lashes made on his cheeks. "I think I do. But there's one more place I have to see," she said. "Will you come with me?"

THAT NIGHT THEY took his car, and the closer they got, the more her breath seemed trapped in her body. Patrick slowed to the parking area below the walkway of the bridge where William had jumped. As soon as they were on the bridge, she felt a hot wire of rage. It was a gorgeous early evening. People ambled along the walkway, holding hands, standing at the rails, and taking in the water. A mother was pulling her son away from the railing. All she could think about was William, coming here at night, when the bridge was all lit up. *You did this. You did this.* She hated him for killing her sister, for leaving her there, swimming in blood, for not turning himself in. He had come here, a coward.

"We don't have to do this," Patrick said. "We can go back in the car."

She looked across the expanse of bridge. "I think I have to," she said. They walked until they were about a third across, not speaking, and then she moved to the railing and looked down at the water. A boat was cruising by beneath them. A few waves churned. All this water went out to sea.

The boat was gone. The water was still moving. Anyone who had jumped from this height into the water would have been killed instantly. It wouldn't have mattered how good a swimmer you were, how crafty a plan you might have. William would never have survived this. Fool that she was, she had thought seeing this would make her feel a release, but instead it all became more vivid.

"I hope it hurt him," she whispered, and Patrick took her hand and covered it with his. "Come on," he said. "Let's go."

Chapter 23

That night, after Charlotte was asleep, Patrick went to the kitchen and poured himself some wine. He wished that they hadn't gone on that bridge, that he hadn't seen all that water and imagined William jumping into it. He kept drinking until he knew he was drunk. He thought of the woman who had given him her number at the farm stand. Shelley Kostner. She was a librarian and he liked her, but the whole time he was talking to her he kept glancing over at Charlotte, the way she glided through the aisles of the stand, the way she tilted her head up when she was thinking. He imagined Charlotte's hair, rich and dark as chocolate, her full, pretty mouth, her straight nose, like a Modigliani. How he wanted to touch it, to touch her. He took another drink. Charlotte was leaving tomorrow, and she had no more reasons to come back, which meant he had no real reason to be thinking about her. Better to think about Shelley Kostner.

He hadn't wanted to be a monk. He had dared to think that there might be another woman in his life, that he might be happy again, or maybe it was just that he thought another woman would cover the pain he felt because of Vera. He had tried. He went to parties and bars, and women came up to him and talked, and sometimes a woman seemed kind and funny, and for a moment, possibility glinted in front of him, and then he would think about bringing her home, but he couldn't quite do it, not until one night, when he found himself talking until three in the morning in a bar with a woman named Sandy. She was a third-grade teacher with a shock of black hair cut into a pixie and big black eyes, and the more he talked to her, the happier he felt. She told him knock-knock jokes that made him laugh, not because they were so funny, but because of the delight she took in them. *Knock, knock. Who's there? Cash. Cash who? No, thank you, I'd like an almond instead.* Her laugh was like a peal of bells. He asked her home with him, she spent the night, and it was sweet and warm, and he fell asleep with an arm around her. He woke in the middle of the night, and she was up, too, and they went into the kitchen to have tea, and she asked him about Vera, and he felt so relaxed he told her. But as soon as he did, he wished he could bite back the words. Her eyes filled with tears. She reached across and took his hand, clamping it in hers. "You know why I love that story?" she said. "Because if you've had one great love, to me it means you can have another."

She took him to her place, a sad little efficiency by a railroad track, with a chipped tile floor and a crack racing along the ceiling. She waved her hand. "I never bothered to fix it up because I figured I'm getting married someday, so why bother?" She smiled at him. "I could fit my whole place in your living room just about," she said. "Think of the money we could save if we lived together."

She kept pressing. "What can I say? It's lonely living alone," she told him, and it made him feel that he could be anyone, and he stopped calling her.

For two weeks after that, he dated a second-grade teacher named Betsy, and at first he thought it might work because she was so happy all the time that it made him feel good to be around her. But then one night, his wedding anniversary, he couldn't hide his sorrow. He told her briefly what was going on, and she sighed.

"You know, happiness is a choice," she said.

"Excuse me?"

"You have to take control," she told him. "You can't let yourself sink into the mire or you'll stay there." She nuzzled against him. "I bet I know how to cheer you up," she said. She reached for his zipper, and he caught her hand.

She pulled back. "I've had enough sadness in my life," she said. "I don't think I need more. I need to be around someone with positivity."

After that, he stopped trying to date. He told himself that if something was going to happen, it would happen like a surprise. He didn't think about the future anymore. When he had lived on the commune, people were always talking about how there was no future because there was no time, and it had comforted him, though he didn't really believe it at all. The only thing he knew for sure was that things could happen suddenly and it was better to brace yourself for the ride. Maybe he'd find someone to be in a relationship with when he was old. Maybe it would be great to have a companion instead of a soul mate, and he would make his peace with that. It might be nice to have someone sharing his bed, his kitchen. Or maybe he wouldn't ever have that. Maybe he'd stay right here and build up the farm stand some. Maybe all you got from life was that one little sliver of brilliance, and the light from that happiness had to shine across your whole life. But wasn't he lucky to have had it at all? To have had a love like that?

It was two in the morning, and Patrick couldn't sleep. He went to the bathroom and splashed water on his face, and then he passed Charlotte's room. Charlotte hadn't asked him for anything except that one night when she asked him to go to the bridge with her. She didn't want him to rescue her. She wanted to rescue Lucy.

Her door wasn't completely shut, and he glanced in. She slept so funny. Her head was on the side of the bed, her legs were sticking out on the other side, and she was tangled in blanket. The whole time she was sick with flu, he had sat by her bed, keeping watch. She had soaked through the sheets and the T-shirts she was sleeping in, and he knew he had to change her clothes. He had to see her naked. He had carefully undressed her, as quickly as he could, as if he were a doctor himself, gently cooling her body down with a cloth, putting her in his nightclothes, and then positioning her under the covers. She moaned, feverish. Her hair kept falling in her face, so he got a rubber band and piled the hair on top of her head, startled to see how high and lovely her forehead was, how small her ears. He had called his doctor friend, Gus, the second she had collapsed, and made him come out and take a look at her. "Simple flu," Gus said, but Patrick knew illness was never simple. He had watched over Charlotte and had made Gus come back to check on her when she hadn't moved in four hours. "She's sleeping. That's what she needs to do, doofus," Gus told him. "Let her heal."

He had sat by her bed, reading to her at first, and then he began to tell her stories about his childhood, about meeting Vera, about leaving school. She never responded, but it still felt good to tell her.

He was drunk now. And Charlotte was well. He walked away from her room. Being drunk was the only reason he was thinking about kissing her, the only reason he remembered seeing the slight, perfect swell of her breasts, the curve of her bare hips. Or maybe it was because he knew she was leaving, going back to Brandeis soon, to her other life. It was easy to want things when you knew you couldn't have them.

He stood in the kitchen, rummaging in one of the cabinets,

pulling out another bottle of wine. He'd have just one more glass and then maybe he could sleep, too.

He got out the corkscrew and it flew from his fingers, and when he turned to pick it up, she was there in the doorway, in one of his white T-shirts, which grazed the bottom of her thighs. He didn't bother to hide the bottle of wine or the glass, and he waited for her to say something about it, but instead she picked up the bottle and the corkscrew and got a glass and poured herself some wine and drank it down. He watched her. His heart was racing too fast. His breath was too thin. He was caught in a dream. Her skin seemed lit from within, her mouth was impossibly lush, and he wanted to touch her stomach, her breasts, the small of her back. He wanted to touch her face, to inhale her, and then she walked toward him, stumbling, as if she were still asleep, and she pressed her mouth against his, and he was kissing her back.

IN THE MORNING, he bolted awake in his bed, the light streaming in. His head was thick with a hangover, and his mouth felt as if it had sprouted mushrooms. He turned to get up, to make coffee, and then he saw her, naked and asleep beside him, her mouth faintly open, and he jolted out of bed. What the fuck had he done? He had been drunk, and she had been upset, and then there was all that wine.

He carefully got up, quietly pulling on his jeans and his T-shirt, and then he went into the kitchen. He got out eggs, and bread for toast, thinking food might settle his stomach. He opened a window. He thought of her smooth, flat belly, the curve of her hip, and he swallowed and forced himself to consider the coffee he was making, the eggs. Normal things that would put the world back into order.

• • •

SHE CAME INTO the kitchen, in a T-shirt and shorts, her feet bare, and he cut his glance from her. He didn't want to see the arch of her back, her long, graceful legs. "Patrick?" she said. "Is this all too weird?" He didn't know what to say to her. Of course it was. She was Lucy's sister. When he tried to speak, the words were frozen in his mouth. She came over and rested her head against his shoulder, and he couldn't help it. His hands found her hair.

It didn't matter what he did or didn't want. She'd go back to work and then, in September, back to school. She'd have her pick of smart, ambitious guys in a big, burly city where anything might be possible for her, and he'd become a story she'd tell her friends, the grad-school dropout who ran a farm stand in the middle of nowhere. The guy still pining for his dead wife. After a while he'd turn into a memory for her and not a person, one she wouldn't want to keep thinking about because all of it was soaked in Lucy. He pulled away from her.

"I know this is crazy," she said. "I'm not sure how I feel about any of it, and I bet you're the same, right?"

"It's weird," he admitted.

Her shoulders rose. "Come back with me." She swallowed. "We can spend some time in Boston. See how things go."

"I don't know if that's a good idea."

"It's a wonderful idea. Your staff can easily watch the stand for a few days, right? You can explore Boston, meet me for lunch. We'll have our evenings."

"We've known each other only a little while."

"Doesn't it feel like longer to you? Don't you feel you know all you need to know?"

"Charlotte—"

"Maybe there's more to find out right in Waltham. I could go talk to Diana again. You could come with me."

"That's a horrible idea."

"Why is it horrible? She was so quick to get me out of her house. Maybe there's something she wasn't telling."

"She wanted you out because you reminded her that her son is gone. You can't always make things be the way you want them to be. Believe me, I know. You have to stop this."

"I have to find out what really happened."

"You know what really happened. What did it get you, coming here, going to William's school, going to the bridge? Did you learn anything new? Did it bring Lucy closer to you?"

"Shut up. Please shut up."

"You're chasing so many ghosts you're in danger of becoming one. You know you can't fix it. Some things just stay fucked and you have to deal with it."

"Like you deal with Vera?" she said, and he flinched, as if she had punched him. "You're the one chasing a ghost, not me."

She dug her hands into her pockets. "Fine. Okay, if you won't go, then I can come back."

"Charlotte, I don't think I'm looking for a relationship. Especially not a long-distance one."

"I don't understand. What was last night, then? Was that just a moment?"

"We were both drinking. It was something that happened."

"No. No, I've had times like that, and this wasn't one of them."

"How do you know?"

"Because I feel it. Because I know you."

"No, you don't. Not really."

"Go ahead and think that, but we both know that isn't true. I know you're hiding out here. I know you drink, and Lucy knew it, too. I know that you can't let go of Vera, that you won't let yourself because you're full of blame. You think I'm wrong to keep asking questions about Lucy, to try to piece together the life she was living, to visit all the places she might have been. You think that's a waste of time, and that I'm obsessed and acting crazy, but at least I have a goal. At least I'm doing something."

"And there's nothing more to do."

"How do you know that?"

"Because I've seen you trying."

She sank against the wall. "I was too late," she said quietly.

"For what?"

"I should have come sooner. And I didn't. I didn't know how bad things were. She called me to come get her, and I knew she could be a drama queen, expecting me to drop everything and do what she wanted. I was scared of losing my job. I didn't go until the next morning, and look what happened." She rubbed her eyes. "Please don't look at me like that. I know what I did."

His stomach was sour from all the wine. He met her eyes and held them. "You still came. You still drove out to get her. That's what matters."

"No, it doesn't."

"Look, I could have taken my car and driven her back to Waltham. I could have immediately called the police when I thought something was off. But I didn't. Don't you think I wish I had?"

She was quiet for a minute. "I wish you had, too. I can't lie about that."

"Well, I was too late, too. When Vera was sick. I was busy with school and wasn't paying attention. She wanted to go see a doctor, and I said it was just stress, because we had so many bills, and she agreed with me. What does that say about the way I loved her?" As soon as he said it out loud, he felt himself sinking.

"Why is Vera's death your fault? Why isn't it Vera's?"

He looked at her, astonished. "You're blaming Vera?"

"She could have gone to a doctor on her own. She could have taken care of herself. That makes her responsible."

"I think you should stop talking," he said. "I think you need to stop right now."

"Really? Are you sure? Why was it all up to you? Why were you the one who had to take on all the burdens? Make all the decisions? She was an adult. Why didn't she take care of herself?"

"I could say the same about you and Lucy."

"Oh, really. Lucy was my *baby* sister. I practically brought her up. I watched out for her because she sure as hell couldn't watch out for herself. I was the one who was supposed to be looking out for her, not you. I fucked up. She called me! Lucy called me! If I had gotten here sooner, if I had come when she called—"

"Jesus! You can't control everything!"

"Neither can you! So Lucy wouldn't let you help her. How were you supposed to know what was going to happen next? So Vera was really sick and you didn't know that, but you didn't cause it. It wasn't your fault."

He shook his head. "This is crazy. We don't understand each other."

"Yes, we do—"

"You think what we have is a relationship? You think we owe each other something? We're thrown together because of a horrible tragedy, and you think either one of us is undamaged enough to have a bond?"

"I think you like me. And I like you."

"I do like you—"

"I said that wrong." She sucked in a breath. "I think maybe you more than like me. And I think the real reason you won't leave with me is that then you'd have to admit that you actually might be capable of loving someone else, and that terrifies you because of what you lost."

"You're crazy. What is this, something you learned in your psychology class?"

"You have to let it go—you have to open yourself up. Tell me that what I'm saying isn't true. Tell me this isn't all about protecting yourself, that you aren't starting to have real feelings for me. I can admit it, even though it scares me, too."

"I'm not protecting myself," he said, but he wasn't looking at her.

"You just said that you are with your body language, the way you jumped out of bed so quickly this morning, the way you're sitting there so rigid you might as well have steel bars in all your bones. You don't let yourself feel your feelings. You just—"

"Charlotte, for Christ's sake!" When she tried to touch him, he jerked away. "You think you get to finish what Lucy started? That I couldn't love her but I'll love you? You think we're going to save each other, is that it? Rewrite the script and get a happy ending? It doesn't work that way."

"So what happens to us, then?" she said.

"You go to Boston and I go back to work. That's what happens."

"Are you serious?"

"It's not real. It's built out of Lucy, our grief. It was a moment—a lovely moment—but now it's time to get back to our lives. Mine is here, and yours is in Boston."

"A moment? Is that what you think? Is this all you want? You have this little life here, this little job, this little heart—"

"You don't think you have a little life, too?" he said. "Always taking care of everyone else, using that as an excuse not to really focus on yourself, on what you want. Not to risk anything."

"I'm telling you how I feel about you. You think that's not a risk?"

"You want something I can't give you."

"Really?" she said. "Say you don't have any feelings for me. Go ahead. Say it."

She had her arms folded around her body, as if any moment she might fly away. Her hair was falling into her eyes, and he wanted to brush it away, but what good would that do? Instead he jammed his hands into his pockets. "I don't have any feelings for you," he said.

She turned and went back to the bedroom, and he could hear her zipping her bag. He heard her in the bathroom, in the cabinet, the clink of bottles. He put his head in his hands, but he didn't move until he saw her, now dressed, striding outside into the blistering morning heat, and then he went outside, too. She got into her car and put the key in the ignition. He didn't call out her name or tell her to stop, and she didn't look at him as she pulled out onto the road.

AT FIRST, AFTER she was gone, it was a relief. He took all the sheets and towels and threw them in the laundry and then he cleaned so that the house smelled of lemon polish instead of her. His place suddenly felt too big. Everything felt different, as if a layer of life had been pulled away. Now he wouldn't be able to look at the kitchen table without remembering Charlotte drinking tea. He wouldn't be able to sit on the porch without thinking of her sitting beside him. He wouldn't be able to lie in his own bed.

Well, now she was just another person to miss.

ALL THE REST of the month, he kept busy at the stand. And then it was the end of August. It was too hot to hand-weed now, but he had to do it. At work, when he needed the ledger, he called her name until he remembered she was gone. Customers asked for her. "Where's that nice young woman?" one woman said. "Oh, I'm so disappointed. She promised to give me her recipe for peach muffins." At night he went through a bottle of wine on his porch before he was drugged enough to sleep. And then he dreamed that Charlotte was there, whispering something in his ear that he couldn't quite hear.

He bolted awake, rubbing his hands across his face. Soaked in sweat, he went to the dresser and pulled open a drawer for a clean shirt, and there was the photo of Vera and him on the beach. She was, so alive. So beautiful he couldn't believe his luck that she had loved him. That he had got to love her. He could remember the smell of that day, the salt in the air, the dazzling heat. If he shut his eyes, he could bring that day back, he could feel her behind him, the past nipping right at his heels. He had read that the reason there were ghosts was that the living tethered them to life, that the dead lingered not because they needed closure but because the living did. And the living needed to do only one thing for the dead: let them go. And they could never do it.

A jab of pain hit him, flowering into anger.

He went to the kitchen and got a bottle of wine and opened it. He was halfway through it when he started crying. He stood up, his legs shaking. Vera used to tell him that if he died, she'd live a horrible, haunted life, and at the time he had loved her for saying that. It had sounded so romantic. But grief wasn't romantic. He thought of being an old man, sitting on this porch alone, remembering the one great love he had once had. The little life he had now. That's what Charlotte had called it.

Charlotte was so young. If they had stayed together, he would have ended up being her project, and he couldn't do that to her. She was the kind who needed full-on, uncomplicated love, the kind of love that he had had with Vera. Charlotte could never have that with him because he no longer trusted it.

He walked into the bedroom, swigging from the bottle, and

went to the box in the closet that held Vera's jewelry and some
of her clothes. The wine was old and sour with vinegar, but he
gulped it anyway. He took out the silver rings he had bought
her, the bracelets she had bought herself. He gathered up the
blue flowered dress that was her favorite and held it to his face.
It didn't smell like her anymore. It was just cloth.

He thought of Charlotte tromping from one place to another, hurtling through Lucy's past, even though she was hurting as much as he was, and nowhere she went ever made her
feel better or gave her any information that might help her, but
she kept going anyway, and he didn't know whether that was
brave or stupid, but at least it was hope. He thought of Vera's
parents, what it must have cost them to lose their only daughter. To lose him, too, though that had been their doing.

He dug deeper into the box and pulled out the notes and letters he and Vera had passed in school, the letter she had written
to him on their wedding day, promising him all sorts of things.
I will never hog the covers. I will always hold your hand. There
was a letter from Vera's parents. They had written him one,
too, for that day, and they had read it out loud at the reception.
You are our son. We will always love you as our own.

But they hadn't. At first they had gathered with him in sorrow, but then he had felt them both separating from him, a
gulf opening between them. There were all those questions, the
endless hammering. Why didn't you know? Why didn't you do
something? And he couldn't tell them the truth. They had shut
him out when he needed them the most, blaming him, acting
as though it were all his fault. And of course, it was. And he
needed to own up to it. He hadn't helped Vera when he could
have. He hadn't helped Lucy. He was a tiny piece of the whole
equation, but this was one way he could own up to his part,
take responsibility.

Maybe Charlotte was right, and his life was a lie. All this

time, Vera's parents had thought it was his fault, and he had denied it. He hadn't told them that yes, she had been sick; yes, he had seen her symptoms and had done nothing about them; yes, he had told her she didn't need to see a doctor because he was so worried about their bills. He had lied to them because the truth was too terrible to bear. He had known that if he told them, he would lose them, that they would hate him. But that had happened anyway. He had been trying to figure out a way to live with all of this for years, and nothing had worked. You don't let yourself feel your feelings, Charlotte had said, but she hadn't realized how big his feelings were, how dangerous.

His hand shook. He was so drunk. He was so tired. He wanted to talk to Charlotte and explain himself, but he didn't know where she was right now, how he could reach her. He wanted to talk to Vera's parents. He was swimming through air. He picked up the phone and dialed Vera's parents' number, one he had called endless times, and when Vera's mother picked up the phone, her voice jolted him, and he hung up before she could.

He hadn't taken time off in years, but he could do that now. He had a whole staff who could run the stand. He could drive there in less than three hours. He could tell them the truth. He owed that to them. He could ask for forgiveness, though he knew he didn't deserve any. I can't leave, he had told Charlotte, and the look she gave him had made him feel impaled. Well, here he was, doing it.

Chapter 24

One day in July, while Charlotte was gone, Iris got tired of what she called waiting for the end. Every day was the same. She'd wake up and think: I'm still here. She'd go to bed early because there wasn't that much to do, and she'd try to count her blessings.

One evening, Iris came downstairs and noticed a man playing the piano, a bad rendition of *Moonlight* Sonata, but what caught her was how he didn't care that he flubbed notes, how it even made his smile beam more brightly. He flung his long white hair back dramatically, and she liked that, too. When he finished, he caught her eye and she walked over to him. "You play beautifully," she said. The words tumbled out.

"I'm Joe," he said. "And thank you." He got up and bowed and then glanced toward the front door. "I'm so sorry, but I have to go," he said, and he walked toward a group of people.

She began to notice him more and more. When he played the piano, she sat down and listened, and he always turned and smiled at her. "Any requests?" he said, and whatever she named—Beethoven, a little Bach—he played for her. A few times at dinner, she sat next to him. She was surprised how comfortable she felt with this Joe. She told him about Doug and Charlotte, but she couldn't bring herself to tell him about Lucy. He mentioned how he had three big, strapping sons, all of them lawyers at different firms. He liked all their wives and all their children, and he thought they liked him. "I don't ask or pry. I give them room, and that way, they tell me things," he said. "I'm just so lucky they all settled in Boston. What would I do if they were in California?"

"Then you'd be with them there," she said.

"Yes, I most certainly would."

Dinner was almost over. It had been another glutinous meal. Joe was getting up when Iris touched his arm. "Would you like to have dinner at my apartment tomorrow? Say, around six?" As soon as she said it, she felt stupid. She couldn't look him in the eye. He considered her, frowning, so that she began to think she might have made a mistake. "So, would you say that this is a date?" he asked.

She was about to tell him no, of course not. It was just two people sitting down, sharing a meal. But she was so tired of always having to make up a story, skirting around the truth, telling people that her eyes were red because of allergies. "Yes," she blurted out. "It's a date."

His smile widened. "I was hoping it was," he said.

THE FOLLOWING NIGHT, Iris stood at her stove, panicking. She had chicken breasts roasting in the oven and string beans frying in olive oil. She had made a salad with dark lettuce instead of iceberg and had thrown in some walnuts to make it different. Her little table was set with her good china and silverware, and she was wearing a rose-colored dress that Charlotte had bought her. She'd fixed her hair with a rhinestone barrette, which she hoped didn't look ridiculous. She kept looking at her watch, and then at the door, and once or twice she even opened it to peer down the hall, which was silent as a bottle.

What if he forgot and didn't show up at all? Or what if he changed his mind?

Or what if she had forgotten and he wasn't supposed to be coming tonight at all? She had been getting mixed up lately, forgetting her apartment number, once coming down to dinner at six in the morning. When she tried to figure out her checkbook, the numbers blurred. But everything always went back to normal within minutes. She found her apartment. She realized her dinner mistake and balanced her checkbook. It was just stress.

She told herself it didn't matter, she wouldn't care whether Joe came or not. She'd eat this fine dinner all by herself, thank you very much. And afterward she wouldn't pine in her room. She'd march downstairs and sit in the common room and read a book, as if that were just what she'd wanted to do all along, and if Joe happened to mosey by, she'd pretend that she had forgotten she'd asked him to dinner and that in any case it didn't matter to her one whit. She was about to peel off her apron and take his plate from the table when there was a knock on the door, and when she opened it, there he was, in a suit jacket, his hair combed back so she could see the rake marks from his comb. He handed her a glossy page from a magazine, a photograph of a roomful of roses. "I couldn't get to the store," he apologized, and she laughed, and then his whole body seemed to relax, and he laughed, too.

He insisted on helping her serve dinner. He poured them some wine. And when he put his fork down, she was pleased to see that he had eaten every bite of the chicken. "I've seen your daughter here," he told her. "First thing I thought was, Why, she's a beauty like her mother."

Iris flushed. Her hands flew to her hair. No one had called her beautiful since Doug.

Joe helped her do the dishes, washing while she dried and put the plates away, and the whole time, he kept talking, telling funny stories about all the places he'd visited: In Barcelona, they sold huge pig legs, called *jamón*, in all the supermarkets, complete with the black hooves. "Some Spaniards keep the leg in their kitchen, peeling off what they want," he told her. "Others kiss the damn thing for luck." In Istanbul, he had bartered in the Grand Bazaar for an embroidered pair of boots for his wife, and when he walked away because the price was too high, the vendor had run after him to make him a deal.

"Well, my world is smaller now," he said, and then he met her eyes. "Or maybe not."

She caught her breath. She could see from the windows that it was dark outside. Most of the residents were back in their rooms. Most went to bed ridiculously early, but here was Joe in her apartment, and all she could think about was that she wanted to kiss his mouth. How she wanted to lose herself. Just for half an hour. Just for a few minutes. All she dared hope for was to forget her life for a little while, to forget that she was in an old people's home, that Lucy, her little Lucy, was dead. Joe yawned and Iris felt her mouth grow dry. "Do you want to lie down?" she said. Her voice sounded tinny to her.

"Lie down?"

"We'll have a rest," she said carefully. She stood up, balling her hands into fists to stop her trembling, and then she walked into her bedroom and stretched out on the bed. Who knew what would happen? They might just lie together and talk. Or sleep.

The world was crazy now. Here she was in this place, and young kids, barely out of high school, were fighting and dying in a ridiculous war in Vietnam. They were burning their draft cards, and Iris didn't blame them. There were those horrible Manson murders, those crazy girls who worshipped him. She had read in the news that Manson had actually been able to pass Linda Kasabian a note in court, after she was given immunity. He was trying to charm her back into the family. "Love can never stop if it's love," he wrote. And there was free love. Wasn't that what Charlotte and Lucy had told her about? At the time, she had been shocked. How could you sleep with someone you barely knew? No one knew how long anything would last. This was crazy. She'd shame herself, and everyone in this place would gossip about it.

She didn't care. She had lost so much already.

She looked up, and Joe was easing himself onto the bed beside her. She grabbed his hand, her heat rocketing in her chest. A flame rose in her cheeks, but she didn't care: Just a little while. Just let me have this for a little while.

He cupped her face in his hands to kiss her. Would he know that her top teeth were a dental bridge? Would he care? Were his teeth his own? He held her hand, and she suddenly wished she had turned out the lights, because the darkness would be more forgiving. "It's been a really long time for me," Iris said.

"For me, too."

He took her hand and placed it on his chest. She thought of the times she had been with Doug. They had loved each other, but kissing had felt unnatural with him, as disappointing as a torn sock. And no wonder. As soon as she discovered he loved men, they stopped having sex altogether. Who needed it? she had thought. She had grown content with his companionship, but now, here beside Joe, she wanted to rip off her clothes. She wanted to feel her bare skin against his, and it scared her a little.

When he leaned over and kissed her mouth, she felt a shock of need. She kissed his neck and he turned toward her, and then she carefully took off her dress and she felt his eyes on her. She knew how many flaws her clothing masked. Her skin was tissue, her veins popped out, and nothing was really in the place where it used to be. "I'm sorry," she said to Joe.

"For what?" Joe said.

"For not being twenty," she said. "You should have seen me when I was young."

"I see you now."

"I'm eighty years old." As soon as she said that, she felt astounded, because how could that be?

"I always liked younger women," he said. "I'm eighty-two."

He kissed her again and she felt a jolt, as if this was something she had been waiting for and she hadn't even known it. He sat up and took off his shirt, and then his pants, letting them fall to the floor. She saw him suck in his belly, the same way she was holding in hers, and it made her like him more. His hands were shaking, and she reached over and kissed his palms. "I don't know if all my parts are in working order still," she said.

"I don't know about mine, either," he said.

He lowered himself over her and gently kissed her shoulder, the curve of her neck, the hollow behind her knee. "Is this all right?" he kept asking, as if he needed permission. His breathing grew ragged. He wasn't fully hard, but she guided him into her. His eyes were open. He was looking at her, searching her face. He cares about me already, she thought, as if she were a young girl. She started to cry, and he pulled away, alarmed. "I'll stop," he said.

"No, no, please—" She had never felt so bold, so wanted. She moved so he was deeper inside her. She felt her whole body blazing like Christmas lights.

AFTERWARD SHE LAY against him, unable to speak. When she looked at him, his eyes were damp with tears. "Are you all right?" she asked, alarmed. "Did I do something wrong?"

He kissed her nose, the tip of her chin. "Sleep," he said, facing her, pulling her closer.

WHEN SHE WOKE, the light was streaming into the bedroom. For a moment she forgot where she was, and then she turned around and Joe was there and he was smiling. "Come on. Let's cause a scandal and go to breakfast together," he said.

She got up, wrapping the sheet around her, and padded into the bathroom. She studied her face in the mirror. The puppet lines around her mouth seemed to have softened. Her lips looked fuller, richer, as if they didn't need the color she always painted on every morning. Love. What it did to a person.

They walked downstairs together, and when they got to the dining room, he took her hand, and she saw the other residents looking at them, felt their hot stares. Let her give them something to talk about. She kissed him right at breakfast, over the soggy French toast, which had never tasted more delicious.

After that, they had a routine. Mornings were the hardest times for her because she would wake and for a minute she wouldn't understand why she wasn't in her home, why she was in this apartment, and then it would come back to her. Lucy dead. Charlotte getting over the flu in Pennsylvania. Iris was so old she didn't recognize herself anymore. But before she sank under the covers in despair, there would be a knock on her door, and she would hear his voice, like a lasso. "Good morning, honey," he'd say, when she let him in, and she would throw her arms around him in gratitude. He escorted her to breakfast, and then they would see whatever movie the place was showing, and Iris never paid attention because she was simply basking in having Joe beside her, the feeling of her hand in his. Sometimes, if it was a nice day, they'd walk outside, around the perimeter of the building. Evenings, she cooked him dinner, and they sat on her couch and talked or read, her feet in his lap. And nights. Oh, the nights. She shivered just thinking of them.

The only time it was hard for her was when his family came to visit on Sundays. It was difficult enough to see the complex filled with family, but because it was Joe's family, it made it more personal to her. But she still couldn't bring herself to tell him about Lucy, to let him know just how much she had failed her daughter.

Three handsome grown-up sons and their wives and kids came to be with Joe for the day. Their faces lit up when they saw him. This wasn't just a visit that they had to make. They loved him. As soon as she saw that abundance, she felt nothing but loss. She wanted to have Lucy there flinging her arms around her, the way Joe's grandson was with Joe. She wanted to clap her hands to her ears so she wouldn't hear Joe asking his granddaughter Pearl about her art classes, wanting to know how she liked using the oil paints he had bought her compared with watercolors. Iris watched the way his grandchildren ran to him, all of them in big wide bell-bottoms, the girls in puckered tube tops and those noisy, uncomfortable-looking clogs, and the way he held on to them with delight. It all made Iris's heart ache with longing. Lucy would never have children.

Joe's family warmed to her, including her in their chitchat, talking about Tricky Dick Nixon, and the best restaurants in Boston, and that new food, sushi, and how the heck you were supposed to eat it, because it wouldn't stay on your fork and it was too big for chopsticks, and why the Red Sox were the best team in the United States.

One day they all insisted that Iris accompany them to Legal Sea Foods for dinner. Joe beamed at her, and all those faces turned to her like sunflowers. "That's so kind, but I'll let you have this time to yourselves," Iris said, because all she wanted to do was go back to her apartment and shut the door.

"Don't be silly," Joe's son told her. "You're important to Dad, you're important to us."

Iris looked at Joe. How lucky he was to have this fine, beautiful family, but if she went to dinner, she'd take Lucy with her. She wouldn't be able to concentrate on anything anyone was saying, because all her energy would be going into hiding her misery. Plus, what if they started asking her questions and they found out that she was the mother of the murdered girl they had surely heard about? Then Joe would know she'd been hiding this from him.

"I think I'll bow out of dinner, too, then," Joe said, but Iris touched his elbow. She didn't want him giving up a minute of his family for her. She knew how quickly it could be taken away from you.

"You go," she urged. "I have some leftover chicken that'll go bad if I don't eat it tonight. I'll see you later."

She practically pushed him out the door. His face crumpled, but if she dared to speak, she knew she'd cry, so she just waved him away. As they left, one of his sons took Joe's arm, and she felt suddenly sick, because that's what Lucy had always done in the winter when Iris was in danger of slipping on the ice.

While he was gone, she restlessly moved through the apartment complex, crying. How could Lucy be dead while Iris was still alive? How did that make any kind of sense? Suddenly none of her life felt true. Not this apartment instead of her house. Not a young girl senselessly murdered.

She couldn't sit still, so she went down to the piano and she began to practice the piece Joe had taught her, Beethoven's *Moonlight* Sonata. Her fingers stroked the keys, but the notes sounded sour, the melody listless. A few people came to listen. "Not ready for Carnegie Hall yet," someone said, and Iris stopped playing. She got up and went to her room to wait for him.

It was ten when he came to her room. "What was that about, Iris?" he said quietly. "You don't like my family? You don't want to know them?" His mouth twitched but she couldn't tell whether he was angry.

She felt the punch of tears welling up again and shook her head. "That's not it," she said. He came and sat beside her, his mouth a line. "Then maybe you should tell me," he said.

What would he do if she told him? Would he be disappointed that she had lied? Would he be shocked? And didn't she have to take that chance? If she said nothing, he'd pull away from her.

"My other daughter was recently murdered. She was seventeen," she said finally.

She heard his sharp intake of breath, but he moved closer to her, and then she told him the whole story, and when she was finished, he had both arms around her, as if he were keeping her from flying away from him.

"I'm here," he told her. She felt as if she had no more tears, but Joe was holding tight to her. He was like a door opening, showing her some light, and all she had to do was push it open a little more.

"Then I guess I'm here, too," she said, and she rested her head on his shoulder.

THE WEATHER GOT hotter, and then it was mid-August and Charlotte was coming home. Iris had worried so much when Charlotte was sick, and she still wondered about that young man who had called to tell her, but when she had asked Charlotte the last time they spoke on the phone, Charlotte had glossed over it. "He owned the hotel where I stayed," Charlotte said.

Well, Charlotte would be here this Friday night, when most people visited, and Iris had so much to tell her. And she wanted Joe to be there with her when she did.

A half hour later, Charlotte knocked on the door. "Oh, honey," Iris said, folding Charlotte into her arms. "I'm so glad to see you. So glad you're home." She stepped back. "Are you all right? It feels like you've been gone so long." She smoothed Charlotte's hair from her eyes. She saw Charlotte staring at Joe.

"This is Joe," Iris said. "You probably saw him before."

"Her boyfriend," Joe said.

Charlotte started. "What?" she said.

Joe beamed at Iris. "Your mother's like sunshine. I've never met anyone with such a joy of life. And I'm so happy to meet you." He held out his hand and she took it for a moment.

He got up and headed for the door. "Well, I'll leave you two alone. Iris, I'll see you later. Charlotte, it was a delight to meet you. I hope we can all have dinner together soon so I can get to know you better." He bent and kissed Iris good-bye.

After he left, Iris bustled in the kitchen, putting away the low-fat crackers Charlotte had brought her, the tins of tuna.

"I know what you're thinking," Iris said. "I'm too old. He's too old. It took me by surprise, too." Iris turned, a package of cheese in one hand, and looked at Charlotte. "He takes care of me," Iris said quietly. "We take care of each other. "

"Well, then, that's good." Charlotte moved as if she were dazed. She opened the refrigerator to put food away and saw that it was stuffed with juices and cheese and produce. "Where did this come from?"

"We walk to the supermarket. We plan meals together."

Charlotte shut the door and leaned against the counter. "No wonder you never picked up your phone."

"I'm just learning to live," Iris said.

"Do you want to hear about Pennsylvania?" Charlotte asked.

"Sit. Talk to me."

Charlotte told Iris about visiting all of Lucy's old haunts, about meeting the rude lady who lived in Lucy's old house. "I couldn't find out anything new," she said, and then she began to cry.

Iris put both arms around her. "There's nothing else we can

do. Don't go down there again." She smoothed Charlotte's hair. She felt the weight of her girl against her, the way Charlotte burrowed her head against Iris's shoulder as she had when she was little. Iris let her rest there, and when Charlotte finally pulled away, Iris wanted her back.

"All of this—" Charlotte said, wiping away tears. "Are you sorry you ever took us in?"

"Never. Not for one moment."

"Why did you? Did no one else want us?"

Charlotte was an adult now, Iris thought, a young woman. Didn't she deserve the truth, the way Joe did?

"Because I had to," Iris said. She saw the flash of hurt and anger in Charlotte's face. It would be so easy to brush it away, but she couldn't stop herself now.

"Why did you have to?" Charlotte asked, her voice flattening.

"Because—because we shared a father."

"What?" Charlotte's forehead bunched. She looked at Iris as if she didn't know her.

"Your father. He was my father, too."

"That's insane. How could that even be possible?"

"He had all these different wives after my mother, each one younger than the rest."

"Don't you think I would have known that? He never mentioned any other kids."

Iris flinched. "He was my dad, the same as he was yours," Iris said. "Except he left my family when I was little. He never wrote. He never called. He never sent money. He erased us. The last I heard of him was when he and your mother died. I never told anyone. It was too hurtful, and I certainly never wanted to tell you or Lucy. You were both so little. You both loved your parents. You were grieving. How could I tell you and spoil what love you had for him? Why shouldn't you continue to love your father, to think of him only in a good way?"

Charlotte's hand flew to her face. "We're half sisters? You and me?"

"We're blood," Iris said. "Does it change things for you? I bet it does."

Charlotte frowned. "Of course it does. You lied to me. For all these years. You lied to Lucy. What else are you lying about?"

Iris tried to touch Charlotte, but Charlotte jerked away from her.

"That's the only thing I've lied about. I'm so sorry. I should never have opened my mouth about this—"

But Charlotte was already gathering her things and heading for the door. She let it slam behind her.

IRIS SAT DOWN. So this is what can happen when you tell the truth, she thought. Joe had been so warm, so understanding, she had thought that Charlotte might be, too. Instead Iris had made things worse. All these years she had thought she was protecting the girls, and now she realized she had just been protecting herself, because here it was, that hot shame flowing over her, that terrible secret: My father didn't want me. Was that what it was all about, raising those girls, getting them to love her the way their father had not? Needing to be the parent she herself had always yearned for?

She told herself she'd give Charlotte time. She'd call her later, explain. She'd talk to Joe about it and see what he suggested. But an hour passed and then another, and finally Iris turned on the TV and stared at whatever was on, unable to concentrate. Just before dinner, she heard a knock on the door, and when she opened it, there was Charlotte. It looked as if she had been crying, because the little red birthmark on her face had appeared again. Iris opened her mouth, though she had no idea what to say, how to make this right, but Charlotte held up one hand. "Let me talk," she said.

Iris waited.

"I thought about it—all of it," Charlotte said. "I walked around and around, being angry, feeling cheated, and then I realized that I wasn't cheated at all. That I had a wonderful childhood. And that it doesn't matter what you call yourself. I don't care. I just know that you're my person, my family, my mother." And she stepped forward and sank into Iris's arms.

Chapter 25

That night, in her sublet, Charlotte cried. She realized how much it must have cost Iris to keep that secret, how terrible it was to have had a father who didn't want you. She cried, too, because Lucy would never know that Iris was her half sister, that Iris was in love. And she cried for Patrick, the way he had dismissed her.

She sobbed until the knot in her chest loosened and then she turned on the TV. There in the news were the Manson girls, the same ones Lucy wrote that she had been obsessed with. The girls camped outside the courtroom. They held hands and sang songs Charlie had written. "We're waiting for our father to be set free," they told reporters. "The girls worshipped him, just would die to do anything for him," Linda Kasabian said on trial. She switched the channel, and there was a protest at another university, a building blown up in Madison, killing a physics researcher. She turned the set off.

The next morning, Charlotte felt hungover from crying. She really knew who she was now. She knew who Iris was. But instead of feeling cheated, she felt a new clarity, as if the revelation of one truth could bring about more truth.

She had been about to give up her search for answers, but now she felt wired. She went outside into the steamy August heat and got into the car and drove to Diana's block. When she stopped at Diana's house, she saw that the curtains were drawn. There was no car in the drive. Without thinking, she got out. Her sneakers sank in the spongy grass lining the sidewalk.

She peered through the window, but the house was dark. She rang the bell, her heart pounding, but no one answered. As she turned to leave, she noticed the mailbox, open, stuffed with mail. Charlotte looked around the empty street and then back at the house, and then carefully, quietly, she slid out the mail. Bills, junk mail for a National Cheese Festival, and then a postcard, a beach scene that said WELCOME TO CALIFORNIA. The postmark was smeared, but it looked as if it was from Dennisport on the Cape. She turned it over, and there, like a shock, was William's handwriting—she recognized the slashed crossed *t*'s, the big loops, from his scrawling across the papers she'd written, which he'd never quite liked enough. *Think harder*, he always wrote to her. On the postcard it said: *Will try to see you soon. Much love.* There was no signature.

The postcard was shaking, and then she realized it was the tremble of her hands, and she tightened her grip. Iris had lied out of love, and maybe Diana had, too. She pocketed the card and got into her car.

AT HOME, SHE called the Pennsylvania police, but the officer she spoke to was uninterested. "This is no proof of anything. Anyone could have written this."

"I recognize his handwriting."

The cop sighed. "You know it's a federal offense to go through other people's mail, don't you?" he said, and Charlotte knew he'd be no help.

"Thanks for your time," she said.

She had the name of a town. She got her old yearbook, hidden at the back of a shelf, and opened it to the teacher section. As soon as she saw him—the overly serious face as if he really cared about his students, his hair falling into his collar—she wanted to rip the photo in shreds, but instead she carefully tore it out and put it in her wallet.

ON THE DRIVE, she veered back and forth between thinking this was a great idea and thinking it was a stupid waste of time. The cop was right. She couldn't be sure the card was from William, and even if it was, how did she really know he was in Dennisport? He could have mailed the card from Wyoming to a friend in Dennisport who mailed it to Diana. And Dennisport wasn't exactly a tiny town. He could vanish into it. Or he could already have gone, moved on, to some other place. To some other girl.

She needed to focus before school started up again, to line up a tutor. She had two more weeks of work left, and she had to do a stellar job in order to get Dr. Bronstein's recommendation so she'd get a grade. She had never let things go like this, never muddied her plan for the future. She wanted to get back on track, she did, but at the same time she thought, what good was it to think ahead anymore? You could plan all you wanted, but the world cracked open around you and it was all you could do to remember to breathe.

She kept driving.

What would she do if she found him? He would have answers, and she needed answers. But then what? Did she really think she could just grab his arm and he would willingly go right to the police with her? If he even spotted her, wouldn't he just take off again? Or hurt her, the way he had Lucy?

BY THE TIME she got to Dennisport, it was nearly evening. Despite having grown up in Boston, she had never been to Cape Cod before. Charlotte had imagined it was all going to be sand dunes and weathered wood fences, with tall marsh grasses and gulls. Instead there were all these tawdry stores, with beach chairs and flip-flops festooned in the window, right next door to all-you-can-eat greasy spoons. Everyone seemed to be tanned too darkly, and the air was drenched in suntan lotion and salt and fried food. Summer people came in and out like tides, but she bet the people who lived here year-round would know one another. That could be a plus.

She wasn't sure whom to ask for information. She concocted a story to make inquiries: she was his old student, he had been a great teacher, she was vacationing on the Cape and realized he was here and she wanted to find him to say hello. It sounded innocent and boring enough to be believable.

But he could be anyone here. He could have shaved his head, or dyed his hair, or grown fat or thin, and she wouldn't recognize him. Maybe she had walked past him already and hadn't even known it. She turned around, blindly. A man, his face hidden by a straw fedora, strode past her. Another man was hunched in his coat, and it wasn't until he turned that Charlotte saw the wrinkles etching his face, the shock of white hair.

She tried the diners and the bars, but most of the people glanced at the photo and then shrugged. "Doesn't look familiar to me," a waitress at a steak house told her. "And we pretty much get all the regulars, so I'd know."

Eventually she got tired and hungry. No one seemed to know anything. She had talked to managers and a hostess, and a few had even asked the customers who were still eating if they knew him. Maybe this was a fool's errand, Charlotte thought. Maybe people who didn't want to be found always escaped and there was nothing you could do about it. She went to the first motel she could find that had a vacancy sign, the Candy Cane, which had a small room on the second floor that overlooked the parking lot.

BY THE END of the second day, she was worn out. She had walked around Dennisport so often some of the shop owners now nodded at her as if they knew her. "Gorgeous day," they said to her. At the Busy Bee Coffee Shop, the waitress had Charlotte's coffee with cream and two sugars on the table before she even sat down and asked for it. Charlotte told herself that if they knew her after two days, surely they would know William.

She had gotten into the habit of cutting her eyes from side to side before she stepped into a place. What if William was in there? What if he wasn't? One night she stopped at Jackie's, a local bar. It was cool and dark and nearly empty, with a pool table standing in the back and a dartboard on the wall in the shape of a mermaid. No William, but you could never be sure. She sat at the bar. She was just going to order a Coke, but looking around, she could see there were some serious drinkers here already, and she thought she'd have more luck if she fit in. "Rum and Coke," she said. The bartender was younger than she was, with a high brown ponytail and too much blue eye shadow, and when she smiled at Charlotte, Charlotte saw a flash of braces. "You're here early," the girl said.

"Pardon?"

The waitress wiped the counter. "Most folks don't come here until past nine usually. That's why it's so quiet." She folded the rag over to the clean side and wiped the counter down again.

Charlotte glanced over her shoulder and then brought out the photo and put it on the table. "Do you know this person?" Her voice cracked. "Does he come in here?"

The waitress frowned. "Doesn't look familiar to me," she said. "Sorry." She held the photo closer to her face, as if she were nearsighted. "What do you want with this one?"

He murdered my sister. She could say that, and if she did, the waitress would definitely be on the lookout for him. But what if she didn't believe Charlotte? What if she thought she was crazy? Then if she saw William, she might tell him. Charlotte drained her glass. She never drank. She had no tolerance, and now her brain felt fuzzy. "I just want to find him," she finally said.

She was on her second glass, a little tipsy, when a man sat next to her. She smelled him first, tobacco and wet wool, and she could feel his stare.

"My name's Jack. Where you from?" His voice was polite, with a soft accent, and she turned. He was in his fifties, his hair long and curly, a blue watch cap pulled over his forehead, casting a shadow across his cheeks.

"Boston," she said. "And I'm married."

"No, you're not," he said, his smile widening. He tapped her finger. "No ring."

"Not everyone wears one."

"Yes, they do. Especially women. They want to show the world they belong to someone. And if they don't, you can see the white line where the ring was."

"Got me," she said. His grin widened. She pulled out the photo to show him the picture of William. And then she saw it, a flicker that came over his face, but he stayed silent.

"You know this guy," she said, trying to steady her voice. She put one hand on top of the other to keep it from shaking.

"He your boyfriend?"

"Him? Not a chance."

"Then why are you looking for him?" He readjusted himself in his seat so he was closer to her.

"He was an old friend. Haven't seen him in a long time."

The guy tilted his head at her, as if he were trying to figure her out. He leaned his shoulder against hers, and though everything in her wanted to jerk her body away, she stayed still. Maybe if she were friendlier, he'd tell her more. She leaned toward him. He smelled like cigarettes and whiskey, but she let her mouth graze his cheek, heard his intake of breath.

"Come on. I told you the truth about not being married," she said. Then she pulled away.

"Well, now that we're getting closer, I'll tell you. I don't know him that well," he said. "But I know that's Eddie. Works at the food kitchen down on Central Avenue in Harwich Port."

Charlotte took the photo back. A food kitchen. It was the best way to stay hidden, because who would see you there except for people worse off than you were? "Do you know where he lives?"

"We aren't that close. I just know him to say hi."

"Well, if you see him, don't mention I was asking for him. I want to surprise him." She forced herself to smile and hoped it didn't look like a grimace. The guy gave her an oily grin. "You do like him," he said. "Just my luck. But I bet I could change your mind." He stroked a finger along Charlotte's cheek, and she willed herself to stay still for a moment.

Then she dug in her pocket, spread a few bills on the counter, and got up.

"You're going? After I helped you and all?" He clamped his hand around her arm. "That's not friendly."

"Neither is this." She nodded at his hand and he let her go. "You did help me," she said. "And I said thank you. But yeah, I'm going."

"I'm here every night," the guy said. He held up his hand and showed his bare finger. "I'm single," he called after her. "No white lie, either. Tell me your name at least. A beautiful woman like you."

"Oh, I'm sure I'll see you again," she said.

"Yeah, you will," he said, winking at her. She waved to him. She made herself move. When she turned around, she pushed out her breath. She saw he wasn't following her. She'd never come into this bar again.

THE NEXT MORNING, she found the food kitchen at the end of a quiet block, a mix of houses and businesses. The food kitchen was a one-story brick building, set off with pine trees, and there was already a queue of people waiting outside. The air was hazy, or maybe it was just because she hadn't been able to sleep the night before. All that rum had made her queasy.

When she tried to get to the door, a woman shoved her. "There's a line here," she said.

Charlotte brushed herself off. "I'm not here for food," she said. "I want to find someone—"

"There's a line," the woman repeated.

Charlotte went to the back of the line. It was a wet day, and she wasn't dressed warmly enough and she was shivering. "Stamp your feet, it helps," the man in back of her said, and she did, grateful. By the time she got inside, her hands were pink from the cold. The room smelled like eggs and toast and forced heat. There were long wood communal tables and chairs, already filling up with people carrying trays, and at the front of the room was a serving station with four people in aprons ladling out food, too far away for her to see their faces.

Someone nudged her. "Take a tray," a woman ordered, and Charlotte picked up a blue plastic tray, which was still wet.

The smell of the food nauseated her. The tables, as she passed them, looked greasy. The line was moving quickly, and the closer she got to the servers, the more anxious she became. What if he was there? What would she say and do? She took another step closer and she could make out the servers, all four of them. A woman with a long gray braid down her back. A man who was so fat his apron wouldn't tie around him, and two teenage boys in rock-and-roll T-shirts. None of them was William. A man ladled scrambled eggs onto a plate and handed it to her, and she didn't know what else to do, so she took it. "Is Eddie here today?" she blurted out. Her voice sounded strange and foreign to her.

The guy looked at her, surprised. "Eddie? Didn't come in today."

She thought, He knows William. She couldn't meet his eyes, so she looked down at the eggs, the specks of parsley on the top like a Morse code she couldn't decipher. "Is he coming tomorrow?" Charlotte said.

"Beats me. Hope so. We're always shorthanded."

She couldn't wait any longer. "Please," she said. "Do you know where he lives? I really need to find him." She set the tray back on the counter.

"You don't want food?"

She shouldn't be taking food from someone who needed it. "Not really," she said. "Eddie's just an old friend and he told me he worked here."

The guy studied her and then sighed. "All I know is he was camping at some guy Buzzard's house, and now he's not. They had some falling out, but maybe Buzzard would know."

"Do you have Buzzard's phone number?"

"I don't even know his last name."

"Where's he live?"

He looked past her at the people waiting for food. "You got a good memory?" he asked. "Because I don't have a pen or paper and I'm too busy to get one. Anyway, all I know is it's the one place on the six hundred block of Mott Street that has a porch. At least that's what Eddie told me."

She nodded and got out of the line. Who knew whether Eddie was even telling the truth? Plus, Buzzard's name made her nervous. She could imagine the type. Tattoos. Beer bottles stacked up in the dining room. What if he refused to talk to her? What if he was dangerous?

But William might be there. If she could just glimpse him and then get to the cops. If she could just know he was alive.

IT DIDN'T TAKE her long to find Mott Street. The houses streamed into one another. The ground under the car seemed spongy, as if her tires were sinking. The street seemed endless, but at least it was busy with people, a few sitting on their front steps, two women with coffee cups in their hands talking. There. There was the porch. She squinted—number 600—and then she jerked the car to a stop. Breathe, she told herself. Breathe. Nobody knew she was there except the guy at the food pantry. If anything happened to her, at least he would know whom she had come to find.

Buzzard lived in a small blue clapboard house with two metal chairs on the porch. She got out of her car and rang the bell, two brief chimes, and then she banged on the door and it opened and there was William, staring at her.

Her heart seized up.

His head was shaved and he had a beard, but the eyes were the same. He was in an old flannel shirt and jeans and sneakers that looked as if they were on the far side of new. There were wrinkles around his eyes and mouth, even on his throat. And then she noticed that he didn't even look shocked to see her. He just stood there, looking at her. "Charlotte," he finally said. His face was flat, like a penny under the wheels of a train. He opened the door wider. "You might as well come in."

She felt herself gathering, ready to spring into a run. Down the street, over to the two women. She would clutch their arms and tell them to call the cops, that a murderer lived on their block. She put one hand on the railing to give herself leeway, and then he sighed.

"You want to call the police on me, go ahead. But why don't you listen to me first."

Her grip loosened. Every word out of his mouth was poison. How would she even know if he was lying? "Why should I?"

He nodded to the house again. "Come on inside. I'll make coffee."

"I'd rather stay here," she said.

He shrugged. "Suit yourself," he said, and he came out and sat on one of the metal chairs, and then she did, too, feeling the cold through her jeans.

"You don't seem surprised to see me," she said.

"Jack told me a woman was asking about me. He described you, but I wasn't sure because he mentioned long hair, no bangs, but then he talked about your eyes, so I knew."

Jack. She should have known he'd tell William. "And you stayed, anyway."

"Where would I go?" He shrugged. "How did you know to look for me?" he asked. "Everyone else thinks I'm dead." He gave a sharp laugh. "I am dead."

"Lucy. Her journal."

Something lit up in his eyes. "You have her journal?" He leaned toward her.

Charlotte nodded. "It was her journal that made me think you were alive. Lucy wrote all these things about how you were terrified of the water, that you'd never go near it. So I thought you wouldn't have jumped. You must have staged it, or gotten scared and left. Then I went to visit your mother, and she said Lucy had lied, that you loved the water. She showed me photos. So I wasn't sure anymore."

He stood up, his face darkening, and for a second, Charlotte readied herself to move fast.

"You went to my mother's?"

"She said you were always asking to go to the beach. Was she lying for you, covering up that you were alive?"

He shook his head. "She told you the truth. I did clamor to go, but it doesn't mean I really wanted to."

"What does that mean?"

"What Lucy wrote was true. My father saw I was afraid of the water, and he insisted I conquer my fear. He'd drag me deep into the ocean and leave me flailing in the water, swallowing the salt, terrified. Sink or swim. That was my dad. I'd manage to get to shore, or someone else would help me, and my father would say, 'Next time.' I knew what that meant. So I began to thwart him. I'd run into the water as if I loved it. I'd splash around for ten minutes, completely terrified, and then I'd race out. I knew my limits, how much I could stand. If I could control it, it was easier for me. And then he'd leave me alone."

Charlotte stared at him.

"So how did you find me?" he asked.

"I went to the food kitchen. Someone told me Buzzard would know where you were."

He laughed. "There's no Buzzard. I made that name up. I had too much to drink one night and by mistake I gave out the street, so I said I was staying with this guy Buzzard, that I was moving the next week. I didn't want people dropping by." He laughed. "But here you are."

He looked down at his hands. "So, is this it? Did you call the cops already? Am I just waiting to be picked up now?"

"What do you think?" Something prickled along the back of her collar. She had been so incredibly stupid. She should have called the police before she came over here. Even if they didn't take her seriously, at least they'd know where she was. She should have told someone she would be here, called Iris to fill her in. She hadn't thought it out, and now here she was. If she left to find a phone, he could leave, too, and she might never find him again. If she screamed, would a neighbor help her?

"Charlotte, I didn't do it," he said.

"That's what guilty people always say, right?"

"I loved Lucy. You can't imagine how much I loved her. I never would have hurt her."

Anger flamed in her chest. How dare he talk about love? "You killed her."

"I didn't. I swear that I didn't."

"I don't believe you."

"Would you just listen to me for a moment?" he said. He put one hand to his face and then let it drop to his lap. "Please," he said. "I know I don't have the right, but I'm begging you."

"Go ahead," she said. "Tell me some lies."

Chapter 26

Everything had died months before Lucy did. William knew it when he began to wake up alone in their bed. He was used to her unfurling beside him, her arms stretching out over her lovely head, her feet twisting against his, her breath against his neck. He loved the sound of her hair rustling on the pillowcase. Mornings were his favorite time to make love, too, when he could see her in the light, and she could see him. One morning—months ago—he put one hand on her side of the sheets, still warm from her body, and then got up to find her. There she was, pale and beautiful in the kitchen, still in her nightgown, her feet bare, hunched over the table, scribbling. She must have been up for a while, because there was a red plate, dotted with crumbs, with half an English muffin on it, and a teacup pushed to the side. She was so involved that at first she didn't see him, not until he stepped on a creaky wood plank and she started. He saw the fear swim across her face. Why would she be afraid of him? He loved her, he would have done anything for her.

"What are you doing?"

She put one hand across the page. "Writing."

"But that's great." Maybe that explained why she was up so early. She wanted time and quiet. He could understand that. Maybe it had nothing to do with him at all. He had tried to write himself, even with the demands of his new job. He had told himself he'd carve out a half hour in the morning, while the kids were rambling around, but when he'd sat down, all that had happened was he had doodled Lucy's beautiful face on the page, over and over. He had thought about all the things he wanted to tell her about his day. He had felt bad enough when he had stopped writing, though he told himself he'd pick it up later. Everything had a time and a season, as that old song said. He didn't know where his drive to write had gone, but it seemed to have been replaced by Lucy, and to him that was a good thing.

He pulled up a chair and sat beside her, and she shut her journal. "It's okay if you keep writing," he said, but she shook her head.

She used to show him her work, almost desperate for his suggestions, gnawing her nails as he was reading, pacing the floor sometimes. "Do you like it? What do you think?" she kept asking. He could feel her panic, and it was his job to calm it all down. She used to welcome his help—the way he showed her how to build a character, how to keep the plot spinning. "Throw rocks at your characters," he advised. Even little things, like spelling and grammar help, she was grateful for.

But by March, she had started changing, and maybe he had, too. He knew that she felt isolated, that she was lonely, but what was he supposed to do? He had told her they had to lie low. She knew all the reasons why, and at first she had been just as excited as he was about their new life. "Just a little while longer," he kept telling her, but she looked more and more as if she didn't believe him.

He kept hearing those stupid songs on the radio—rape songs, he called them—about older guys and younger girls, and every one of them seemed directed at him, like a finger, pointing. He could tell himself all he wanted that Lucy was mature, but she didn't know how to use an iron. She couldn't cook. She was seventeen, and even if she would be legal in another year, that was still months of worrying every time he saw a cop, every time the phone rang.

WHEN SHE WAS out of the house, he looked for her journal, but he couldn't find it. Sure, he sometimes read her writing on loose leaf paper, but it was always only beginnings of stories, snippets of dialogue. Where was her blue journal, the one she thought was so special? Would she really go so far as to actually hide her writing from him? He knew it was a rough patch for them, but didn't all relationships have them? Couldn't making it through those shaky spots actually strengthen a bond? That night, he came home with wildflowers that he had picked by the school, a bouquet of tiger lilies that he put in a glass for her.

And then, a few weeks later, while looking for his glasses, he found a magazine shoved under the bed, just pages stapled together, and a name, the *RagTag Literary Review*. He had been the one to tell Lucy to read what was being published, to study it, but he meant places like the *New Yorker*, the *Atlantic Monthly*, the *Michigan Quarterly Review*. He leafed through it. Some bad poetry, two stories. He idly started reading a story by someone named Berry Moss, thinking maybe he could finally find time for himself and send off his own story. He recognized a phrase. And then another. He felt something slam shut in his head. It was Lucy's writing and it was about an older guy and his younger girlfriend living in an isolated town in Pennsylvania, and then the guy hits the girl. It was published. He grabbed the magazine, went to the living room, where Lucy was reading, and held it up, watching her face pale. "Do you realize what you've done?" he told her. "Do you want people to find us?"

She stared at him. "I didn't use my real name—"

"But someone could call the magazine and ask. They could

make up some story to trace you. And you must have given them our address—"

"No one will find us," she said. "No one has."

"How could you publish this?"

"Because it's good! Because I'm good!"

"I'm glad you're writing again, but don't write about us. And you don't publish right now. It's too dangerous. Save your stories until you're eighteen, and then publish them, and then no one can touch us."

She grabbed the magazine back from him, wincing when it tore in his hand. She smoothed the pages. "Fine," she said stiffly. "Fine." She left the room, and he sighed. She'd get over it. She'd come to see that he was right, that he was doing this out of love, because he needed to protect her. *To protect them.*

But more and more, she was out of sorts. One month passed and then two and three, and things were no better. "What do you want?" he asked her, and she always said the same thing. To live in a city. To drive. To get her GED. Things he couldn't risk giving her. And then everything had come apart.

His job was more and more terrible. He couldn't handle the kids, they didn't listen to him. He had to come up with a new plan, but what?

The night before Lucy died, when he reached for her, she pushed him away. "I'm tired," she said. When he persisted, stroking her back, nuzzling her neck, he felt her stiffen. When he turned her to face him, her eyes were blank, and his desire faded. He smoothed her hair and kissed her forehead. "Sleep, then," he told her, and when she did, he stayed awake, his mind racing. She used to chatter when she made breakfast, but that morning she was silent, setting down his oatmeal thinned with organic milk, a slice of the corn-and-molasses bread he was addicted to. "Eat with me," he said, but she shook her head. "I ate already," she told him.

She ate without him? Why? The school had taught that eating together was a privilege, that it bound people together. Weren't they a couple? Didn't they do things together? They didn't have that much time together, so why didn't she prize the time they did have? He took a deep breath. "Well, keep me company, then," he said, in as pleasant a tone as he could manage. She sat in the chair opposite him. He sat eating, looking around the house, which was a wreck. Dust bunnies floated along the floorboards. Laundry bred in chairs. But when he suggested—merely suggested—she clean it, she got that look on her face, as if he were pressing a great stone down on her chest. "Okay, never mind for now," he said. "We can both clean it up later. Or I'll do it." He finished his breakfast, but when he went to kiss her good-bye, she dipped her head so that he had to tilt her chin up to get to her mouth, her dry lips.

"Bye," he called to her, and then he was out the door.

Maybe, he thought as he drove to school, it was this place that was ruining them. Lucy could be right: maybe they needed a fresh start. They could move to a better place, with a bigger garden. Or he should really teach her to drive, get her her own car. He trusted her to drive now, didn't he? It wasn't the same situation as when she was younger and wilder, and he was so afraid something might happen to her. She was sturdy stuff. And he could track her by the mileage. He could know where she went, so he could keep her safe.

When he got to work, William was still trying to figure out what to do. As usual, he walked into his room and it was chaos, with two kids, Rain and Doobie, shouting at each other. "Come on, let's learn about the kings of Europe!" he said, trying to sound encouraging, and Rain made a face. "Fuck the kings," she said cheerfully, and he lost it. "Shut up! I can't hear myself think!" he said, and just as he said it, the head of the school walked in.

"Did you just say 'shut up' to a child?" he said, and he started lecturing William on the pacifist nature of the school, on how teachers were supposed to be loving and kind, and William threw up his hands. "You can shut up, too," William said, and he was fired.

THE MAGNITUDE OF what he had done didn't hit him until he was in his car. He didn't have a job anymore. There'd be no money coming in. He couldn't even get unemployment because the school was set up so that everyone's hours were part-time.

What in God's name would he tell Lucy? That without a steady job, there was no way that he could pay the rent on their place anymore? That he wouldn't be able to take care of her? He pulled over to the side of the road, trying to calm his breathing, the way Mimi, the school's yoga teacher, had shown him. He leaned his head on the steering wheel. "Ideas will come to you if you breathe properly," Mimi had said, but all that he could see were bills piling up on the dining room table and Lucy's disappointed face.

He straightened and began driving again. He and Lucy had each other. They were healthy. They were young enough to walk into any place and find some kind of work. What did it matter what the work was, as long as there was money coming in? And hadn't he been thinking about moving farther out, where it was cheaper? They could grow their own food, give back to the community, really live all their ideals.

He felt a flash of hope. He pulled the car over and picked some wildflowers on the side of the road. Lucy loved them.

BY THE TIME he got to the door, he was anxious to see her pretty face, to tell her everything, to make new plans. He opened the door and saw Lucy's coat and a stuffed backpack in the middle of the floor. "Lucy?" he called.

And then she came into the room, her face pale as a sheet of paper.

"I know. I'm home early." He glanced at the knapsack. "Where are you going?"

She hesitated.

"Luce?"

"I'm leaving you," she said. Her voice was fragile, like a mirror with a crack in it.

He put the flowers down carefully. "No. No, you're not. That will never happen," he said quietly.

"Are you listening to me?" Her voice rose. "I'm leaving. You can't stop me."

He tried to reach for her. He was sure that if he could just kiss her mouth, he might win her back. But as soon as he had her wrist, she jerked it back from him, scratching him, drawing blood. He blinked at her and then she turned around. "I'll put the bag away," she said, and he felt a hard skip of relief. She went into the bedroom, and for a moment he thought she was going to lock herself in there. "Honey—" he said. She was different, as if something had broken inside her, and he didn't know what to do about it.

And then there she was, the gun trembling in her hand. "Get away from the door. It's loaded," she said.

"Lucy." He said her name like a prayer. He told her how much he loved her, how he didn't know how to be in the world without her. He had bought the gun because Lucy was getting so obsessed with everything she heard on the news, with being alone so much of the time with nothing but the woods around her. He had thought a gun—some protection—would make her feel better, but after the first time he tried to teach her how to use it, she'd freaked. She had never touched the gun again, and he hadn't pushed. He had promised her it would never be loaded, but he couldn't remember now if it was or it wasn't.

She held the weapon higher now.

"Lucy, honey—I love you," he said, and when she laughed, it sounded like a bark. As if it hadn't come from Lucy at all.

"You don't love me. I don't belong to you anymore," she said.

"I understand your pain," he said slowly. "But I need you to understand mine—"

"Be quiet! Just be quiet!" she cried.

Her eyes blinked hard. Her hands shook. How could she be this desperate, this frightened of him?

"People know about you. What you did to me!" Lucy shouted.

"What people?" he said quietly. "And what did I do to you?" He thought of the story she had published. "Who did you tell about us, Lucy?" When he reached for her arm, she jerked free, but he took hold of her again. He twisted the gun in her hand, wanting to grab it, to hurl it outside. "Lucy," he said. "Lucy—" She struggled in his arms, kicking his legs, bending down and biting his hand, so he felt a shock of pain. He wrenched her arm back at a funny angle, and then the gun went off, like a shout in his ears, and he saw a star of blood on his sleeve. A shell clattered to the floor.

He looked at her in wonder. Her features had rearranged, so that she was all eyes and her mouth was a line, and her whole body crumpled against him and fell to the floor, the blood spreading across her chest.

He screamed, and then he dropped down, frantically probing her pulse points, her wrist, her ankles, the base of her neck. "Lucy! Lucy!" he shouted. He breathed into her mouth, pressing himself against her until he was covered in her blood. She didn't move. He wiped a hand across his face, his eyes so wet with tears that the world faded around him. Finally he got up.

The floor was spattered with red. The gun was in the corner and it had both their fingerprints on it. He knew what it looked like. *People know about you.* That's what she had said.

No one would believe him. He had taken Lucy over state lines when she was a minor. It wouldn't matter that they had loved each other, that they were planning to marry. The cops would blame him. And for this, too. They would blame him.

He started to cry again. He couldn't go to prison. He couldn't. He'd die in there. But he couldn't live without Lucy either.

He LEFT EVERYTHING the way it was, jammed the gun into his pocket, and then ran out to his car. His shirt was spattered with blood. His hands. He glanced in the mirror, and though his face was clean, he looked like a stranger to himself. He drove around and around, trying to think what to do. A car beeped at him and he turned, and it was one of the mothers from the free school, waving hello, and he didn't know what to do, so he just waved back, moving his hand like an idiot until he remembered the blood dappled across his fingers. He hastily wiped them on his shirt, hoping she might think it was finger paint, and then stopped, because really, what did it matter now?

He kept driving, out of town now, not sure where he was going. Hours passed. The sky darkened and the air took on a clammy chill. A horn blared and he looked up and a truck swam into his field of vision, coming toward him head-on, and he wrenched the wheel to the right. His car skidded onto a shoulder, and he bumped up against the roof of the car, banging his head, feeling the star of pain, and the car slammed to a stop. He sucked at the air. He was all right. He was alive. And Lucy was dead.

It was funny how calm he got after that. How he knew what to do. He drove to the Ben Franklin Bridge, a place that had always scared him. Whenever he had to drive across it, he would wonder, What if the bridge collapses, flinging cars and people into the dark waters? He still couldn't swim, any more than he could when his father had flung him into the water when he was a child.

He couldn't save himself. Not then, not now.

He parked by the bridge. In the backseat was an old sweatshirt, and he took off his bloody shirt and put the sweatshirt on so he'd look ordinary. Then he got out of the car, leaving the keys in it, his wallet. He took the shirt and balled it in his fist, and he forced himself to walk up the stairs. The bridge had a walkway. Walking across it was always mentioned as one of the fun things to do in the area, but the day was cold and clammy and the walkway was pretty empty. The cars were zooming by, too fast for anyone to really notice what he was doing. He walked over to the edge of the bridge. He was terrified of water, and so this was the way he had to die. His punishment. He wavered, bracing for the wave of nausea. One, two, three. He'd count, and then all he had to do was let go, falling, and it would all be like a dream. Or maybe he'd jump and fall and then there'd just be nothing more than a blanket of night to tuck him in.

His whole body trembled. He threw the shirt into the water. Then he lifted up one foot on the railing, hoisting himself up.

"Hey! You!"

He jerked back from the edge.

"What are you doing there? Hey!"

He heard the voice, but he couldn't see where it was coming from.

"Hey!" This time the voice was female. There was a couple there, farther down on the walkway, and they were coming toward him. Running. He quickly turned, dislodging a stone, which splashed into the water.

He ran, too. His breath roared in his ears. Huh, huh, huh. His muscles ached, but he took the stairs three at a time, running, stumbling, so he had to grab the rail, skinning his palm. He kept running, past his car, onto the road, toward a train station.

Coward. He had never hated himself more than he did at that moment.

He left the car. He made it to the train station. No one paid him any attention. His arm throbbed where she had bitten him. Lucy. His Lucy. He stopped at a drugstore, bought a cheap pair of scissors, a razor, and a clean T-shirt, and headed for the men's room. It was the middle of the night, and no one was there. He had never had his hair short, but he began cutting it as close to his head as he could, and when he was finished, he took the razor and shaved the rest. He ran one hand over his skull. He didn't look like himself anymore.

He heard a noise suddenly. A man strode in, hungrily kissing a woman wrapped around his neck, moaning. Neither one of them looked at him. William ran the water, washing the hair down the drain, then took off his old shirt and put on the new T. Then he walked out the door and, with the money he had in his pocket, bought a train ticket to Boston.

HE WAS THERE by morning. He hadn't slept on the train because he didn't want to be defenseless, and now he could barely see straight. He didn't have money for a hotel, so he went into the men's room and found an empty stall and sat on the toilet and shut his eyes. Just for a moment, he told himself.

SOMEONE WAS BANGING on the stall door. "What, you living in there or what?" a voice said. He stood up, shaky on his feet, glancing at his watch. Had he slept a whole day? How was that possible? He opened the door, and a man in a custodian's jumpsuit glowered at him. "This ain't the Ritz," he said.

The world swam before him. People in work clothes were rushing for trains. Couples were kissing. He glanced at his watch. How could he have slept so long? It was now the next day. He passed a newsstand and picked up a paper, and there it was, a scream in his ear:

TWO DEAD IN MURDER-SUICIDE.

They thought he was dead.

He saw his name and his photo, the one from the high school yearbook, where he was sitting at his desk, looking contemplative. And beside his picture was Lucy's. She was laughing into the camera, so beautiful that he wanted to weep. An unnamed guy had called and said he and his girlfriend had seen someone jump into the river. The guy had called out, but the person had vanished. They had heard the splash and seen the rings of water, and they had seen enough to identify William by the picture. Then they had found his car, the keys in the ignition.

Something knocked in William's head. There, farther down, the head of the school gave a quote about how William had been fired, and William flushed with shame. Reporters had talked to his neighbors, who said that he was quiet and that he and Lucy were a lovely couple.

And William thought, We were. We were a lovely couple.

They talked to Lucy's family. But the family refused to comment, and well they should, because what did they really know about what Lucy and he had been to each other? And they talked to his mother, who couldn't believe he had done such a thing. "It's not in his nature," she said. She said that she hadn't heard from him in a while, that she knew he was in Pennsylvania but she knew nothing about a girl.

A girl.

He had, of course, told her he had a new job in a tiny rural town, a dot on the map. He hated lying to her, but he couldn't trust that she wouldn't mention to someone what he was doing and where he was. He knew she didn't drive, so he knew she'd never show up. He had even lied to Lucy, telling her he had a two-day conference when he was really going to visit his mother. She hadn't seemed to mind. He had driven all the way to Boston to see his mother. They had ordered food, and she hadn't had enough money, so she saw his wallet and went to get money and noticed the photo of Lucy that he carried, and then another of the two of them kissing. She held up the photo. "You want to tell me about this?" she said quietly, and when he couldn't speak, she touched his face. "I only want the best for you," she said, and he believed her. The whole time he told her, she was quiet.

"What about her family? They must be going crazy."

"They don't care about her. But I do. I love her," William said. "As soon as she's eighteen, we're getting married." He saw the fear buckling his mother's brow. Her hands flew up like birds. "You'll meet her," he promised. His mother came toward him and hugged him. "If you love her, I'll love her, too," she said, and then he knew it was all right.

Now he put his head in his hands. He knew his mother. The shock she must have felt reading about Lucy's death. About his. He couldn't let her think he was dead.

He called her from a pay phone. He heard the shock in her voice. "You're alive," she cried. "Oh my God. The police were here—the newspapers . . ." She burst into tears.

"Don't cry," he begged. "I'm sorry. Mom, I'm sorry." He waited for her to stop crying. "I didn't kill her. It was an accident."

He heard her blowing her nose. "Listen to me," he said. "The newspaper stories aren't true. I loved her." He pressed the receiver against his head. "You have to believe me."

"Where are you? You have to tell the police you're alive—"

"They think I did it," he said. "The newspapers already have me in jail. Right now, it's better if they think I'm dead."

He could hear her breathing. "Honey—" she said.

"It was an accident, I swear on my life. You have to believe me. You can't think I did it."

"We'll get you a lawyer. The best one in Boston."

"You don't understand. They've already convicted me. If I go in now, they'll think I planned it to look like I was dead. I'll look guiltier than ever."

She was quiet again. "You must need money," she said finally.

"I'll find work. I'll be all right."

"Go far away," she said quietly. "And then somehow let me know where you are."

IF HE WAS going to vanish, he should do it in a place where there were lots of transients, where he'd blend in. He wasn't sure where that would be yet. His mind was filled with Lucy. He thought of that moment when he was standing on the lip of the bridge. He should have jumped.

HE COULDN'T RISK renting a car, plus he didn't want to use up the rest of his money. Instead he stood on the edge of the highway, hitching. A beat-up red sedan pulled over, and a kid, his hair tied back in a ponytail, waved at William to open the door. "Where you headed?" the kid asked.

"Where're you going?"

"Dennisport. I need some beach."

Cape Cod. There were lots of transients there, summer

people who came and then left, and who could keep track of any of them? William opened the door. "That's where I'm going, too," he said.

By the time he got there, he had given himself a whole new identity. He was Eddie James. He was thirty-one years old, born in Oregon; his parents had been sheep ranchers and now they were dead. He had no siblings. No cousins. He worked odd jobs. He had never married and had no kids. The more he told himself the story, the more he began to like it, to think of himself as Eddie, to like having such a simple, spare life with no one attached to it.

He'd grow a beard. He'd keep his head shaved.

William's luck was terrible, but Eddie found a job at a soup kitchen the day he arrived, hired by a woman named Marianne, her frizzy yellow hair caught in a kerchief, who also helped him find a room he could afford and gave him an advance on his earnings. When he thanked her profusely, she clasped his hands in hers and said calmly, "Oh, honey, we've all had hard times."

HE NEVER STOPPED missing Lucy, but it hit him hardest at certain times. When a young woman with curly blonde hair came into the soup kitchen, he stopped to stare at her and then gave her extra soup. One day, when a couple came in holding hands, gazing at each other, he felt like a broken elevator, catapulting to the bottom, out of control. And at night he dreamed about her, always the same scene with the gun, and he'd bolt awake, bathed in sweat, calling her name, missing her so much it was driving him crazy, but she never answered.

He never stopped being afraid. *I didn't do it. I didn't do it.* It was like hands constantly clapping. One day a cop wandered into the kitchen, and William, stirring a big silver pot of chili, froze. There was no place to run except through the kitchen and then outside into a dead end, a wall so high he'd never even try to climb it. He kept his head down, pretending to concentrate on the food. The cop sauntered toward him, and William felt himself sweating. He dared to meet his eyes. "Chili today, hot tamale," the cop said, giving a little laugh. He patted William on the shoulder. "Just dropped in to make sure everything's copacetic." William nodded, forcing himself to smile, to look as if everything was easy. The cop wandered over to talk to Marianne, tilting his head, flirting, but William didn't relax until the cop left.

A month after Lucy died, he walked to a pay phone and finally risked calling his mother again.

"William—" She said his name as if she didn't believe it was really him. He listened to her cry on the phone. She told him to set up a PO box so she could send him money. "No one will trace it," she cried. "No one's looking."

"Make it out to Eddie James," he told her.

"I love Eddie James," she said. "I know Eddie James is a good man." And then she hung up the phone, and he listened to the dial tone and tried to believe that Eddie James was a good man, too.

MORE AND MORE he noticed the regulars in the soup kitchen, and they began to talk to him. A single mom told him how she and her son were living in a cardboard box, and he called the shelter for her and got her a room. A guy who had been fired from his job told William about his wife, how she had left him when their bankbook was depleted. "My heart's punched full of holes," he said, starting to cry, and William reached over and took the man's hands in his.

"It helps to have a sympathetic ear," the man told him.

William stayed late and got to the soup kitchen early, and he worked seven days a week because what else was there to do? And before long, he would walk down the street in the little town and people would call out, "Hey, hey, Eddie," and wave to him.

And after a while, he felt himself becoming that guy, becoming Eddie. Eddie would never marry, would never have another woman, but that was his penance. He had dared to believe it could be possible to be someone brand new.

Chapter 27

Charlotte waited until William was finished talking. "You think I believe you?" She blinked back tears. "Is any of this story true?"

"It's all true," he insisted.

"Your mother knows you're alive?" She thought of how innocent Diana had made herself out to be.

He nodded.

"Why should I believe you?"

"Why would I lie now?" He was looking at her the way he used to when she first came to his class, his eyes deep pools. She jerked her gaze away from him.

"You have to ask me that?" she said. "There was a lamp smashed on the floor."

"It wasn't a struggle. She knocked it over before I even got there." He leaned closer to her, so that she could feel the heat of him.

"She was the one who put bullets in the gun," William said. "Not me. Never me."

"Lucy wrote a lot of things," Charlotte said. "I have her journal." She tried to remember whether Lucy had said anything about loading the gun, but all she could remember was how terrified Lucy was, how much she wanted to get away, and how she'd risk anything to do it.

William stiffened. "Lucy wrote fiction."

"She was afraid of you," Charlotte said. "Patrick told me."

William frowned. "Who's Patrick?"

"She worked at his farm stand."

"Now who's the one telling stories?"

"She wrote that you were controlling," Charlotte insisted.

"What's controlling? Is loving someone so much you try to make everything perfect for them controlling?" He shook his head. "You knew me, Charlotte, from high school. You know what kind of person I was. You think I changed so much from then?"

"I didn't know you," she said, but she thought back. She remembered the thrill of being in his class, how the air crackled because you never knew what he was going to teach or how he was going to teach it. He came dressed up like a monk to talk about Chaucer. He once ran around the room, leaping from desktop to desktop, chanting, "Da-da-da-da!" to explain Dadaism to them. And she remembered how so many of the girls liked him, how they dressed better and wore their shortest minis to his class. She was one of those girls who had a crush on him. She had wanted him to make her feel special.

"I remember."

"Do you?" he said. "You were sort of unaware."

"Fuck you. I was the smartest person in your stupid class."

"Then you would have known that it was you I loved first."

She felt something, like a small electric shock. "What are you talking about?"

"Back then, Lucy was so unsure of herself. She was all over the place, like wildfire, taking everything in its path. But you— you were like a compass. You knew just where you were going. You were true north. Just shining out there."

"I don't understand—"

"You came into my class and you sat in the front and you were so smart."

She remembered how she had wanted to impress him. She was always asking him questions, but when he answered he seemed to look right through her.

"You seemed older. You knew all these books. You knew who you wanted to be in life and you had this plan for how you could become it. I didn't know how you did that, and I admired it. I couldn't wait for you to come to class, to hear what you might say or ask or do. And you were so . . . lovely."

She felt sickened. "I don't—"

"Don't you know how awful it was for me? To feel those things? I knew it was wrong, and I was glad when you left my class. But Lucy never left."

He put one hand on her leg, and she couldn't move. He looked directly into her eyes so she could see how sorrowful he was, and then for a moment she felt a pull toward him, as if his voice, soft and low, were an undertow tugging her deeper, grabbing hold. "You and me, we were always alike. Wanting to fix things, to make them better, including ourselves."

"Shut up," she said, but his voice, so low, so deep, nipped at her.

"We both lost Lucy," he said, and she recoiled, jerking her knee away.

"I was never going to tell you how I felt, but then one day we were talking about Fitzgerald in class, and you stood up to me. You said my thesis was wrong, and you wouldn't back down. It unnerved me, that stubbornness. The way you kept insisting you were right. I didn't love it. I hadn't seen it before in you and it didn't seem right. I decided it was better to leave you alone, and then you left. The next year, Lucy came in, and after that, there wasn't anybody but her. I never even told her about any of this."

"You shouldn't have loved either of us."

"Things never turn out the way you think, do they?" he said.

Charlotte stood up, nauseated.What if she had known back then that he liked her that way? She knew the answer. She would have been as excited about it as her sister had been.

"I have to go," Charlotte said. She couldn't breathe. There wasn't enough air.

"I didn't kill Lucy," he said. "Do you believe me?"

"I don't know."

"I'm already in hell. Are you going to turn me in, anyway?" William said.

"You don't have the right to ask me that." She couldn't look at him anymore. She felt hot and dizzy. Even if he hadn't shot Lucy deliberately, if it was really an accident, he had killed her in other ways, isolating her, taking her from them. If she had lived, he was going to move them farther out, Lucy getting smaller and smaller until she shrank to a dot. Or maybe he had shot her because she was leaving him, and he was the one who would vanish into nothing without her.

She stared back at him one last time. The collar of his shirt was ripped and his face seemed broken.

She walked toward the car, waiting for him to grab her, to try to stop her. He didn't move to follow her.

She sat in the car, her hands gripping the steering wheel. She would drive to the police and tell them where to find William. She would turn him in and let the police decide whether to believe him.

SHE HAD ALWAYS thought she would be the one to redeem her sister by finding William. And maybe the bigger truth was that she had hoped she would redeem herself as well. And now it seemed too complicated and impossible and she didn't know what was true or right anymore. She didn't feel better; she felt worse.

Charlotte cried, thinking, I was coming, I was. How could

Lucy not have known she was coming? When had she stopped
believing that Charlotte would always rescue her?

Charlotte tried to wipe away her tears, but she was sobbing
now. She couldn't know for sure whether William was telling the truth. Even if William went to prison, how would it
change anything that had happened? Lucy was dead. William
was dead inside. This would never be all right. Not for Lucy.
And not for her. And she was a fool to think otherwise. All that
was left for her to do was to go into town and find out where
the police station was.

She'd tell them everything. Her foot was easing down on the
gas when she heard a shot. The echo reverberated in the air,
and she clapped her hands to her ears, slamming on the brakes.
She leaped out of the car. Already, a woman from across the
street had come out of her house in a floral housecoat, staring. A dog was barking. Charlotte ran to William's house and
yanked at the door, but it was locked. She banged and banged
on the wood until she heard the whine of a police siren, the
sound of neighbors coming out of their houses. The cops pried
her fingers away.

The police wouldn't let her in the house. A detective stood
outside with her and took down her story. Charlotte stood
with both her arms crushed around her body. Another cop was
talking to neighbors, and Charlotte heard bits of conversation.
Eddie had been quiet. He kept to himself. He was friendly. He
was standoffish. He sometimes had girlfriends. He had never
had girlfriends. The cops wrote everything down.

When the detective came out, he walked over to Charlotte.
"Vultures," he said, pointing to a car that was pulling up. The
doors opened and a woman in a tight red suit climbed out, a
notebook balanced in her hand.

Charlotte nodded, her whole body tight as a wire.

"Single bullet. To the head. No note."

She heard the click and whine of the cameras. A flash of light in her eyes made her squint. "Look, innocent guys don't shoot themselves," the detective said quietly.

"How do you know?" Charlotte said, but the detective had turned away from her, pushing aside the microphone thrust in his face. No one was looking at her. No one knew who she was. She slipped back into her car and drove.

SHE HAD ASKED the cops not to contact Iris, to let Charlotte at least be the one to break the news. Iris didn't get the newspapers anymore, and she rarely watched the news, but by the next morning it would be in all the papers. Dr. Bronstein would know. Her friends. Everyone. The end of a manhunt, an announcer said. She clicked the radio off.

She found Iris in her apartment, the sunlight splashing across her kitchen table, and as soon as Iris saw her, she gave her a hug. She doesn't know yet, Charlotte thought. "Can we sit?" Charlotte said quietly.

"Of course we can, honey." Iris pulled up a chair and waited, her hands folded.

The whole time she was talking to Iris, Iris stayed completely still. Charlotte had thought Iris would yell at her for being so reckless, but instead she was rigid, tears streaking her face.

"That horrible monster," Iris whispered. Her fingers were threaded together so tightly that Charlotte could see the whites of her knuckles.

"It's over now," Charlotte said, though of course she knew it wasn't.

Iris got up and brought out cheese and bread, but Charlotte shook her head. "I'm not hungry."

"You have to eat," Iris said, but she didn't touch the food either.

Charlotte stayed with Iris all that evening. They played a

game of cards. They finally ate the cheese and bread, and then, when Iris yawned, Charlotte got up to leave.

"You'll be starting school soon," Iris said. "I've been thinking about that."

Charlotte had been thinking about it, too. There was so much she had to do. She needed to talk to Dr. Bronstein and get his recommendation. She'd have to find her zoology professor and see how much it would count for her grade. And even though she had saved money from her job, it wasn't enough to pay for an apartment for a whole year. She'd have to move back into the dorm unless she could keep working, even part-time. Maybe Dr. Bronstein would let her. But could she keep her same apartment, or would she have to find a new one?

"Are you giving up your sublet?" Iris asked, as if she had read Charlotte's mind. "Do you want to go back to the dorms? Could you stay there during vacations and breaks?"

"No one wants to be in the dorms except the seniors, who get singles. Maybe I can keep subletting."

Iris's mouth curved. "I'd like to see you in your own apartment."

"I'm going to look."

"And I'd like to pay for it for you."

"You can't do that," Charlotte said. "And I have a little money from my job."

Iris shook her head. "Not enough for a nice place. A bigger place."

"A studio is fine."

"No, it isn't."

"I won't let you. You need your money."

"What I need is to help you. And you need to let me."

Charlotte blinked hard.

Iris stood up. "I want you to invite Joe and me to dinner in your new place. I want you to fix it up and make it pretty and feel at home and know that it's yours. You can live there all through school, and in the summer, and even when you graduate, if you choose."

Charlotte covered her mouth with her hands. She thought of not having to pull out the couch to sleep on every night, of actually having an extra room, with a door she could close. She would have a real kitchen, not just a tiny stove and fridge stuck in the corner. And it would be hers. Really hers. "Are you sure?" she asked. "It won't be a hardship for you?"

"It'll be a hardship if you don't let me help you."

"Then September fifteenth," Charlotte said.

Iris raised her brow. "What's that?"

"The day you and Joe will come to dinner at my new place."

Chapter 28

By the time he got to Cleveland, Patrick was tired and hungry. Every woman he passed reminded him of Charlotte. The way a hand brushed hair out of her eye, the way she might smile, the corners of her lips turning up. He stopped at a diner to get a grilled cheese sandwich and had a beer, downing it in one gulp, and then ordered another. He drank until he was good and drunk. He was exhausted but he didn't want to stop, because then he might think better of seeing Vera's parents. Well, if all the doors in his life were closing, he might as well be the person to close this next one himself.

The last time he had been to the house was right before he moved out of the apartment in Ann Arbor. He hadn't had the courage to call them and say he was dropping out of school, so like the coward he was, he had written a note. Maybe it wasn't the best note, but he didn't know what else to say. All their lights were on. The grass was patchy and overgrown. The flowers Ellen had fussed over were wilting or dead. He had stopped the car. He had heard music coming from inside. He had idled the motor and was about to get out when he saw the curtain moving, a shadow behind it. Someone was there. He had driven away, the note on the seat beside him.

Now he drove down the street and stopped at the familiar blue house. How many times had he come here with Vera, for a family dinner, everyone laughing and talking around the table? How many times had they all sat out in Vera's childhood backyard?

He swallowed. He got out of the car and walked up the walk. He couldn't imagine her parents would want to talk to him. Well, he would say his piece and then leave. Sometimes just being heard was all you could do, the only kind of forgiveness you might get.

He rang the bell, and then the door opened and there was Ellen, her hair golden and cut to her chin, a pale blue cashmere sweater wrapped around her. "Patrick," she said. Her hand flew to her mouth. "Look at you." He couldn't tell whether she was glad to see him. "Come inside."

He didn't know what he had expected, that the house would be rundown, or a mausoleum, but instead it smelled like cinnamon. Everything here was new to him, a floral couch and matching chairs, a deep rust-colored carpet over polished wood floors. She led him into the living room, and there was Tom, leaner now, his hair gray but longer and styled. "Patrick," he said, and he held out his hand.

"Come have a seat," Ellen said, and then he noticed the photos on the mantel. Vera and her parents at the beach, their hair dark with water. Vera at six in a party dress, her hair in pigtails. And then he saw a photo of his wedding, Vera on his arm, and he had to stop himself from going over and touching it.

"That was always one of my favorites," Ellen said quietly.

He stared at it. Vera had insisted on wearing a blue lace dress instead of white, and when his mother had asked her, baffled, "But how will we know the bride if you aren't wearing white?" she had laughed. "If you don't know, you don't belong at my wedding." He remembered that day. How beautiful she had been. How ridiculously happy they were.

"It's been a long time," Tom said.

Patrick swallowed. "I came to apologize."

"For what?" Tom said.

"No, no, let me talk. I need to tell the truth. It was my fault."

"Patrick—"

"She wasn't feeling well. She asked me if I thought she should go to a doctor, and I said no."

Ellen slowly sat down on the couch and took Tom's hand so he would sit with her. She threaded her fingers through his.

"We had these bills. College and the rent, and they were all just building up and building up. We were trying to have a child . . ."

Ellen shut her eyes and then opened them. "I didn't know that," she said slowly. "About the child. About the bills. We could have helped you with money. With anything. All you had to do was ask."

"I waited too long. For everything—"

"Good God, Patrick," Ellen said quietly. "She had a bad heart. It's no one's fault."

Patrick swallowed. "Yes, it is, and you were right to blame me."

Ellen and Tom exchanged glances. "You know," she said slowly, "we blamed everyone. You. The mailman. The checkout girl at the market. Do you know how many friends we lost because of the way we were? I argued with my best friend because she hadn't been able to come to the funeral. I shouted at our dentist because I knew there was a connection between teeth and the heart and I thought maybe he should have known something when he examined Vera. I picked fights. After a while, people didn't call as much. They didn't come by. And I blamed them for that, too. Tom and I—" She looked at Tom. "We nearly split up. One night, I got in the car and drove for two hours and stayed in a hotel. But I woke up in the middle of the night, missing my husband so much I came home, and when I did, he wasn't here, and I thought everything was ruined."

"I was driving around looking for her," Tom said.

"It was just too hard to be around anyone," Ellen said. "All that grief. All that rage. And the person it was hardest to be around was the one she had loved most. And that was you."

Patrick sat down, putting his head in his hands.

"Tell us what you're doing, how you've been," Tom said quietly, and Patrick began to talk, telling them about leaving school, about the commune, the farm stand. Tom and Ellen didn't move. At one point, when he mentioned how small his town was, Ellen put one hand on Tom's arm.

"You left school?" Ellen said.

"I couldn't handle it."

"But you'll go back?"

"I don't know."

Ellen straightened, and for a moment he saw the old Ellen, the way she used to fuss over him and nag him.

"Do you know how proud Vera was of you?" Tom said. "She'd come over here and talk about you, and her eyes would just shine. She'd be so upset to see you like this. To know you had given up everything you two had worked for to live on some crummy patch of land and work a shop—"

"Hey," Patrick said. "Hey, hey—"

"She'd think she had failed."

"I'm the one who failed! I failed!"

Ellen was quiet for a moment. "Tom and I went to therapy. We had help. There were days I wanted to die, and days I wanted to kill you, but every time I felt that way, I thought about what Vera would think if I did either of those things." She looked at him with deep sadness. "You can't kill your life, Patrick. Our daughter was a tragedy, but it pains me to see that you are, too, because you're alive and acting like a dead man."

Patrick laughed, a short, snuffling sound.

She reached over and took his hands, and he was shocked at how warm her fingers were, how when she let his hands go, he wanted her touch back again.

"We mourn her every day," she said. "But I've found that when I plant my flowers—you saw them, right?—or when I stand up in front of a class, I feel her, and maybe it's just me being crazy, but I feel that she's seeing what I'm doing."

They wanted to know whether he was staying in town, what hotel he was at, whether he would have dinner with them, but he felt overwhelmed. He needed to be by himself. "I've got to go," he said.

Ellen handed him a piece of paper and a pen. "Not without giving us your address, you don't," she said. He scribbled it down and she looked at it. "This time we're not going to let you vanish from our lives. That was our fault, too."

She hugged him, the way she used to, and then, to his surprise, Tom, who had always given him a hearty handshake, hugged him, too. "Let us know where you land," Tom said.

Patrick walked out of the house into the bright, clear day, and they came out after him and stood on the porch. "It was good to see you," Tom said.

He sat in the car, unable to move. He looked back, and Tom and Ellen had their arms around each other. They waved at him.

HE DIDN'T WANT to go back to his hotel yet, so he drove around town, the same town where he and Vera had fallen in love. Everything was different now. There was a gourmet brownie store where KrickKrack Records used to be. Paolino's, his favorite pizza place, was gone.

Time was passing. People changed. And what was he doing? Why wasn't he changing, too? He turned the wheel. He caught sight of his face in the rearview mirror, the wrinkles starting to web his eyes. He kept driving, past them, past the bar. The thirst was still there, but he wasn't going to listen to it. He turned on the radio. He opened up all the windows in the car and let the air breeze in.

BY THE TIME he got home, everything looked tired and familiar. The farm stand. His house. The isolation. He went inside and looked around and he knew he couldn't do this anymore. He hadn't realized how sadness was clinging to everything. Lucy had seen it, but he hadn't been able to recognize it. Charlotte had seen it, too, and he had chased her away.

He didn't want to watch the years keep sweeping by. He didn't want to find that he was forty and alone and still selling vegetables and fruits. He got up and went through the house, emptying out the bottles of wine he had. He knew that it wasn't that easy, that he could wake up tomorrow and go to the nearest liquor store and replenish his stock, but right now it felt as if something new was starting, and maybe that was enough.

He began to clean the house, putting away the photo albums of Vera, clearing out books he didn't want, and the more he cleaned, the less he wanted to live there anymore. The more wrong it felt. He was going through a shelf when a picture of Lucy drifted out. He lifted it up. He had never taken a picture of her. Charlotte must have left it by accident. Or maybe Lucy did. She was sitting in the grass, smiling up at the camera, and the light was haloed around her hair. She was posed in a way that was meant to be seductive, her hip lifted, her chest pushed out. But to him she looked fourteen and innocent, as if she would jump up and go get a burger and fries with her friends and then dream about the huge, bountiful life that was unfolding in front of her.

He studied the photo. He didn't have a photo of Charlotte, but he didn't need one. He would always see her eyes, her mouth, her hair, like a pour of ink. He'd always wonder whether she had been drawn to him just because Lucy had been there, because she was desperate for a connection to her sister.

He rolled the photo of Lucy through his fingers, but it was Charlotte's face he still saw, even after he put the picture back on the shelf. He found an old pad of Charlotte's on the table, a list of all the things she had done that day, crossed out. Ice cream place. William's school. He had laughed at Charlotte for her lists, but now he opened the pad to a brand-new page and picked up a pen and began to write out his own.

Chapter 29

By the last week of August, just when Charlotte despaired of finding anything, she stumbled on a great apartment, a small one-bedroom on South Street, with high ceilings and wood floors, and she could move in immediately. To her surprise, not only did she have Iris's financial help, but she also had help from Dr. Bronstein, who wanted her to keep working for him weekends and had even given her a raise. She'd painted the bedroom a creamy blue and the kitchen a bright yellow, and she'd even bought some furniture. Sometimes she just stood in the middle of the room and thought, this is mine.

Charlotte began eating better, because it seemed an affront to the apartment not to cook herself nice meals. She put her sister's journal on a shelf so that every time she walked into the room she'd see it, but she would never read it again. She didn't need to. She heard Lucy's phone call to her in her head, every day, and the only way to stop it was to go out for a run and exhaust herself. Nights, she threw herself into her studies.

In September she went back to school, taking the exams she had been supposed to take in the spring. Her zoology professor gave her credit for her work at the vet's, and to her surprise, she passed all her exams.

For a while she half expected to get a postcard from Patrick, a phone call. She was easy enough to find. But then it began to feel more and more as if the two of them had happened in another life, as if love could really be finite. What would he now say to her, really? What was left? Everything felt changed. She still saw leaflets protesting the war all over campus, but she also saw far fewer black armbands, and the activity at the strike center had petered out. Things were slowing down, and kids seemed more interested in school now. All that effort, and the war was still raging. The Manson Family was still on trial, though the Manson girls had been denied access, and the news kept flashing pictures of them holding vigil outside. They carved x's into their foreheads, they shaved their heads bald. The trial, they told reporters, was "the second crucifixion of Christ."

Students gossiped about their summers; they talked about their courses and who they were sleeping with and who had the best dope. If anyone knew about Lucy, they didn't mention anything to Charlotte. They might have read the papers, formed their own ideas about the case and about her. It might make them think differently about Charlotte, but she couldn't help that. Instead, when they saw her, they said, "Like your hair," which Charlotte now wore in a single braid down her back.

ON SEPTEMBER 15, Charlotte went to pick up Iris and Joe for dinner at her place. She was a little nervous, but she had scoured her apartment, waxing the kitchen floor, mopping the wood, polishing every surface. She wasn't sure what to make, so she decided on spaghetti with a sauce she had made herself the night before, from real tomatoes, with basil and mushrooms. She could cook it quickly when they arrived, and she had already made the salad.

As soon as Iris stepped into the apartment, she opened her

arms wide, beaming. "Will you look at this wonderful place!" she said. Iris and Joe examined everything—the books on Charlotte's shelves, the braided rug she had bought to give the place warmth, and the wood table set with red dishes.

All through dinner, Joe kept one arm around Iris's shoulder. Charlotte liked them together, their easy banter, the way they looked at each other. And Iris looked different, in a slim pair of dark tan pants and a cashmere cardigan. "Where are you getting all these great clothes?" Charlotte asked, and Iris blushed. "Joe and I walk down to the mall and shop," she said. "He has an excellent eye."

When dinner was over, Charlotte cleared the dishes and led everyone to her couch. She noticed that Iris was walking more slowly, but before she could get to her, Joe gently took Iris's arm and guided her. "Did we have our meal yet?" Iris asked, and then Charlotte saw the fear float across Iris's face. "It's okay," Joe said. "We had a delicious meal."

He helped Iris sit down and then kissed her cheek. "My girl," he said.

Charlotte didn't know what to make of it all. The way he took care of her. The way she looked at him. Charlotte had heard of late-in-life romances, people hurling themselves into love because it was their last chance, or because they wanted companionship, or maybe because they were just discovering that everything that had kept them from real love no longer mattered anymore, but this felt different. She sat opposite the two of them in a floral side chair she'd found at a vintage store, and a kind of heat seemed to radiate from them. They were both in their eighties and maybe they didn't have so much time. Iris was forgetful, and it might get so much worse, but it might also stay the same. Joe's memory could fray, too. And so what? None of that had happened yet. Wasn't it better to have love for a little while than not at all?

Iris's smile grew. "Honey," she said to Charlotte, "this is a special night."

"I think so, too," Charlotte said.

"Not just this wonderful dinner. Honey—" She paused. "Joe and I—we're getting married."

Charlotte started. Joe nuzzled Iris, who shut her eyes in pleasure.

"What?"

"November ninth, so save the date," Iris said. She yawned and rested her head on Joe's shoulder. "It's getting late for us, honey."

Charlotte leaped up and hugged and kissed both of them, over and over, ignoring their laughter. Imagine that. They were getting married. Just last week, one of Iris's friends had been moved to a nursing home by her family because she could no longer remember who she was or why she shouldn't come down to dinner wearing nothing but a pair of blue floral socks. Another man, two days after he had arrived, had been found dead in his apartment, the TV blaring a game show. But here was Iris, stubborn as a ray of light, and Charlotte hoped beyond hope that she might be just like her.

"Let me drive you two lovebirds home," Charlotte said.

AFTER CHARLOTTE DROPPED Joe and Iris off, she stood outside before getting back into her car. It was dusk, the air milky with stars. When Charlotte was little, she and Lucy used to wish on them all the time. They'd squint their eyes so the stars would look as if they were spangling across the sky, making the wish stronger. Charlotte always said her wish out loud because she thought it gave it more power: you never knew who might be listening, and you could use all the help you could get. Sometimes, too, even though it had never happened, she thought Iris might be listening and could get her what she yearned for. Charlotte never asked for anything impossible. Charlotte wanted to pass her math test. She wanted Bobby Adams, the boy who lived down the street, to know she existed. Her dearest wish was to own a big white dog she would call Larry. But Charlotte only wished for things that might actually happen. Lucy's dreams were wild. She wanted to travel all over China. She wanted to be a movie star and live in a palace and have a pet zebra. But Lucy didn't just dream. She went out and tried to make her life happen, no matter the cost, like running away with William. She wanted to write something that would change people, and she had, because look at Charlotte now, not knowing what direction to go in or whom to hold on to.

Every way that Charlotte had known to live her life felt like a sweater she couldn't pull over her head anymore. Maybe Lucy had acted dangerously, but at least she had acted, jumping at life, taking chances. If Lucy had lived, she'd have come back to Waltham and gone to school, but Charlotte bet it wouldn't have been Katie Gibbs. No, Lucy would have found a writing program. She would have turned herself inside out every night to write, and she might even have published a book. She might have found love, too, but with the right person this time, a man who might have looked at Lucy and blessed the universe for giving him the great luck of knowing her. And maybe, too, Lucy and Charlotte could have been friends again, the way they used to be. *Us against the world.*

Charlotte would never know what had really happened to Lucy, whether William had been telling the truth. She'd never know whether she could have saved her sister. She might still have gotten there too late even if she'd left right away. Or she might have brought Lucy home and Lucy might have run off again. Charlotte had tried so hard to control everything, but she knew now how wrong she had been. Control wasn't freedom. It didn't protect anyone, not you or the ones you loved, and if anything, it kept you from living.

Sometimes you couldn't fix things, you couldn't make them better, and you had to live with that. It didn't make you a bad person, the way she had thought. It made you human.

Charlotte got into her car and drove, following the highway, burning with restlessness. She tore off her heavy earrings and flung them to the backseat. She rolled all the windows down so that the crush of honeysuckle came into the car. The land began to look familiar—the green hills, the thick trees—and soon she knew she was headed for Patrick's, and maybe it was a stupid idea and maybe it wasn't, but it was what she felt like doing right now. It was what Lucy would have done. She wanted to see him, if only to apologize for the way she had left, so furious she couldn't speak. She didn't expect anything from him now, not even for him to be glad to see her, and she wasn't sure how she'd feel seeing him, either, but seeing Iris so happy had made her yearn for a deeper connection to someone, even if it was messy. Even if it was just for half an hour.

THERE IT WAS, the road to Patrick's. It was late and she knew the stand would be closed. She didn't know anymore what she'd say. Hello. I'm sorry about the way I left. Hello, my mother got engaged. She's actually my sister, too. Hello, William killed himself, and I'll never know if he really killed Lucy. Hello, I'm sorry I said you had a little life. So did I, really.

She pulled into the driveway, trying to imagine what Patrick would be doing. Having coffee. Reading. Then she saw the new sign. DAVE'S, it said.

She got out of the car, her legs trembling, and walked over

to the house, climbing the porch, peering in. The floors were swept clean. The walls newly painted a soft white. There was a box in the center of the room, with a name she didn't recognize. She leaned against the house.

Was there anything left of him here? Fred, the big coleus, was gone. The chairs on the porch had vanished, but the porch swing was still there. He hadn't taken that, and to her surprise, he hadn't taken the funny-ugly macramé hanging either. She stood to look closer at it, and then she noticed something white hooked among the ropes. She pulled it out, a square little envelope with her name on it. He had left her something, just in case. She smoothed the paper with her fingers and then opened it up.

> *By the time you read this, I will be back at school in Ann Arbor. I wanted to thank you. You pushed me into having a life and living it. If I never hear from you again, I will know you're happy. That you are out there doing what you are doing, living a full, big life. And that would make me happy. I wish that for you. Wish the same for me.*
>
> *Love,*
> *Patrick*

Charlotte's hands shook. He had given her love and attention when she felt so alone in the world, and she had given him that, too. That would have to be enough.

There was something else in the envelope, and she teased it out. A small color photo. Lucy, sitting in a field—a picture she had never seen before. Charlotte started to cry.

She carefully put the letter back in the envelope and tucked it into her pocket. Then she got back into the car and put Lucy's photo on the visor. How beautiful her sister had been. How alive.

SHE PULLED OUT onto the road. The air had a filmy cast, and then for a moment she felt dizzy. It was just hunger, she thought. But there, in the dusk, she swore she saw Lucy, like a mirage, running toward her across the lawn, her hair like a marigold against the blue of her nightgown, a glow inside her body. Charlotte lurched the car to a stop, so that her head whipped back, but she didn't take her eyes off Lucy, whose mouth was curving now. "You came for me! You really came!" Lucy cried. Then the radiance dimmed, and just like that, Lucy was gone.

Charlotte blinked hard, searching. She sat there in the car for ten minutes, waiting, but there was nothing but grass and night sky and a dog barking in the distance. The whole wide, alive world.

For the first time, she had no real idea what might happen next for her, how she'd now manage to live her life. She only knew that she'd go back to her apartment and study. She'd do better. She had it in her, and she had Iris and Joe, too. She'd try to get to know more people this year, to let them know her. She would hear from Patrick or she wouldn't, or she could track him down, and when he asked, What are we doing? Where are we going? she'd tell him that for the first time she didn't know. That sounded like a good start. She'd have to be patient to see what might come next for her, but somewhere, when she didn't expect anything, she'd find her answers.

She started the car again, taking one last look back, where Lucy had been, and then she turned her focus to the road stretching ahead of her, shining in the moonlight.

Acknowledgments

I'm so lucky and so blessed to have the incredible, warm, funny, and smart Gail Hochman as my agent, cheerleader, adviser, first editor, and friend. And huge undying thanks to the rest of the agency, too.

I can't say enough about Algonquin Books, because they literally saved my life, in addition to being the best, most revolutionary publisher on the planet. Huge thanks to all the gods and goddesses: Elisabeth Scharlatt, Craig Popelars, Brunson Hoole, Michael McKenzie, Carol Schneider, Katie Ford, Lauren Moseley, Emma Boyer, Ina Stern, Debra Linn, and every other person there.

And I think I would be totally lost if not for the brilliance and warmth of my editor, Andra Miller, who turned this novel inside out and unlocked it, who kept me centered through the hours of work, when I was so overwhelmed I was hallucinating between the story world and the real world and couldn't tell the difference.

For research help beyond the call: To Bonni Miller, for telling me everything she knows about chickens and farming, and to Ross and Brigid Ferkett, Cathy Segedy, and Lucine Sihelnik, and the wonderful folks at Gravel Farm Road and Four Season Farm. Lee Breslow, Elliot Maggin, and Ted Diamandopoulos talked me through the student strike at Brandeis in the early seventies. Kate Mallow, Paula Feria, and Kristi Holmes Espineira gave me their free school experiences and much more.

For help about forensics and guns and the law, multi thanks to Emily Hammerl, Gail Knowles, Chris Henson, Sherri Koster, Joseph Clark, Jill Goodman, and Matt Bayan. John McDonough willingly spent hours on the phone with me to tell me everything I needed to know about police procedure. Natashia Deón not only helped me with legal issues but is also helping me with my next novel—she has my undying love.

Cooper Gallegos and Christine Valenza shared their Manson Family stories with me.

To my tough and loving first readers, I can never thank you enough: Gina Sorell, Rochelle Jewell Shapiro, Jeff Lyons, Leora Skolkin-Smith, Victoria Zackheim, Linda Corcoran, and Jeff Tamarkin.

And for help and support, thanks to my beloved tribe of writers and friends: Clea Simon, B. A. Shapiro, Jo Fisher, Dawn Tripp, Jessica Brilliant Keener, Yona McDonough, Gina Frangello, Litsa Dremousis, Suzanne Finnamore Luckenbach, Meg Waite Clayton, Robb Forman Dew, John Truby, Leslie Lehr, Jenna Blum, Ann O'Brien, Kathy L. Murphy and the fabulous Pulpwood Queens, Lisa Cron, Julia Fierro, Nick Belardes, Ron Rice, Mary Morris, Anne Lamott, Sarah McCoy, Gayle Brandeis, Laura Strachen, Larry Ely, Wendy Orange, David Henry Sterry, Arielle Eckstut, Regina Joskow, Holly Cara Price, Jane Praeger, Michael Taeckens, Yvonne Prinz, Nancy Lattanzi, Peter Salzano, Eileen Oliver, Carolyn Zeytoonian, Cindy Smith Bokma, Julianna Baggott, Jordan Rosenfield, Robin Kall Homonoff, Ilie Ruby, John Valerie, Suzanne Simonetti, Alice Eve Cohen, Ann O'Brien, David Marks, Susan Henderson, Tracey Becker, Sonia Taitz, Maxine Leighton, and Susan O'Doherty.

Thanks to my mom, Helen Leavitt, who fell in love for the first time at ninety-three; my supportive and loving sister, Ruth

Rogers; and the amazing, wonderful Strongs: Hillary, Cotie, Charlotte, and Owen. And thanks to everyone who followed my agonies and exhilarations on Facebook and Twitter and gave me hope, cheer, and support.

Thanks, too, to Stanford and to UCLA Extension Writers' Program, the brilliant naming company Eat My Words and Alexandra Watkins, and to every indie bookstore on the planet.

And finally, with love from here to Jupiter, to my son, Max Tamarkin, who is truly the funniest, smartest, and most talented and interesting young actor I know. I can't wait to see what you're going to do next.

And for Jeff, my partner in crime and my everything, who sings me silly songs, makes me laugh, and always cheerfully shares his Mallomars. How could I possibly love you more?

Cruel Beautiful World

Shedding Light on the Dark Side of Love:
A Note from the Author

Questions for Discussion

Shedding Light
on the Dark Side of Love
A Note from the Author

For me, every book starts with a longing, with something that haunts me so fiercely that the only antidote is to write about it. But sometimes, the book isn't ready to be written—not yet. It was that way with *Cruel Beautiful World*.

The seeds for the novel sprouted when I was sixteen. I went to a rough high school in a working-class neighborhood where being smart and different in any way was a curse. But I had a few allies. In study hall, my protector and friend was this girl I'll call Sally. She was pretty and kind, and at sixteen, she had a boyfriend who was in his thirties. "Oh, it's fine," she always insisted. "Age makes no difference." They had been going out for years, she told me, and her parents loved him, though her sister felt he was too controlling. "But what does she know?" Sally said, laughing. They were going to be married as soon as she graduated.

I was in my first year of college when I heard the news. She had decided not to marry him; she wanted to play the field, to be a girl instead of a married woman. She was going to tell him when he came to her house that night. Instead, they both vanished, never to be heard from again.

Sally's parents began to fall apart, but her sister kept searching for answers. What happened that day? And why? And how?

Sally's story and her sister's search haunted me, but I didn't know how to write about it. Not then. I hadn't experienced that kind of loss.

And then, years later, two weeks before my wedding, my fiancé died suddenly of a heart attack. I grieved for months, unable to eat or sleep or write. One especially debilitating night, I realized I couldn't grieve anymore. I had to move forward, so I decided the only thing that might help is if I got involved in another relationship.

I met a man who seemed pretty nice, smart, and he wanted to be with me all the time, which kept me so busy that I didn't have time to grieve. And it was this man who made me understand what storms might lurk inside a bright exterior. Though he always spoke in a sweet, loving voice, he controlled every aspect of my life—from what I ate to whom I saw—as if it were perfectly normal. I finally left him after he went into my computer and rewrote a page of a novel I was working on. It was then I realized that even the closest relationships had to have boundaries.

Years passed. Eventually, I got happily married. I had a son. One day, I happened to see a message from Sally's sister online. She was still searching and wanted to know if anyone had any news. The past flooded back to me, and I knew then that I could write this story. I understood what it was like to be haunted by loss. I knew what it was like to be controlled under the guise of love. I just had to burnish it into fiction.

Cruel Beautiful World is about a young woman named Charlotte, a disciplined college student searching for the truth about what happened to her wild little sister who had run away with a much older and controlling boyfriend to live off the land. But it's not just a quest for answers; it's also a journey

of self-discovery and change for Charlotte, who begins to realize she can't fix everything that's broken in her life, and the
truth might be more fluid than she ever imagined. Because
this is a book about the positive and negative kinds of love,
I felt there was no better time period to set it in than when
the free-loving, freewheeling sixties morphed into the tumultuous seventies with Altamont and the Manson family murders.
I began researching the Manson girls, how they were willing
to do anything he asked, how their love for him bordered on
worship. I researched the back-to-the-land movement of the
late sixties and early seventies, when magazines like *The Whole
Earth Catalogue* told you you could get rich by raising worms
for fun and profit. I found story after story about runaway girls
who thought the world was going to be their Utopia. They were
seeking adventure and freedom but instead ended up scaveng-
ing for food or sleeping on the streets. I wrote about someone
like my friend Sally, a young girl swept away by a heady romance who couldn't see the dangers a controlling man could
bring—something I knew about firsthand. But not everyone in
that era was a flower child, and so I created Charlotte, who had
been responsible for her sister growing up and was desperate to
find and save her—from herself and from the times.

Cruel Beautiful World explores dangerous relationships, just
as I did in my own life when I was young. But, like my characters, I learned from those connections what I really wanted
and needed in a partner, and what I didn't. There's also real,
hard-won love in my novel—and in my life—and I know now
that it would not have shone as brightly had I not experienced
a darker side of love.

Questions for Discussion

1. Why do you think Leavitt called this novel *Cruel Beautiful World*? How does the title relate to the themes of her novel?

2. Leavitt's novel is told from the points of view of five characters: Charlotte, Lucy, Iris, Patrick, and William. Do you think the novel is more effective told this way, from a closed point of view, or do you think it would have had more impact if she had used a third-person omniscient narrative? Why do you think Leavitt chose this way of telling the story, and how would the novel have been different if she had taken a different approach?

3. Leavitt is deliberately unclear about what really happened to Lucy and whether William was really culpable. Why do you think she left it open-ended, and what do you think really happened—and why?

4. How does the time period in which the novel is set, the late 1960s and early 1970s, lend itself to the themes that appear in *Cruel Beautiful World*, especially in terms of love, family, and a remarkably changing era? If the story were set in contemporary times, how do you think it would it differ?

5. In her novel, Leavitt investigates family, what it means to be part of one, and what it means to bend the rules about what "family" really can mean. Which of the families in *Cruel Beautiful World* seem to you to be the most successful, and why? What do you think Leavitt is saying about the nature and importance of family?

6. An underlining theme of *Cruel Beautiful World* is how we can control some things and prevent others, but must sometimes simply yield to life and let it happen. Do you agree with the author's position? Why or why not?

7. There are so many what-ifs in *Cruel Beautiful World*, and characters seem to wonder constantly how life might have been had things been different. Given the situations the characters find themselves in, do you think they could have made different decisions that would have changed the outcome, or would everything have played out just as it did? Do some of the characters seem to feel trapped by their circumstances? If so, which ones, and do you think they could have done more to effect change in their lives?

8. The shadow of Charles Manson and his "family" seems to provide a kind of backdrop to the book. Why is Lucy so affected by the distant characters? Do you feel she is similar to those in Manson family? Why do you think the fascination with these young women continues to this day?

9. Leavitt writes about many different kinds of love, and as one early reviewer of *Cruel Beautiful World* stated, the novel "is all about love until it's not." What do you think this reviewer meant? In writing about the many faces of love, what statement do you think the author is making about love in general?

10. Leavitt has said in interviews that she likes to have what she calls "never-ending story" endings, where nothing is neatly tied up and the reader is left to wonder what is going to happen next. Did you feel the ending of *Cruel Beautiful World* was satisfying? What do you imagine will happen next in the lives of these characters? What questions for you were unanswered?

JEFF TAMARKIN

Caroline Leavitt is the author of eleven novels, including the *New York Times* and *USA Today* bestsellers *Is This Tomorrow* and *Pictures of You*. A book critic for *People* and the *San Francisco Chronicle*, Leavitt teaches writing online for Stanford and UCLA. Her work has appeared in the *New York Times* and other publications. Visit her at www.carolineleavitt.com